A *New York Times* bestselling author, Gregg Olsen has written eight non-fiction books, six novels and contributed a short story to a collection edited by Lee Child. The award-winning author has been a guest on US and international television shows discussing crime.

Also by Gregg Olsen

Victim Six
Heart of Ice
A Cold Dark Place
A Wicked Snow
A Twisted Faith
The Deep Dark
If Loving You Is Wrong
Abandoned Prayers
Bitter Almonds
Mockingbird (Cruel Deception)
Starvation Heights
Confessions of an American Black Widow

Closer than Blood

GREGG OLSEN

ROBINSON

Constable & Robinson Ltd
55–56 Russell Square
London WC1B 4HP
www.constablerobinson.com

First published in the US by Pinnacle Books,
Kensington Publishing Corp., New York, 2011

First published in the UK by Robinson,
an imprint of Constable & Robinson Ltd, 2012

A copy of the British Library Cataloguing in
Publication Data is available from the British Library

ISBN: 978-1-78033-288-8
ISBN: 978-1-78033-289-5 (ebook)

Printed and bound in the UK

1 3 5 7 9 10 8 6 4 2

For Jessica Rose Wolf

ACKNOWLEDGMENTS

The author wishes to thank the following for their help with *Closer Than Blood*: Annette Anderson, Tina Marie Brewer, Charles Turner, Bunny Kuhlman, and Debra Gelbach.

And special thanks go to Michaela Hamilton, who came up with a wonderful solution at the eleventh hour, proving once again why she is my forever editor.

And finally (really), to Jane Dettinger, who knows that seeing double is sometimes a very, very good thing.

PROLOGUE

Kitsap County, Washington
Fifteen years ago

If Kitsap County's road engineers had wanted to seek careers as Disney Imagineers, they might have served up Banner Road as proof positive that their designs could deliver the requisite thrill. The ups and downs of the Bactrian-camel-on-'roids roadway were only matched by its highs and lows. The stomach-in-throat feeling that came with motion and speed was delivered there every day without fail.

Truth be told, the roller-coaster effect owed more to the topography of that stretch of the south county, which chases up and down the hills as it careens along a nine-mile path just east of Colvos Passage from Sedgwick Road to the Olalla Bay Bridge. At about its midpoint, near the intersection with Fragaria Road, was a spot locals had long dubbed the Banner Jump. The Jump was a patch of asphalt that eggs on the lead-footed, as it literally *begs* those who traverse it to fly. A quick descent down the hill is followed by a slight rise, and then another drop. Even at the posted speed of 40 miles per hour, a driver and passengers can feel that tickle in the tummy that makes some people queasy and little kids cry for more. For as long as there have been teenagers with something to prove or fathers yearning to give their kids what they've wanted, there has been the invitation to push the pedal to the floor. Those with a '70s TV or film reference flash on the opening moments of *Starsky and Hutch* or possibly the famed chase sequence of *The French Connection*.

Kids called it "going airborne."

The Banner Jump was a buzz that required no alcohol to deliver the goods. No amusement park fee. Just a not-so-lazy drive past modest homes, equestrian estates with sprawling pastures, and mobiles, to and from Port Orchard. In rural places like South Kitsap County, cheap excitement was frequently the order of the day.

The thrill could be as short-lived as a spark.

A decade and a half ago, it was also quite deadly.

Mikey Walsh no longer cared what time it was. What *day* it was. *Where he was.* It was a week before Thanksgiving, and Mikey had little to be thankful for. He'd been tweaking for a week. Or maybe it was just three days. He'd never be able to swear to it. Not in court. Not anywhere. Crystal meth had been the solution to a problem of his own creation and he knew it. Certainly, it wasn't his fault that he hurt his back at a construction job site for a new Taco Bell in Bremerton, a half hour to the north. But the fact that he'd tested positive for drugs *was*. He'd violated his employment contract—and that meant he had no insurance, no compensation. Mikey sat in his double-wide mobile home on a twisty gravel road in South Kitsap and started to contemplate just how it was that he'd be able to get himself out of the debt that threatened to take over his life. As far as he could tell, he had two choices.

Cooking methamphetamine or turning his life over to God.

Mikey thought about it long and hard, and in a moment of weakness and despair, he did what any addict would do. He didn't choose God.

Crank, as most in his crowd called it, was like anything illicit. At first a thrill, then a curse. It kept him going when he wanted nothing more than to stop. Mikey was never a handsome figure, but bit by bit meth took every ounce of his youth. His hair thinned. His teeth yellowed. His eyes became languid pools of emptiness. When he wandered the aisles of the all-night Albertsons off Mile Hill Road in Port Orchard, everyone knew he was a tweaker. His empty stare, his bamboo limbs, and the fact that all he ever purchased was beer, chips, salsa, and wings were the giveaways that checkers make casual note of in the ceaselessly boring hours of a late shift.

The night everything changed for Mikey, he landed behind the wheel of his 1979 Chevy Silverado with a shudder and a thud. It was almost midnight when he found himself headed down Banner Road toward his mobile in South Kitsap. The roadway was shiny and he considered the possibility of frost. It was only for a moment. Meth impairs its users with a sense of invincibility, bravado, as it sends a steady flow of energy and false signals of well-being into a shell-shocked system. Mikey had been out on a drug run late that night, delivering, selling, and sampling his wares as he went from customer to customer swapping Baggies of drugs for crumpled twenties. He wasn't tired. Hell, he *never* got tired.

Down the long hill from the intersection at Willock Road, Mikey reached over and turned the knob to the defroster to clear the condensation off the pickup's cracked windshield. The combination of his watery eyes and the low skirting fog made it hard to see. His gaze returned to the road and he shook his head.

It couldn't be.

A girl was waving frantically from the center of the road just at the Banner Jump.

Jesus! You dumb shit! I'm going to kill you!

His eyes riveted to the figure in the roadway, Mikey slammed on the brakes.

Get. Out. Of. My. Way!

The Silverado's nearly bald tires laid a smelly patch of rubber and slid toward the shoulder. Gravel spit out from under its tires, and in that instant Mikey thought that he was going to meet his Maker. Not in the way that he'd imagined lately. Not in the flash of an explosion in the toolshed where he converted the raw materials—the very flammable raw household materials—that turned a toxic brew of chemicals into money. Making meth was part chemistry class flunkout and part short-order cook. Mikey had assumed that if he died young, it would be in a blaze of glory.

A literal blaze.

As he skidded to avoid the girl in the road, Mikey did what he hadn't done in a long time. He said a silent prayer.

The sound of branches scraped the side of his cab. The sparkle of broken glass glittered in the wet road like a busted snow globe. All came at him in the strangeness of slow motion. All came at him in the instant that he would later say was the beginning of a turning point.

The girl in the center of the road rushed at him. She was pulling at the handle of his door and he sat still and scared.

"We need help. Our friend's hurt. My sister might be hurt, too."

She was a teenager. Pretty. Scared. *Very scared*. Her words pelted him between big gulps of air. Mikey thought he detected the odor of beer, but he wasn't sure if he'd smelled himself or the remnants of a can of Bud that had ricocheted from the drink caddy on the floorboard to the passenger seat. Reflexively, he reached down and tucked the beer under the seat. His priorities were warped by trouble, which followed him like a shadow. Trouble had been his soul mate. Personal disaster, his closest companion.

Mikey didn't need another dose. He didn't need a DUI.

The girl pulled open the driver's-side door and lunged at him. She was blond with ice blue eyes. Everything about her was stunning—the kind of girl who got noticed in a crowd. The kind of girl he might have asked out on a date if he hadn't ruined his life. A splash of blood trickled down from her temple, but otherwise she looked fine.

Scared, but oh-so-fine.

Mikey pulled back, but the seat belt held him in her grasp.

"What are you doing?"

"We need help! You have to help us."

The young man pushed himself from behind the pickup's steering wheel. He swung his legs to the ground.

His vision was fuzzy and he wiped his eyes with his palms as the girl dragged him to a silver '92 Taurus on its side. Steam or smoke poured from the car's crunched engine block. It was an instance in which there was no color. Shades of gray, black, silver. The girl's black shirt was wet and he looked closer at it.

Was it water? Blood?

More steam erupted from the stomped-beer-can Taurus.

"This is gonna blow!" he said. "We got to get out of here."

"Not without my sister, we're not," the girl said.

"Hey, I don't care about your sister. I care about being blown to bits."

"We need an ambulance. The sheriff!"

Mikey loathed the concept of wanting the sheriff in any proximity whatsoever. He had been arrested twice before and, despite the numbing haze of his addiction, he did not want to join the "Third Time's the Charm" club of tweakers and drunks.

He pulled back, but the panicked girl grabbed his wrist.

"Over here," she said. It was nothing short of a command. "Hurry! What's the matter with you?"

He looked over and rubbed his eyes as the second girl, hunched over a body, looked up. He shook his head. The second girl locked her eyes on his. He rubbed his eyes. Even in the dim glow of a broken headlight, it was apparent that she was a dead ringer for the first girl.

Was he seeing double?

"Get moving! You have to help!"

What he saw next, he'd never forget. And never speak about.

Who would believe a tweaker like him?

One of the twins leaned closer to another figure on the roadside, a teenage boy.

"Help," he said. "Help me, please."

Fifteen years later, Detective Kendall Stark looked at the e-mail that she'd printed out on the Kitsap County Sheriff's Department laser printer. It was brief, puzzling, and, the detective had to admit to herself, a little concerning.

THE TRUTH SHALL SET YOU FREE.

It was e-mailed to the Class of '95 reunion website.

"That e-mail you forwarded was interesting," she said, when she got Adam Canfield on the phone. Adam's various responsibilities with the reunion committee included managing the website.

"You mean the truth one from the Bible?"

"Yes. Any idea who sent it?"

"Nope. It came from a Kinko's copy center. Some loser from our class must work there."

"All right. See you at the next meeting."

She hung up and put the e-mail away. She wondered which one of their classmates had sent it and, more important, just what *truth* the writer had in mind.

Kendall had no idea that she was on the edge of a whirlpool, about to be sucked in.

CHAPTER ONE

Tacoma, Washington

It was close to midnight and Darius Fulton couldn't sleep. He found himself on the couch watching TV. He wasn't sure if it was the somewhat suspicious aioli he slathered on left-over crab cakes or the general malaise of his life. He was queasy *and* uneasy. He scrolled through the satellite guide. Hundreds of channels were listed there, but nothing was on. *Nothing good, anyway.* It was a cool spring night, the kind that made the inside of a historic North End Tacoma home chill down. *Fast.* Sometimes it felt like the walls were more colanderlike than solid. Outside, gusts shook the feathery tops of bright green pampas grass in front of his North Junett Street house, partially blocking the neighbors' view.

Oh, yes, the neighbors.

Darius had heard them arguing earlier in the evening. Since they'd moved in a year and a half ago, they seemed to never miss the opportunity to seize the attention of everyone within earshot and eyesight. New car. New landscaping. New this. *New that.* Darius had been divorced for more than a year and knew that his days of keeping up with anyone were long gone. At fifty-five, Darius was going to have to make do with the residual trappings of the life he'd once known. Before the jerk with the Porsche scooped up his wife and left him in the dust.

He hoisted himself up and went to the kitchen, where he poured himself a glass of wine, dropping an ice cube into the slightly amber liquid. He didn't care if ice cubes in wine was some grand faux pas. *Hell, it was Chablis out of a box.* He returned to the couch and restlessly flipped through the channels before settling on an *Oprah* broadcast that celebrated all the things he'd need to do to have his "best life."

My best life was five, no, ten years ago, he thought.

Another sip. A guzzle. Ice cubes collided with his teeth. And he hoped that sleep would come right then and there on the couch that he and Greta had picked out together. That was back then. Then, when she still loved him. Then, when he was climbing the corporate ladder with the vigor and grit of a man who knew that he'd have the world in his hands. Always. Forever.

He thought he heard a sound at the door, and just like *that* his pity-party-for-one was over.

His ex-wife's cat, Cyrus, scooted under the dining table in the other room. How he loved that cat. At times, he found himself talking to him as if he were his only friend, a feline confidant. It was as if the silver tabby understood every word. Darius hoped that Greta would allow him one little consolation in the bitterness of their split. He wanted to keep Cyrus.

"What was that, Cyrus? Too late for a visitor," he said.

The cat stayed put, but cocked its head in that knowing way that cats do.

When he heard the sound a second time, Darius looked at his mantel clock and determined that he had not misheard.

Next, the sound of a fist bumping the rippled window-pane on the front door.

The glass is a hundred years old! Be careful! he thought,

Greta's admonition when he washed the windows coming to him.

Darius pried himself from the couch.

"Who'd be over at this hour?" he said, turning on the overhead lamp.

The glass door was smeared with red.

Jesus, what's happened?

He moved closer to get a better view. In that instance when reality is suppressed for a more plausible, a more *acceptable* scenario, he allowed himself to think that a bird might have lost its way in the dark, hitting the window and splattering blood. Yet at once it was obvious that there was too much red for that.

The bloody smear was a big red octopus on the center glass panel.

Or the shape of a human hand.

The underemployed, cat-loving executive turned the lock and swung the door open.

Wilting on the front steps was a woman in her nightgown. It must have been a white nightgown, but now it was red. She was lying there, shivering, making the kind of guttural sounds that people do as they fight for their last breath. He knew her. Tori Connelly lived in the Victorian across the street.

"Good God!" Darius said, dropping to his knees. "What happened to you?"

Tori curled in a defensive ball, lifted her damp head. Her hands were smeared with blood.

"Help," she said. "I need an ambulance."

"Of course," Darius said, his adrenaline pumping. "I'll call for one now."

"Not for me," she said. "My husband. Alex has been shot, too. We've both been shot. He needs help. Oh, God. Help me. Help *him*!"

"What happened?" Darius asked.

Her eyes were terror filled. "A man got in. Our security system is down. He got inside the house to rob us. He shot us. He shot Alex."

Darius bent down and pulled her inside. It was all happening so fast. He was slightly drunk from the crummy wine he'd consumed, and he knew it. He wasn't sure right then if he should go for his phone—charging in the kitchen—or get something to help stop Tori's bleeding.

"Are you going to call for help? I need help, too!" Tori said.

He slammed the door shut and turned the deadbolt. The SOB who'd shot his neighbor was out there. His heart pounded and he thought of getting his own gun. But Greta had a thing against guns, so the firearm that he'd bought for protection was in a lockbox in the carriage house. He couldn't get to it, even if he'd been under attack himself.

"Yeah, dialing now," he said.

Tori began crying loudly, loud enough to be heard by the 911 dispatcher.

Darius knelt next to her as he gave his address. He looked into the woman's fearful eyes. Her skin was white. Her eyes glazed over.

He pulled a knit throw from the sofa and pressed it into her bloody thigh.

"It's my neighbor, Tori Connelly. She's been shot. Her husband Alex Connelly's been shot, too."

The dispatcher confirmed the address and told Darius to stay calm.

"How's Ms. Connelly doing?"

"Not great," he said, his heart racing toward what he was sure would be a heart attack.

"What's her color? Can she speak?"

"She's pale, and, yes, she can talk. Please get someone here fast," he said.

"Are you applying pressure to the wound?"

"Yes, I think so. I'm doing my best."

"They're on the way. Stay with me," the dispatcher said.

"Stay with me," Tori echoed. "Please stay with me."

"I'm not going anywhere," Darius said, gently touching her shoulder. "Hang on. You'll be fine."

He wasn't sure if he was unintentionally lying or hoping for the best. With the spatter of blood drenching her nightgown, it was hard to say just what her chances were.

CHAPTER TWO

Seattle, Washington

Lainie O'Neal awoke as the clock app on her iPhone rolled like an old-school digital alarm clock to 3:00 A.M. She drew in a breath and held it a moment before exhaling. It was an exercise that was supposed to return her to slumber. Once more. *Please.* Her eyes were wide open and the pinprick of light coming from the slit in the window shade found her like a searchlight's beam. Spring rain pelted the window.

Why now? Why can't I sleep? She took another breath. Something felt wrong. Lainie just couldn't get comfortable. She flipped the pillow over and over, on the hunt for the cool side. *As if that would matter.* Lainie shut her eyes with a decided force, almost a wincing action, which she knew was more than needed. Although the bedroom was chilly, she kicked her covers to the floor.

Whenever the first indication of insomnia hit her, as it had the night before, a twinge of panic came with it. She was never sure if the dreaded sleeplessness would last a night or a week. *Maybe longer?* She'd been through counseling. She'd seen a doctor. In fact, she'd seen *two.* Nothing worked.

She sat up and threw her legs over the edge of the bed. She cradled her face in her hands.

Lainie knew the reason for her insomnia, and no counselor or doctor could quite grasp what was so obvious to her.

For the past several days, she'd been thinking about Tori. More than usual. It was as if her twin sister wouldn't let her sleep. It was as if the twin she hadn't seen for years had her hand on her shoulders, shaking Lainie as she tried to fall toward that desperate and dark space.

I'm not going to let you. You better listen to me.

She went to the medicine cabinet, took an Ambien, and looked inside the pill bottle.

Only one more.

She checked the date. She had a week more on the prescription. She'd have to resort to an over-the-counter sleep aid to get her through refill time.

She drank some water and set down the paper cup.

The mirror swung shut, and the haggard face that met her gaze belonged to another.

Tori.

She shook her head, turned away, and looked back at the mirror.

She blinked. It was her own face.

Lainie steadied herself a moment.

Me.

She padded back to her tousled bed, hoping that the pill would work its magic and send her to the restful place she needed.

And not, she prayed, to the nightmares that visited her all too often.

Ten minutes later, the lid of darkness shut over her supine body.

*   *   *

Setting the stage was as crucial as it was easy. All one had to do was think like a crime scene investigator or a cop. Maybe a little like a nosy mother-in-law. The woman pondering that scenario had had a few of those to contend with, too. Ultimately, she knew that no detail was too frivolous. Even the mundane had to be considered, very carefully. The point of setting the stage was to ensure that *she* was in the final act.

The act that had her getting everything she ever wanted.

The plasma screen over the fireplace was playing *The O'Reilly Factor*. The man glued to the TV loved the political commentator's take on politics, business, and culture. He even drank from a "Culture Warrior" ceramic mug.

The woman considered the TV analyst an insufferable blowhard.

A chime from a grandfather clock sounded.

The woman felt the chill of the air from an open window as she stood nude behind the sofa.

"Babe, how about a piece of that pie?" he said, his eyes fixed on the screen.

"Right here," she said.

Yet there was no pie.

She put the barrel of the pistol to the back of his head and fired. Blood spurted like from a stomped-on ketchup packet. Specks of red dotted her glove-covered arm. There was likely more blood than she could see with the naked eye, but that was fine. She knew how to handle it. She'd planned for it. He gurgled a little, but it wasn't the sound of a man fighting for his life. That was over. It was the sound of air oozing from his trachea. He slumped over.

She made her way to the shower, which was already running. She pulled off the glove and set it inside a trash can lined with plastic. The water was ice cold by then. Even for her, it had taken considerable effort to summon the nerves to do what she had wanted to do.

Gunfire was messy.

Blowback is hell.

Spatter matters.

And only time will tell.

It was a kind of verse that she'd conjured that moment, and she allowed a smile to cross her lips as the icy water poured over her. She looked down at her legs, long, lovely. Flawless.

But not for long.

The water had gone from crimson to pink to clear, swirling down the drain between her painted toes. She turned off the shower and reached for a towel. As she patted her face dry she caught a glimpse of herself in the mirror.

Still lovely. Still rich. Even more so at that very moment than she'd ever been in her life.

She poked her arms through the sleeves of a sheer white nightgown and let the filmy fabric tumble down her body. This was part of setting the stage. Her augmented breasts— not freakishly so, just enough to arouse a man when she needed to—would protrude only slightly. She'd act modest and embarrassed, but if the cops on the scene were under fifty, they'd be looking where they shouldn't.

A distraction. One of many.

She poured a plastic cup of bleach down the shower drain and ran the water while she counted to ten.

Taking the trash can liner that held the glove and the empty plastic bleach cup nestled inside, she hurried back into the living room and surveyed the scene. Exactly seven minutes had passed since she pulled the trigger, propelling the slug into her unsuspecting . . . pie-wanting . . . TV-watching . . . husband. It was important to get on with it. The pool of blood around his head would congeal, and her story would not seem so plausible. She knocked the contents atop the coffee table to the floor. Using her hip, she pushed over a potted button fern. A trickle of black soil scattered over the rug. A drawer in a sideboard was pulled to the floor. Knives fell like gleaming Pixy Stix.

It looked like a struggle. Not much of one, but one that could have taken place in the moments that she'd later describe.

Next, she put on a second rubber kitchen glove—the long kind that ran from fingertips to elbow—and picked up the gun. She was grateful for all the things that money could buy just then. Pilates. Yoga. Tai chi. She'd taken all those courses with the other rich bitches. They never accepted her, but that didn't matter. She wasn't there to get to know them. She was there to limber up. She bent down and twisted her shoulder as she pointed the gun at her leg and fired.

She didn't cry out.

Instead, she bit her lip and started toward the door. She was no longer concerned about blood and where it fell. In the throes of her imagined escape, there could be blood anywhere. *His or hers.* She left the door open, and started to pick up the pace by the koi pond that had been a labor of love, apparently, of the previous owners. She didn't love anything or anyone. Except, of course, a brimming bank account. She bent down, her nightgown now more red than white. She'd missed her femoral artery, of course. But she hadn't expected that much blood.

Good thing Darius is still up, she thought, looking up the walkway of the property across the street. The violet light of a TV slashed through the manicured foliage framing the window.

She tucked the gun into the plastic bag, dropped in a three-pound lead weight, and deposited all of it between lily pads in the pond. She dropped the bag containing the gloves into the storm drain on the street—it was a risk, but one that she'd take.

Each time she moved her leg, she let out a yelp. Then a scream. Finally she turned on the tears.

One notch at a time.

She caught a glimpse of a figure between the house and the hedge, and she smiled.

Lainie's eyes fluttered, struggling to open, weary slits reacting to light they wanted to avoid. She looked at her phone. It was now 4:00 A.M. She felt the chill of the early morning air and pulled up the sheet. Groggy from the pill, she had a million things to do in the morning . . . and she was going to look like hell. She reviewed her list as she tried to find her way back to slumber. *Just fifteen minutes more. Only fifteen.* There was an interview to conduct for an article she was writing for a blog, an overdue errand to the dry cleaner, and a ferry ride over to meet with the high school class reunion committee in Port Orchard. She exhaled, closed her eyes.

The dream shook her. They always did. Dark. Violent. Specific and ambiguous at the same time. They always led back to thoughts of her sister. Her heart pounded. She knew her dream had been a nightmare, but there was no way to analyze what it might have meant. If, that is, she was still the kind of woman who would do that sort of thing. She could not recall much about it . . . except the gun, the figure running . . . and the face that was hers when she looked in the mirror.

CHAPTER THREE

Tacoma

Police and ambulance sirens serve to warn others that danger is near. *Stay away. Move aside. Let us through. Get the F out of here!* In truth, the shriek of the siren only ensures that people will congregate *toward* the commotion. A siren is like a rising curtain and the switch on the panel of stage lights. There is no stopping the casual onlooker when the siren screams. People can't help themselves.

Everyone wants to see what the fuss is all about.

Everyone wants to see the show.

It was surely that way that cool spring night in Tacoma when Tori Connelly and her bloody nightgown arrived on the front porch of Darius Fulton's North Junett Street home. Without waiting for a second, Darius reacted with the instinct that comes with the injection of adrenaline into the bloodstream. He comforted her and dialed the police, who in turn called the paramedics.

Darius had flipped the switch.

Woman injured. Shot. Bloody. Hurry.

"When will help get here?" Tori had asked over and over.

She'd only been in his house five minutes. *If that.* But she was slipping away.

"Hold on," Darius said, cradling the limp Tori in his arms, now on the sofa. "I hear help now," he said, speaking to the 911 dispatcher as much as to the now nearly unconscious woman who had bled all over his sofa.

"You can hang up," the dispatcher said. "They're in front of the house now."

Darius snapped his phone shut, slid a pillow from the sofa under the woman's head, and flung open the door as a team of young, jacked-up, soul-patched paramedics swept inside.

"Hurry," he said. "She's lost a lot of blood."

"What's her name?" asked a young man with a port-wine stain crawling from under his bright white T-shirt collar.

"Tori Connelly. She says her husband's been shot, too. You got to get over there. Across the street. There's a madman out there somewhere."

"Already on it, sir," he said, as two other paramedics ran her vitals.

Darius stepped back to give them room. "I hope she's going to be okay. I didn't know how to stop the bleeding."

"You did fine," the first paramedic said. "Wound looks worse than it is."

The second paramedic nodded. "Color's not so good, but she's stable. Let's transport her now."

Tori murmured something unintelligible as they rolled her out the door into the strobe of the aid cars and police.

"Take care," Darius said.

In less than two minutes, the living room that had been the scene of the unthinkable was empty. Drops of blood still freckled the floor, the sofa, and the pillow that Darius had offered Tori. The TV droned with an infomercial for a chamois. Adrenaline still routed through Darius's veins, but with less intensity. It had gone from chaos to quiet.

A light switched off.

He stood in the foyer facing a pair of cops, one middle-aged, one younger. Both rightly grim-faced. As they prompted him for details, Darius Fulton gave a statement about what had occurred. How he'd heard the knock, saw the terror on Tori's face, and the story she'd conveyed about the intruder.

"Did she say anything about the man who shot her?"

"No. Just that he shot her husband, too."

The younger cop noted the info on a pad.

"Who was shot first?"

Darius didn't know and said so.

"Did she say how it was that she was able to escape?"

Darius shook his head. "No. I just assumed that she might have startled the intruder and was able to get out of the house."

"Things like this just don't happen around here," he said.

The older cop shook his head knowingly. "Maybe not on this street," he said. "But, yeah, this kind of stuff happens."

Not usually around here.

"No, not here. Yeah, I mean, the Hilltop is ten blocks away, but this isn't *there.*"

The meaning was clear and not without merit. The Hilltop neighborhood of Tacoma was the center of most of the city's violent crime. While things had improved somewhat due to a consortium of police and community groups who sought to clean it up, it was still rough. Indeed, it was a world away from this tony neighborhood. This was a street more known for dinner parties, book club meetings, and wine tastings. It had always been so. Tacoma's North End had once been the address of the most notable names in Northwest history, chief among them the Weyerhaeuser family. The lumber baron's stately mansion was but a couple of blocks from North Junett.

*   *   *

Edmund Kaminski, a Northwest native who lived in nearby Spanaway because on a detective's salary he couldn't afford rent in Tacoma's better neighborhoods, was on his way to investigate. He gave a quick check to his shirt collar and tie in the rearview mirror.

Looking sharp.

Kaminski had just turned the big 4-0. He'd taken up running to shed what his teenage daughter, Lindsey, called his "middle jiggle."

"Better a middle jiggle than a full-fledged spare tire," he playfully shot back, though Lindsey's words stung a little— in the way that truth frequently does.

"I don't know, Dad. You don't watch it, you'll be shopping for clothes at Sears automotive."

The extra poundage was a symptom of a life off track. He knew it. Lindsey knew it. He'd found solace in long runs along the Thea Foss Waterway, with its views of Commencement Bay and Mount Rainier. *Time to think.* Time to wonder if he'd made any mistakes that could have altered the dissolution of his marriage to Maria. She'd given him the old "it isn't you, it's me" song and dance, and it just didn't sit right. It didn't give him a chance to play the role of the fixer. Even so, he doubted if he could make her love him if she no longer did.

He threw himself into his work while trying to negotiate the realities of being a Weekend Dad. On Saturdays he'd pick up Lindsey and they'd spend the day doing something fun together. Lately that meant a lot of time roaming the shimmering halls of Tacoma's Museum of Glass. Seattle Mariner games were no longer as much a draw for a girl who'd had her nose and eyebrow pierced and dyed her tawny brown locks a fireman's-boot black. Lindsey loved her dad, but she was changing.

The notion of all of that crushed him.

He popped a Rolaid into his mouth and immediately bit

down. Detective Kaminski never waited for anything. Not even for an antacid to dissolve. He turned down a side street, and a bag of yard waste that had rolled from the curb acted like a speed bump, reminding him to slow down a little.

Always in a hurry.

While Kaminski didn't know the specific house that had been referenced in the 911 call that evening, he surely knew the neighborhood. Lindsey had dragged him there when she was obsessed with actor Heath Ledger. The actor had filmed *Ten Things I Hate About You* in Tacoma, and a house on North Junett had been the home of his character's love interest, played by Julia Stiles in the film.

"Heath didn't really want to change Julia," Lindsey said as they stood in front of the three-story white bungalow that had been featured in the movie. "He just wanted her to be, you know, herself. Changing someone never works."

"Really," he said, looking at Lindsey, pondering what it felt like when she blew her pierced nose.

"Yeah, changing someone isn't love, Dad."

Kaminski considered a hidden agenda wrapped up in his daughter's words. *Was this something that Maria had said about him? Had he really tried to control her? Was that what she'd meant by it not being about him, but her? That she could no longer take being the perfect wife, the detective's wife?*

"I can't imagine, honey," he said.

Lindsey looked at him and he sized up her expression. Like her mother, Lindsey was hard to read. *Harder every day.*

He turned down Junett and went just past the house used in the movie. Every light was on, and the place looked like it was floating above a perfectly coiffed front lawn. A Mercedes and a Lexus were parked in the driveway.

Living large in Grit City, he thought, his mind flashing to his one-bedroom condo in Spanaway that could be swallowed up in one gulp by the parlor of any home on this grand street.

It wasn't hard to find the Victorian where the crime had occurred. It was a birthday cake explosion that screamed to the world to pay attention to its gingerbread curlicues and overwrought paint color scheme. That night, the bouncing red and blue lights of the police and ambulances in front of the carriage house tinted the already garish colors akin to a Tim Burton fantasy. How that house could coexist across the street from the impeccable lines of the more simple and elegant bungalows and brick Tudors was a colossal mystery.

Though it clearly was not the biggest mystery on the street at that moment.

Kaminski parked his black Toyota Prius and approached a couple of blues who'd secured the scene. One a slightly haggard veteran and the other an eager beaver.

"Guys," he said.

"Evening, Ed," said Tracy Smart, the more seasoned of the two.

"The female vic in there?" Kaminski indicated the ambulance as the door closed and the driver stepped inside.

Tracy shook his head. "She's en route to the ER."

"Going to be okay?"

"That's what I hear," said the younger cop, a kid with an earnest demeanor that reminded Kaminski what it was like to be fresh out of the academy. *The top-of-the-class syndrome*, he thought. *The eager beaver's need to raise a hand, make a comment, just to be sure to be a part of the conversation.*

"Thanks, Tracy . . . and . . ." He looked at the kid.

"Officer Caswell."

Kaminski grinned. "Yes, officer. You got a first name?"

"Robert," he said, nodding, like he was confirming some major mystery of life.

Kaminski nodded back and looked up over the lawn at the front door of the house. "Got it."

Not Bob. Not Rob. But Robert.

"Call me Detective," he said over his shoulder, stopping a beat to look up and down the block as he made his way up the painted gray steps.

He nodded at another officer by the door.

"House is secure?" he said.

The officer nodded. "Yeah, neighborhood canvass at work, too."

Kaminski pulled the knob and stepped inside. The foyer was grand, *museum-entryway* grand. The floor was burnished oak topped with a powder blue and gold oriental rug, its pile so thick that the soles of his shoes nearly levitated as he walked to the sitting room. The coffered ceiling seemed a mile overhead. He looked up; pale blue insets filled the voids between dark oak mullions. The staircase was curved, sweeping from the first floor to the second like an anaconda. A series of portraits artfully illuminated by unobtrusive spotlights added to the museum vibe.

Not my taste, he thought. *But who knows what a man will do with the dough if he has too much?*

He glanced in the direction of the pocket doors, pulled open to reveal the activity of the murder scene. The smell of blood and gunpowder was unmistakable. Sweet and smoky. Not like barbecue, of course, but more like the scent of a Fourth of July picnic. A Tiffany fixture overhead sprayed gold light from its mushroom shades; Kaminski could see the coroner and assistants in clean suits, assuring that whatever evidence would be gathered from the deceased would not be anything they brought in from the outside. There was never a time when that procedure didn't make sense, but it didn't become official until a case a dozen years before in which a defendant claimed chain-of-custody issues when a detective's Persian cat's fur was discovered on the corpse.

If a person visiting an open house was required to wear disposable booties, then no one should argue the need for initial criminal responders to suit up.

Kaminski caught the attention of forensics specialist Cal Herzog, hunched over the area by the sofa where the body had been found.

Cal, a balding man of about fifty, who began working in the forensics unit at the Tacoma Police Department after a reasonably distinguished career in the military, was crouched over the dead man.

"Evening, Cal."

"Just in time. Medical examiner's about ready to bag him," Cal said.

Kaminski stepped closer. "Let me have a look."

"Point-blank," Cal said, indicating the wound on the back of Alex Connelly's head. The place of entry for the bullet was like a bloody borehole that cut through the man's skull and into his brain. Death, no doubt, was instantaneous. Alex Connelly, sitting in his robe, facing the television, might not even have had an inkling that the gun was going to fire.

"SOB didn't struggle," Cal said. "Didn't even *know* this was going to happen."

Kaminski crouched behind the camelback sofa and looked up at the TV over the mantel.

"I don't know about that," he said. "Pretty good reflection off that plasma. Almost like a mirror."

Cal looked up. The TV had been on when the blues arrived and secured the scene, but it had been loud and one of the cops shut it off.

Kaminski fixed his eyes on the victim. He wore a blue and gold robe. It was a flimsy, silky fabric that he wouldn't be caught dead in.

Which, of course, Alex Connelly had just been.

He had slippers on his feet. Nothing else.

"What does the vic do for a living?"

"Works for an investment firm downtown. About middle on the high-up scale, if you ask me. You know, makes enough dough for a lease on this place, but not enough to buy it."

"Lexus, actually a his and hers, in the garage, er, *carriage* house," one of the cops said, correcting himself. "Not a Porsche."

"Almost feel sorry for him," Kaminski said. "You know, not being able to get a Porsche."

It took three men to move the body to the split-open bag. In doing so, the robe slipped to reveal the victim's chest. A tattoo of an eagle with artillery and olive branches in its talons soared over his right pec, which, given his age, was well defined.

"Nice ink," Kaminski said. "Looks like navy."

While the techs and cops worked together to process the scene for evidence, Kaminski took a tour of the house. It was late by then, but the place seemed as if it had been ready for a Realtor's open house. Nothing was out of place. The kitchen, small by the standards of what modern people wanted, was nicely redone to include the niceties that big-bucked folks wanted. A Sub-Zero refrigerator was clad in white cabinetry to match the rest of the kitchen. A Viking range was another giveaway that the place had been redone. Nothing was out of place on the plane of soapstone that served as the counter.

Upstairs, Kaminski entered the master bedroom. A Rice bed that in someone else's house would have been ridiculously oversize commanded the large room. The bed had been turned down. All perfect.

The dead guy was in a silky robe and slippers.

Where were his clothes?

The bathroom was also show-ready. He went inside and a

flash of red caught his eye. On a hook on the back of the door, a woman's teddy.

Nice, he thought.

As he moved the door, the fabric fluttered, like a red flag.

He opened the shower door and caught a whiff of cleaner. The marble surface was slick, *dripping* wet.

Cal appeared in the doorway.

"Everything diagrammed, photographed. ME is taking the body now. Some blood in the hallway, fair amount of spatter on the wall behind the couch. We're dusting everything. Place is pretty clean. Must have a maid."

"All right. I'm going to the hospital to see Mrs. Connelly."

"Techs are there now."

"Gunshot residue?"

"Hands have been swabbed."

Kaminski nodded. "Prelim?"

"Clean."

The two started down the stairs as the body was being carried out, bagged and tagged, on a gurney. A breeze from Commencement Bay filled the air with marine smells, a welcome reprieve from the odor of blood and gunfire.

"She talk?"

"Not on the way to St. Joe's. Didn't say a word. Told the neighbor that a guy broke in, shot her and her old man. Nobody's seen anything to approximate a break-in."

"Security system?"

Cal watched the ambulance doors as they closed on Alex Connelly.

"Looks like it was turned off," he said.

The sirens started and about ten onlookers started to head back to their homes.

"Show over," Kaminski said. "At least for now. I'm going to the hospital."

* * *

Most who inhabit such a fine street as North Junett would consider the most dominating piece of artwork that hung in the Connelly living room as something incongruent with the home's stature or the place in society that its inhabitants surely held. It was a bourgeois depiction of a stone cottage in the midst of a snowstorm. The artist, Thomas Kinkade, was known for a popular, albeit kitschy, style that stoked memories of a long-ago time when skaters wore fuzzy ear-muffs and free-flowing scarves as they skimmed over the surface of a frozen pond.

This Kinkade print on canvas was called *Evening Glow*. Besides its stone cottage, it featured an illuminated gas lamp that appeared to emit an orange red glow. In fact, such a fea-ture was the hallmark of Kinkade's paintings. He was, his aficionados insisted, "not an artist, but a painter of light."

None of the men and women from the Tacoma Police and the Pierce County Coroner's offices at the crime scene paid the lush accoutrements of the Connelly household much mind as they went about tagging and bagging the victim and the assorted evidence they'd need to run through the lab.

If they'd have looked closer, they would have noticed that Thomas Kinkade's ability to trick the eye with illumination techniques was in better-than-average form. The light on the top of the lamp standard twinkled.

As it did so, the discourse among the interlopers on the scene continued.

"What do you make of the lady of the house?" a cop asked a forensics tech.

"Meaning?" a woman's voice answered.

"A lot younger than the husband," the man's voice said. "Better looking, too."

The same woman's voice responded. "I guess."

"I'll tell you what I guess," the man said. "I guess that when they do a GSR test on the missus they'll find that she was the shooter. Honestly, the wound on her leg was a graze. Self-inflicted. Betcha a beer."

"I don't know," the woman said. "I don't like beer."

CHAPTER FOUR

Kitsap County

The Lord's Grace Community Church was a converted metal Quonset hut in Kingston, Washington, that had once been used to store floral greens for a long-since-closed brush-cutting operation. The structure was so close to the edge of the road, it had been the frequent and unfortunate recipient of more than one car's broadside. In fact, a makeshift memorial of a cross marked the location, adorned with faded photos kept mostly dry inside Ziploc bags, a red plastic lei, and stenciled letters that read C-A-N-D-Y. The tribute's central feature—the cross—was so solid and substantial that a passerby unfamiliar with the events might assume that the cross belonged to the church. It had been seven years since Candy Turner slid on the pavement and crashed her cherry red '69 El Camino pickup truck.

Locals who didn't attend there called it the Candy Church, the home of "My Sweet Lord."

Inside, Pastor Mike Walsh got on his knees and looked up at the big Douglas-fir cross. He'd been contacted weeks ago and the conversation stayed with him. Like a leaky pipe tucked away in the ceiling, quietly, steadily doing damage.

It was a woman, a crying woman, who'd contacted him. She recalled a traffic accident that he'd happened upon a decade and a half ago.

"You could have told the truth," she said. "But you didn't."

"I was scared. I wasn't the man that I am now."

"I'm sure the passage of time has made you a better person."

"A better person, but not a perfect one," he said.

There was a short pause before the woman made her point.

"It is never too late to do what's right."

Pastor Mike couldn't help but agree. "But I made a promise," he said.

"That was a long time ago. Things change. The *truth*, Mikey. The truth is all that matters."

It was a troubling, haunting conversation, as if the woman on the other end of the line was merely testing his resolve. He wondered if she'd taken Jesus into her heart so that she'd be free of what had happened. Forgiveness was so powerful. He prayed for guidance and the strength to do what was right.

He remembered what happened that night.

As he knelt down to help the girl who had been driving, he watched the other one hurry over to where the boy was sprawled out on the gravel. He was saying something to her, though Mikey couldn't hear a word of it.

He heard the sirens coming from the end of Banner, a good four minutes away.

The girl standing over the boy was yelling at him.

"I hate you. I wish I'd never met you," she said.

"Help me," said the girl in his arms. *"Help my sister. My boyfriend."*

Mikey tried to soothe her. His brain was fried and it was so hard to concentrate on what was happening. The smoke. The headlights still on, punching through the blackness of the night. The sirens getting louder and louder.

"They're okay."

"It's all my fault," she said.

He patted her hand. *"It was an accident. You were probably going too fast for the Jump. It happens."*

"Are you sure they are okay?"

He looked over at the other girl. She was yelling at the boy.

"Goddamn you! I hate you!"

What he saw next would haunt him forever. The other girl clenched her hands around the boy's neck.

"You're a piece of shit, Jason!"

"What's happening?" the first girl said.

"I don't know. Nothing!"

The lights of the sirens came down the hill like fireflies on steroids.

He looked over and the boy had stopped moving. The other girl's eyes locked on Mikey's and she came toward him.

"You say anything and you're dead. I'll make sure the sheriff blames you for all of this. That you crossed the center line and forced us into the ditch."

"You're a crazy little bitch," he said.

"I've seen you around. You're Mikey Walsh. You're trailer trash, a drug addict. A loser. No one would ever believe you over me."

The girl went over to her twin, leaned close to her ear, and whispered something. A moment later, a deputy sheriff and the commotion that comes with the sirens and lights arrived.

* * *

It was late evening and the silhouette of Blake Island was outlined by a halo of lights from Seattle on the other side of Puget Sound. Kendall tightened her frame to stay warm as she sat on the old madrona stump with a glass of wine. She'd been quiet since coming home from the sheriff's office. In fact, she'd been quiet the last few days. Steven brought the bottle and a glass outside in search of his wife. It was a cool night, but late spring in the Northwest guaranteed such weather. A sweater and a blanket were kept in a storage bin by the back door.

"I haven't seen you like this in a long time," he said.

Kendall looked up and smiled.

"I'm sorry. I guess I'm not good company."

"You're always good company, honey. But sometimes you're very quiet company. What's going on with you? Is it the case?"

The case.

Those words were often volleyed among the spouses of those in law enforcement when they tried to dig into the source of whatever it was that had stolen all the attention. Steven didn't mean it in that way, of course. He'd long accepted that Kendall had a purpose in life nearly as great as mother and wife—putting away monsters so they'd never hurt or kill again. It was that simple. It didn't matter one bit if the victim was a child, an old man, a person of wealth or not. All were equal in her mind.

He sat next to her and poured himself a glass. "Want more?" He extended the bottle and Kendall nodded.

"I'm trying to sort things out."

"Can I help?"

"Not really."

She wanted to say something more; she wanted to tell her husband that she was wrapped in lead-lined clothing and she could barely breathe. But she didn't. She just couldn't.

"Make a wish," he said, looking at the quilt of stars over the inky-black island. "A falling star."

Kendall looked skyward and did just that. She wished that she didn't have to say anything to Steven, ever. Not the truth. It just hurt too much.

CHAPTER FIVE

Kitsap County

Kitsap County Sheriff's Detective Kendall Stark looked at the text message on her cell phone. It was from Adam Canfield and marked urgent. She pondered if it was something about the fifteen-year high school reunion that, in the scheme of things, was anything but urgent.

Annoying, yes. Urgent? Only to those with something to prove.

Her short blond hair was damp from a morning towel-dry as she stood in the kitchen of her Harper, Washington, home and considered the rest of her morning. There had not been any major cases in a while, at least none that hadn't already wound their way from investigation to the prosecutor's office. There was a lull in Kitsap County, and that alone made her a little nervous. Kendall Stark believed in the concept of calm before the storm.

Every criminal case started that way. From nothing to something. With a gunshot. A knife. An electric cord wrapped around the neck.

Kendall's phone buzzed again. She sipped coffee and listened to the radio as it recounted more news about a stumbling economy, a soggy spring, and a shooting in Tacoma.

She opened the first message:

CHK OUT PAPER. TORI O SHOT. HUSBAND DEAD. L8R.

Then the second. Adam had a penchant for drama and never used one exclamation mark when several would do.

Can u believe it?!!!!

Kendall couldn't, or rather didn't want to.

Tori O'Neal had been a student at South Kitsap High. Her sister, Lainie, was on the reunion committee, along with Adam, Kendall, and Penny Salazar. No one—not even her sister—had heard from Tori in years. Her name was the proverbial "blast from the past," and, in Tori's case, a cold blast indeed.

I hope Lainie's all right. This is the last thing she needs, Kendall thought as she retrieved the paper from a stack ready for the recycling center on Burley-Olalla Road. Her husband, Steven, hadn't gone running that morning, and that meant that the morning's edition hadn't been picked up from the tube at the end of the driveway.

Tori O'Neal? Shot? Dead husband?

She unfolded the paper and scanned for the story.

The article was tucked near the bottom right-hand corner next to articles about toxic rainwater runoff in Commencement Bay and a tragic accident involving a church bus and a semi in Terre Haute, Indiana.

Man Dies in North Tacoma Shooting, Wife Injured

An intruder shot a North Tacoma couple in their home early this morning. Police are unsure if it was a home invasion or a robbery gone wrong. The man, an executive with an investment firm, died at the scene. The woman was transported to St. Joseph Medical Center for treatment.

"We're still piecing together last night's events," Sgt. Tammy Lewis said. She cited privacy laws when declining to provide the prognosis for the woman. "There did not appear to be much of a struggle so we don't consider this a home invasion."

Lewis's remark referred to several cases involving intruders who held their victims captive. The most recent case pending involved a trio of young people who'd murdered and tortured victims they'd met through Craigslist when they feigned interest in purchasing jewelry or other items.

"We can't say anything about her condition other than to say she was taken to St. Joseph Medical Center for treatment. She was admitted sometime after midnight."

The article's abbreviated content was more a reflection of the timing of the shooting than what had actually occurred at the residence and who the victims had been. If it had taken place earlier in the day—and provided there were decent photos—it easily would have found itself above the fold on the front page of the *News Tribune*. Cutbacks at the *News Tribune* and other papers had shifted more editorial effort to the electronic side of the news operation. Frequent updates, blog entries, and even video supplied by "mojos," or mobile journalists, would be featured there. Partly because her husband was in the media business, working for a hunting and fishing magazine, the Starks still subscribed to print editions of three newspapers: the *Kitsap Sun*, the *Port Orchard Lighthouse*, and the *Tacoma News Tribune*.

She set the paper aside and opened her laptop on the kitchen table and clicked over to the web page, where the update included the victim's name, Alex Connelly. There was also a photo. He was a handsome man with a square jaw and dark hair that he wore combed straight back. His eyes were intense and very blue. Piercing blue eyes, even in a photograph. The image appeared to be a business portrait. In the casualness of the Pacific Northwest, a suit and tie were seldom worn unless it was for work or a wedding.

In the comments section someone had posted:

RIP, Alex. You were a great guy. It was an honor to serve with you.

Although the paper said he was an executive with an investment firm, it was clear that Kendall's first impression was right on the money. She instantly saw the unmistakable deliberateness that came with a military background. A military man's eyes never failed to telegraph directness. He looked straight at the camera. Unblinking. Sure. Confident. She wondered where Tori had met him. Had it been across Port Orchard's Sinclair Inlet in Bremerton where the navy decommissioned old battleships and aircraft carriers? Or maybe Fort Lewis south of Tacoma? That was army. Or McChord Air Force Base right next door?

More than anything, she thought about Tori.

How was it that she was able to escape when her husband was likely trained in self-defense?

It was close to 8:30 and she needed to finish drying her

hair and scoot out the door to work, a ten-minute drive away. That it had been a slow spring, crime-wise, was just as well. She wasn't the kind of cop who'd signed on because she was an adrenaline junkie. She knew that type and felt they'd missed the whole point of law enforcement.

"We're here to help people, not ride the wave of others' misfortune," she once told her frequent partner in investigations, Josh Anderson. "Do you really need to smile so much at a scene?"

Kendall went outside to the patio, following the sound of her husband and son in the yard. She glanced at the stump of the madrona that had once arched over the backyard with its distinctive red-and-green striated bark and canopy of waxy green leaves. It had silvered in the weather of the past couple of seasons, and a series of fissures ran from the center of the cut outward, like spokes on the wheel of an old ten-speed bicycle. The cool air from Yukon Harbor blew against her face and she touched her damp hair, wondering if she'd be able to avoid the blow dryer and just tousle it with her fingertips. It was short and she could get away with that technique most days. She was still young and attractive, but time was creeping at her and she knew that fingertip hairstyling and a light swipe of lip gloss was no longer a wise go-to regimen for the morning.

She watched Steven and their nine-year-old son, Cody, burn deadfall in a fire pit on the edge of the yard. For most, it would have been too early in the morning for such an endeavor. But not for those two. Father and son were early risers. Kendall was the opposite—the last one out of bed on a Saturday morning. The one to turn out the lights of the house in the evening. The one to check the door locks and the security of the windows.

A smile broke out over her face as she caught her son's gaze. Cody was quiet, leaving the conversation to his father.

As always.

"Let's get that bunch of branches from over there, son. Let's get this thing going good."

Kendall moved across the wet grass. "Isn't there a burn ban?" she said, half kidding.

"You going to arrest us?" Steven said, winking at his son.

Cody remained mute, but the flicker in his eyes indicated he'd understood the irony of his dad's comment.

"I might have to," she said.

Steven poked the fire and put out his hand to push Cody back a step. "Full plate today?"

"Barring a catastrophe with the committee at lunch, it won't be a long day," Kendall said. The reunion was a week from Saturday at the Gold Mountain Golf Club in Bremerton.

As far as Kendall was concerned, the next nine days couldn't pass quickly enough.

"We've got it handled, babe," Steven said, giving her a short kiss.

"You smell like smoke," she said.

Steven grinned. "You smell beautiful."

Cody set a nest of grapevines at the edge of the fire pit.

"Be careful, Cody." The boy nodded and Kendall kissed him.

Steven patted their son on the shoulder. "He's good."

Cody's autism was fickle, cruelly so. Sometimes he'd speak plainly, even spontaneously. Not that day.

Kendall climbed into her white SUV and started to back down the driveway, Cody and Steven looking smaller and smaller as she pulled away.

She hadn't mentioned to Steven what she'd read about Tori and she knew the reason why. Tori was connected to a part of her past that she'd just as soon never revisit. She knew she'd have to say something eventually. Once it broke that their old high school friend was the wife of the murder victim, Tori's name would surely find its way to the pages of the *Lighthouse*, the local paper.

She could feel her heart rate quicken and willed herself to relax. This was a stressor she didn't need. She thought of a note on the back of a card that had come through the mail when the save-the-date and early head count cards went out six months prior. It too had bothered her. It made her a little paranoid. She hated even admitting to that kind of feeling. It was only eleven words.

I KNOW EVERYTHING. SEE YOU THERE. IT'LL BE LIKE OLD TIMES.

Just what did the sender mean? And to which committee member had it been directed?

Kendall wasn't sure if the card was a threat or just someone's idea of a joke. She didn't tell anyone—not Sheriff McCray, not Josh, not even Steven—that she'd taken the card to the crime lab and processed it herself. No fingerprints but her own. No postmark. No identifier whatsoever. Later, she pored through the stack of cards to see if it had come in an envelope that she'd misplaced somehow, but she came up empty handed.

She wondered how that card got to her if it hadn't been mailed. She also wondered if it was related to the Kinko's e-mail.

THE TRUTH SHALL SET YOU FREE.

Earlier that same morning, a very tired Lainie O'Neal stared at the void of her computer screen. French roast coffee perfumed the confines of her home office, the second bedroom in a two-bedroom apartment she'd rented for five years on Seattle's Queen Anne Hill. She watched her Siamese fighting fish, Rusty, blow bubbles on the surface of the brandy snifter that was his home. It was just before 7:00 A.M., and she had time to polish a chapter of a book that she'd been working on—with renewed vigor—since the *Seattle P-I* shuttered its newsroom after more than a century of being the "newspaperman's newspaper." She'd dreamed that a book would get her out of the endeavor that was killing her with each fifty-word nugget she had to write. She was a "content provider" for a number of travel websites. She was literally writing for food, each word, one bite at a time. On a good day she pounded out twenty-five of the inane little travel tips that the freelance employer sought. Everything from how many mint sprigs and limes should be muddled in a mojito to the best fish tacos in Los Cabos.

She hated the whole lot of what she was doing, but reporters like her had been shoved out the door in an age that no longer seemed to value context, nuance, and depth.

Everything was free, and fast. Even the news.

Her cell phone rang and her eyes darted to the tiny screen, but she did not recognize the number. It was too early for a source to phone. Neither was it the number for one of the other reporters who'd regularly called to commiserate about their bleak futures in a post-newspaper world. A moment later, the caller tried a second time.

It must be urgent, she thought. She clapped the phone to her ear.

"Hello?"

"Lainie?"

The voice was a whisper.

"Yes, this is Lainie O'Neal," she said.

A second of silence and the sound of a deep breath.

"Lainie, it's me. Your sister."

Lainie no longer needed the early morning jolt of a mud-thick French roast coffee from Starbucks. The words were a cattle prod at her heart.

"Tori?"

Silence.

"Tori? Is that you?"

Another hesitation on the line. "I'm in the hospital. I've been hurt. I need you."

"Where?"

"Tacoma. I've been shot."

"Oh, wow, but no, *where* are you?"

"St. Joe's."

Lainie felt her adrenaline surge, slowly, then a tidal wave. She needed more information. She had no idea in which city her sister resided. They were twins, but they hadn't spoken in years. Just how many, Lainie didn't know. She refused to count the number anymore. It hurt too much.

"What happened?"

"An intruder last night. Late. I was shot. My husband was killed."

Husband? Lainie had no idea that Tori had married again.

"Will you come? I need your help."

Again, an awkward silence, the kind that invites the person waiting to hear to press the phone tighter to her ear.

"They're whispering about me . . . I think they think I did this to myself," Tori said. "To him."

"I'll be there," Lainie said. "Right away."

"No. Not now. Wait a day or two. I'll be okay in the hospital. I'll let you know when to come."

"Are you sure? I can come visit you now."

"No. Good-bye."

Lainie hung up and looked across the room at a photograph of two little girls posing in leotards on a balance beam. Their hair was blond, eyes blue. Everything about them was the same, but in reverse. Like looking into a mirror. Lainie's hair parted naturally on the left side of her face, Tori's on the right. Lainie's upper left lip had a mole. Tori had had hers—on the right side—removed when she was fourteen. Their mother dressed them alike until fourth grade, when both girls rightly rebelled. No one could tell them apart. They were so close. *So seemingly identical.*

Yet they were not the same.

Not by a mile.

She wondered about her sister living in Tacoma, too. An encounter with an old classmate the previous fall came to mind.

Lainie O'Neal felt a tap on her shoulder as she stood in line at a Queen Anne drycleaner. Her mind was on her job-hunting suit and the stuffed-mushroom stain from September's "networking" meeting for displaced media professionals.

She turned around to a somewhat familiar face.

"Lainie, it's me. Deirdre Jericho, now Landers, from South Kitsap."

Lainie paused as the synapses fired and the memory returned. Fourteen years ago, Dee Dee was a sullen girl with blue streaks in her brunette hair and a penchant for scoop-neck tops that dropped a little low for South Kitsap dress codes.

Except for the disappearance of those blue streaks, she hadn't changed all that much.

"Oh, yes, Dee Dee! How are you?"

"Better than last time I saw you," she said.

Lainie nodded. "Back in high school," she said. "It has been a long time."

"No, not then. In Tacoma at the bar in El Gaucho. You were there with your boyfriend and you, well, you acted like you didn't know me."

Lainie shook her head. "I've never been to El Gaucho," she said.

"It was you. I'm pretty sure. You treated me like a total bitch."

"Honestly, Dee Dee, I never would have done that."

Dee Dee smiled. "That's what I thought."

Dee Dee Jericho had come in to South when the navy transferred her dad, a commander, in the beginning of her senior year of high school.

She barely made an impression on anyone.

Kendall Stark knew she'd loathe the endeavor almost from the moment she agreed to do it. She would have rather been back home burning yard waste with Steven and Cody. In fact, she would rather be poking around the most gelatinous decomposing body than working on her South Kitsap High School class reunion committee during lunch. It was a quagmire of hurt feelings, unfinished business, and the kind of tedium that comes with agreeing on even the minutest of details. The news that one of their old classmates was involved in a shooting made all of it seem more trivial.

Who cares about what color the napkins are?

The question was rhetorical, of course.

Penny Salazar's steely stare and finger tapping on a planning binder said everything about what she thought commanded supreme importance.

"Look, people," said Penny, who was a sawed-off, square-shouldered brunette and ran the Port Orchard deli that had been the committee's meeting place since the first of the year, "details are what people remember when they remember a special event."

Kendall looked at the other committee member, Adam Canfield. Adam had always been a sensible ally, from high school on the drama team to the Kitsap Cutter serial-killer investigation when he supplied some key evidence from his Bay Street collectibles shop. He had texted Kendall with the news that Tori had been shot, but he and Kendall agreed not to mention it.

Penny could find out about it in the *Lighthouse*. She was an incorrigible gossip.

Adam tugged at his gray lamb's-wool cardigan.

"Yes, details," he said. "I'm glad we approved maroon and white, with maroon the *accent*."

Adam swallowed the last of his Diet Coke and waited for Penny to disagree.

She'd made it a point to disagree with anyone's idea that didn't mirror her own plan for the fifteen-year reunion. She'd even come up with a theme: *Fifteen Minutes of Fame*.

Fifteen Minutes of Blame, Adam had thought before acquiescing to Penny's ill-conceived plan.

"But shouldn't the napkin design have been the other way around? I mean, our cheer uniforms weren't white. We'd have looked like nurses if they had been."

It was Penny again, once more using the opportunity to remind the group that she'd been a cheerleader.

"Lainie texted me," Adam said, not surprisingly, unable to hold his tongue. "She's not going to make it to the meeting."

"The ferry?" Penny was referring to the most common excuses people employed when they gave their regrets about missing an event, party, or appointment on the other side of Puget Sound from Seattle.

"No. She wanted me to tell you that her sister's in some kind of trouble."

Penny's eyes widened. "Tori?" she said, taken aback by the mention of the name. Lainie's sister hadn't been heard from for years. Not by Lainie, not by anyone in Port Orchard. She'd vanished.

"What kind of trouble?" Penny asked.

Adam looked anxiously at Kendall, who had stuck to her word. She didn't want to say anything about Tori O'Neal.

Penny reached for her binder and started writing something down. She looked up, satisfied, and smiled.

"Now we can invite Tori. I thought she'd dropped off the face of the earth. You know, another dead end. About half the class is a dead end one way or another."

"That makes number two," she said, again doing some updating in the binder.

"She's a very unlucky girl, our Tori O'Neal," Adam said.

Kendall looked at Adam. She knew he was making a statement swathed in irony, his forte since high school, but she didn't like it.

"No one is *that* unlucky," she said, unable to resist adding her two cents.

"Poor Lainie," Adam said. "Torrid was fun to watch in high school, but I wouldn't have wanted to be her sister."

"Her *twin*," Penny said, drawing the connection even tighter. "Yeah, that would totally suck."

Penny didn't have a way with words, Kendall thought, but she was right. Tori O'Neal came with more baggage than an airport skycap.

"I wonder what happened this time?" Penny said. "And where is she, anyway?"

"Tacoma," Adam said.

Penny was clearly surprised and there was no hiding it. Tacoma was across the Narrows from the peninsula, barely a half hour away from Port Orchard. "That's weird," she said. "I had no idea she was still in the area. I thought she'd left for California or Alaska or anywhere but around here. She hated it here."

"Yeah, imagine that," Adam said, looking at his phone as if it would force Lainie to send another text. "Tori's been hiding in plain sight."

* * *

Kendall Stark returned to her office and dialed the number for the Tacoma Police Department. She identified herself and asked for the investigator in charge of the Connelly murder case, and Eddie Kaminski got on the line. She told him that Tori had roots in Kitsap and had been associated with the death of a young man, Jason Reed.

"You say it was a car accident?"

"Yes, but some things seemed odd about it."

"Odd in what way?"

Kendall didn't have anything specific and she felt foolish just then. "One witness said he was talking—alive—then suddenly, dead. Internal injuries can be like that. Other talk, too."

"We deal with more than talk here in Tacoma," Kaminski said. "We deal with facts."

Her cheeks went a little pink. "Of course. Did you know that her first husband died, too?"

There was a short pause.

"It might have been mentioned to the other investigators," he said. "Yes, I think it was."

"Can we meet? I could tell you more."

Again a slight pause.

"Hang on for a sec." He put the phone on mute and returned a moment later. "Busy here, sorry. Sure. Maybe you can come over this way?"

"All right. I'll figure out a time and get back to you," she said.

After he hung up, Kaminski turned his attention to the medical examiner's report on Alex Connelly. The sum of all the dead man had been reduced to the weights and measurements of his liver, his heart, his kidneys. *His gunshot-addled brain.* All were unremarkable. He was fit, healthy, and struck down in the prime of his life by a masked assailant.

A bullet to the brain had killed him instantly. The second shot was merely icing on a murderer's cake.

He scanned the report—fifteen pages of diagrams and notes made by a pathologist who knew it was best to include every detail, mundane or not. Alex Connelly's right earlobe bore the telltale puncture of a scarred-over piercing. As he read, Kaminski touched his own lobe, feeling the tiny lump of a scar from his own youthful indiscretion for the sake of fashion. Except for the fact that Connelly made five times Kaminski's salary, the detective and the victim were so very much alike. Height and weight were the same. The victim had had a vasectomy. His tonsils had been removed.

Check. Check.

There was really nothing remarkable about Connelly, other than the horrific and violent way that he'd died.

By the time the body was processed and released, his widow had already arranged for his cremation. It was as fast as one of those Pyrex commercials that crow about moving something from the freezer to the oven without a second in between.

CHAPTER SIX

Tacoma

It was the weary time of day when the world is sleeping and the digits on the clock are small and stand alone. Except for the crying from down the cavernous hallway toward the elevators, the fifth floor of St. Joseph Medical Center was quiet. No visitors. A nurse with a citrus yellow scrub over a red turtleneck studied the chart and checked the bag of fluids that circuited from a tube overhead into the vein of the woman everyone at the fifth floor nurses' station was talking about. The gossip at the station centered on the tragedy that had unfolded on North Junett Street. Nurses have well-deserved reputations for caring and nurturing, but the reality of their world is that they see so much that it is hard to force a tear for every misfortune that rolls down the high-gloss linoleum floors.

Diana Lowell, the nurse wearing the yellow smock, chatted a moment with a younger woman fresh out of nursing school. Her name escaped the veteran nurse, out of the unfortunate acceptance that young people came and went. Few became lifers like her. Diana was friendly, but only enough to get the job done. They spoke in hushed tones. It was the kind of casual chatter that characterized a lot of admissions at St. Joseph's. Probably true of any hospital in any city. The exchange was somewhat lighthearted despite the subject matter at hand.

Frivolity constantly played against tragedy at the nurses' station.

"Her husband was shot," Diana said. "An intruder, I guess."

"Yeah, right in the face, I heard," Corazón White, the younger nurse, said. "I have a friend in the morgue. I'll ask for details."

Diana smiled slightly as she observed an exasperatingly slow computer screen morph from one patient's file to the next.

"Nice to have friends in low places," she said wryly.

"Yeah, I guess," the newbie said without a trace of humor. "Last person most of us see is the morgue attendant."

"That's why you must always look your best," Diana said, playing with the girl now.

"Anyhow, is she going to be okay?"

"Yeah, fine. Barely a graze, really. Three stitches. Lucky girl, she is."

Diana picked up a clipboard, the last vestige of the days when she was in the newbie's position. Several nurses carried electronic clipboards, but Diana was lagging behind on her required training. She started toward the corridor that led to Tori Connelly's private room, 561D, arguably the best room on the floor. It was smaller than the others, and because of that it, was never converted to a tandem. There was no sharing of a bathroom. No feigned interest in one patient's malady from across a curtain suspended by grommets and a steel tube. Diana Lowell let her eyes wander over the woman in the bed. She could tell that the patient was watching her every move, though her head stayed stationary. Diana could feel those eyes follow her as she rotated the bag containing clear liquid that was a mixture of saline and anti-anxiety meds. Not enough to knock her out. Not enough to keep her from complaining. If the woman in 561D was a complainer, that is.

In time, most were.

Diana flipped the crisp new pages of the printed chart and scoured its contents. Tori Connelly certainly had the pedigree to be a complainer. Her home address was an exclusive street in North Tacoma. Her hair was cut with the messy precision of a stylist who probably charged half of what Diana made in a day. The color was good, too. Blond, the hue of wheat on a bronze-lit summer day. Not the DIY color from the bottle that Diana and her sister used because they were "worth" it.

"How are we feeling?" Diana asked, catching the patient's stare. "You slept all day yesterday."

"We," Tori said, moistening her parched lips. "*We* have been shot."

Diana smoothed a bedsheet. "Of course, I know that. How is the pain? You know you can increase the dosage by pressing the button."

Tori was annoyed. "You are pressing my buttons now," she said.

"I didn't mean to," she said. "Just trying to be helpful."

"I want to know if my husband's okay. He was hurt, too."

Diana knew what had happened to the patient's husband, of course, but it wasn't her place to say anything. The doctor could tell the new widow. A cop could.

She set the chart down and focused on Tori.

"The police are here now," she said, moving toward the hallway and catching the eye of the man lingering by the doorway. "They'll tell you everything you need to know."

"The police?"

Diana looked at her. "Yes. The shooting, remember?"

"I look like a wreck," she said. "Besides, I've already answered questions galore."

This one was going to be memorable in every way.

"You look fine. You know, considering all you've been through."

Tori ran her fingertips through her hair. In doing so, she tangled the tubes taped to her wrist. She indicated the IV line.

"This hurts," she said.

Diana bent closer and unwound the tubes from the bed rail. "Let me help you." She gently splayed them out from Tori's wrist to the bag of solution.

"Will I be all right?"

"You'll be fine," Diana said. There were times when that phrase was said as a white lie, only to bolster a patient's dwindling prospects. But Tori Connelly would be as good as new. At least physically.

"I bet I look like twenty miles of bad road," she said.

"Not hardly." Diana studied Tori. She'd been shot, yes. She'd lost blood. Yet somehow she held herself together enough to allow her vanity to come into play. The woman in 561D was one of those women with nerves of platinum and an unbending concern for how things appeared.

A man appeared in just inside the doorway and Diana motioned in his direction. It was Eddie Kaminski.

"She's resting comfortably, but she can talk, Detective," she said, walking out the door and past the detective.

Kaminski knew that the victim's recollection of the crime would be most accurate closer to the event, rather than later. Tori Connelly's doctors told him that she was on pain medication and fluids, but was lucid and given the circumstances would be able to share what she knew about what had transpired.

"Ms. Connelly," Kaminski said, ducking into her room. "I'm sorry to disturb you."

She barely looked at the man in a seasonally questionable black overcoat, dark slacks, and a rumpled white shirt.

"Ms. Connelly?" he repeated, this time a little louder, but modulated for the hospital setting. "I'm Detective Kaminski, Tacoma P.D. I'm here to talk about the shooting."

She moved her lips. Her eyes fluttered.

"Yes," she said.

He found a place by her bedside. Not so close as to invade her personal space, but with the narrowest of proximity to hear her words. Tori Connelly's hair was swept back and her skin quite pale. Her eyes rested in charcoal hollows. She was fine featured. Despite her ordeal, however, she was an attractive woman.

She looked up, eyes damp. "There was so much blood. Everywhere."

He nodded. "Yes, there was."

She lowered her eyes and then looked out at the Tacoma skyline. "He didn't make it," she said, more a statement than a question. "My husband, I mean."

He shook his head. "No, I'm afraid not."

A tear rolled from the corner of her eye, leaving a shiny trail as it traveled to the white linen of the hospital pillow.

"But *you* did," he said.

She held her words inside a moment.

"Yes, yes, I did."

Kaminski took out a notepad and started writing. He'd given up the idea that he could remember every word uttered by a witness. It wasn't that he was struggling with early-onset Alzheimer's. It was simply the recognition that a notation was a safeguard against forgetting when it came time to tap out the report.

"Did he suffer?" she asked.

Kaminski stopped writing and looked up. "The coroner doesn't think so. Death was instantaneous or thereabouts."

She stayed quiet for a moment and then let out a long breath. "That's a blessing."

"I'd like to talk about what happened. From the beginning, if you don't mind. I know you're exhausted."

He didn't really care that she was tired, but he'd come off a two-day sensitivity training workshop that had him primed to all but hug a felon.

"We'd been out to dinner," she said. "It was just one of those lazy evenings. We never expected anything to happen."

"Of course not," he said. "Where was dinner?"

"Oh, a little Italian place on Pacific we'd never tried before, and we're never going back." She caught her mistake. "I'll never go back. No, I won't."

His stare bore down on her. "Anything happen at dinner?"

"What do you mean? *Happen*?"

"Out of the ordinary? I'm just trying to capture what happened before the shooting."

She stared at him. "Did we argue? Is that what you're hoping for, Detective?"

Kaminski was taken aback by her sudden shift to an undeniably defensive tone. "No, that's not what I was inferring, Ms. Connelly."

"Implying," she said.

"Excuse me?"

"Implying, not *inferring*."

"Fine. Okay."

"I want to know if Alex suffered long, or at all. If he was able to say anything."

The detective hated this part of his job. More than anything. "I'm sorry, Ms. Connelly, but your husband was dead at the scene. I thought you knew."

She looked away, toward the window.

"I knew. I just wanted someone to say it to me." She looked at Kaminski, her hollow eyes now flooded. "I knew when I ran out that door that I'd never see him again. Never again." The words tumbled out. "I loved Alex so, so much."

"I know. I need to know what happened," he said.

Tori looked at him, almost pleadingly.

"I don't want to relive it."

"You are the only living witness," he said. "You want us to catch the killer, don't you?"

"Yes, of course I do."

"Tell me. I'm here to help you," he said.

She told him that she was in "another room" when she heard a commotion and the "popping" sound of a gun.

"I mean, I know it was a gun now, but honestly, I thought it was a champagne cork popping. Alex could be like that, you know. Surprising me."

"I'm sure he was a good man. I'm sorry for your loss. Then what happened?"

"I went into the living room and a man was standing there by Alex. I screamed and he started to run to the door."

"How'd you get shot?"

She looked at him, irritated and emotional. "I'm getting to that. Do you mind?"

"Not all, please. Just trying to help, Ms. Connelly."

"Then it was over. He ran out the door and I followed. I went over to Darius's place and he called for help."

"What did your assailant look like?"

"It happened so fast," she'd said. "I think he had dark eyes, but they might have been dark blue or green."

The response could have not been more ambiguous.

At least she didn't say "red," thereby ruling out an albino assailant, he thought.

"Could you determine his ethnicity?"

She looked at the reporting officer, almost blank eyed.

"Not really. He had on a mask."

This was the first time she'd mentioned a mask. Kaminski underlined that.

"Ski mask?" he repeated.

The wheels were turning now. Tori was retrieving some information. A pause, then an answer. "Not sure. More like a panty hose. I could see his face, but his features were smushed by the fabric."

"Had you seen anyone in the area who matches—to the best of your recollection—what you saw that night?"

The question was bait, and usually good bait. A suspect frequently takes the suggestion and runs with it.

"He looked like a gardener."

"A man who delivers groceries."

"A transient I've seen a time or two nearby."

Tori went limp. A tear rolled down her cheek.

"You're going to have to give me a minute. This is extremely difficult."

Kaminski waited for her to collect herself. Her eyes were damp with tears, but none flowed down her cheeks. She was a coolheaded woman, a logical woman. She'd expected the worst and had prepared herself for the moment when she'd knew with certainty, with utter conviction, that she was alone in the world.

What came from her lips next would have been stunning to the most veteran detective.

"I'll need a lawyer," she said. "Won't I?"

"Why would that be?" he asked.

"Just call it a hunch," she said, this time looking directly at him. "You'll focus the investigation on me. I understand it. I know how things are done. In the end, you'll have to look elsewhere because I had nothing to do with any of this."

"No one is looking at you," Kaminski said.

She looked past him once more, breaking the gaze they'd held. "Not now. But tomorrow somone will. Someone will say the ugliest things and your minions will circle me and my tragedy like a school of sharks. Each after a piece."

She stopped talking.

Kaminski stood there in uncomfortable silence.

"Detective," she finally said. "I want to know one thing."

"What's that?"

"How am I supposed to live without him? He was my soul mate. I loved him."

Tears started rolling down her cheeks.

"Again, I'm truly sorry for your loss," he said, taking a couple of steps backward before turning for the door.

She looked back at the sky through the window, turning to the blush of a new day. "Thank you, Detective," she said.

The beige Princess phone next to Tori O'Neal Connelly's bedside rang. She smoothed her covers and disregarded it for a moment. But the ring was persistent and altogether annoying. She reached for it, wincing with the pain that came with stretching skin that had been sutured. She assumed it was a nurse or, as she liked to call them, an *attendant* from the hospital. She planned on telling whoever it was that she would make an outgoing call if she wanted anything. Tori was never shy about indicating whatever it was she wanted. Her heart's desire was hardwired to her mouth.

As she clasped the receiver to her ear, nurse Diana Lowell entered the room.

"Hello," Tori said into the mouthpiece. She shifted her body in the bed. Immediately, her face froze. She turned away from the nurse who was emptying a plastic bag liner brimming with used tissues and other nonsharps into a large disposal can.

"Yes," she said.

Her voice was low. Not a whisper, but if Diana Lowell had actually tried to listen, it would have taken considerable effort.

"Understood," she said, her eyes fixed on the nurse as she rolled the disposal can from the room to the bathroom.

She turned away.

"Don't ever call me here again," she said, her voice, decidedly firm.

She pressed the button to disconnect the call. The line went dead, but she didn't put the phone down just yet.

"Don't worry. I will be fine," she said, her eyes purposefully catching the attention of the hospital worker. "I miss you, too. I can't wait to see you."

The nurse who frequently didn't see a need to hold her tongue just looked at her.

Tori shifted in the bed. "My sister," she said. "She's coming to see me."

Diana nodded and smiled, that practiced smile that didn't really betray the fact that she thought the patient with the dead husband was a B.S. artist of the highest order.

CHAPTER SEVEN

Tacoma

The *Tacoma News Tribune* ran a follow-up to the shooting in the morning's paper:

Police Question Widow in
North End Shooting

Tori Connelly, the wife of a Tacoma financial consultant, was questioned by police in conjunction with the shooting death of her husband, Alex.

"We're satisfied that this case will reach a proper conclusion soon," said lead investigator Edmund Kaminski. "Ms. Connelly has been cooperative."

A tech working in Tacoma Police Department's state-of-the-art forensics lab had taken a swab of Tori Connelly's hands for gunshot residue particles at the scene of her husband's murder. An analyst at the lab compared the particles captured by the swab to determine if the woman who'd been injured was the shooter. Law enforcement in Tacoma and elsewhere had become wary of gunshot residue in the past few years. There were several instances on the law books in which men had been wrongfully convicted when they tested positive for GSR when they'd only *handled* a gun, or had recently been in the proximity of one that had been fired. There had also been a famous Northwest case that was botched when it was determined that the GSR found on a shooter's jacket had been the result of contamination from a police detective who'd been at the firing range before going out to the murder scene.

Tori Connelly's white nightgown was next. It had been hanging in the biohazard room drying since the shooting. Specialist Cal Herzog spread out the garment on a table under fluorescent and ultraviolet lights to see what story it might tell.

Eddie Kaminski stood over the garment next to the tech, a young man in his late twenties with hair heavy with product and teeth that appeared all the whiter as the ultraviolet light bounced off the fabric of the filmy nightgown. The blood had already dried to a dark wine, almost chestnut, color.

The younger man, Rory, smoothed out the fabric, took a series of photos, and cut two small square patches from the bloodiest part of the material. He made a few remarks about the blood's pooling and how gravity had dragged a pair of rivulets down to the hemline.

"Can't be sure until we analyze it, but it doesn't look like there's anything here other than what we see. No semen. No other fluids," he said.

"What's interesting is right here," Cal said. His hands were gloved, but he didn't get close enough to the nightgown to really touch it. He motioned to the fabric, though his eyes stayed on the young man.

"What are you getting at?" Kaminski asked.

"Look closer."

"I *am* looking closer," Rory said, his teeth flashing like a cotton bale bound by steel wires. "I don't see anything."

"Precisely. There's nothing to see."

"So? I'm not blind," the young man said.

Cal rolled his eyes, enjoying the moment.

Kaminski held his tongue. What he wanted to say was something about the kid having earned his degree in a correspondence course or that whatever training he really had was B.S. He expressed his irritation because, well, it was fun to irritate the kid.

"If she was shot like she said she was, I'd expect a bullet hole, a tear, something in the nightgown, wouldn't you?"

Point made.

"Yeah, I guess I would."

With the new widow still in the hospital, Eddie Kaminski returned to the scene of the shooting on North Junett. He'd noticed a koi pond near the walk up to the Connellys' front door the night of the shooting, but it wasn't because it was sinister. His former wife, Maria, had wanted to have a gold-fish pond installed in their backyard early in their marriage. When they couldn't afford a landscaper, she dug the pond herself, shovel by shovel. Kaminski remembered coming home from a long day on patrol, and how happy she was that the inexpensive feeder goldfish she'd bought by the bucket had laid eggs. It wasn't the only news she had to share. She was pregnant. It was the happiest day of his life.

The last time he saw the pond was moving day, when all the happiness had literally drained from the Kaminskis' life.

The pond had turned green and was full of Douglas fir needles, a decaying symbol of their dying marriage.

He walked up the pathway to the door of the stately Victorian and the koi pond. Just below the surface a fragment of red and white caught his attention. Kaminski bent down to get a better look. It was the edge of a plastic bag. The red, a half circle filled with another, smaller one, appeared to be the familiar logo of Target. He wondered what was more incongruent—a Target bag in that neighborhood or the presence of plastic refuse in a pristine pond.

He looked around for something to help retrieve the bag. The yard was perfectly landscaped with not a tool lying around, not even a garden shed. Nothing was handy, so the detective did his best to wrestle with some bamboo that had been artfully planted along the pond's farthest edge.

Another reason to hate this annoyingly invasive plant, he thought.

A piece snapped in his hands, and he poked the end through a small void in the lily pad–studded surface. It took some finessing, and he figured ice fishing north of Spokane with his dad had served him well when he snagged the bag and managed to pull it out.

It was heavy.

It didn't belong there.

He knew what he had. The bag conformed to the shape of its contents.

A gun.

"Not just *any* gun," Kaminski said to himself, his heart pumping with a little more vigor. "The murder weapon."

It had started in the kitchen with his back to the soapstone island. Tori wore a thin blouse that allowed her nipples to show. She opened the refrigerator and let the cold air pour over her body.

As if she needed to call attention to what she was selling and how good it would be.

Is there a more beautiful woman on the face of the earth? Not in magazines. Not on TV. The movies. Nowhere, *she thought, always the best marketer of her own charms. She spun around and latched her hands around the small of his back, pulling gently, teasingly.*

"You seem a little excited," she said, looking at her lover. "That's lovely."

He wanted to speak, but he didn't want to say the wrong thing. She was in control and he was going along for the ride, happily, hungrily.

Her fingertips slipped under his shirt and caressed his chest.

He leaned backward, pushing his pelvis toward her.

"I know what you want," she said. Her voice was soft, yet playful.

"Yes, I know you do," he said.

She undid his belt, then his jeans. Her fingers found his zipper and she pulled.

"A little tight," she said. "Sorry."

"That's okay."

"Yes, it is," she said, dropping to her knees.

He was breathing heavy by then. He closed his eyes and she put her mouth on him.

She stopped.

"Keep going," he said.

"I will. I'll get you there. Just let me do what I do best."

And she did.

CHAPTER EIGHT

Kitsap County

Cooking dinner in the Stark household was the kind of communal endeavor that artists so charmingly sketched for the *Saturday Evening Post* and that modern-day advertisers with buckets of guilt and products to sell still employed to remind people that the family that ate their meals together *stayed* together. Kendall and Steven alternated the roles of sous chef and head chef. On days when she was up to her neck with criminal investigations and the people who populated the files of her in-basket at the sheriff's office, Kendall liked the feel of a sharp knife in her hands as chief chopper. She enjoyed the way carbide made its way through a potato or an onion. The cut felt good.

A release.

The day had been consumed by thoughts of the reunion, Lainie, and, of course, Tori. That her partner Josh Anderson was coming to dinner might drag the day to a new low. She pulled herself together.

Focus, Kendall. Good things. Happy things.

She looked around the kitchen. Things didn't get much

better than what she saw. It was—her son, her husband, her *home*—what she had dreamed about as a girl in Port Orchard.

The Starks had recently remodeled the kitchen, with Steven doing most of the work except the fabrication of the limestone slab countertop. Kendall sanded the cupboards before Steven lacquered them with a creamy white, but quickly learned that there was no glory in sanding. Increasingly, it was clear that the kitchen had been designed with Steven's preferences in mind, anyway. Kendall didn't care. The backside of the new island had, by default, become her domain. She prepped the salad—a mix of arugula, romaine, and fennel—and looked at the clock.

"You don't mind, do you?" she asked.

Steven stirred the contents of a saucepan.

"You mean an evening with To-Know-Me-Is-to-Love-Me?"

"I felt sorry for him," Kendall said.

"Josh almost cost you your job. But, no, if you can forgive him, I can, too."

Kendall turned to Cody, who was sitting at the kitchen table working on arranging dried pasta into an intricate design that suggested both chaos and order. Kendall was unsure if it was a road in a mountainous landscape or something else. Pasta was linked up, one piece after another, and fanned out into a kind of swirling shape. Cody had always been adept at puzzles—sometimes putting them together with the reverse side up, using only shapes and not imagery to fit each piece together.

"You doing okay, babe?" Kendall asked.

Cody looked up, a faint smile on his round face. Whatever he was thinking about at that moment was a pleasant thought. It might have been dinner. It could have been the stars in the sky. Cody spoke, but not often. He was not an alien like some spiteful people consider those with autism, but a gentle spirit who had an awareness of everything around him—even when it seemed he let no one inside.

"Good. I'm good," he said.

"I know you are," she said.

Cody had become more verbal in the past few months. And while his responses weren't exactly lengthy, they did get the point across, and they gave his parents and doctors hope that his particular form of autism might not be as severe as once thought. It was true that he'd likely never be able to function without continued support and guidance; he wasn't going to end up in some hospital somewhere. He was only nine, of course, but the Starks feared the day that they were gone and what their son would face in life without the love of those who knew him.

"Lasagna's ready to come out," Steven said.

Kendall squeezed a lemon into the salad dressing she was mixing with a wire balloon whisk in a small glass bowl. She dropped in a little Dijon, some minced shallots, and a sprinkle of cayenne. With the tip of a spoon, she tasted the dressing, made a face, and added another squeeze of honey from a plastic bear-shaped bottle.

"Perfect timing," she said, catching the sight of a BMW as it moved into the parking area behind the house. "Josh is here now."

Josh Anderson had been an infrequent guest in the Stark residence for the past year. He'd heard about the remodel and had even offered to help out, but his proposal was half-hearted and the relationship was somewhat strained following their last major case, the so-called Kitsap Cutter, and subsequent media brouhaha. He stood at the doorway, bottle of Oregon pinot noir in hand and a somewhat nervous smile on his face. At fifty-two, Josh no longer looked like he was trying so hard to be the ladies' man that he'd once been. The gray at his temples was more pronounced, as though he'd given up on coloring it to "just a touch of gray." His jacket, an ill-advised tweed with elbow patches that seemed a little more "professor" than "detective," was a little tight around the middle.

"Ninety-two points on this one," he said.

Steven took the bottle. "I'd probably like it if it had sixty points."

Kendall motioned for Josh to come inside. She looked at Steven and rolled her eyes. It was a playful gesture, not to repudiate him for a lack of knowledge.

"My husband, the wine connoisseur," she said.

Steven, however, took the bait. "It isn't that I don't like a good bottle of wine," he said, "I just don't usually know the difference between the notes of this or that."

"It was twenty bucks," Josh said, hanging his jacket over the back of a chair. "I buy by price, not points."

"Something we have in common besides Kendall," Steven said.

Josh ignored the sarcasm, intended or merely the result of Steven's attempt at making a quip.

"Hi, Cody," he said.

Cody looked at him, but said nothing.

"How's he doing?"

"He's doing better. Every day is better," Kendall said.

"Wish I could say that about me."

Josh Anderson may have been knocked down a peg in the past year, but he was still surprisingly adept at putting himself back into any conversation as its focus.

Steven uncorked the wine and poured it into the bulbous globes of Kendall's grandmother's stemware—the only thing they had in the house that was reserved for company. Josh somehow rated. Steven almost said something about that, but thought better of it. He kind of liked a kicked-to-the-curb Josh.

"Cheers," Steven said, swirling the syrupy red liquid in his crystal wineglass.

Three glasses met in the clinking sound that comes with the promise of a good evening.

They went into the living room with its windows taking in glorious nighttime views of Puget Sound. The choppy waters had been sliced by a passing boat, leaving a foamy V from its engine to the rocky shoreline. They had a few moments before dinner and they chatted about the weather, the view, the things that they were doing around the house.

"How's that class reunion coming along?" Josh asked.

Kendall set down her wine. "Don't get me started."

Steven looked at Josh and grinned. "Don't get *her* started."

Kendall laughed. "Since you brought it up, Josh, I'll ask you to remind me never to get involved in another committee." She glanced in Steven's direction. "Someone here could have saved me a lot of trouble."

"Don't get me involved in this. You're a Wolf through and through," he said, invoking the name of the South Kitsap High School mascot.

"So, really, how's it going?" Josh asked. It seemed that he wanted to talk about something other than himself or the gossip around the sheriff's office, which was fine with Kendall. There was a subject she really didn't want to get into, though she knew the conversation would go that way eventually.

She talked about the process of selecting everything with a group of people who had nothing in common other than they came from the same graduating class.

"Ask me about napkins sometime and I can bore you for a good two hours."

"Napkins can be tricky," Josh said. "Not that I'd know much about that."

"I was thinking the same thing," she said. "You seemed more the kind of guy who'd use your shirtsleeve to wipe off your mouth." She paused. "Not that there's really anything wrong with that."

They laughed a little. It was always fun to zing Josh. Zinging the pompous was always a good time.

With a lull in the conversation, Steven spoke up. "You did have one thing worth talking about today. Tell Josh about your old schoolmate, Tori."

"She was your old schoolmate, too," she said. "I told him."

Josh looked at her. "What's up with your old pal? Win the lotto or something?"

Kendall shook her head. "Not hardly. I mentioned it today in the office. Tori's husband was shot and killed in Tacoma. She was shot, too. Her sister Lainie's on the reunion committee."

Josh narrowed his brow and Kendall's demeanor had changed. If Kendall had mentioned it, it had been so fleeting that he'd missed it. He could have called her on it, but there was no point in that.

"What's up with Tori?" he asked. "I'm getting the vibe here that she's not in your top ten."

Years on the job had allowed Josh and Kendall to understand each other only too well. He could read her and she didn't like that. Not at all.

She set down her wine. "We had our moments. I won't lie. But really, I was better friends with her twin."

Kendall seemed uncomfortable and that made Josh dig a little deeper.

"Twins?"

This time Steven jumped in. "Yes, exactly the same, but completely different."

Kendall looked at her husband, quietly acknowledging what he said was true, then turned her attention back to Josh.

"I like Lainie," she said. Her tone was surprisingly defensive, as if she needed to back up the so-called good twin. For some reason or another. "And honestly, I have no idea how she could share the same genes with her sister."

Kendall stood to go to the kitchen.

"Dinner's ready," she said. "Be prepared, Josh, to have the best lasagna made by a non-Italian. My husband's a pretty good cook."

She faced the lasagna pan and started cutting, the sharp knife slicing through layers of pasta and cheese, clear, distinct strata of white and amber. Each piece came from the pan in a perfect rectangle. There would be no messy, ill-shaped portion served for the cook or his wife.

"So what's the prognosis for Tori?" Josh asked.

Kendall handed him a plate. As steam curled from the food to the ceiling, he breathed in the garlic and oregano as if it were a drug and smiled.

Steven beamed. He knew he was a pretty good cook.

"I don't know," Kendall said. "I really don't know much more than what I've told you."

"Did you call Tacoma PD?" Josh asked.

When Kendall didn't answer right away, Steven echoed the question. "Did you, Kendall?"

She looked at her husband. It was a hard look, the kind of expression meant to shut down that line of questioning before it went too far.

Josh picked up the subtext of the conversation and pounced. "I didn't know you were that close," Josh said.

"Tori and I were schoolmates," she said. "End of story."

"We all were," Steven said, taking a bite. "But then so was Jason Reed."

Jason Reed. Kendall let out a quiet sigh at the mention of his name. She really didn't want to discuss Jason in front of Josh Anderson. Talking about Jason always brought back a flood of sad memories. Sometimes it brought tears, and with tears came too many questions.

Steven spoke up. "Tori was driving a car that killed the guy. Back in high school."

"Parm? I have some shredded in the kitchen," Kendall said, in a completely ungraceful attempt to alter the direction of the conversation.

"Killed the guy?" Josh said, putting down his fork.

"It was an accident," Steven said. "Wreck on Banner. At the Jump. Tori actually did some time for it in juvenile detention. Some people thought she did more and deserved more time. Not all accidents are accidental, you know."

"Some class you SK Wolves must have had back then," Josh said.

"I guess so. Jason's death hit us hard," Kendall said, putting herself back into the conversation, seeking control. "He was so young and it was so final."

"So, are you going to look into Jason's case?" Steven asked.

Kendall shook her head, a rote response to a question she'd already considered. "No," she said, watching her son slide into a chair next to her. "Of course not. But I am worried about Lainie."

The shift in conversation interested Josh. It was like the second half to an ongoing dialog that Steven and Kendall must have engaged in earlier.

"Why dig into it now?" he asked.

Again, Steven answered for Kendall.

"You cops like the word *hinky*, don't you? Something about the case that bothered people. Rumors. Gossip, whatever. There's always a lot of time for speculation in Kitsap County. Not a lot of other things to do."

Kendall didn't want to cause an argument at dinner, but she was irritated with her husband.

"There were some rumors, yes," she said.

"Look," Josh said, leaning closer to her, "I know you. You're gonna dig."

Kendall knew he was right. They both were.

"All right. Probably. Four deaths around one person, that's pretty remarkable odds."

Josh knitted his brows as he swallowed his 92-point pinot—a number he'd exaggerated when he presented the bottle at the front door. It was only an 88. He held out his fingers and wiggled three of them.

"Four?" Josh ticked off two of them. "Jason Reed and her husband in Tacoma? That's two."

Steven nodded as he prepared to drop the bomb. "And the husband before that. Never knew the guy. None of us did. And her mother—that was quite a few years ago. A suicide."

Josh nearly spilled his wine. "You're shitting me."

Kendall looked over at Cody, who was happily enjoying the gooey top layer of his lasagna.

Seeing the boy, Josh Anderson's face went a little red. Despite what everyone thought about him, he knew better than to curse in front of a kid.

"Sorry," he said, lowering his voice. "But you're kidding, right?"

"Afraid not," Steven said. "Husband number one bit the dust on a Hawaiian vacation a few years back."

Josh leaned across the table toward Kendall. Clearly, he was enthralled by the conversation. "Nice. That Tori seems like trouble."

Kendall didn't respond and Steven poured more wine into each of their glasses.

"Yeah, as I recall, that Tori was like a whirlpool," Steven said. "She can suck everyone down in her misery."

"I guess," Kendall finally added. "Like a whirlpool."

Kendall Stark rinsed the dinner plates of the sticky residue of pasta and ricotta before aligning them just so into the open grate of the dishwasher. The breeze had kicked up a little and the flowering plum by the window had lost most of its petals, sending a creamy pink drift across the patio. Josh had gone, and Cody was tucked in down the hall of the old house. She slid the dishwasher shut with her hip as she dried her hands on a white-and-red checkered towel.

The evening had not been bad. Not one hundred percent bad, anyway.

"Look," Steven said after Josh left, "I know you cared about Jason. I get that. He was special to you and he's gone. I'm not threatened by that."

His words were undeniably heartfelt, yet they made Kendall feel uncomfortable. There were areas that had been off limits even in a marriage as good as theirs had been. Jason Reed was one of those areas.

"I know," she said, lying a little to make him feel better. The minute she said it, she questioned it.

Why do I do that? she thought. *Why do I care about making someone feel better all the time?*

As the dishwasher started to hum and Steven went to turn off the lights, Kendall thought of Jason and how she'd been so haunted by his death more than fifteen years ago. The dinner that night. The talk about Tori's latest tragedy, if that's what it was, had released old feelings.

Feelings she avoided.

She wondered what her life might have been like if Jason hadn't died. She wondered what everyone's life might have been like.

Most of all, she felt sad that those thoughts hadn't evaporated over time. Not as she'd been told they would. Not as they should have. Fifteen years, she assured herself, was long enough to grieve.

With Cody already asleep, Kendall turned off the red, white, and blue tugboat lamp by his bedside. She brushed her lips against his straw-colored hair and kissed him good night. She lifted the always-sticky double-hung window a crack to let in a little night air. Not too much. Just a trickle of cool. Cody was one of those kids who slept hot, often kicking off the covers by morning.

Sleep, my baby, she thought.

By the time she got to their bedroom, Steven was already in bed, smelling of toothpaste, and looking at his sales call sheet for the morning. Kendall had a visit with her mother in mind for the next day, but given the late hour, it *was* the next day.

"Don't you ever take a break?" Kendall asked as she undressed.

"When you're on commission," he said, "there's no such thing as a break. Particularly in this day and age."

The publishers of the magazine Steven represented had made a big push to focus on electronic advertising. Steven had gamely gone along with the change. The results were not as encouraging as he'd hoped. It appeared that hunters and fishermen didn't necessarily take their laptops when they went out in the sticks. It appeared that Wi-Fi had not caught up with the great outdoors. Sales were down sharply and he was feeling the pressure.

"Tomorrow's a busy day all the way around," she said, slipping into a chambray blue pair of pajama bottoms and an oversize T-shirt. "I'm going to see Mom. Run some errands. Solve a crime."

"Sexy look, girl," he said, eyeing her as she crawled next to him.

"I'll show you sexy." She kissed him. That was all the cajoling Steven needed. He set down the paperwork that had held his attention. His hands found the softness of her skin underneath the T-shirt. She let out a sigh. They were tenderly entwined, tangled in the bedsheets.

"Didn't take much," she said. "Did it?"

Steven's stubbled face skimmed the surface of her breast as he slid lower into the bed.

She still felt the excitement that came with the touch of her husband.

"No, baby. Not much."

Neither one said another word about Jason Reed. If his ghost had hovered around the dining room only a couple hours ago, he'd vanished once more.

CHAPTER NINE

Tacoma

Tears filled her eyes and there was no stopping them.

I shouldn't feel this sad, but I do, Laura Connelly thought. Her ex-husband's death had left her feeling bereft in a way that she would have told someone a week ago was completely impossible. Alex had left her for another woman. Betrayed her. Left their son.

And yet my heart aches? Why?

At her home in Fircrest, just south of Tacoma, a broken-hearted Laura moved about her seventeen-year-old son's bedroom, picking up what he'd carelessly left on the floor. It was early in the morning, and Parker hadn't come home. He'd been doing a lot of that lately—staying with his best friend, Drew. Laura was a petite strawberry blonde, with green eyes that she made the color of clover with tinted contact lenses. In her mid-forties, she was a single mother with no prospects for being anything but. Her world was about her son. It had been that way for a very long time. Until that week, Parker had his dad, too.

But no more.

She shook her head as she looked around. Parker was no more a slob than any boy his age, but she'd noticed a little improvement in areas that mattered. He'd asked her to buy new jeans and a couple of new shirts. He even wanted new underwear.

"Not boxers, Mom, boxer briefs. They fit better."

Point taken. In fact, everything Parker wanted those days seemed to reflect a need to improve his appearance. He'd been working out, bulking up his adolescent frame to one that showed the definition of a young man's physique. Not quite six-pack abs, but getting there. When he wasn't Skyping on his computer, he was out running or lifting weights in the basement.

Parker was growing into a young man, and whatever she thought of Alex, she knew that only in death—senseless, untimely, tragic—would he leave his son behind.

A pair of Tacoma police officers came the morning after the shooting to let them know what happened. Parker got up from the breakfast table and bolted for the door. He didn't say a word. He didn't even take his backpack to go to school. He just left.

Come home, baby, she thought over and over. *I'm still here. I won't leave you.*

Everything in her son's room took on an unbridled poignancy. Laura smiled when she came across his cache of personal hygiene products on top of the cherry highboy. A bottle of body spray, a tube of acne medicine that he'd begged her to buy off a TV commercial, and a hair product called Bèd Head. Her teenage son was growing up. He was still somewhat distant, but the signs were there. He was interested in girls. That was good. While her relationships with men had not gone the distance—her failed marriage to Alex was only one of four longtime relationships that had ended—she hoped that Parker would have better luck in that arena. His relationship with his father and stepmother had also improved. The cellular phone bill indicated a sharp increase in phone calls to his father's.

That was good, too.

In putting away his neatly matched socks in a top drawer that was only organized when she did the arranging, she noticed a flash of red and white, a greeting card. Its red heart with an arrow indicated a valentine. She opened it and read the message:

> *Our love is forever. I will wait for you. Will you wait for me?*

It was signed, somewhat cryptically, *Me*.

Tears flowed freely as she thought of Alex and how they'd met on the stainless-steel dance floor at the Black Angus in Bremerton. He was young, handsome. *Attentive*. A naval officer with plans for the future that included getting a master's degree in finance. The message on the card reminded her of their own love story. Alex was transferred to San Diego for a year.

And, yes, she waited for him.

When he returned to Bremerton the following year, he had a new tattoo on his chest and a diamond engagement ring for Laura's finger.

Underneath the first card, she found a second one. This one featured the image of two swans, their necks forming the shape of a heart.

It was wrong to invade Parker's space and his mom knew it. Yet she couldn't help herself. Her son had been so unhappy, so wounded. Few mothers can resist the urge to learn more about the girl who had given her boy a reason to smile.

> *When one swan dies, so does the other. I can't live without you.*

The handwriting was a neat script, the same script as on the other.

Teenagers. Everything is so dramatic, she thought, closing the drawer.

Before Alex's murder, Laura considered Parker's eighteenth birthday as a personal and financial game changer. The substantial child support that Alex had faithfully sent each month since their divorce would cease. It was far from a gravy train, but its derailment was going to be tough. She was unsure exactly what she would do to get by. It was true that she had investments and a decent nest egg, but the cash flow that came from Alex's account to hers was the kind of money that made the difference between being comfortable and having strained finances. She could buy what she wanted. Eat out whenever she liked. She could even afford to have her car detailed once a month.

All of that would be off the table when the support checks stopped.

Alex wasn't blameless in all of that, of course. And, though she loathed to admit it to herself, she'd once hoped that Alex would drop dead of a heart attack. He had a sizable life insurance policy and she was the beneficiary. She could have lived nicely on that. She could have avoided the embarrassment of giving up a big house, European vacations, and platinum tennis bracelets. But Alex didn't drop dead before they were divorced.

And there was clearly no stopping Tori. She popped into her husband's life at a time when Laura and Alex were at odds, when the excitement of their marriage had faded into a world of obligation.

She saw Tori as a schemer who used her considerable charms to snare a man who wanted that last gasp of youth that comes in one's forties. A wife the same age was only a mirror to the passage of the days and months of his life.

Laura hated Tori for coming into their lives. The blonde with the perfect body had wriggled her way into their affairs like a beautiful virus. She wanted what she saw—a husband with a bank account that would keep her in expensive clothes, a nice house, and a car that would be the envy of those who care about such things. Alex had other affairs during their marriage, but none lasted. None had morphed into anything other than sex and secrecy.

Yet Tori would have none of that. She played to win. As Laura saw her, Tori was one of those women who knew that the power in their beauty was a commodity that was never to be given away without something in return.

"Don't worry, Laura," Tori had said over the phone, when Laura had called to discuss Parker's declining grades. "I don't want to take your place."

"Really? That seems to be exactly what you've done."

"I mean with Parker. I don't want to be his mother and I won't even try. I want him to think of me as a friend."

"He doesn't need another mother, and to be frank, he doesn't need a friend, either. He has plenty."

"That's good to know," she said. "He seems a little lonely. He shares so much with me that I just want to be helpful. It isn't easy being a child of divorce. I want to be there for him."

Laura held her tongue, which was the only thing a decent person could do. Tori was Alex's problem. Certainly she wanted to blast the bitch and say something about the fact that *she* had caused the divorce, but there was no point in that.

"Thanks for your concern," she said before hanging up. She seethed a moment and went for a vodka tonic.

Absolut vodka today, Brand X tomorrow.

All of that had felt so foolish now. All of her worries about how she was going to survive after her son's birthday were an embarrassment now. She'd never say a word to anyone what her hopes had been.

No one would understand.

CHAPTER TEN

Port Orchard, Washington

The Landing at Port Orchard was the newest assisted-living residence for seniors "who need a little extra care" in the small city on Puget Sound. The first floor was beautifully if predictably appointed: leather couches, wingback chairs with brass nailhead detailing, and a gas fireplace that was perpetually on. The river rock–faced hearth was outfitted with a raffia-bound bundle of birch twigs and an old-fashioned popcorn popper, the kind that would be used over a campfire. Above the fireplace, illuminated by a trio of halogen lights, was a three-foot model of a red canoe. Most of the design—from the colors of the fabrics and walls to the nostalgic artifacts placed around the entire first floor—was in what the center's director called "memory chic." None of it was real, but all of it was designed to help residents and visitors recall a time when they could remember. When they didn't need a schedule or a prompt to remind them what to do next.

In reality, the ambiance of the Landing was that of a slightly overdone theme restaurant in which artifacts were used to suggest, rather than to recall, specific memories.

Bettina Maguire had been at the Landing for more than three years, having survived a car accident on an icy road in northern Kitsap County that killed her husband and Kendall's father, Ben. A retired high school shop teacher, Ben had been driving when a deer stepped out of the shadows; he did what he told his daughter and wife never to do: he swerved, his own advice of "hitting the animal will kill it, but hitting a tree will kill you" unheeded.

Bettina's brain had been damaged in the accident, as had her once indomitable spirit. She'd also taught school for decades, specializing in art. Before the accident, she often talked about the lovely mosaic that she helped the children create; it had been featured in the *Seattle Times*. Bettina's depiction of Port Orchard's history was told through the tiny shards of broken pottery, glassware, and one very upset student's mother's prized wedding platter.

Kendall arrived at the Landing feeling tired from a sleepless night full of thoughts about a criminal case in which she had no stake.

Tacoma PD can deal with the likes of Tori, she thought.

She had parked her SUV and headed inside to sign in when her cell rang. She looked down at the display. The incoming call was from Adam Canfield. She pushed the button to send it immediately to voice mail, then she reached for one of the pens embellished with roses that were stuck in a flower pot on the reception desk.

"How's my mom?" she asked Samantha, the young woman whose name tag suggested she was a "Landing hostess" and not a desk clerk.

"You know the way it is around here. Good days, bad days. Your mom's having a bad one."

Samantha's voice was chirpy and relentlessly upbeat.

"I'm sure."

"One thing I'm sure about is that she will be so very happy to see you!"

So very happy.

Kendall made her way to Room 14, on the first floor of south side of the building. She passed by a group of old women moving puzzle pieces on a tabletop and smiled at the one who looked at her. The building's three floors told the story of an occupant's status. Those on the upper floors were, generally, in better health. Mobile. Put together. *Cognizant.* Those attributes dwindled closer to the first floor. Bettina Maguire had stayed on the second floor for only two months before they moved her to the first floor, close to the medical staff. Her health had been failing, and failing fast.

"It's better for everyone," the director had said. "Easier, you know, if she needs help."

The steel door that was more hospital than residential was open, and Kendall went into her mother's room.

Bettina was in bed, her face turned away from the window. Her right hand held the steel tube of the bed rail. Her fingers no longer looked like the mother's hands that had once caressed her daughter. They were gnarled sticks, dipped in a milky blue. Her once-marmalade hair was now white.

"Mom?"

Bettina's head turned, her eyes flickering with recognition.

"Kendall, you're here."

Kendall bent down and kissed her mother's rice-paper skin.

"You warm enough?" she asked, fussing with the pale yellow coverlet that had been her mother's favorite.

"I'm fine, dear. Daddy and I were talking about you last night."

A nurse had told Kendall that correcting her mother was not necessary and, if it didn't bother Kendall too much, to play along.

"You can't change what a person knows, even if it is wrong," the nurse had said.

Kendall patted her mother's feet.

"What were you two conspiring about?"

Bettina smiled. "Just how proud we are of you."

Kendall shook her head and poured some water from a white plastic pitcher on a stainless-steel tray that the staff had brought in. She glanced around the room, noticing that her mother's collection of miniature porcelain shoes had been boxed up. The room was looking more and more institutional.

Bettina lifted her head and sucked on the straw, her lips groping the tube as if she were feeling it instead of attempting to drink. Her eyes met Kendall's with a look of warmth, appreciation. She nodded as she leaned back on her pillow, which Kendall had fluffed slightly in the moment that she had been able do so.

"You're a good daughter, Kendall."

"I try. Would you like me to sit with you?"

"That would be nice. Tell me, dear, what are you working on?"

"Same old, Mom. Bad people doing bad things."

"Sending lots of people to jail, I hope. Might do them some good."

"Some, not all," Kendall said. "Remember, sending people to jail doesn't make anyone better."

Bettina smiled. "No, it doesn't. But it makes me *feel* better."

It was funny how that moment would recur between Kendall and her mom now and then. She was an officer of the court, a detective no less, and she could clearly see that her mother and she had both been right: sending someone to jail didn't do much for the inmate, but it did make everyone else feel a little better.

She thought of Tori and Jason. She hadn't been sure if she would bring it up to her mother. Bettina had known both of them back in the day. She'd be interested, for sure. She might even be a little judgmental. Her mom could be that way.

"Mom, we got some news that Tori O'Neal's husband was killed."

"That was a long time ago," Bettina said.

Kendall shook her head. Her mother was having a very "good" day indeed. "Not the husband in Hawaii. Her *new* husband. He was shot in their home in Tacoma."

"Tacoma?"

"Yes."

"I never liked that girl," Bettina said.

Kendall nodded. "I know, Mom. You've told me. Tori's latest trouble made me think of Jason."

"Jason was very handsome, wasn't he?"

"Yes. He was."

Kendall didn't allow her eyes to tear up. She couldn't start that now.

"I loved him, Mom," she said.

Bettina's washed-out blue eyes studied her daughter's face, looking for something, but not seeing it. "I'm sorry that things turned out the way they did," she said.

Kendall nodded. "I know. I'm just not sure about everything back then. If . . ." Her words trailed off.

"I know where you're going, honey," she said. "And we can't talk about it."

"Can't we talk about it now, Mom? It has been such a long time."

"Leave it alone, honey. Keep doing the right thing. You were made for doing the right thing." Bettina closed her eyes, her signal that she was either tired or the conversation was over. Kendall couldn't quite be sure.

"All right, Mom," she said, leaning down to kiss her

good-bye. They had never been able to talk about it. It was clear that no matter how much time had passed, there would be no good time to discuss Jason or any of it.

Heading out the door, she played her message from Adam.

"Kendall, you've got to find out what's up with Tori. Don't you have a friend over there in Tacoma? Someone you can call with some kind of police referral? I don't know anyone, or I would. See you at the meeting. Only seven days to go and we get our freedom back."

Kendall didn't need a nudge to find out what was up in Tacoma with their old classmate. She'd already decided she'd do so as a professional courtesy.

After all, she thought, *they probably have no idea who they're dealing with. Tori was always pretty good at fooling people.*

She had written down the name of the lead detective on the case: *Eddie Kaminski*.

A guilty conscience can be akin to a thermos of black coffee at midnight. Eyes cannot stay shuttered. Muscles cannot relax. Sleep is a quest beyond the grasp of those who wrestle with the wrongs they've done. The clock is a snare drum.

Darius Fulton couldn't sleep. He'd tossed and turned the entire night. A loose bedsheet nearly encircled his neck and choked him. He'd wished that it *had*. Every time he almost drifted off to sleep, he saw the smear of red on Tori Connelly's nightgown. It had pooled above her thighs in a swirling pattern that he was certain was caused by her hurried run across the street to his house. Her skin was white. *Paler than he'd ever seen*. She wasn't a serial tanner like so many of the younger women he'd dated after his wife had dumped him. She had seemed classier, kinder.

And while her charms were more than just her physical attributes, those were unquestionably the reason why he'd slept with her.

It was only *one* time. It was a mistake and he knew it. She was married.

Yet it felt so good.

They'd come across each other at a lecture at the Washington State History Museum in downtown Tacoma. The museum was in a completely refurbished 1911 train depot and was considered—along with a new museum dedicated to glass arts—a cornerstone of the city's rebirth. They'd noticed each other going inside.

"We're neighbors," she said, walking toward him, "at least I think so."

"Welcome to the City of Destiny," he said. "I guess I should have brought over a pie or something."

"Oh, does your wife bake?" she asked, looking at the pale band of white skin where his wedding ring had once been.

"I'm separated. That's why I'm here alone."

"My husband is a workaholic," she said. "That's my excuse. And I'm sticking with it."

Two days later, he was over at her house ostensibly because she was having problems with the alarm system.

Tori put her hand on his shoulder, letting it loiter as he peered into the wiring with a flashlight. She let her hand slide down his back, landing at the leather of his belt.

He turned around and looked at her.

Her touch was an unexpected invitation and Darius took it. He leaned closer and kissed her.

"I'm so lonely," she said.

"I am, too."

They kissed again.

"Tori, this isn't right."

"It seems right to me," she said.

Ten minutes later, they were sprawled out naked under the canopy of a big bed in the guest room. She was, without question, the most beautiful woman he'd ever seen. It was as if he'd been captured by some kind of superior being from another world. Her touch was electric. Her voice, her breath, all of it made his body throb with pleasure.

"Tori," he said, "you are an amazing woman."

"Let's not get carried away," she said.

The next day, her husband out of town, Darius showed up with a bottle of wine. She met him at the door, but she didn't invite him inside.

"Darius," she said, "I think you might have the wrong idea here."

"I wasn't being presumptuous," he said, before reading her body language and the cool expression on her face. "I mean, I'm sorry."

There was no smile on her face, no trace of anything that indicated any kind of sympathy for the awkwardness of the moment.

"I'm not interested," she said.

He lowered the wine bottle to his side.

"We're not lovers," she said. "What happened was fun, but only a little bit fun."

His face went red. Tori Connelly was *dismissing* him. If he'd felt that he might have gotten his game back the night before . . . if he felt that whatever his cheating wife had done to him was now erased by sex with a beautiful woman, he was misguided.

"I'm sorry," he said. "I guess I made a mistake."

Darius didn't know it at the time, but he was so right about that. So very, very right.

And now Alex Connelly was dead.

He dialed the number Detective Eddie Kaminski had left

the night of Alex Connelly's murder, the night that Tori Connelly had been shot. It went to voice mail and he did as commanded.

"Darius Fulton here. I want to come in and talk to you. In person."

CHAPTER ELEVEN

Tacoma

Corazón White rolled a cart with a snack for Tori Connelly, a task that a nurse would never have to do if not for the budget cutbacks that left the hospital short staffed. Mrs. Connelly had somehow managed to make a bad situation worse. The gunshot victim's latest annoyance was her request for an egg white omelet and side of whole wheat toast "no crust please" and "a dark juice of either acai or pomegranate."

"We have orange, tomato, or pineapple," Corazón said while she took her order and did her vitals for the doctor's rounds earlier that morning.

Tori frowned and fussed with the IV line again. "This is a hospital, isn't it?"

"Yes, of course it is."

"Surely, you've heard of the benefits of dark juices."

She wanted to play dumb and say her name wasn't Shirley. Mrs. Connelly was getting on her nerves.

"Yes, I have."

"Well, your dietician here ought to have his or her work permit pulled. The juices you offer might as well be colored sugar water, because you're not giving your patients anything of value."

The "work permit" phrase was a slam and Corazón knew it. She'd also waitressed through nursing school and knew that such arguments can never be won.

"I'll see what I can do," she said.

It turned out she could do next to nothing. Mrs. Connelly wasn't getting any pomegranate juice. She was getting orange like everyone else on the floor.

"Best I could do," Corazón said, wheeling the tray into the room.

"Your best is not going to be noted on my comment card. If you have one here. I guess one would be surprised if you did."

Corazón wanted to say something rude back, but she held her tongue. The woman with the wound on her thigh and the perfect haircut thought she was in a spa or hotel, not a hospital. She sure wasn't acting like a woman who had just lost her husband in a violent shooting.

She started to pull the curtain, even though the room was without a second bed.

"I know you'll want some peace to eat your meal, Mrs. Connelly."

After her encounter with "the bitch in 561D," Corazón did only the minimum required. She saw the patient. She tried not to engage her. The woman on the other side of the perma-drawn curtain didn't seem to mind. Being alone and being the subject of hospital gossip didn't trouble her one iota.

Corazón stalled when she came to get the food tray. Tori Connelly was on the phone and Corazón didn't want to disturb her. Instead, she parked herself a few steps inside the doorway.

"Do not call me back," Tori said.

A short pause.

"Are you listening? I do not want to talk to you. Not for a while."

Her tone was demanding and exceedingly direct.

"I won't say another word about it and neither will you."

The next pause was a bit longer.

"You will do what I say. Good-bye."

Corazón wasn't completely sure what she heard, but she'd been browbeaten by Tori Connelly once and that was enough. She waited a second, and then made her presence known by rattling the metal cart.

"Hope you're feeling better," she said.

Tori looked at the young nurse when the curtain parted. She was wary. Her eyes fixed on Corazón's.

"Talking to my sister just now."

"Oh, your chart says you don't have any family," Corazón said, careful not to sound like she was anything but bored with her patient. She disliked this lady, but she knew the type. They'd make trouble for anyone they could. Making trouble was a sport for those who could afford to play the game.

"She's coming from Seattle," Tori said.

"Seattle's pretty."

"And boring. You'd like my sister."

Corazón wasn't sure who was the subject of the put-down—the sister or *her*. She was just glad that whenever Tori Connelly was discharged, she'd be rid of her. Her sister, poor thing, was stuck with that woman for the rest of her life.

"I want to see the doctor. A real doctor. Not a nurse. Not a trainee." Tori pulled herself up. "I want out of here. I can rest more comfortably at home."

Corazón figured they both could.

"The doctor will be in soon. Just rest, okay?"

She left the room glad that the patient wanted to leave and feeling sorry for the sister who was stuck with such a . . . *Class-A bitch,* she thought. *Yeah, that's what she is.*

There was something oddly gratifying about the e-mails— knowing that she would see them, react to them, and they'd make love.

I miss you. I miss how you feel in my arms.

You are being cold to me. How come?

What have I done?

I saw you yesterday outside. I waved but you ignored me. I don't get it.

Your husband is a fool. He's not taking care of you. Not like I would.

Please. Don't do this to me. Give me another chance.

Not every message got a reply, but those that did were unfailingly direct.

Stop.

I don't want to see you again.

My husband knows what happened and he loves me enough to forgive me.

It is over.

Smooth jazz played from the stereo in the other room, but it did little to abate the tension in the air. The lovely little house in Fircrest never held a vibe that matched its charming Cape Cod exterior. Laura and Parker Connelly were mother and son, but they were increasingly at odds. Alex Connelly's brutal murder on the other side of town had done nothing to bring them together. The two residents in that little house knew firsthand that times of crisis aren't always measured in the positive. Sometimes there was no bright side.

"Honey," Laura Connelly said, putting her hand on her son's shoulder as she cleared the dishes from the kitchen table, "I'm worried about you." She had fixed him his "unhealthy favorite" fish and chips with chipotle mayo and a carrot-and-cabbage slaw. It was a thousand calories a serving and the house smelled like a fast-food joint. Laura didn't mind. She noticed a widening gap in their relationship and she wanted more than anything to win him back. Whatever secrets he'd been keeping had been wearing on her.

"I'm doing okay, Mom," he said unconvincingly. He fished a French fry off her plate as she started for the sink, a wobbly stack of dishes in hand.

"Are you, really?" Without turning around, Laura started rinsing plates in preparation for loading the dishwasher. Avoiding eye contact was a strategy. Her son hated confrontation. "You haven't talked much about your father's death."

Parker pushed back his chair and looked over at his mother. "There isn't much to talk about."

She turned off the faucet and reached for a kitchen towel. Again, no eye contact. "It would be all right to be mad at him, if that's what you're feeling."

"I am mad at him, but I really am not having any kind of struggle about him dying. He treated all of us like a big jerk. You, me, Tori."

"Tori?"

"Yes, her, too."

"How did he treat her? I thought they'd been happy."

He shook his head. "I'm not going to get into it, Mom. Tori's a private person. I just know stuff."

"What kind of stuff?"

Parker knew that on some level his mother had every reason to hate Tori. Yet he wanted her to know that she was wrong for doing so. Tori was a victim, too.

"Dad was cheating on her," he said.

Laura didn't say it, but she wanted to. *What goes around comes around.* "All right, let's change the subject. Tell me about this girlfriend of yours."

"Have you been spying on me again?"

"A mother looking out for her son isn't spying, Parker."

"She's just some girl. She's cool. That's all you need to know."

"When do I get to meet her?"

"I don't know, Mom, maybe never."

Part of him wanted to shout it in the middle of the mall that he and Tori were lovers. But his mother would never, ever understand. He didn't think anyone could understand. He also knew that what he and his stepmother were doing was illegal.

"If she's so cool, why can't I meet her?" Laura asked.

"Because you can't," he said.

"I don't want to see you get hurt."

The idea of his mother dispensing that kind of advice set him off. His face went red. She could be so stupid. Tori warned him about women like his mother.

They say they know best because they don't want you to find what eluded them, she said the first time they made love. *I know best. I can give you what you need.*

"Jesus, Mom, there's no chance of that. I've found my soul mate. Look at you. You're alone. You don't have a freaking soul who cares about you. You think I want to end up like you?" He got up from the table and started for his bedroom. "And I don't appreciate you going through my stuff, Mom. That's over the line, even for a control freak like you."

Laura didn't dissolve into tears, though she felt like it.

Her son was growing up. He was trying to find his own way. He was such a good, sweet boy. She was sure that whatever girl he was dating was going to be just like him—good, sweet.

She could not have been more wrong.

Parker's phone buzzed. He looked down at the text message and took a deep breath.

HAVE U LEFT YET?
THE SOONER THE BETTER.
MISS U.
LOVE, ME.

CHAPTER TWELVE

Kitsap County

Kitsap County forensic pathologist Birdy Waterman kept a completely well thought-out workspace, even if her surroundings suggested more of the makings of a gruesome garage sale than the offices of the county coroner. The house at 704 Sidney was exactly that, a *house*. County commissioners and law enforcement had resumed talks about the need for a state-of-the-art facility, but money remained in short supply. Recently, jail and administrative offices had been renovated and rebuilt, and clamped-handed conservative taxpayers were not in the mood to shell out more so soon. So the sad little house pressed into service by a tight budget had been the place of a thousand autopsies in its dank, cement-floored basement.

Like Hollywood deaths, Kitsap deaths often came in threes.

That month the tragic ending to a trio of lives had already crammed the first week in May of the coroner's calendar. The first was a Southworth toddler who'd been run over by her father as he backed out of the driveway in a hurry for work. The second found its way to the basement morgue in the remains of a Port Orchard man whose hand had become tangled in a fishing net with no time to free himself before being pulled underwater just west of Blake Island. The third was a Poulsbo woman who had packed up all of her belongings to make her getaway from a husband who'd used her as a punching bag whenever he drank—which was daily. She'd made a run for it one night, but she wasn't fast enough. He severed her jugular with the splintered end of a Monarch vodka bottle.

That last one echoed scenes from Birdy's own childhood. Not the murder, of course, but the darkness that came with living in a household in which booze was the dominating force behind every act of evil done to her mother.

And there were too many of those moments to forget.

Outside, Kendall Stark peered into the small window of the basement autopsy suite of the Kitsap County Coroner's Office. It was dark, which was in its own way a relief. Kendall didn't mind dealing with the aftermath of an actual crime scene when gathering evidence. Those moments came with a kind of adrenaline surge to ensure that everything was done with complete urgency, as if a dead person's life depended on it.

Which it did.

On the other hand, autopsies were slow, mechanical, and sad. Though they were often the start of the real investigation, they held no adrenaline surge for the practitioner or observer.

The hemline of Kendall Stark's black slacks wicked water from a puddle as she went around the coroner's office toward the front door. The detective always felt a little funny about going inside. Walking up the wet sidewalk between the overgrown shrubberies, up the concrete steps to the front door, felt like one was visiting a friend, not a county government office. She buzzed, identified herself, and went inside.

From the small foyer, she passed the desk of the administrative assistant, a capable silver-haired woman who'd been with the office longer than anyone. Kendall smiled at Pamela, who was on the phone negotiating a warranty on a Stryker saw that had gone kaput. She walked toward Dr. Waterman's office, across green hi-lo carpeting that had been splattered with stains made by God-knew-what.

Leaking bags of bodily fluids? Or the dribble of tea from the kitchen in the back of the office?

Birdy, her black hair swept back by a bright red clip, hovered over her work. A plastic and foam tote holding the fragments of a woman who'd been shot three times in the head by her estranged boyfriend sat on her desk, the focus of her attention. She was in the midst of marking chain-of-custody paperwork that would take the tissue samples to the state crime lab in Olympia, where toxicologists would examine everything for drugs—prescription or otherwise.

"I thought you might be downstairs," Kendall said. "Heard about the crash on the highway last night."

Birdy looked up. She slid a manifest about what was being dispatched to Olympia into a glassine. She scooted the tote aside.

"The girl was seventeen. Died at the scene. Broken neck. Honestly too many broken bones to count, but I logged in every one. Once you find a severed spinal cord, you don't need to look for another cause of death." Birdy let out a sigh and ran a line of evidence tape down the center of the tote, over the glassine, and under the bottom of the container. "Driver, a drunk from Gig Harbor, walked away without so much as a scratch."

Kendall sat in one of two old typing chairs being used for visitors in a place that seldom had many, or rather, many visitors who were *living*.

"Seventeen," she said. "That's so young."

That's the same age as Jason.

"Almost everyone who comes through here has died too young, Kendall. But you're right. This is a heartbreaker of the worst kind. The girl was a straight-A student and captain of her tennis team. Pretty. Smart. Athletic. The kind of girl you'd want your daughter to be."

Fifteen years ago, Kendall *was* that girl.

"Notification?" As Kendall slid her coat off her shoulders and let it fall over the chair back, its sleeves tumbled to the awful green carpet and she pulled them onto her lap.

Birdy nodded. "Handled. The parents were at the scene when they brought her in."

The words were so painful, Kendall was grateful that this was one notification she didn't have to make.

"Nothing is more difficult," she said.

Birdy looked at the clock on the wall behind Kendall. "She's in the chiller. The guys from Rill's Chapel will be here in an hour."

The doctor and the detective were friends, and they used a few minutes of their time to catch up. At forty, Birdy had married the owner of a Port Orchard restaurant the previous summer. Her life had seemed to run in a series of long-delayed changes. She never looked happier. A sparkle in her eyes. A smile on her face. Birdy Waterman was a late bloomer, a woman who'd put her career ahead of personal aspirations and desires. She once told Kendall that she'd forgone marriage and all that went with it out of a sense of duty, a need to achieve all she could.

"You know," she said. "Because of where I came from and how what I do reflects on my people."

Kendall had understood, yet there was nothing to which she could personally relate. She'd had the nice middle-class life in Small Town, America. Her parents adored her and her sister, and they'd never really gone without. If they needed something, they got it. It wasn't always the best quality, but growing up in Port Orchard, they didn't necessarily know the difference between Walmart and Nordstrom.

Birdy had been born on a reservation to an alcoholic mother and a father she barely knew.

"My people need something to hold on to, and every time I go home, I am reminded of that. It is loud and very, very clear."

Kendall knew that was true. One of the rare times was when she'd been over to Birdy's new place on the bluff overlooking the Southworth ferry landing, she'd overheard bits and pieces of a phone conversation.

"Are you all right, Mom?"

"Have you been drinking?"

"Mom, just go to bed. Just crawl under the covers."

"No, there is nothing I can prescribe for you; you need to see Dr. Bergman."

"Mom, don't do this now."

Kendall had seen the hurt and fear in Birdy's eyes after she hung up the phone.

Awkwardness had penetrated the air.

"I'm sorry," Birdy said. "My mother has problems."

Kendall considered Birdy one of the most accomplished women she'd ever known. Certainly, she knew she'd grown up poor, but somehow she hadn't let it pass through her mind that the stunning black-haired woman with the medical degree had any battles left to fight.

"I'm sorry," Kendall said. "If there's anything I can do . . ."

The offer had been genuine, but words uttered in that sequence rarely carry much weight. People mean well most of the time, but sometimes they only mean to put a period on an uncomfortable moment. An offer of kindness that will never be cashed in, never be due.

"You're not here about the crash vic this morning, are you, Kendall?"

Kendall shook her head. "No. Something from quite some time ago. You probably don't have it."

Birdy smiled. "I sense a little trepidation there. You must know about our wonderful filing system." She looked toward the stairway to the attic.

"I'm sure it's better than ours," Kendall said, recalling the difficulty the sheriff's office had when the records division went to a fully computerized system some years ago.

"What's the case? And, almost more important, *when* was it?"

"November or October 1994. A fatal accident on Banner Road. The victim was a seventeen-year-old-boy named Jason Reed."

The forensic pathologist took in the information, but her face was without recognition.

"Doesn't ring a bell," she said. "It'll take some looking. I can dig around this afternoon."

Kendall thanked her, stood, and reached for her coat, a long lapis peacoat that was more suitable for winter than for spring.

Washington weather for you, she'd thought, when she put it on that morning. *Never warm when it should be.*

"No big rush," she finally said to Birdy, though she really didn't mean it.

Kendall walked back from the coroner's office across the parking lot toward the rear entrance of the Kitsap County sheriff's offices. The rain had slickened the lot, leaving a dozen puddles swirling with the iridescence of motor oil. She drew her hands into her pockets to hike up her pant legs. She needed to do something about those pants. Ordering on-line was easy, but the fit was never right.

She wondered how it was that so many years had passed since she thought of Jason and the night that he'd died. In the months following the accident, she doubted that a day went by without her thinking of it.

Jason Reed's death had changed the trajectory of so many of their lives. Especially her own.

It took about two minutes for the staff in the Tacoma PD crime lab to validate that the gun recovered from the Connelly residence had been, in fact, the murder weapon. Three casings retrieved from the scene and slugs from Alex Connelly's brain were fired from a 357 Ruger. DNA analysis on the gun had confirmed it. Traces of blood and hair—belonging to Alex Connelly—were found on the outside edges of the barrel. A second person's DNA was also captured along the underside of the gun's barrel. There was a partial print, but it was barely there at all. Also missing were the weapon's identification numbers. They'd been somewhat crudely scratched out.

"An attempt to obliterate the serial numbers was made by someone," a technician named Carol-Ann told Kaminski when he sidled up next to her behind the counter, where she'd placed the gun under a microscope outfitted with a camera.

He leaned as close as he could without interfering with her personal space. Carol-Ann could be touchy. "You read anything?"

She barely glanced at him before answering. "Of course. That's my job. I'll run some prints for you, but the printer's in its god-awful cleaning cycle—ten minutes or ten hours."

"Just read 'em. I've got a pen."

She read out the numbers and Kaminski jotted them down.

"Wonder where this will lead?" he said.

"Back to Connelly's front door," Carol-Ann said. "I'm not a detective, but I'd say a random intruder might shop at

Target, but I doubt they'd bring the bag to the crime scene and dump it off right in the bushes or pond or whatever."

He almost corrected her by calling the store Tar-*zhay*, as Lindsey did, but he didn't think that would get Carol-Ann to smile.

Nothing ever did.

CHAPTER THIRTEEN

Kitsap County

Kendall hadn't suggested any real urgency, but Birdy Waterman was never the type to hear a request made more than once. She found the 1994 Jason Reed file in the attic in a plastic tub of other files that had never been converted to microfilm or destroyed as a matter of disposal protocol. That wasn't unusual, given the cost of the conversion process, but it was fortuitous. She went into the coroner's office kitchen with its view of the county's administrative buildings, courthouse, and always-jammed parking lots. At one time the homeowners who lived there when the house was new probably had views of the Olympics and Sinclair Inlet. She poured some coffee from a formerly white, then brown Mr. Coffee machine that had been there longer than she had.

The file folder was thin: a single X-ray film, a death certificate, and a partial police report covering the basics of the accident. Tori O'Neal had been the driver, with the victim Jason Reed in the passenger seat. Her sister, Lainie, had been in the backseat. The twins' statements were identical. They'd been to a party where there had been drinking. The roadway was wet. Tori was driving at least ten miles an hour too fast—but, she insisted, not much more than that. The file was interesting for what it didn't contain—an autopsy report. Yet, a death certificate had been issued. A predecessor had signed off on it—internal injuries the result of impact in a car accident.

Birdy set the film against the light box and flipped the switch. It was an X-ray of Jason Reed's chest, indicating several broken ribs. The fractures were consistent with the crash described in the report. She looked closer, fumbling for glasses she still was not used to wearing. The fractures did not indicate that they'd splintered and pierced any organs. Nor was there any pooling of blood.

She looked closer yet. Although the previous pathologist had likely meant only to cover only the dead boy's chest, at the top of the frame Birdy's dark eyes fastened on the horseshoe-shaped hyoid bone. It had been broken. In a boy the age of Jason Reed, that particular bone was not likely to have broken in the impact of the crash—it was known for its flexibility as it hadn't completed the process of ossification.

Yet Jason's was broken, crushed, *smashed*.

She set down the film and called Kendall.

"You in your office?" she asked.

"I am."

"Good. I feel like taking a walk. I've got something to show you."

Birdy Waterman smiled at the photo of Cody and Steven on Kendall's desk. It was an image Kendall had taken of the two of them crabbing off the dock in Harper. Though they hadn't caught anything of consequence, it was clear that father and son were enjoying the sunny weather, the water, and the pleasure of just hanging out and having a good time.

"Cody looks happy," she said, taking a seat.

"That was a great day. We're having a lot of those lately," Kendall said, not wanting to jinx it, but happy to acknowledge that life had become better, more joyous, over the past months. Hers was not like anyone else's family, but she was feeling a lot better about their lives and the road that they'd been on since Cody's autism diagnosis.

"I have something to show you," Birdy said, turning the banker's lamp on Kendall's desk upward. She pulled the film from an oversize envelope.

"Jason Reed," she said.

Kendall nodded and looked on. "I knew you'd find him."

"I don't want to lie and tell you it was difficult. There seems to be a method to the madness in the attic."

"Sounds like a horror movie," Kendall said.

Birdy missed the reference and looked unsure.

"*The Madness in the Attic* starring some TV actor."

"Yes, Tony Danza."

Kendall laughed. "I like it. Random, but I like it."

The forensic pathologist held the film to the light, darkening the room. She pointed out her discovery.

"Is this conclusive?" Kendall asked.

Birdy didn't think so. "Not at all. But given what we know about Tori O'Neal now, it might be wise to take another look."

"Why didn't they catch that the first time?" Kendall asked.

Birdy shook her head. "I'd like to say that I'm a lot better at my job than any of my predecessors, but I won't. Mistakes happen."

"Are you thinking, what, a second autopsy?"

Birdy's dark eyes flashed. "Yes. And sadly, you know what that means."

Kendall's eyes landed on Cody's photo, his halo of blond hair, his blue eyes, and the smile that spoke of a cherished moment and the promise of more to come.

"No mother should ever have to go through that twice,"
she said.

Mary Reed knew that the rhythm of her life had been interrupted. At fifty-nine, she was a woman who had always
liked order. She'd found comfort in ensuring that everything
lined up in ways that it ought to. She did that for more than
twenty-five years as a custodian at the Kitsap County Courthouse. All of her cleaning supplies were set on her swiveling-
caster cart in a sequence that made perfect sense. She always
worked from top to bottom: glass and mirror cleaner (no
streaks), counter surface cleanser (disinfects, too), and the
industrial floor cleaner that she was sure would give her lung
cancer someday, despite assurances that it was not toxic to
humans. Mary, a woman of some girth and muscle, considered the sequence of things in everything she did. And yet,
she knew there was a great failure to her theory that one
thing should always follow the other.

A child should never die before his or her parents.

Never should a mother watch her baby's coloring move
from the pink of life to the blue of death.

Never. Ever.

As she rubbed out the spitty spray above the sinks in the
second floor's women's bathroom, she saw her own reflection for the first time in a long while. She was no longer a
young woman. New creases bolted from the corners of her
pale blue eyes.

The same color as Jason's.

She pulled back a fallen strand of her dark-from-the-
bottle brown hair.

The color of her hair belonged to no one, not anyone on
earth.

She rubbed at the streaks with greater vigor, first with her

fingertips, then with the heel of her palm. *Harder. Faster.*
The streak was getting worse, not better. The damn mirror
cleaner was no good.

Probably eco-friendly. Damn!

She stopped for a moment and turned around.

"Are you all right, Mary?"

It was Grace, another custodian.

Mary shook off the intrusion.

"I'm fine."

Grace, a Korean woman of about twenty-five with too-
short bangs and overwhitened teeth, stepped a little closer.
Her brown eyes were intense with concern.

"But you're crying," she said.

Mary dropped her cloth and blotted her eyes with the inside of her elbow.

"I'm fine," she said. "Give me a second, Grace."

The younger woman, not really convinced whatsoever,
nodded and backed away.

Mary wasn't fine, of course. She'd been thinking of Jason
and how he'd be in his thirties had he lived. A husband
maybe? A father? A police officer? A lawyer? A TV star?
She would never know what he would have been because he
was gone, a tight, sad slipknot in the sequence of what she
knew to be the proper progression of things in an ordered,
fair world. There was no one to talk to about it anymore. It
had been nearly fifteen years. Mary's husband, Doug, had
specifically told her on more than one occasion, maybe a
hundred occasions, their son's untimely death was no longer
a subject he'd consider for conversation.

"I feel as you do, babe," he said. "But we have a daughter.
We have a marriage. Our lives can't be about the loss we've
suffered. Our lives should be about the joy we had with
Jason and the future that Sarah brings to our lives."

She knew Doug's sentiments came from the survivor's

part of his heart, the little place that somehow recognized that with each beat of life, a person must go on. With a daughter at home there was no other option.

No curl up and die. No way she could pour a handful of pills down her throat and pray that God would forgive her for what she'd done.

Mary Reed studied her image in the mirror once more. The whites of her eyes were now braided with the tiny fissures of red that come from crying. She wrapped her arms around herself. It was as if she could pull herself together in a way that felt as though someone, Jason maybe, had given her a hug. She took a deep breath into her former smoker's lungs and conjured the memories of her baby.

The one taken from her in a bloody crash Tori O'Neal caused on Banner Road.

Kendall Stark knew where to find Jason Reed's mother. She'd seen Mary Reed at least once or twice a week at the courthouse when she was chatting with deputies working the security detail by the main entry, or when she was headed into court to testify.

It was just before her shift when Kendall found Mary in the locker room in the courthouse basement.

Mary smiled when she saw the detective.

"Great minds think alike," she said.

"Hi, Mary," Kendall said. "How so?"

"I've been thinking about you lately, wondering if we'd be talking."

"You've been following Tori O'Neal's case, have you?"

Mary nodded. "Like everyone else." She pulled on a deep-pocketed smock and stuffed a cleaning rag and a small squeegee into the front panel.

"Let's sit," Kendall said, indicating the bench. Mary complied.

"I used to feel sorry for Tori, so young, so pretty. Her whole life ruined by an accident. Not anymore. I never thought she was that sorry. She seemed sorrier about missing senior prom than the fact that she killed my boy."

"I was only a teenager then," Kendall said. "I remember things about the accident, how sad we were about losing Jason. I don't know if I ever told you how sorry we were. I was at his funeral, but I just didn't know how to tell you."

"That's all right, Kendall. I know you care about people. I know that's why you do what you do. Me, I've spent my life cleaning up the mess. Maybe it's because I could never clean up, *make right*, what happened to Jason."

Kendall didn't completely understand, but she put her hand on Mary's. It was a gesture that was meant to comfort, and it did.

"I know. I wanted to talk to you about something very important, but it is also very difficult."

Mary fixed her eyes on the detective's, but she stayed quiet, letting Kendall speak without interruption.

"We're looking at Jason's death with fresh eyes. It isn't that we think that there is anything there other than a tragic accident, we just want to make sure."

"Because of Tori's husbands?"

"Something like that."

"I wasn't there that night, and I don't know what happened."

"I know. But I need your help."

"What kind of help?"

"Dr. Waterman wants to do a full review of Jason's case."

"All right. That's fine. You mean reinterviewing people?"

Kendall narrowed her focus and looked Mary in the eyes.

"More than that," she said. "We want to conduct a second autopsy on Jason."

Mary's eyes started to flood, but she didn't cry.

"How can you do that?" she asked.

"That's the hard part and that's why I'm here. I want to ask you something that no mother would ever want to be asked. And I don't take it lightly," Kendall said. "I want to ask you for permission to exhume his body."

Mary shook her head. "I don't know about that."

"I know this is hard, Mary," Kendall said.

"No, I won't allow it."

"You want to know the truth, don't you?"

"We know the truth, don't we?"

"I'm going to tell you something very important and something very confidential."

"What is it?"

"The file on Jason is very, very scant on information. We have the accident report and a single X-ray. No photos. No nothing."

"Yes."

"The X-ray shows a slight irregularity," Kendall said. "It appears that Jason's hyoid was compressed, broken."

Mary looked confused. "Hyoid?"

"A bone in his neck," Kendall said.

"From the accident?"

"Not likely."

Mary looked down at the chamois that she'd been absent-mindedly balling up in her hands.

"I'll have to think about it a while. My baby's been undisturbed for fifteen years."

Kendall Stark looked at her phone. There was still plenty of time to get over to Tacoma to talk with Detective Kaminski. The round trip across the Tacoma Narrows Bridge and back took about an hour. She dialed his direct line and he answered right away.

"Not a good day today," he said. "Things stacking up a little on our case. Maybe later in the week?"

Kendall understood completely. She knew how impossible it was to get everything done, every procedure done correctly, in the beginnings of a murder case.

"We have an exhumation in the works," she said. "An irregularity appeared on the films of the dead boy."

It felt strange to call Jason the "dead boy" when she knew him. It seemed so impersonal and she didn't like the way it came out of her mouth. But it also struck her that Jason would always be a dead boy, never a man. Never anything that he had dreamed about.

"Interesting," Kaminski said. "But just so you know, we don't like your friend for this shooting. In case that's where you're going with this."

Kendall took a moment. "No, not at all. Going for the truth, that's all."

"That's the name of the game," he said. "What else are you doing on the Reed case?"

"There's not much we can do. Only three witnesses, an addict who came on the scene and the two sisters."

"Addict around?"

"As a matter of fact, he is. He's a pastor of a church in Kingston."

"Parker, you let me down once," Tori Connelly said, her voice decidedly stern, the kind of icy, emotionless tone that reminded the teenager more of his mother.

"You can't do it to me again. You need to be a man now."

"I am a man," he said.

"You're acting like a loser. I want to be with a winner."

"I can't do it. I couldn't do it then. You know that. I'm not like you."

She let out an exasperated sigh. "What's that supposed to mean? I've given you everything I have, my heart, my soul, and you have failed me time and again. I don't know why I bothered to fall in love with you. I wish I didn't. I wish that I'd fallen in love with a man who would protect me. Save me. Take care of me."

"I don't know."

Tori seemed exasperated, possibly a little bored. "You will. Parker, your fingerprints are on the gun used to kill your father. Your hair is on that ski mask."

"It isn't *my* hair," Parker said. "It's *his* hair."

"It *is*, baby. I had to do something to make sure that you'd stay strong and fight for me."

There was a long silence.

"Parker?"

"Yeah, you did that to me?" His voice was shaky. He wasn't a man after all.

"Pull yourself together, Parker. Are you listening to me? I did it because I love you. I love us."

CHAPTER FOURTEEN

Kingston

It was late, the time of day when Mike Walsh wanted nothing more than to go home to his little house in the woods, feed his cat, and watch some reality-show trash. The reality-show TV schedule was key. Those shows that reminded him that not only were there others to save out in the world, there were many who could not be saved. On the bulletin board facing his computer screen was a bumper sticker that riffed on the motto of AA, an organization that had helped save his own life.

ONE SOUL AT A TIME.

He heard footsteps and a knock on the door.

"Come on in, Susan," he said. " 'Bout ready to leave for the night."

The door lurched open. "I'm not Susan."

"Son, do I know you?"

Parker stood still, his eyes dark and lifeless, the kind of eyes that refuse to divulge or betray any emotion. His hands were tucked inside the front pockets of his Western Washington University hoodie.

"I'm new. Are you Pastor Mike?"

"That I am," he said, looking down and noticing that the teen was rocking slightly on his heels. *Was he drunk? High? Nervous? All three?* "What can I do for you?" Pastor Mike smiled. It was a wide smile, but a jarring one. His teeth had been damaged by years of drug abuse. They were more gray than white. In the illumination pouring in from a solar tube skylight, it was clear that his skin had been ravaged, too— pockmarks long since healed dotted his cheeks.

"Will you pray with me?" the teenager asked, as he started to cry.

Pastor Mike felt the surge of emotion that comes from seeing a person in need make that step to the Lord.

"Let's pray side by side in the Lord," he said.

Parker didn't say anything as Pastor Mike led him from his office out to the sanctuary. Its pink-hued fir woodwork cast a warm glow, even as the darkness fell in the woods that framed the Quonset hut church.

They both knelt down. The pastor closed his eyes and folded his hands, but Parker didn't. He needed to see what he was doing. He wanted to hold that hunting knife. His hand shook as he gripped it. The minister was deep in prayer.

The prayer was for him.

Parker knew that he needed it. He also knew that what he was doing was the only way he could ensure that his dreams come true.

That he would be with her.

"I need you to stop that."

"I'm praying for you."

"I don't want you to do that."

He showed the blade.

"What are you doing with that?"

"Lie on your stomach."

Pastor Mike shook his head. "You don't want to do this. You don't need to do this. We don't have much money, but you can have what we have. It's yours."

"Get on your stomach now."

His eyes now filled with the solid black of his pupils, Pastor Mike complied.

"Hands behind your back."

He did so.

Parker unspooled the bright red duct tape from the pocket of his hoodie. He climbed onto Pastor Mike's back and started to bind him. It surprised him that the man on the floor didn't fight.

Didn't he want to live? Had his own dad gone so willingly, too? Was it that easy to take a life?

"Why are you doing this? There are other ways to make money, son."

Parker was doing his best to follow the plan but the walls were closing in on him. Fear was taking the place of the excitement of the moment.

"This isn't about money. This is for love. And I'm not your son. My piece-of-shit dad is dead."

Parker plunged the knife into the side of the minister's neck. Blood immediately started to shoot forth. It was a darker red than he imagined. Like the color of the wine that Tori had shared with him the first time they'd made love in his father's bed.

Parker pulled back and then shoved the knife into the minister's side, then again. And again.

The room was turning red.

"I'm sorry. But I have to do this. You are in the way."

Mike tried to speak, but he couldn't. He was choking on his own blood.

"Help me," he said, the words sputtering from his bloody lips.

"Jesus will help you. Jesus loves you," the teenager said, without a bit of irony in his voice. He suddenly felt strong, empowered. He stood up and looked himself over. He was clean. There was blood everywhere, but not a drop on him. It was as if God had been watching out for him. For his love. For his soul mate.

All of this was meant to be.

As the syrupy pool of red spread over the floor, Parker stood there. Scared, happy, excited, and proud. It was all good. He was the man that she needed him to be.

The money pouch from the week's collection sat on the pastor's desk.

What he did was for love, not money, but the teenager grabbed the pouch anyway.

A little cash could come in handy on the trip that would take him and Tori to their new lives. A little money was always a good thing.

Something wasn't right. Laura Connelly knew teenagers either took inordinately lengthy showers—or none at all. But after Parker returned to Fircrest from a day at the skateboard park in Port Orchard, he'd taken a half-hour-long shower. He also loaded the washing machine and washed his jeans, T-shirt, and underwear. Clean was good, of course, but such devotion to helping around the house was out of character.

"Honey, what is it?" she asked Parker when she found him holed up in his bedroom. He was in bed, facing the wall.

"Leave me alone, Mom."

"Parker, did something happen today?"

"No. Nothing." He pulled the covers up over his head.

Laura stood there a second, wondering if he'd been having trouble with his girlfriend. She'd considered asking Parker if he wanted to invite the girl over for dinner, but she doubted he was in the mood for that. When he said he wanted to be left alone, she didn't doubt it.

"All right," she said. "I'll have some dinner for you later."

"I'm not hungry, Mom. I'm going to sleep."

When his bedroom door shut, he lifted the covers. Despite toweling off after his marathon shower, he was damp again. Sweat collected on his chest and beaded in the small of his back. He felt a wave of nausea come over him. He rocked himself, like a baby, gently and slowly.

He remembered what Tori said to him the last time they made love. "You will never understand the lengths people will go for true love until you do what needs to be done to keep us together. I've done it. I will never let you down."

"I love you, Tori," he said, as tears came to his eyes.

Laura Connelly paced in the kitchen. She put his dinner into the refrigerator and wondered what she could do. She had worried nonstop about Parker after Alex's murder. She had suggested counseling, but he'd insisted that he was working through it on his own. She assumed that, whoever his girlfriend was, she was a good listener. He needed that. Laura couldn't reach him. She couldn't seem to get him to open up to her.

She went to the laundry room and unloaded the dryer. As she folded her son's clothes, she considered if she'd been a good-enough mother. Had she given him what he needed to get through a difficult time?

"I love you, Parker. I want to help you. It seems you are drowning here. I'm your mother, your lifeline. Give me a chance."

For the first time, she noticed a small vinyl pouch tucked into the bottom of the hamper. She picked it up and read its faded label.

LORD'S GRACE COMMUNITY CHURCH

Where did this come from? she thought, as she unzipped it.

It was a packet of one- and five-dollar bills.

Where did this come from?

Her heart rate picked up. She zipped it fast, like closing it quickly would make the whole thing disappear.

Parker, what did you do?

CHAPTER FIFTEEN

Tacoma

The headquarters of the Tacoma Police Department was tucked amid strip malls and chain restaurants on a bleak stretch of South Pine, not far from the Tacoma Mall. And if it is true that all police departments have their own vibe, Tacoma's was unique in its very blandness. One in Arizona could pass for a Mexican restaurant and one in Florida had a stream running through it that made it seem like a tourist attraction. Aside from the fact that the building was built and operated with green technology, Tacoma's distinction was the fact that its Fleet Services division was housed in a renovated Costco warehouse store.

That's right. A Costco.

One woman arched her brow while looking at the new three-story building that loomed above the old warehouse parking lot.

"I remember when I could get a hot dog and a Coke here for a buck fifty. I guess they must be dispensing justice in economy size here now," she said.

Eddie Kaminski chugged a tepid Mountain Dew in his

cubicle on the second floor. Included among his many lifestyle changes after his wife dropped him was giving up coffee. It wasn't good for him, and sipping tea seemed a bit fey for a police department's must-have machismo. That the soft drink he was swilling was nothing but a citrus, caffeine-stoked version of coffee without the brown color wasn't lost on Kaminski. He simply saw the drink as a small but necessary step away from a java habit that left him jittery and anxious.

"Like using a nicotine patch to wean a guy off smoking," he told Lindsey when she caught him chugging the sweet stuff after a run along Ruston Way.

"Dad, that's dumb," Lindsey said. "There's tons of sugar in that and as much caffeine as a couple of cups of Charbucks."

"Maybe so. But it's one third the price."

"It's gross, and price isn't everything."

You sound like your mother, he thought, but he didn't say it.

While he waited for Darius Fulton to show up, Kaminski tidied up his desk. The neighbor had seemed cautious on the phone.

"What I need to say to you needs to be said man to man."

The choice of words was peculiar.

A half hour later, he met Darius in the lobby. When they shook hands, the detective noticed that Darius's hands seemed clammy. The weather outside was cool, unseasonably so. Sweaty hands usually meant nervousness or anxiety.

"Let's talk in an interview room upstairs," Kaminski said.

Darius nodded. "The lot was full. So I left my car in a one-hour visitor's spot across the street. Is that going to be enough time?"

"That depends on what it is you have to tell me."

The interview room was as impersonal as could be, purposely so. It was, like all good interview rooms, set up to keep distractions to the minimum. It wasn't an unfriendly place, just decidedly blank. Slate blue carpeting, nothing on the wall, blue molded chairs, and a mirrored viewing window.

"Take a seat," Kaminski said. "Need anything? Water?"

"You really drink that crap?" Darius said, indicating the can of Mountain Dew that the detective carried with him.

Kaminski smiled. "Long story. But, yeah. Want one?"

"Pass. Water is fine."

Kaminski retrieved a bottle of Dasani and a notepad.

"You said something was bothering you when you called me."

"Right."

"And what is that?"

"This isn't easy. I feel pretty stupid. And it might not be anything. But you know I've been thinking a lot about what happened over at Tori's place."

Tori's place. The words resonated in an exceedingly familiar way.

"You have? Good. You should. You, Ms. Connelly, and the shooter are our only witnesses."

Darius nodded. "Yeah, that night."

"Have you remembered something new?"

Sweat collected above Darius's eyebrows. "It isn't that. It's, well . . ."

An attractive female officer walked by the sliver of a window in the door and Darius used the pleasant visual distraction to stop the conversation. His eyes met Kaminski's and, if he had expected some kind of vague semblance of male bonding, it was not the right time or place.

Not in the middle of a murder investigation, for sure.

"Dude, get to it," Kaminski said. "What are you trying to tell me?"

Darius looked down. His eyes were awash with worry. "I don't want to get involved in this mess. But I don't think I have any choice. I've weighed the implications of my silence and, well, I guess I have to come out with it."

The detective set his pen down. His eyes fixed on the man on the other side of the city-issue, Formica-topped desk.

"You involved in this?" he asked.

Darius waved his hands as if pushing away the accusation. "Oh, hell no. Not at all."

"Then what is it?"

"I had an affair with Tori. I mean, it really wasn't an affair. We messed around a little. Only once."

If Eddie Kaminski or any other cop had a five-dollar bill for every time someone said whatever they had done was "only one time," they'd be on the beach in Maui with a mai tai and a beautiful babe at his side.

"Can't say as I blame you," Kaminski said. "She's easy on the eyes."

Darius nodded. "Tell me about it. I mean, yeah, she is, and that's probably the biggest part of it. You know, look at me, I'm not young. I'm not really handsome, though I looked a lot better in my day. I'm just a big fool."

"You aren't the first, and you won't be the last. Tell me, if it only happened one time—"

"Yes, that's what I said."

Kaminski leaned back; he hadn't been trying to push the guy, but it was clear that's how he'd taken it. "Okay. Tell me."

"She invited me over to help her with some bogus project. She gave me the look, you know."

"The look?"

"The *look—I'm lonely and you'll do.*"

Kaminski took a drink. "Yeah. I know it."

"We ended up having sex right then and there, but that was it. I wanted seconds the next day—like a dumbass thinking all of a sudden I had something some woman wanted other than my wallet."

Darius talked about how they'd met at the lecture at the museum, how she'd told him that her husband hadn't been paying attention to her.

"She flat-out said she wanted some fun, no strings."

"But you wanted more. You wanted a repeat."

Darius looked away, briefly.

"Yeah, but she didn't," he said. "End of the story. I thought you'd want to know. You know, in case she tried to pawn herself off as the poor widow. Missing her man."

"I get that. I need to know something else. I need you to be straight with me."

"I *have* been."

"Maybe so."

"No maybe. I *have* been."

They talked about the specifics of the crime scene, a subject of keen interest to Kaminski.

"Are you remembering anything different about that night?"

"Look, I resent what you're trying to imply."

"Not trying. Just asking."

"No, nothing different. She arrived on my doorstep bloody and crying, and I called nine-one-one."

"Did you kiss her?"

"What kind of a question is that?"

"Just asking, remember."

Darius Fulton's face went white, then red. "No, I did not. She was hurt. I called for help. Your guys came."

The detective leaned closer, pushing the limits of the man's personal space. "Did you have anything to do with her husband's death?"

"Hell no! That's why I'm here. I knew that if the word got out that I tapped her, I'd be on the chopping block."

"Tapped" her? It was like an old man using a younger person's vernacular. It didn't fit. It made him look older and

more foolish. As Kaminski saw it, the move on the woman across the street was probably as much about being still in the game as it was about having sex. Darius hadn't wanted to be left behind, thrown away.

It was a scenario that mirrored his own. Though he had a ten-year cushion, he was damned if he was headed that way.

"I'm going to need to write this up," Kaminski said. "You're going to need to sign it."

Darius Fulton nodded.

"Yeah. I'll sign it. But this isn't going to be in the papers, is it?"

Kaminski shook his head.

"Not hardly. Last time I looked it was legal to mess around with a neighbor's wife. Tacky, sure. But, yeah, totally legal."

Lindsey Kaminski knew her father didn't take care of himself when he was deep into a case. She remembered when growing up that she and her mother had more than their share of meals without him. He'd be out on a case, at his office, and, at the end of his marriage, away in some bar drinking too much.

"Daddy," she said, when she reached him on the phone that evening, "want to get some Chinese?"

"You know I would love to, babe, but I'm up to my neck in alligators."

"How's that case going?"

"Making some progress," he said.

She knew when her dad did and didn't want to discuss a case. Usually it was because it wasn't going all that well.

"Good," she said. "But you have to eat sometime, you know."

He let out a sigh. "I'm going to be at the office for a while. I'll get something later."

When Lindsey hung up, she went about the business of putting together a care package expressly for her dad. The year before her mother dumped him, he'd tried to get back into the fatherhood role in earnest. *Trying so hard to win over his daughter.* He used to make care packages for her when she had a big calculus test. She hated calculus, and her dad's thoughtfulness made it a lot easier to endure. Her mother was out with her boyfriend, and Lindsey went through the fridge and pantry to try to put together something he'd like. She knew he was working on losing weight, but he also loved Fig Newtons—and since she hated those cookies above all others, they were easy to part with. She added a couple of bottles of water and an "encouragement" card that she'd bought for a friend whom she no longer wanted to encourage. She'd never seen the inside of his apartment, but maybe he'd invite her in.

Just before she started to knock, she heard voices.

Her father's and the softer voice of a woman.

Lindsey was thrilled that, just maybe, her dad was seeing someone.

It was about time.

She left the package by the door and stepped quietly away. Later that night, she texted him about her foiled delivery.

He texted back right away.

I WISH! THAT WAS LANDLADY! NEIGHBOR ABOVE HAD LEAKY SHOWER. LOL. MY LIFE SUX.

With Parker's eighteenth birthday only days away, Laura Connelly fretted about what she might do to celebrate the milestone. Every time she broached the subject, her son just dismissed it. He said that he didn't want any fuss.

"Drew and I will go out and do something, Mom. I'm not a kid anymore."

"I wasn't suggesting Chuck E. Cheese, Parker."

"Whatever," he said.

"What do you mean, *whatever*? What do you want to do? Maybe I could meet this girlfriend of yours."

"I highly doubt that, Mom."

Later, Laura would beat herself up over how blind she'd been to what was going on in her son's life. How she'd missed all the signs that he was slipping away. He'd been more remote than ever and she had no idea what he'd gotten himself into. Or what that pouch of money from the church meant.

Part of her didn't want to know.

CHAPTER SIXTEEN

Tacoma

The cab ride from Seattle to Tacoma was a bleary-eyed mess. Lainie O'Neal had sold her Ford Focus for cash, thinking that she'd be able to get by on Seattle's overhyped bus and light rail, Sounder Transit. The money helped in the short term. But not right then. She had expected to get to the hospital in an hour, but a recent miscalculation by the engineers working for the Washington State Department of Transportation had turned the primary link between the two cities into a parking lot as five lanes merged to one.

It had been three days since Tori called, telling Lainie that she needed her to come, "but not right now." Everything, even an emergency, was ruled by the whims of her twin sister.

As the yellow cab waited behind a minivan with two children watching a DVD, Lainie thought once more of the last time she'd seen her sister. It had been years. So many, in fact, that she'd stopped thinking of Tori every day as she had when she first made it clear that she had no room in her life for any family member.

It was a dark time, seared in her memory like a hot blade against her cheek. Unforgettable. Unstoppable. She fought the memory as the traffic in the so-called fast lane crawled southward to Tacoma.

Maybe this is a new start, she thought. *She needs me.*

As traffic centipeded past the Tacoma Dome, a message envelope appeared on the screen of Lainie's cell phone. It was from Tori. If anyone had asked Lainie a week ago if her sister had ever called, Facebooked, MySpaced, or texted her, she would have laughed out loud. She might even have asked, "What sister?" But not right then. Tori had, indeed, called and texted. She was making up for lost time and using whatever means were available to reel in a sister she'd ignored for years.

IVE BEEN DISCHARGED. MEET ME AT 222 N. JUNETT.

Lainie gave the driver the address.

"Nice part of town," he said, glancing in the rearview mirror.

Lainie looked out the window. "Figures," she said.

Tori always knew how to get what she wanted.

When Lainie thought of her sister and how she became the way she did, she was transported back to the times and places of their childhood in Port Orchard. In her mind's eye, Lainie saw Tori as she saw herself. As twins, they'd come into the world as a matched set. They'd been dressed alike. Voices were often mistaken for each other, particularly when answering the telephone. For the longest time, when they were elementary-school age, Lainie thought they were the same person—replicas of each other. Lainie assumed that their feelings mirrored each other's, too.

Why wouldn't they?

A few things stood out that she could pull from her memory and revisit.

They were ten. Their father, who literally couldn't kill a fly, had the misfortune to back over the O'Neals' ancient, bag-of-bones Siamese cat, Ling-Ling. It was a Sunday morning and they had been on their way to church when the bump and crunch occurred. Their dad sprang from the driver's side as if he'd been jolted by a hot wire. Their mom followed. Tori and Lainie were in the backseat, at first unaware. Lainie caught the look of anguish on her parents' faces and watched her father bend down to pick up the cat. She was limp, bloodied, lifeless.

It was apparent only then what had transpired—what the bump had been.

"Daddy ran over Ling-Ling," Lainie said, starting to cry. She unbuckled her seat belt and swung open the door, dropped her feet onto the pavement of the driveway. She swiveled and looked in the direction of sister.

"Are you coming?"

Tori didn't bother to look up. She had a Sweet Valley Twins *book in her lap, her eyes fixed on a page, as she continued to read.*

"Tori, Daddy ran over Ling-Ling!"

"He didn't mean to and the cat was old," she said.

The cat was *old, and their father hadn't* meant *to kill it. Lainie understood that. Everyone understood. But Tori's observation came with a disturbingly cool demeanor.*

Snow on ice.

That afternoon when they buried Ling-Ling under a pear tree that never fruited, Lainie let the tears flow. Her father held her hand and squeezed. His eyes had moistened, as had their mother's. Tori's eyes had puddled, too. Lainie thought that the wave of emotion that swept around them as they placed an avalanche of pink and white dahlia blossoms on the tiny grave was genuine.

"I thought that you didn't care about Ling-Ling," Lainie said later when the twins tucked themselves into their beds that night. "You cried. I saw you."

Tori rolled onto her side and her blond hair tumbled onto the pale blue pillowcase. She looked at Lainie.

"A cat is a cat," she said. "I know she meant a lot to you, Mom, Dad. We'll have other cats, other pets. She's an animal and she was going to die soon anyway."

Lainie didn't know her sister. Later, she'd play the scene over and wonder if she ever had. Tori's matter-of-fact take on things seemed clear and emotionless. She was right about Ling-Ling. The O'Neals did have other cats. What resonated with Lainie was not about the cat at all. It was about how devastated their father had been by killing Ling-Ling. The cat was a pet, for sure. She was, in fact, very old. But none of that mattered. Their father was so sorry for what he'd accidentally done. Lainie's tears were really for him. She didn't think Tori ever got that part of it.

"She never understood how other people really felt," Lainie confided to a friend many years after the incident. "It wasn't in her to really, really look into the heart of another person to see their suffering. Or even their joy."

Pewter-colored Commencement Bay faded from view as the taxi headed up the hill from downtown toward the Stadium District, then on to North Junett. Lainie hadn't spent much time in Tacoma, having fallen victim to the prejudice that came from thinking that Seattle was the Northwest's only real city. Tacoma had been the butt of jokes since she'd been a child. The "aroma of Tacoma" was a favorite derision of those who didn't live there, as it evoked the stinky smell of the old pulp mills and copper smelter that no longer spewed any stink. The jokes, like a residual smell, still lingered. It never occurred to her that her sister lived there. In fact, it never crossed her mind that she might bump into her in some random way like that. They'd been apart so long, the ties felt irrevocably severed.

The phone call from the hospital changed all of that.

She nodded off in the deep dark of the taxi's backseat, only to awaken as the car slowed in front of the gargantuan Victorian. She rubbed the sleep from her eyes and looked out through the fingerprint-marred window. A swirl of apricot blossoms clung to the large turret that overlooked the street. It was a gingerbread house with sugar. It was Candy Land. Chutes and Ladders. The house was a girl's fantasy of the most charming home ever imagined.

And her sister lived there.

"I guess she married well," Lainie said to the driver as she swung open the taxi's door. A blast of cool air smacked her in the face and she pulled back a bit.

The driver nodded. "Oh yeah, that she did. She had it good. Real good. You know, until the end."

He must have read the news paper or saw the story on TV, she thought. She noticed a fluttering remnant of yellow crime-scene tape on a walkway lamppost. That also might have tipped him off.

She reached for her purse and started to rummage for her wallet, full of maxed-out credit cards and four twenties. She paid the man and, with suitcase trailing like a dog on a leash, Lainie trudged up the brick herringbone-patterned walkway to the front door, which was already parted to let her inside. Ten steps away, her heart pounded as she braced herself.

Immediately, she saw her face.

Her face.

The door opened wider.

"I knew I could count on you," Tori said.

It was Lainie's voice, too. The voice that confused any

who called the O'Neals' wanting either of the girls from elementary to high school.

"I'm here and it's cold outside," Lainie said.

Despite a recent violent injury and a hospital stay, Tori had pulled herself together. Her makeup was flawless, understated. She wore a white robe with what appeared to be egret feathers—a little *Sunset Boulevard*, Lainie thought. Her hair was chic and lighter, almost the color they'd shared when they were little girls and looked exactly alike. Lainie wasn't sure, at least not completely, but as she ran her eyes down her sister's body, it looked as though Tori had breast implants. She wasn't heavy in the face, but she was definitely heftier up *there*.

"When did you get those?" Lainie asked, staring at her sister's breasts.

Tori shrugged. "A while ago. Already jealous and you just got here."

"Jealous? Of you?"

"You've always wanted whatever I had."

Lainie regretted her original comment and ignored her sister's tone. Getting off on the wrong foot was not her intention. It was easy, *too easy*, to slip into old habits.

"I came because you said you needed me," she said.

Tori's face softened a little. "I know," she said. "Leave your bag by the stairs. I'll take you up later and show you to your room." The door shut behind them and the sisters studied each other in the foyer, quickly so as not to be peculiar, but the rapid once-over that twins sometimes do when taking stock of how they might appear to others.

"The police are treating my house as a crime scene," Tori said. Her voice was low, almost a whisper.

The remark was ludicrous. Lainie wondered if it was a sedative talking.

"That's because that's what it is," she finally said.

Tori's eyes flickered. *A glare or look of confusion?* With Tori, Lainie could never be sure.

"That's not what I meant," Tori said. "I mean they are treating me and my space as though I've done something wrong."

Lainie studied her sister's lips. They also seemed a little fuller than her own. Not that she thought she had particularly thin lips, but her twin apparently thought so. She'd had them plumped with some ghastly filler, a permanent pout that she undoubtedly felt was sexy.

Youthful. Pretty.

"It all happened so fast," she said.

"Of course it did," Lainie said. "Did you get a good look at whoever did it?"

She paused and looked past her sister.

Lainie knew that the tone of her words hadn't matched what she'd meant to convey. The word *whoever* had come out slightly accusatory. She didn't know why it did, but it did.

"You look tired," Tori said. "Hungry?"

Lainie was, but she knew that her sister didn't care about that. She'd asked only because it was the right thing to do. The expected thing.

"It was a long ride, ten times longer than necessary," she said. "But what about you? Are you feeling all right?"

"My injury is severe, of course, but not so much that I can't manage." Tori's eyes glistened. "Alex didn't make it, and that's the part that hurts so much. And I know that it will for a long time."

The two sisters were suddenly in the moment, the reason why they'd been brought back together. Lainie reached over and patted Tori's hand. It felt cold, and she gripped it a little. Tori pulsed back. Lainie wanted her to warm up, be better.

"I'm so sorry, Tori," she said, feeling sorrow for a man

she'd never even met. "Do you need me to call someone? Alex's family?"

Tori, her eyes dust-dry, looked at her sister, searching. "He has a sister."

"Parents?"

Tori shook her head. "No. Just a sister."

"All right, a sister."

Lainie waited for more instructions, a name or a number. Something that would let her know what she was supposed to do. There was a coolness between the pair. Such an interaction wasn't exactly foreign. At their greeting, there was no full-on embrace. It was more tentative, casual, almost impersonal. On the ride to Tacoma Lainie had let it pass through her mind that her sister would need her. *Want her there.*

After all, she'd *called* her.

"What's her name? Where does she live?"

Tori's eyes drilled into Lainie's. "I can't stand her."

Lainie knew that meant that Alex's sister couldn't stand *Tori.*

"Okay. Why is that? Why can't you stand her?"

"It's complicated. But, yes, you need to let her know about Alex. Her name is Anne Childers. Husband is a sales manager or something. They live in Portland. One of the suburbs. Beaverton, I think."

Lainie could hardly believe her sister's disclosure. "You don't know?"

"Not any more than I have to. Trust me. Anne is a bitch. But, yes, call her, tomorrow. She is family, after all."

Tori tenderly touched her thigh, indicating that she was in pain and the conversation was over.

"Let's lock up," she said, "and I'll show you to your room so you can freshen up."

They walked across a blue, gold, and cream oriental carpet in the foyer. Tori seemed only a little hesitant in her gait, not in wincing pain as she had when she first appeared in the doorway. Lainie watched her sister tap out a code on the alarm system hidden behind a panel in the foyer.

"Did that go off the other night?" Lainie asked.

Tori sighed. "No, it didn't. Alex must have forgotten to set it. He was always doing that. It's amazing that I've survived this long."

"It isn't like you were suffering, Tori."

"I'm sure it looks fine from your perspective. Your view of things was always a little cut-and-dried. You know, average."

It was meant to be another sucker punch to her psyche, given by a sister who probably wanted to see if she still had the ability to hurt. Tori never liked to waste time.

Lainie shook it off. "Are you afraid your attacker will come back?"

"Why should I be?" Tori shut the panel. "You're here."

The remark was unsettling, though it shouldn't have been. It probably wouldn't have been if they were any other pair of sisters. Lainie wondered if Tori was suggesting that since she had arrived, the assailant might become confused and snuff out the wrong twin.

"That's right, I'm here." She picked up her carry-on.

They slowly walked up the grand staircase and down the Persian-rug-padded hallway to the first bedroom, dominated by an antique canopy bed. Tori pulled back the coverlet and drew the floor-to-ceiling moiré silk drapes, the color of bloodred tulips, like the ones their mother had grown in pots on the back deck of their home in Port Orchard.

"Lainie, I'm so glad that you came."

"Me, too," Lainie said, watching her sister disappear into her bedroom just down the hall. Lainie dressed for bed, brushed her teeth. When she discarded a length of floss into wastebasket, a glint of foil caught her eye. It was square with a circular indentation.

A condom wrapper.

Whoever last stayed in the guest room had a lot more fun than I'm going to have, she thought.

Under the covers in the old mahogany bed, Lainie scrolled through her e-mail messages. Her eyes were as tired as they'd ever been. Some messages—too many of them, really—were related to the job she was doing as a content provider for Media, Ink. Her production contact wanted to know if she'd be able to file an extra forty blurbs on Mexican vacation hot spots for a new site the company had recently launched. She fast-forwarded to the end of the message. She hated what her journalism experience had been reduced to.

The last message was from Adam Canfield.

Hey Lainie! You know how I feel about your sister, so don't say hi from me. I know this must be a rough time for her, but I don't care about her. Hope you're doing OK!!! Been lots of talk about Tori around here. Anyway, hope your sister is fat now. Call me when you can. Here's a link to an article about what happened.

She clicked on it.

It was from KING-TV, the NBC affiliate in Seattle. It linked to a video that didn't want to download on her phone's media player. She scrolled through the article.

"*. . . The intruder or intruders circumvented the security system by cutting the wires to the power source. . . .*"

Lainie wondered why her sister had lied to her about the security system, saying that it had only been switched off.

Accidentally.

She gleaned one more bit of information from the story. Alex had a son from a previous marriage. The piece didn't say specifically where the boy lived, but Lainie figured it was with his mother somewhere. She made a mental note to ask about that, too.

As she drifted off to sleep, Lainie knew that her sister had a knack for misstating the truth. Lying convincingly had always been one of Tori's specialties.

The truth was Tori had so many gifts. Some good, some evil. Sometimes it was hard to tell exactly which.

Lainie O'Neal got off the phone and sat still on the edge of the bed. She could scarcely believe the conversation she'd had with Anne Connelly Childers, the sister of the brother-in-law she'd never met. It was unbelievable in its content, brevity, and overall awkwardness.

"My brother didn't trust her, so, that's what he got. Dead."

"What are you saying?"

"You know. *I know.*"

"My sister never would have—"

"Really? That's interesting. Ask her about the life insurance. If the money goes to her and not his son, then you know what kind of a woman she is."

"She wasn't even all that beautiful, if you ask me. I told him that she thought she was God's gift to men, but I bet she was a plain, if not ugly, little harlot when the makeup came off."

Still playing the conversation in her head, Lainie went downstairs and found Tori in the living room. As she watched her walk to the cherry cabinet that held an elaborate media system, Lainie couldn't help but think that her sister was using the moment to conjure up something appropriate to say. She put on Erik Satie's Gymnopédie No. 1, a plodding piece of piano that seemed to fill the room with more sadness than the moment really required.

Tori pulled her robe closer around her voluptuous torso as if the air was cool.

"Are you hungry?" she asked.

Something was off, but it was hard to figure. Lainie studied the room. An enormous flatscreen TV over the mantel dominated the space. Antiques that were too good to be re-productions were positioned tastefully. In fact, all of it was tasteful, with the exception of the cottage painting that hung behind them. All of it expensive.

"I talked to your sister-in-law just now."

Lainie feigned interest. "Really? How was she?"

"She hates you. But that wasn't the biggest revelation. You've made a habit of pissing off people, haven't you?"

Tori said nothing.

"You neglected to tell me that you're a mother," Lainie said.

Tori looked hard at her sister as she stood clad in another filmy Old Hollywood robe, pink as a flamingo's feathers. Tori led them to the kitchen, where coffee was brewing into some expensive Italian carafe—not an espresso machine. That would require too much work. Tori liked to sit back and have things happen for her.

"You mean Parker?" She finally answered.

Lainie stood across the expansive soapstone island. "If that's his name."

Tori pretended not to hear. "Want something to eat? I'm not a meal person, but I seem to recall you were."

"I'm fine, Tori." Lainie knew that was one of Tori's old tricks, a way to point out that she was two pounds heavier than she. *Two freaking pounds!*

Tori poured them both a cup. "Look, he's the stepson from hell and I try to forget about him. Blamed me for everything—the breakup of his parents' marriage, the fact his father was a workaholic. I don't know anything and everything. But yes, and Parker has a mother, too. They live in Fircrest."

The town's name caught Lainie off guard.

"That's so close by," she said.

Tori shrugged. "Yes."

"Aren't you going to call him? Call his mother?"

"Taken care of, Lainie. I asked the police to handle it."

Lainie let the comment pass without another remark. Her sister had a way of sifting out responsibilities and leaving the hard things behind for others to do.

"Sugar?"

"No. I'm trying to lose some weight," Lainie said, lying.

"Good idea," Tori said.

CHAPTER SEVENTEEN

Tacoma

The lobby area of the Tacoma Police Department was a mini-museum to all the men and women who donned a uniform to serve and protect the people of Grit City. Kendall sipped a mocha she bought in the Mug Shot Café by the front door and perused the uniform and badge exhibits in the clean, brightly lit space of a big-city station. It was a far cry from the Kitsap County Sheriff's Office.

"Detective Stark?" a man's voice said.

She turned around.

"I'm Eddie Kaminski," he said.

Kaminski was a handsome man, dressed in a gray suit and silver-and-blue tie that would have made Josh Anderson envious.

"I didn't know I'd be so fascinated by this, but I am," she said, indicating the history display.

"Lots of great history on these walls. We joke around the office that one day there'll be pictures of us up here."

"I'm sure there will," she said.

"How are things in Kitsap?" he said, motioning for her to

follow him to the elevator. He swiped his badge and they got inside for the quick ride to the second floor. "Nice area. My in-laws, or rather my ex-in-laws, have a place on Beach Drive."

"As small towns go, pretty good place to live and raise a family."

"Your hometown? Tori Connelly's hometown?" he said.

"Right on both counts."

Kendall followed the detective to a spacious conference room that was most notable for an entire wall of photographs of police officers, most in uniform.

"Every commissioned officer and then some," he said. "I'm somewhere in the middle, but don't point me out. That photo was twenty pounds ago and I'm vain enough to admit that I don't like looking at it."

Kaminski picked up a Mountain Dew he'd been drinking before she arrived.

"Tori Connelly is that well known in South Kitsap?" he asked.

"You could say that, yes. Unforgettable, absolutely. She's one of those people we know will always pop up. Not often. But always in a big way when they do."

"You've heard we've got a person of interest in the shooting, and it isn't her."

Kendall slid a plastic straw into the cup and drank. "Right. The neighbor."

"You have kept up on it," he said.

"Sure, Detective," she said. "Like I said, Tori is kind of a legend in around here. I'm friends with her sister."

"She's the stuff of legend? How so?"

Kendall sat down. "She's never had it easy, and she's never responded to a situation in a way that was predictable. You probably know that she's had some family and personal tragedies."

"Her mom? Her boyfriend in high school?"

"Those, yes. But also her first husband. Died in Hawaii in an accident. She's had more heartache than just about anyone I've ever known."

Kaminski retrieved a notepad and started writing.

"What about that first husband?"

"Accident. I didn't investigate it, but the Honolulu police were thorough."

"Right. Thorough," he said. "What about the dead kid in high school?"

"Jason Reed was his name. He was seventeen. Tori and her sister Lainie were involved in a car crash. Jason died at the scene."

"Sounds tragic. But an accident, no?"

Kendall shrugged slightly. "Not sure. It was a long time ago. There are some irregularities and we're working it."

They talked a little longer and agreed to keep the lines of communication open. He gave her copies of the Connelly autopsy and the police reports as a show of good faith for their promise to work together.

"Keep me in mind," he said, "if anything shakes loose with the Reed case."

Jason Reed's death indicated a potential homicide and Alex Connelly's was the clearest example of a homicide—a bullet in the head. They were years apart, miles away in time and space, but were connected by a woman named Tori Connelly.

Josh Anderson noticed the Tacoma PD documents on Kendall's desk later that day.

"Anything of interest there?"

Kendall shook her head. "Not really. I don't know what I was hoping to find. Thought maybe there would be something in the tox screen that would indicate Alex had been drugged."

Josh sat down. He smelled of cigarette smoke, but Kendall didn't say anything. If he was going to quit smoking, he'd have to do it on his own. She was a mother to Cody, but not to Josh Anderson. That was Mrs. Anderson's substantial cross to bear.

"You're thinking that a woman would have poisoned him."

"Most do. Women rarely use a gun."

Josh flipped through the report. "You've been reading up."

"Like a crime junkie," she said.

"Why are you assuming that she's involved?"

She bristled a little at the question. "I'm not assuming anything. I want to know what happened to Jason more than I want to know what happened in Tacoma. I knew Jason. We all did. He was a good kid. Birdy thinks it is highly likely his hyoid was crushed intentionally, Josh."

"I get that, but that's not enough to do anything with. If she'd been charged with the Tacoma case, then you'd have the nexus to make your case that there is something worth piling on some resources. Remember, we are a little light on funding these days."

"Don't remind me. I could use a raise."

Josh continued to run through the pages of the printout. "Tell me about it. My Bimmer is in need of a tune-up, big time, but it'll cost me seven hundred. I might just go to Grease Monkey and get it done."

Kendall suppressed a smile. Josh had an uncanny knack for bringing his BMW into every conversation.

"So he had the snip," he said. "Just wanted the one kid. I did that, too. Sure regretted it. If I'd have had more than one, I'd have better shot of someone giving a shit about me when I'm ready for the rest home."

Kendall leaned forward and reached for the report.

"Hey, I'm still reading that," he said.

"Sorry. You say he had a vasectomy?"

"Yeah, so?"

"There are plenty of other explanations, of course. But Lainie told Adam that there was a condom wrapper in the guest bedroom at the Connelly place."

"So?"

"A couple of things, Josh. Think about it. Wouldn't the Tacoma criminalist collect that?"

"LAPD missed OJ's glove."

"Okay. But why would there be a condom wrapper in the house? Alex Connelly had a vasectomy."

"Maybe he had an STD."

"Blood's clean."

"Maybe *she* did?"

Kendall closed the folder. "Doubt that," she said. "Lainie told Adam that Tori didn't want to have kids because she didn't want to ruin her body or something along those lines. Something typical for Tori."

CHAPTER EIGHTEEN

Tacoma

It was after four in the afternoon when Lainie heard the doorbell buzz. She waited for her sister—painful stitches in her thigh or not—to come down the staircase to answer it.

"Tori?" she called from the foyer.

No answer.

Tori had been holed up in her bedroom all afternoon Skyping, or e-mailing, or surfing the Web. Lainie wasn't sure. It wasn't funeral arrangements. No services, as far as Lainie could tell, were in the offing. They planned to go to lunch at the restaurant in the Hotel Murano before Lainie met with her lawyer that afternoon. She hadn't been charged with a crime, but the rumblings were out there.

Earlier that morning, Lainie heard Tori talking on the phone in her bedroom.

"Don't you get it? What part of this don't you understand? Is it the combination of 'do' and 'not'?"

Lainie hadn't been sure if the call was to her lawyer or a confidant. It dawned on her as she moved past Tori's bedroom door that she still knew next to nothing about the dead husband or Tori's life after she left Port Orchard. Questions were not answered; they were brushed aside like crumbs on a dining table.

Lainie saw the figure of a man through the leaded-glass sidelight and turned the knob. It was Eddie Kaminski.

"This spring's colder than a witch's—" he said, not finishing the line. "You know, really cold."

She nodded as the unseasonably cold marine air from Commencement Bay scratched her face and neck.

"You look like you're feeling better," he said.

Lainie had never seen this man before. This was one of those moments she hadn't experienced in a very long time. The man on the front porch thought *she* was Tori.

"I'm Lainie," she said. "Tori's my twin."

Kaminski shook his head. "You really are a ringer. Gals at the hospital said you were, you know, coming to lend a hand."

"Are you a friend of hers?" Lainie asked.

"Not exactly." He pulled out his ID and showed it to her. Lainie's eyes lingered on it longer than it took for her to read. She was thinking.

"I'm Detective Kaminski. I'm working your brother-in-law's murder and your sister's assault."

"Tori's upstairs, but she's not feeling well. She's tired." Lainie started to close the door.

The detective took a step forward. "I'm not here to talk to her. I want to talk to *you*."

Lainie shrugged slightly and the space in the doorway tightened. "I don't know anything."

Kaminski ran his eyes along the vertical space that offered a glimpse of the young woman behind the door. She was slender, pretty. She wore dark blue jeans and a rust-colored sweater over a light cream blouse. As she gripped the door, he could see she wore no rings.

"Don't you want to help your sister? Help her find out who killed her husband?"

"A stranger killed her husband. And of course I—*we*—want to help."

"Really. Are you really sure?"

Lainie didn't like the detective's accusatory tone. "Please let go of the door now," she said, pulling the door closed.

"Are you so sure?"

She had one more shot. "She told me so." The words could not have been emptier, but Lainie found herself in an old, decidedly defensive mode. It was not an unheard-of place for her. In fact, when it came to her sister she'd been there many, many times.

"Ask her if she was having an affair, why don't you?"

Lainie shut the door and turned the deadbolt. She looked up, and Tori was standing at the top of the stairs.

"What did he want?" Tori asked.

"Didn't you hear him? It seems to me you were always good at eavesdropping."

Tori started down the steps. She wore four-inch heels, a purple dress, and a coil of black pearls around her neck. She'd done her makeup with a heavier hand than a late lunch necessitated. She was beautiful. And she looked worried. Not in pain, as her injury seemed to take a backseat to the heels and the need to look good. Yet, there was no mistaking it. She was troubled.

"All right," she said. "You know I've never been perfect."

"Were you cheating on Alex?"

"Not exactly."

"What does that mean? *Not exactly?*"

"What happened might be my fault."

Kendall was making a coffee run at the Kitsap County Administration Building for herself and Josh—because he'd actually done the deed the day before—when Eddie Kaminski called to check in.

"Tori Connelly is a tough nut," he said. "All you women in Kitsap are that hard, are you?"

Kendall laughed. "We're the daughters of lumberjacks, you know. Hang on a sec." She put a tip in the coffee girl's tip jar and moved to a table overlooking Sinclair Inlet and the Bremerton shipyard. She set down the cups, wishing she'd wrapped them in paper sleeves. Her fingers stung.

"How's the case?" she asked.

"Case is fine," Kaminski said. "I'm wondering how things are going in Kitsap."

She opened the lid of Josh's cup and added two packets of sugar. "Exhumation on the Reed boy is scheduled."

"Good," he said.

"I don't know what we'll find. But Dr. Waterman says the films indicate an irregularity that could use a relook."

"Court ordered?"

"Yes, but we didn't do it without getting permission from the family."

"Tough and nice."

"Excuse me?"

"I was just thinking that it was good to ask the family what they thought. You know, you're tough and nice."

"Port Orchard women?"

"Yeah, those lumberjacks are good folks."

She smiled. "I'll let you know what we—*find*."

"You almost said 'dig up,' didn't you?"

"Yeah," she said. "You caught me on that. Tough *and* nice."

"What are you reading, Kendall?"

Kendall looked over at Steven from her side of the bed. It was late and their bungalow was still. A book called *Women*

Who Kill was propped up on her lap. It was after midnight and he'd fallen to sleep only to be awakened by her bedside lamp.

"How to kill your husband and get away with it. Or something along those lines."

Her tone was deadpan.

"Should I be worried?" he asked, propping his head up with an extra pillow.

"Maybe," she teased. "Some of these women that I've been reading about went through more men than we go through Splenda around here."

"That's a lot," he said, rolling a little closer to look at the pages of the book. Steven was a handsome man, but never more so than at night when the stubble of dark whiskers peppered his chin. She inched a little closer to him, but continued reading. The book was not a forensic journal, but one of those compendiums of crime that she picked up at the Port Orchard Walgreens. Most cops were loath to admit it, but those kinds of books were a guilty pleasure.

"Who's that?" Steven indicated a picture of a frumpy, middle-aged woman with horn-rimmed glasses and shoulder-length dark hair.

"Nannie Doss. She confessed to killing eleven people."

"That's more husbands than Larry King has had wives."

Kendall laughed. "Not all husbands with that one. She killed sisters, children, her mother. A real wonderful gal."

"So you think Tori is a Black Widow, do you?"

Kendall looked above her frameless readers. "I have no idea, really. But two dead husbands, quick disposal of their remains, and a big cash settlement from insurance companies. A nice racket, I guess."

"Yeah, if you don't mind bumping off those you supposedly love."

"That's just it," she said. "These women don't mind at all."

She went back to her book, reading up about cases of women who did just that. Many did it for money. A more recent case that caught her eye took place in California, where two women in their seventies murdered men living in their boardinghouse.

A cop working the case said, "It was like *Arsenic and Old Lace*, but it doesn't have Cary Grant."

She read the line to Steven and he laughed.

"Isn't it great that you have such fun bedtime reading, honey?"

His words were said teasingly, but there was a little jab in the mix, too. Kendall had never been able to separate the workday from her home life. She and Steven had gone around and around about it. There was a need to build a wall around her husband and Cody, but it wasn't so easy. Not when her responsibility was so great.

"How much did those old gals get?"

"Two-point-eight million," Kendall said.

Steven cocked a brow. "Jesus. That's big bucks, considering how a gangbanger will kill a guy for a pair of tennis shoes and a five-dollar bill."

Another case, even more recent, involved a woman from upstate New York named Stacey Castor. Castor, forty, was convicted of murdering her husband and the attempted murder of her daughter.

"Nothing like keeping it in the family," Steven said.

"She used antifreeze."

"A woman that cold should use it on herself," he said.

Kendall rolled her eyes and nudged him.

"Sorry," he said, though he wasn't. "Couldn't resist." Steven reached over and gave her a kiss. That would be the sum of any affection between the two of them that evening. He'd seen his wife like this on more than one occasion. He called it "fact-finding mode," and once she was immersed, she didn't come up for air until she knew everything she needed to know.

Every once in a while, she'd turn to him and say something about what she was reading.

"Case from Oregon is interesting," she said. "Sami Watanabe was convicted of murdering her husband and trying to kill her little boys."

"Another real sweetheart," Steven said.

"That's right. They see everyone as unnecessary. What is necessary is the money they'll get when their victims are out of the way."

"So that's Tori O'Neal?"

"I don't know, Steven. But look at it, two husbands, a high school classmate, and her own mother. That's four dead people connected to one person."

Steven pushed the book down so Kendall would focus on him.

"Her mother? What are you talking about?"

"I don't know. It just strikes me as odd that Tori was the last person to see her mother alive."

"She died of an overdose, right?"

"Technically, yes. I mean, no doubt. But even so, sometimes an overdose is accidental, sometimes on purpose."

"Jesus, Kendall, you really don't like Tori, do you?"

She ignored his invitation to argue. "I hate not knowing what happened to all the people who died, all the people who trusted her. Steven, really, one after another?"

"You could say that about other people, Kendall. Misfortune has a way of visiting the same people over and over."

Kendall looked away from her husband and back at the book. "I agree. It could be just that. I guess I wouldn't have thought of the first two as potential victims if we hadn't considered the circumstances of the last two—the moneymakers."

"Moneymakers," he said, reaching for the bedside lamp.

His half of the bed fell into darkness. "That's a cold way to think of anyone."

Kendall knew he was right and she wondered if someone she'd gone to school with could really be that evil.

"We'll find out," she said.

Kendall turned another page and started to read, but Steven lifted himself up and reached over to turn off her light. It wasn't a subtle gesture, but he made his point. She wanted to tell him everything that was on her mind since the shooting in Tacoma, but she couldn't. When she heard his soft snore, she felt relief.

Later, she thought. *I'll tell him later.*

CHAPTER NINETEEN

Kitsap County

While many cemeteries in the Northwest feature water or mountain views for those quiet moments of reflection needed with the passing of a loved one, Fraola Cemetery in Olalla held no such distinction. It was flat as a football field, studded by shade trees and tombstones of the type that cannot be mowed over by an overtaxed volunteer caretaker. Fraola's name came from the combination of two once-vital towns, Fragaria and Olalla.

The Reeds lived in South Kitsap off Stormy Lane. When it came time to inter their son, Jason, they buried him in Fraola in a large plot purchased by Doug Reed's family. A pink-hued granite monument loomed in the southwest corner of the cemetery; it was the size and style of a marker used for a wealthy family. The Reeds weren't wealthy at all. Doug worked at the shipyard and Mary at the courthouse. The larger marker was a measure of the importance of their son to their family.

When Mary Reed came to observe the exhumation of her son's grave, it wasn't to throw a fit, cry, or stomp her feet at the indignity of all of that. She was past that. Kendall had told her that the only way they'd know the truth of what had happened that terrible night would be to reexamine his body.

"He's already in heaven, Kendall," Mary said. "I know that what remains in the casket is only flesh and bone. Not him. Not his spirit."

Kendall could scarcely argue. She'd seen the other side of the reaction at the mere suggestion of an exhumation. A young navy wife from Bremerton had insisted her daughter had stopped breathing, the victim of Sudden Infant Death Syndrome, while her husband was on tour in the Northern Pacific. The investigators, the medical authorities, the forensic pathologist, and the coroner all agreed. Baby Natalie was laid to rest at Forest Lawn Cemetery in Bremerton. Two years later, baby Scott died in a similar situation when the father was out at sea. The woman broke down. The detective figured she'd do the same thing if her son Cody had died.

That changed, of course, when the judge issued the exhumation order and the discovery was made that both children had died of ethylene glycol poisoning. She'd stirred three tablespoons of Prestone antifreeze into Scott's and Natalie's baby bottles.

Since a backhoe was too large to get around the Reeds' mammoth monument, four deputy sheriffs had volunteered for the exhumation. Birdy Waterman had outfitted each with a shovel she purchased at Ace Hardware—the clerk didn't ask why she needed four.

"You must dig your work," he said, with an overt wink.

She rolled her eyes playfully at the corny joke. Just to be kind to the clerk. But the fact was the pathologist found no pleasure in disturbing a grave. Birdy believed in the sanctity of a burial and the need for people to say good-bye only once. Putting someone through the nightmare of reliving the worst moment of their lives was never taken lightly. The only thing that motivated her was the hope that if anything had been missed by Kitsap's previous forensic pathologist, she'd be able to see it. She wanted justice to be served, and she knew that sometimes justice was messy and late.

Birdy had reviewed the thin report on the Banner Road accident one more time before coming out to Fraola that morning. If she could have come up with a reason to halt the exhumation, she would. She'd rather be embarrassed before, not after. Everything was in order.

Bones held up pretty well after fifteen years, and if the embalming was good, the tissue would be relatively preserved.

A black plastic curtain cordoned off the area so that any potential onlookers could only see the people working the grave opening from the neck up. After about a half hour of silent digging, one of the deputies moving the sandy soil to a blue tarp spread on the grass hit something solid. He stopped. The sound of scraping metal against a concrete liner was worse than fingernails over a school chalkboard. The coffin was about to be unearthed. After fifteen years in the darkness of a grave, Jason Reed, forever seventeen, was about to be exposed to the bright light of the world.

The forensic pathologist looked over at Kendall and Josh as they stood about twenty yards from the exhumation. Behind them by another ten yards was Mary Reed and Jason's sister.

"Lift it," Birdy said, softly.

Two deputies checked the black plastic curtain to shield the view of the grave. It was time for the curtain to fall.

"It'll take some real muscle," one of them said, "but we can get it out of here."

Birdy spoke to the investigators in a quiet and, as always, dignified manner.

"This will take about two hours. I'll see you in the autopsy suite."

"This is a waste of time," Josh said.

Kendall nudged him.

"Tell that to Mrs. Reed," she said. "She's here for the truth."

Josh looked over and nodded at the mother and sister standing behind them. He'd hoped that neither had heard what he'd said to Kendall. He hated looking like he didn't care.

Even when he didn't.

A white halogen bulb pumped so much brightness onto the mummified body laid out on Dr. Waterman's autopsy table that two of the three observers in the Kitsap County Morgue had no choice but to blink and turn away. *Flash! Dead! Boy!* The cuts and scrapes from the car accident had turned into dark scratches on an oddly smooth and waxy figure. Jason Reed's face was in remarkable condition. He looked lifelike, with a trace of stubble protruding from his frozen-in-time adolescent chin. His eyes were shut, of course, but they did not look as if they'd been forced closed. Narrow slits made it look as if he might just wake up.

Both investigators stood on the opposite side of the steel and aluminum autopsy table from Dr. Waterman.

"I hope I look that good when I'm dead that long," Josh said.

Kendall looked straight ahead. "You don't look that good now."

Birdy ignored Josh, which irritated him. Sometimes it seemed that he said things only to get a rise out of others. It was as if he thought insensitivity was somehow charming.

Kendall braced herself, but she couldn't help but be deeply moved by the sight of the body. He'd been dressed in a Smashing Pumpkins T-shirt and Levi 501s. The last time she'd seen him was at South Kitsap High, on the commons. He was with his circle of friends, jocks mostly. He was a good-looking teenager with curly dark hair that always looked messy and sexy. She closed her eyes a second, imagining him as he was.

"He was a really nice boy," she said.

Dr. Waterman nodded. "Most who end up here are," she said. "At least to somebody." She gently swabbed the rigid, waxy skin over the dead boy's hyoid.

"Dirt?" Josh said.

"No, in fact, Jason's casket had nary a leak. Tightest seal I've ever seen. I'm removing makeup that the funeral home had applied with their well-meaning but leaden hand."

"If you want to look that good, maybe you should use makeup," Kendall said.

Birdy smiled, but didn't say anything.

"Like your buddy, Adam?"

Birdy glanced at Josh. "You know, you'd be better off not speaking at all, Josh Anderson. Every time you open your mouth, you piss me off. And I don't like to be pissed off when I'm wielding sharps here."

She turned the beam of light lower to scatter a spray of light over her work area.

"Look," she said. "Right there."

Kendall went first.

"Those marks? What are those?" Without touching Jason's body, she pointed with a gloved finger to a darkened line four inches long and a half inch wide.

"I'll measure and map them. But my bet is they're the reason for the broken hyoid."

Josh took his turn. "I see it. But what of it?"

"Fingertips," Birdy said. "Somebody cut off his air supply."

"Strangled him? *Really*."

"Yeah, that would be my guess. Of course, it is hard to say with complete certainty this many years later. If we were looking for poisoning, heavy metals, for example, they'd be here and we'd be able to call this a homicide for sure."

She bent lower to get a better look, completely absorbed in the process of doing her job. It didn't seem to matter to Dr. Waterman how close she got to the face of the corpse. She sometimes got lost in what she was studying, considering. The spirit was long gone, but the remainder, the vessel, that had held the spirit also told the person's life story. Jason Reed had a swath of acne above the bridge of his nose that was absent from the photo of the boy handed out at his memorial. No teenager wanted to be remembered for the bad skin that came with a changing body. His senior portrait had been retouched. His blue jeans had a trace of silver paint along the edge of the right-hand pocket. The forensic pathologist wondered if he'd been working on a car, a bike, some other project that had been his passion.

She went back to his face, gently probing the stiffened tissue of his lips, drawn tight, thin, like a rubber band pulled to the point of near-breaking. Braces still held his lower teeth in a neat row.

Had he dreamed of the day those came off? Is that why he didn't have a full-on smile in his portrait?

"So where does this take us, Birdy?" Kendall asked.

Birdy stayed focused on the body. "What?"

Josh spoke up. "Next step?"

She set down the handheld light and looked over at the detectives. "Back to the witnesses, I'd say. But then again, I'm not a cop. That's your job."

CHAPTER TWENTY

Kitsap County

Even for an outsider like Tori, the gossip line from Port Orchard was as reliable as any means of communication, in any age. One time Tori dialed her father and pretended to be Lainie to fish for information on what everyone in town was doing. Her dad didn't catch on. She also called Adam Canfield, and he fell for her ruse. But this wasn't really gossip that day. She looked at the online edition of Port Orchard's weekly paper, the *Lighthouse*.

Body of Local Boy Exhumed

The story reported that the county coroner's office and sheriff's detectives led by Kendall Stark were literally digging into Jason Reed's death and interviewing old witnesses. The case was being reinvestigated because of connection with a more recent case in Tacoma.

Jesus! Why not just name me? If Kendall wasn't a cop, I'd kill her. Lainie entered the kitchen and Tori shut her laptop.

"Coffee?" she asked.

Lainie, sleep deprived and feeling it, nodded.

Tori poured them each a cup.

"Tori, do you ever have dreams?"

It was a simple question, rooted in something deep and foreboding. Lainie wanted more than anything to know if their broken bond was not so broken after all. Tori had called her for help. And while she didn't trust Tori at all, she wanted to. She looked at her sister and waited for something to come from her lips that would bring them closer together. Maybe not as close as she'd hoped, but a little more was all she wanted. Just a few words. That's all.

"What kind of dreams?" Tori finally asked as they shared coffee in the immaculate kitchen of the North Junett house. Tori played it carefully. She always did.

"About us. About me."

Tori laughed. "I'd call that a nightmare, wouldn't you?"

"Can't you just try to be nice? You've invited me back into your life. I'm here. I'm thinking that you want us to be sisters again. And I wanted you to know that sometimes I dream about you."

"That's sweet. You were always the sweet one, Lainie. But no, sorry. I never dream about anything. Not you. Not George Clooney. Not winning the lottery."

Lainie pressed her, gently. To push too hard would get her nowhere. "Everyone dreams," she said.

"Maybe so. But I don't remember any of it."

"Sometimes I dream of things that I feel are happening to you."

"Good things, I hope."

"Not always."

"Like what?"

"I sometimes dream of Jason and what happened that night on Banner. Sometimes about the night Mom died."

"Leave it alone, Lainie."

"I can't. I don't know how."

"Leave it."

"I want to tell you about my dreams. They scare me. They seem real. More than real."

Tori stood up, wincing in pain. "I don't want to hear it. Besides I have real problems now. The media's going to be coming around. Let's ignore the house phone and the front door. I just can't deal with all of this crap."

Kendall Stark could have found the Connelly address without a GPS, though she had it turned on. She'd been in the neighborhood once before when she and Steven took the Tacoma Historic Homes Tour. This time curiosity, not history, brought her there.

It figures that Tori would end up in a place like this, she thought, as she pulled in front of the Victorian on North Junett. *She always wanted more than anyone dared to dream.*

Kendall parked her car and looked over at Darius Fulton's place, which seemed deserted. She told herself she would talk to him only if he was outside. She knew that inserting herself in any kind of investigation going on with Tacoma PD was a major breach. Her only way around it was that she and the victim's twin sister were friends. Lainie was staying there. Seeing her on a personal basis was probably something that others would accept.

As she stepped out of her vehicle, a woman across the street got out of her car and walked over. She was a small woman, but she was walking big, purposeful steps.

"Are you the sister?"

Kendall shook her head.

"No. I'm a friend. Are you here to see Tori?"

"We'll, no one's home. I'm Laura Connelly. Alex was my husband. Rather, he *was* my husband before he divorced me to be with her."

Her. The word was uttered with complete disdain. Kendall smiled slightly. She didn't care much for Tori, either.

Laura swept back her strawberry blond bangs and looked over at the house. Kendall kept her eyes fixed on Laura.

"I wanted to talk to Tori. I don't appreciate what she's done since the shooting."

"What do you mean?"

"She isn't even doing a memorial service. I talked to her on the phone. She says she's too upset. But you know what, she sure didn't sound upset. She sounded more like she just didn't want to deal with it."

Kendall could see the woman was barely hanging on, caught up in the emotions that come with loss and anger. "I'm friends with her twin sister. Lainie told me about the service, or rather the lack of one right now. I'm sure that Tori will come around and do the right thing once she's feeling better."

"You don't know her very well. I mean, you might know her twin, but I can assure you that Tori never does the right thing. She wouldn't know the right thing if it bit her on that lipo-sucked butt of hers."

"You're angry," Kendall said softly. "I'm sorry. I'm sure this is hard for you, too."

In that very instant, the fuse that had been burning ignited and Laura started to cry. She turned away, embarrassed.

"I'm sorry. I'm more worried for my son. He's a special boy and he's torn up over this. I just know that losing his dad is another blow. I honestly don't know what to do. I'm pretty sure that Tori had something to do with Alex's death. I don't know how my son will deal with this . . . he's only seventeen."

There was a lot wrapped up in Laura's words, but there was only one part she could address right away. "The police will take care of it."

"How do you know? They don't seem to care. They just

go through the motions." Laura wiped the tears from her eyes with the back of her hands.

"I'm a police officer," Kendall said. "And believe me, I care. I care about the victim here and those who are collateral damage to a violent crime."

"Like my son."

"And like you," Kendall said.

Laura nodded. "I appreciate that. Thank you. I'm glad that you're working on this case. Makes me feel better."

"I'm not working this. I'm an investigator with the Kitsap County Sheriff's Office. This isn't our case, but I do care. I'm sure that Tacoma Police will do an excellent job." Kendall held out a business card. "You can call me if you want to talk. I'm a mother, too. I know how hard this can be on your son."

Laura accepted the card. "Thanks, I know it might seem silly that I care so much. I know I'm not his wife anymore, and it really isn't that anyway. It's my son. He needed his dad."

"It isn't silly at all," Kendall said. "I know you are grieving, too."

The year before her husband died, Tori Connelly smiled. It was a big, white, sexy grin. Tori liked what she was hearing. She loved it when her ideas were embraced. Indeed, she thrived on it. In fact, the whole world spun in the right direction when others understood her place in the universe. She was the center of it all. Always had been. She knew that the greatest power came when a person took her idea and held it as his or her own.

"We'll need a patsy," he said.

She looked at him with that smile on her face. "What have you been doing, reading up on Chicago gangsters?"

He snuggled next to her and laughed. "You know what I mean."

She kissed him. "Yes," she said, "I do. Someone we can pin this on."

He nodded. "To buy us the time we need."

CHAPTER TWENTY-ONE

Kitsap County

Amy's by the Bay was in fact owned by a woman named Amy, but it did not have a view of the bay. It did, however, look out across Sinclair Inlet toward the Bremerton shipyard with its mile-long row of navy vessels waiting for their turn to be decommissioned and disassembled for scrap. From their table, the reunion committee could see the ships looking like a string of beached gray whales.

"Stunning view," Adam Canfield said, his snarky tone in full swing. "Port Orchard's true best-kept secret is that it is a waterfront town that looks out at a bunch of rusty ships."

"That's the sight of freedom," Penny said, pointing to an aircraft carrier.

"They're still ugly."

"Don't they come in any other color? Taupe?"

Adam smiled. He had that know-it-all Penny right where he wanted her. "Taupe, Penny? Really, Penny? That's so two decades ago."

The waitress came and Penny used the intrusion to ignore Adam.

Kendall ordered fish and chips and a slice of cheesecake to go. She'd bring it to Cody for dessert that evening. He was back on a strawberry kick.

That meant that sandwiches had to have strawberry jam, milk was flavored with Strawberry Quik, and Kendall had to wear a pink coat when they went out together.

"So, Kendall," Adam began, "what's going on with the O'Neal case?"

"I can't really say," she said. "You know that."

"What? Is this some law enforcement code of silence or something?" Penny said, stabbing a shrimp on her salad with a fork like she was on the hunt.

Kendall shook her head. "No, not really. I mean, I really can't talk about it."

"Well, I can," Adam said. "I talked with Lainie last night. You know when I was checking to see if she's coming to this meeting."

"I take it she's not coming," Penny said, looking around the table.

"You should be a detective, Penny." Adam poured a packet of artificial sweetener into his iced tea. "Actually, she told me a few little tidbits that I can pass along."

Kendall was interested in what Adam was about to say but did not egg him on. Adam never really had to be egged on anyway.

"She thinks her sister had a lover."

"That doesn't surprise me. Tori was such a slut," Penny said.

Kendall glared at Penny, then focused back on Adam. "What did she say about that?" she asked.

"She didn't say anything. She found a condom wrapper in the bedroom."

Penny chomped down on the last of her shrimp, wrinkling her nose a little. As the owner of her own quasi-restaurant, she had to show her disdain for the competition.

"Kind of skimpy here on the shrimp," she said.

"Aren't you still trying to slim down before the reunion?" Adam asked.

Penny ignored the remark.

"I know this isn't good food conversation," Adam said. "But what's up with digging up Jason Reed? That's so gross."

Kendall set down her fork. "You're right, Adam, that isn't good food conversation."

"I saw it in the paper, too," Penny said.

Adam motioned for some more sweetener. "I'm glad Lainie wasn't around when you dug him up. They were pretty serious."

Kendall shook her head. "No, you got the wrong twin. Tori was dating Jason. And they were not serious. Not at all."

Adam poured the white powder into his drink and stirred. "I could never get those two girls straight. Who could?"

CHAPTER TWENTY-TWO

Port Orchard

Josh Anderson stood awkwardly outside the women's rest-room at the Kitsap County Sheriff's Office. A young deputy walked by and gave him a strange look, but Josh shrugged it off. The minute the door cracked open and a records clerk exited, he poked his head inside.

"Kendall, you in there?"

A voice came from one of the stalls. "Yes, Josh, do you mind?"

He took a step inside, hoping that Kendall was the only woman in there. "We got to go," he said.

"I'm trying to go now," she said.

"Seriously, Kendall. Mike Walsh has been killed. Church secretary just called it into Cen Com."

"Our Mike Walsh?"

"Yeah, the Reed accident witness."

Kendall flushed.

"Coming now," she said.

* * *

From the street it appeared as if the Lord's Grace Community Church was nothing more than a relic of an old business, an enormous, rusted tin can stuck in the sandy loam of the peninsula. But not so. Outside appearances were so deceiving. The Lord's Grace Church was paneled inside with quarter-sawn old-growth fir that had been salvaged from somewhere. The interior of the building glowed pink, like the interior of an enormous scallop shell. But that day none of that mattered because tragedy had visited there in a very big, bloody way. The church had not seen such commotion and traffic since the funeral for a firefighter who'd been killed in the line of duty the previous summer. An ambulance, a trio of the black-and-white Kitsap County Chevy Blazers, and a horde of onlookers crowded the parking lot. Forensics had already begun processing the scene when the Kitsap County detectives arrived in Josh's blue BMW, one of the rare times when he offered to drive. Josh parked behind the church, and the detectives followed the painted plywood sign that indicated the location of the office.

"This place is a dump. Gives me another reason to be glad I don't go to church," Josh said.

Kendall looked at him before returning her gaze to the celestial Quonset hut. On the edge of the walkway, a box marked FREE was filled with canned goods.

"I don't know," she said. "Church might be a good thing. Surely a needed thing."

"You believe in all that shit?"

"I do. I thank God every day for the gifts he's given me—Steven and Cody."

Josh looked uncomfortable. "I guess so. Not sure what God has to do with any of it. And considering that the pastor was murdered, I'd say God didn't do much for him, either."

Kendall wasn't a regular churchgoer, but challenges in

her life had brought her to the place where she folded her hands and asked for guidance. She didn't say so right then, but one of the people she prayed for was Josh Anderson. She also prayed about things that she'd done in the past, and for forgiveness for any mistakes she'd make in the future. Mostly it was about the past.

"Nice ride," one of the uniformed officers said, indicating the BMW.

"It gets me here and there," Josh said, as the officer held up the plastic yellow crime-scene barrier for the detectives to pass under.

Kendall didn't say a word. Josh Anderson's life had been reduced to one bright spot—a car. She made it a point to let him bask in any attention that came his way. In the office, at a latte stand, or even at a crime scene. Josh had been down so low that a little boost was probably a good thing.

Not too much. But a little was good.

A woman in a khaki jacket stood over by the door. Her face was red, and it was obvious that she'd been crying. A lot.

"Secretary Susan Piccolo," the officer said. "She found him. He's been dead a while."

Just inside the doorway to the church, a tall African American officer whom Kendall had met at a fund-raiser for a crime victims' group greeted her with a smile and a nod.

"Fishing knife," Charlie Turner said, "recovered in the pastor's office." He motioned for Kendall and Josh to follow him inside. Yellow cards had been taped to the fir floor in the pattern that suggested the obvious—footprints.

"Left tracks," Josh said.

Charlie nodded. "Yeah. The scene is pretty clean except for five small imprints left by the toe of a tennis shoe. Tech says Nike. Lab will confirm, of course."

The body had been dead long enough to emit the gasses

and stench that comes with death, but not long enough for blowflies to lay their eggs.

"Cause of death is pretty obvious," Josh said kneeling next to the body.

Kendall crouched closer, pointing to the gaping wounds cut through the fabric of what had been a plain white shirt. It was now dark brown and red. Blood had coagulated in a kidney shape, like an old Hollywood swimming pool, on the floor next to the body.

"He was sliced pretty bad, wasn't he?" she asked.

Josh nodded. "Overkill."

Kendall used her silver Cross pen to point. "Bound at the wrists with tape."

"Red tape," Josh said. "Wonder if the poor SOB was tortured. Maybe this is one of those cases in which the abused choirboy comes back with a blade and a plan for payback."

Kendall stood and scanned the scene. Everything was serene, the lilies, the prayer books, the banner of doves and olive branches to the side of the altar.

"Let's get everything photographed and mapped and get him down to Birdy's table."

Men know it because they were once teenage boys. They know that the power of desire and lust is a steel cable that runs from their penis to the body of a pretty girl. Sometimes *any* girl. If the real thing is not a possibility, the image of a woman in the foldout of a spank magazine is a surefire catalyst for sexually charged fantasy. Teenage boys are embarrassed by the stiffness that comes from the thoughts in their heads. Yet it cannot be helped. Teenage boys think of sex twenty times a minute. No adolescent male can stop himself from standing at attention.

Most teenage girls, average ones anyway, don't understand their true power until their youth has faded and they no longer can command the eye of a horny male. But a beautiful woman always remembers how it's done. How a look, a movement, a voice can excite a male. How she can cause something small to grow in size. Smart beautiful woman never forget. Smart, beautiful, and cunning women, like Tori Connelly, know how to use it.

Sex is joy. Sex is a weapon. Sometimes sex is an ecstasy-filled prison camp.

Tori sprayed on some Attraction by Lancôme perfume, checked her hair and makeup in the rearview mirror of her Lexus, and went into the Tacoma Police Department. If heads turned when she passed by, that was fine. She was used to people studying her with both adulation and disdain.

Look all you want; you can hate me. You can want to fuck me. But you'll never touch me unless I say so.

Kaminski met her in the lobby.

"Detective," she said, "I hope you don't mind the intrusion."

"Mrs. Connelly."

"Tori. That's what people who know me call me."

"Mrs. Connelly."

"Don't be so cold, so professional," she said. "I know you can be friendly when you want to be."

"What can I do for you?"

"I'm not sure. I'm here to clear the air a little." She looked over at the bench in front of the display of an old paddy wagon. "Can we sit? My leg still stings a little."

The detective nodded.

They sat, and she scissored her legs. They were long, lean, and bare. Her calves were among her best features, and she rotated her heel slightly to make sure he got a look. *Leg man?* Kaminski moved his eyes back to Tori's face, catching a look that indicated she'd tracked his gaze.

"I've been hearing things from Port Orchard that you're still investigating *me*, which is odd because I've heard you're about to arrest my stalker for the murder of my husband."

"Just doing some background," he said.

"Fine. So I'm here to answer your questions about my past. And yes, I have one. And even though my so-called criminal past occurred when I was a juvenile and was expunged upon my release, I'll tell you about it. I also previously lost a husband in a tragic accident."

"That makes three deaths?"

"Tic-tac-toe, detective. So what?"

"You feel good about that? About the coincidence of it all?"

"I'm fine," she said. "Two of those deaths made me rich. One made me the woman I am today."

Kaminski chugged his tepid Mountain Dew. "Detective Stark thinks you might be a black widow."

Tori shrugged as though the remark was nothing. "She has an overactive imagination. Comes from being a nerd in high school and fantasizing about being a detective."

"Oh, really? You seem to like her a lot."

She shifted on the bench. "I honestly came here to check in on the investigation. You know, to make sure everything is just fine."

"We're good," he said, noticing a beat cop coming their way. "Thanks for coming by."

The young officer from the crime scene happened by with some paperwork, but his eyes stayed on the beautiful blonde.

Tori got up to leave. She looked Robert Caswell up and down.

"The uniform suits you," she said.

"If you say so," he said, accepting the compliment.

She smiled as she walked away toward the door on a cloud of perfume.

"She's hot," Robert said.

"You can put your hard-on away," Kaminski said.

But yeah, falling for her is slipping into a danger zone, for sure, he thought.

Kaminski noticed Kendall Stark's number pop up on his phone as he walked toward the elevator, but he ignored her.

Not even your case, detective, he thought. *This one belongs to me.*

CHAPTER TWENTY-THREE

Port Orchard
Fifteen years ago

There were lots of bland names for the place. Euphemisms, really. Kitsap County authorities and those who worked there liked to call it a Secure Crisis Residential Center, or S-CRC. It sounded so civilized, so ordered. The facility off Old Clifton Road, tucked behind a curtain of evergreens, was institutionally bland in every way.

Except for the goings-on inside—and the reasons why anyone had been sent there.

Eight units called pods made up the living quarters for the 100-bed juvenile justice facility. Despite the best efforts of the custodial staff, each pod was vile, smelly, ripe with the odors that come with boys who refused to shower, girls who won't change their clothes.

Defiant teens times ten.

S-CRC, not hardly. The inmates who did time there thought of it as juvy, or jail.

The place hadn't been remodeled for twenty years and it

needed it. When government funds finally came through in the late 1990s, it was decided that floor-to-ceiling renovations were in order. New furniture, too. The place was closed and "students" (times had changed and the teens incarcerated there were no longer called "inmates") were sent to facilities in Belfair and Bremerton.

A pair of day laborers who'd started carrying the bed frames out of 7-pod ("Unlucky 7") were the first to notice the messages.

"Check it out," one man said to the other.

The other bent down and started reading.

"Shit. We're talking screwed-up kids, for sure."

"Yeah. Big-time. Wonder what became of this twisted little puke?"

Under the widely spaced wire mesh of the bed frame was a smooth, almost melamine-like surface. The writer was not the first to scratch out words of rage there. Others had done so, too, using everything from a jagged shard of glass to the bloody tip of a fingernail.

I want to kill my family.

Deb is a whore.

My mom cheats on my dad.

Officer Hector is the devil.

All of those things might have been true. The writer, who was adding to the litany of wrath made by others who had lain there to look up at the backside of the upper bunk bed, took out an X-ACTO blade that was contraband of the highest order. Worse than drugs probably, but stupidly available in an art resource classroom down the hall.

Scratch.
Carve.
Scratch.

Particles rained down into the eyes. But the angry scribe kept scratching out a message that would be seen by only a few. Only those who'd suffered. Those were the ones who might understand. Tears, designed to give the eyes relief from the irritants that spiraled downward, only blurred the action at hand.

A hard blink and then more scratching.

No one will ever do this to me again.

It was only three letters.

D-I-E.

Satisfied, the writer slipped the blade into the space between the mattress and the bed frame.

It would always be there at the ready.

Just in case.

The ladies of the Port Orchard Kiwanis Club donated a kit for a three-foot-tall Victorian dollhouse as a project for the teens incarcerated in juvenile detention. The concept was simple and, detractors thought, naive. Give the troubled kids something to do that was constructive in every sense of the word and just maybe they'd see that creating something for a greater cause would lead to improved self-esteem and compassion for others. The world was not always about them, drugs, hot cars, and the erratic behavior that put them behind bars in the first place.

The kit for the dollhouse was prepackaged and labeled by

the manufacturer. It was foolproof. The model selected by the women's group was called "Summer Time" and featured a turret, widow's walk, and windows that actually opened—though they were made of clear Plexiglas.

"Real glass poses a real danger," said the administrator responsible for recreational programming at the detention center, when first approached with the idea.

The woman who had been going over what would be in the kit appeared confused.

"Nothing that can be used as a weapon can be brought into the rec center."

"I see."

"No nails," he went on. "No sharp corners. Nothing at all."

"The shingles are fish scale, so they're rounded," the woman said as if the design had been in sync with the agency's concerns.

"No toxic glue. Elmer's only. No soldering. Burns, you know."

Six weeks after she dropped off the kit, the woman returned to pick up the finished dollhouse. She planned to auction it off that weekend, with the money raised to support a food drive.

The house was a marvel. Better than she thought it could be. It was painted white and blue, with a burgundy trim around the turret. With the help of a custodian, she loaded it into the back of her minivan.

"The kids did a nice job on it," she said.

The custodian agreed.

"Yeah. The girls did all the work. Guys wouldn't touch it."

As she drove away, the woman noticed an acrid smell. She cracked the window of the van.

That paint sure stinks, she thought.

The next morning she noticed that the rusty trim had darkened to almost a black.

"That's odd," she thought.

She didn't know what the stain had been, nor did she see the message scrawled under the front porch.

I KNOW WHO KILLED JASON REED.

No one would ever see it.

No one would know that the red stain had not been wood stain at all.

CHAPTER TWENTY-FOUR

Tacoma

The Hotel Murano was a hipsters' hangout, upscale and oh-so-cool in a city decidedly short on both qualities. Scattered throughout the chic design of the hotel and restaurant was glass artwork, the equal of which could be found in some museums. In the lobby, a life-size glass sculpture of a woman's dress and torso looked as though it had been carved from ice. Lainie eyed it, thinking the size and look might work for Tori.

Cold as Tori.

The pair went up the staircase to the fourth floor to Bite, where they were seated in a semicircular orange-colored booth with a peekaboo view of the Thea Foss Waterway. A waiter in a light blue shirt and dark slacks flitted from one table to the next. Flitting wasn't easy at his age, to be sure. He was old enough to be a grandfather. He reminded Lainie of a waiter at Seattle's venerable Canlis restaurant, which she'd profiled for the *P-I* the month before the paper went under. He'd had that job for forty-five years with no sign of letting up. She'd felt wistful about the man, as if working at the same place for so many years should almost be envied.

I'll bet he still has his *job*, she thought.

As the sisters took their menus, the eyes of a few patrons latched onto them. Some might have wondered if they were sisters who merely looked similar; a few might have allowed themselves to wonder if they in fact were twins. Tori was brighter, shinier, and undeniably more alluring than her sister. It was more than her tight, stylish clothes or her shimmering blond tresses.

There was something about her that transcended all the parts that created that stunning image. She had an aura of sensuality that men could not resist and women—those who chose to be honest with themselves—were envious of to such a degree that they instantly reviled her.

"Gold digger."

"White trash."

"Harlot."

"Slut."

All of those words had been hurled at Tori. She'd deflected them with Teflon-coated talons. A quick flick and away they went.

A new nickname was in the offing and Tori Connelly seemed to know it would take some doing to deflect that.

"Black Widow."

The *Tacoma News Tribune* advanced the story of the Junett shooting that day with a photo of Tori and information about her first husband's death.

DEATH TOOK A HOLIDAY
Connelly's First Husband Killed in Hawaii

Despite her newfound notoriety, she was still in Tori mode. The waiter brought San Pellegrino with lime slices with dingy edges and she told him to take them back.

"You wouldn't want that served to you. Why bring that to me and my sister?"

He nodded and left the table in a blue blur.

"I hope he remembers which glass to spit into," Lainie said.

They were there to talk about what happened the night of the shooting, but Lainie had another topic on her mind. Her sister hadn't once mentioned their father. It infuriated her.

"Aren't you going to ask about Dad?"

Tori set aside her water and poured some wine from a decanter that probably cost a week's salary—if, that is, she still had a salary, Lainie thought.

"How is he?"

Lainie looked sharply at her sister.

"Like you care."

Tori let out a breath and shook her head. "I stayed away because I care."

The response was maddening because, as far as Lainie could see, her sister didn't care. Couldn't, really. It was beyond what she was able to feel.

"Don't give me that, Tori. Remember, you and I have the same DNA. I know what makes you tick, how you feel, what you are going to wear when you go to your closet."

Tori shifted in the booth, buying time to think. Lainie couldn't be sure. "I've always loved that about you, Lainie. You were always so goddamn smug about what you thought you knew about me."

Lainie took a sip, twirling the wine in her near-empty glass. "Don't go there. I'm here because you needed me."

"Right. And I do. And you, my other half, owe me."

Lainie looked at her and said nothing. Her face was devoid of emotion. Tori knew how to feed off others in a way that seemed both remarkable and scary. She could tap into a weakness and drill out whatever advanced her cause.

"You know you do. You're my blood." Tori sipped her wine. "We're probably closer than blood."

There was truth to that, but Lainie didn't want to acknowledge it. The relationship was complicated and it was better to change the subject.

"Did you shoot him, then yourself?"

Tori sighed. "I knew you'd think that," she said.

"Well?"

"Are you my lawyer or my sister?"

"Being your lawyer would be a choice. No, I'm your sister."

Tori looked directly into her sister's eyes. "No, I didn't shoot him."

Lainie finished her wine, and the salads arrived. She would not have another drink. She never wanted to give Tori the upper hand. "Then who did?"

"I don't know." She looked back down at her glass. "Pour you another?"

Lainie ignored her offer. "You seem to be hiding something, Tori."

Tori studied her sister; this time her eyes glistened with tears.

Oh, yes, Lainie thought. *I've seen those tears before. They come whenever she needs to get her way.*

"I'm in trouble. I'm afraid," Tori said, speaking in a plaintive manner that didn't seem like the sister who'd been out of sight but not completely out of mind.

"What happened, Tori?"

No response. Just more thinking, buying time, scanning for the right words.

"What happened?" Again, Lainie restrained herself from ending the question with the words "this time."

Tori told her about the night of the shooting, how she hadn't really seen all that much. How quickly everything happened. She mentioned that one of the detectives had been rude to her, almost suggesting that she wasn't being truthful.

"I really don't know how much more forthcoming I could be," she said. "I was a victim here, too. I was shot. If I didn't get out of there, I probably would have been raped, then murdered."

The old but speedy waiter awkwardly took their order. Lainie selected grilled tofu with a miso vinaigrette, peanut noodles, and curry coconut butternut squash. Tori ordered a pan-roasted organic chicken breast with kalamata and green olives.

"Don't tell me you're a vegan now," Tori said.

"You'd like that, wouldn't you?"

Tori smiled. "It would be so like you not to eat meat."

Lainie changed the subject. She motioned to Tori's leg.

"How many stitches?"

"Three or four. I'll never be able wear a bikini again."

At thirty-three, Lainie doubted she'd ever wear a bikini, and it had nothing to do with a scar.

"What do you want from me, Tori? I mean, really, you call me up out of the blue. You walked out on Dad and me. You didn't even come when he was so sick. He almost died! Where in the hell were you?"

Tori stared into Lainie's eyes. "I have issues with the past. You of all people should know it."

If they were playing a game of chicken, neither was going to blink.

"You can't use that forever, you know that, right?"

Tori held her sister frozen in her stare. "Who says? *You?*"

"Let's move on," Lainie said, realizing she had blinked. "Your husband is dead. You've been shot."

"Yes and yes."

"I don't know anything about him. About Alex, your husband, whose name you seldom use. Honestly, I don't know anything about *you*."

When the words left her lips, Lainie O'Neal knew that she could not have been more accurate in her description of the state of affairs between the twins.

"Fair enough. But I don't expect you'll like much of what I have to say," Tori said, showing no emotion. Her eyes could be filled with charm and sparkle one moment and completely dead the next. She could play the center of attention or the woman no one wants to make eye contact with for fear of a cruel remark.

"You've always been such a bitch, Tori. Glad to see that hasn't changed."

Tori smiled. "Remember," she said, "I'm the bad one."

Lainie didn't take the bait. "That brings me to the next question. Were you having an affair? The detective thinks so."

"It wasn't an affair. It was a *mistake*. A big one. And I think that's the reason all of this happened."

"Who was it? Did your husband know?"

Tori lowered her head and put her palms against her forehead, gently. Not so much that she'd muss her hair or smear her makeup. She rolled her forehead against her hands, as if coaxing the memories.

"My neighbor, Darius," she said, looking up. "I was lonely and stupidly got involved with him. Alex was always working and I was in that big old house all alone. I didn't mean for it to happen. I really didn't. I was . . . just so alone."

Cue the violins, Lainie thought. She'd heard her sister's attempt at contrition plenty of times before. In fact, a cascade of memories poured over her as they sat.

"What happened?"

"He just wouldn't take no for an answer, Lainie. I swear it. He kept coming over. He told me he loved me and that he couldn't live without me. Then he told me that he'd do anything to be with me again. I told him no. I told him that the sex was a mistake."

"When was this?" she asked, thinking of the condom wrapper.

"It has been over for a while. At least as far as I was concerned."

Lainie didn't believe her, but she didn't want to confront her about what she'd found.

"Did he shoot you? Did he kill Alex?"

Tori shook her head. "I wish I could say he did. But honestly, I didn't see the face of who did it. It happened so fast. I heard the gunfire. I ran into the room, bent over Alex . . . a man in a black mask shot me. . . ." She started to cry. At least, tears rolled down her cheeks, and if it was any other person it would have been genuine tears.

With Tori, Lainie wasn't so sure.

"You didn't see him well enough to identify him?" she asked.

"No. I ran over to Darius's house to confront him. I thought it could be him . . . I stood there bleeding and I told him that I would kill him myself. I don't know if it was him. He didn't seem to be out of breath or blood soaked or anything. I passed out, and he called nine-one-one."

Lainie leaned forward to make sure her sister got the point. "You need to tell the police."

Tori looked away, then back at her sister. "I've tried, but considering my history, I'm not sure anyone would believe me."

Lainie knew what she was talking about.

There was the matter of that other dead husband of hers.

Their food arrived and Tori brightened.

"God, I'm so hungry!" She pierced her chicken with her fork. "I feel like I haven't eaten in weeks!"

Lainie nodded. She wanted to say something about how it was so nice that her sister had gotten back her appetite.

"You know, since your husband has barely been dead a few days."

But she didn't.

She didn't dare.

Tori Connelly didn't look like the kind of woman who would need to use a twenty-four-hour Kinko's copy machine or computer, but she was. She made her way into the copier center off South Nineteenth Street. She carried with her a notebook and a purse. She needed neither. She had no intention of using cash or a credit card, and she certainly didn't need to refer to any notes.

She pretended to peruse the stationery section and paper samples while she waited for a caffeine-buzzed student to leave his rented PC for the bathroom. It took her about a minute to pull up a phony Hotmail account.

Stupid idiot, don't you know about computing security?

She typed in an e-mail address and tapped out a message that included a bank account number in the Bahamas. It was typed in reverse order as she'd been advised to do.

The subject line was: You Better Not Screw This Up.

"Hey, I was working there."

The voice belonged to the student-idiot.

She looked up at him and smiled.

"Oh, I'm sorry! I thought you were gone for the night."

"You can see I'm not. I left all my stuff here while I went to take a leak. Do you mind?" He glared at her and waited for her to give up. He looked down at the screen to read what she was doing, but she'd minimized the screen.

She pushed the send button and closed the window.

"Sorry. No harm. No foul."

* * *

She couldn't blame it on the food at Bite that evening. But once more Lainie couldn't sleep. Her eyelids popped up like pulled window shades with broken springs. Lainie O'Neal shifted under the covers and lamented how the drama of the past days had beaten her back to the familiar point of exhaustion and sleeplessness. She still had not renewed her sleeping pill prescription, and it wasn't for lack of trying. Her doctor had said that her inability to sleep might be rooted in some unchecked psychological problem. It wasn't the first time that she'd heard that.

"A pill will only mask the problem, Lainie. You need to address what is eating at you day and night," he said.

She would change doctors again.

In the meantime, she knew the pattern of the past few nights would play out again. Sleep would come after 3 A.M. and so would the nightmares. By 4 A.M. she'd be awake, shivering, and alone to try to come to terms with what she'd seen in her dreams, dreams that always included her sister.

Finally, darkness and slumber came.

She followed the sound of angry voices down the hallway of the house in Port Orchard. She was in a pale pink nightgown, following the sound into her parents' room. She stood there in front of her mother, her fists balled up and tears streaming down her face. As she took it all in, her mind floated to the ceiling where she looked down at the scene playing underneath her. A curtain fluttered. Her blond head from above. Her mother in the bed looking at her, her head propped up on a satin pillow.

"I didn't do anything wrong."

"I didn't say you did."

"You looked at me like I did. That's enough."

"A look isn't the same as an accusation, Tori."

"I know what you're thinking, Mom."

"No, you don't. I told you what I thought, and you seem to think that I've said something otherwise."

"I hate you. I hate *her*. I hate *him*."

"Hate is an ugly word."

"You are ugly. You are stupid. You are boring."

The insults were the trifecta of teenager insults at anyone, especially mothers.

"I'm not having this conversation. If you can't be nice now, come back when you can. We're done here. Leave."

"I wish you were dead."

Their mother closed her eyes and exhaled a sigh.

"I will be someday. I might even be dead now."

The scene stalled, and then crackled like an old 1960s TV clip as the imagery went from color to black-and-white. Lainie watched from above, her back pressed against the popcorn ceiling.

A male's voice interrupted the single moment of quiet.

"What's going on here?"

It was the familiar voice of their father.

"Nothing. She's being mean."

"I'm being truthful and she knows it."

As the images faded and she began to wake, her body drenched in sweat, Lainie could not be sure who had said what. She got up and sat on the edge of the bed. She looked down at her hands, still balled up in a rage for which she had no control.

Slowly and deliberately she unfurled her fingers. There was nothing inside but lozenge- and circular-shaped indentations.

Lainie wondered if she was awake or asleep. If she'd seen herself or her sister. More than anything, she wondered if there was a message coming from Tori at that very moment as she slept and dreamed in the bedroom down the hall.

"Tori," she said aloud, "what is this all about? Tell me. What did you do?"

* * *

Tori sat straight up in the big Rice bed. The clock was ticking toward a deadline that mattered. Not like the seemingly arbitrary IRS deadline of April 15, or the kind of line in the sand that someone adheres to when they insist something has to be done by a certain time. This deadline wasn't like that at all. In fact, some might see it as a time of celebration. A rite of passage.

It was only a few days until Saturday. Once the clock struck midnight, everything would be exactly as she'd wanted.

As *they* dreamed.

CHAPTER TWENTY-FIVE

Port Orchard

Kendall looked over reports from the night of the shooting in Tacoma and the preliminary report Birdy Waterman had completed on the stabbing of homicide victim Mikey Walsh in Kingston. They were not related by methods of homicide, by geography or socioeconomic status.

Yet Kendall didn't believe in the concept of coincidences. Certainly there was a random order to the universe, but when it came to evil there often was a connection.

Evil is rare and not that random.

In instances in which a crime had been staged by a perpetrator, items were often scattered willy-nilly. In fact, *over-scattered*. If Tori Connelly had fabricated the events of the evening, she'd exercised considerable restraint in her cover-up. That very little in the house was disturbed bolstered her contention that an intruder had entered the residence and panicked after coming across Alex watching TV. Any killer who makes the mistake of doing the deed in their own home usually stages every aspect of the crime to ensure that even the greenest detective or crime-scene investigator sees each clue as it is hurtled at them.

Drawers pulled out.

Coffee table overturned.

Jewelry littering the floor like bread crumbs to the front door.

All of those things were right out of the mostly caught killer's playbook of greatest mistakes. Yet very little of that, aside from a single pulled-out drawer and an overturned potted fern, had been found at the scene of the Connelly murder.

Alex Connelly was killed execution-style. But if so . . . who? And why?

Mikey Walsh had been on the scene of a fatal traffic accident fifteen years ago. Within days of the body of the victim being exhumed, he's stabbed to death. Susan Piccolo, the church secretary, indicated that some money was missing.

But was that merely staging, too?

Liver temperature put Mikey's death on Monday. The report also noted that he'd been stabbed five times, though Birdy considered two of the wounds as "tentative" in nature.

Afraid? Weak? Uncertain?

Josh appeared in the hallway and Kendall called out to him.

"I think the cases are related," she said.

"Of course you do," he answered. "You like that sort of thing."

Just when she thought he'd be a decent person, the old Josh was back. "Why are you being dismissive?"

"Look, I know a big conspiracy theory is a lot of fun. But there's no way your Tori stabbed that preacher."

Kendall shook her head. "I didn't say *she* stabbed him. What if someone is helping her?"

"Why would that be? And who?" It was clear that Josh was only playing along.

"I don't know, but Tori is in the thick of this. I can feel it."

Josh picked up the autopsy report and turned toward the door. "What if we look for a meth head that needed some dough and the preacher was a good target?"

Kendall didn't agree at all.

"You're the lead on this one," she said. "You figure it out."

"Tracked down the source of the red tape. It's nothing professional, like I hoped. It's sold only in craft stores. Our killer might be Martha Stewart."

Kendall didn't say a word.

"That was a joke," he said.

"I just forgot to laugh," she said. "It might be because there isn't anything funny about a minister who'd been gutted, Josh."

"I'm afraid." Parker Connelly's adolescent voice came over the phone like a leaky bicycle tire, soft, fading. He was in his bed, the covers thrown over his head like an army-issue pup tent. He had called Tori to pledge his love, to tell her that he missed her. He'd hoped that they'd share a little phone sex. His hand was in the waistband of his Diesel boxers when he dialed, but as the conversation moved from pleasure to murder, he vacated that idea.

"You should be," she said, her voice cool and direct, "afraid that you will never, never have my legs wrapped around you again."

Parker's muscles tensed a little and he rolled over toward the wall, his body wrapped in a cocoon of fabric. It was the kind of position that suggested a desire for protection. He could feel his stomach churn in the way that it did when he had to give a speech in front of the class—times one million.

"That's not what I was talking about, Tori," he said.

"I don't know why we're even talking. *Period*. Every day that this goes on you prove to me that you're not the man that I thought you were." She paused a moment as if to reconsider her statement. "Not the man I thought you would be."

"That's not fair and you know it."

"This isn't about fair, Parker. It is about whether or not you love me enough to find a way to protect our relationship and ensure our future. I know you're young, but honestly, you're not *that* young."

The last part was a slam. It was meant to remind him once and for all that while they had played at being lovers and had talked about a lifetime commitment and a future together, he wasn't quite her equal. He was younger. *Immature*. He was but a boy.

He hated it when she played that way. It wasn't fun. It was cruel and demeaning. It made him feel weak and insignificant. It made him feel like he imagined his mother might have felt when his father kicked her to the curb. Laura tearfully told her son that she wasn't sure exactly why Alex had chosen Tori over her, but that she felt it had more to do with what she no longer possessed—and Tori still did.

The air under the covers was thinning. He couldn't really make sense of what she was asking him to do. Maybe there was no sense needed. It was about love, after all. Love, she had told him over and over, cannot be rationalized or explained.

"By killing someone?" He finally asked. "Killing another person is how we protect our love?"

"Oh, Parker," she said. "I have made a mistake. I've let you love me and I've fallen in love with you. But you don't seem to understand. This is a war we're in right now. We are going to have to do things that no one would want to do unless they were in for the fight of their lives. History is full of examples. Think about the Donner party . . . did you study that in school?"

Her tone was slightly condescending, but he ignored it.

"Yeah, the pioneers who ate each other in California."

"Right. They did what they had to do to survive."

"We're not stuck on a mountain in a blizzard," he said.

She laughed. "No, but we're in a war, and you and I are the only people who can defend our futures. The world will try to stop us. They won't understand. Your dad. Your mom. Whoever."

"My mom isn't a part of this," he said.

"No, she's not. But you have to understand, Parker, if she tried to get in our way we'd have to do something about it."

"Hey," he said, "don't talk that way. I don't know if I can do that last thing you want me to do."

"You have to."

"It would be like killing you. She looks just like you."

"That's right. And that's why we need her gone."

"I don't know if I can do it."

"It's time to grow a pair, Parker. I need a man in my bed, not a boy."

"I am a man."

"Then you'll prove it to me, babe."

"I don't know."

"Look, Parker, killing isn't as hard as you seem to think. I think I've proven *that*. I wish you would have sucked it up and paid attention. I need you."

They'd had a plan. Or at least Tori thought they had one. Killing Alex was going to be a team effort because she knew that in order for her to succeed that time, she'd need a partner. The subject was first broached as she and Parker sat in her car overlooking an empty expanse of Puget Sound one summer afternoon. They'd found a place for sex at the end of a long beachfront parking lot. She finished him off quickly— which was a pretty easy mission to accomplish with a seventeen-year-old boy—because there had been so much more to do.

"I want you to shoot him in the head," she said.

"I hate him as much as you do, but, Tori, he is my dad."

She reapplied her lipstick and turned to face the boy, head-on. "Biology didn't make him a father. You know that. Tell me you know that."

"I know it," he said, repeating her words.

"You're not getting cold feet on me."

"No, it isn't that. I don't want to let you down."

"It isn't about me. It doesn't matter to me that he's screwing that bitch at the office and getting ready to throw me away . . . like he did your poor mother." She leaned closer and touched his chin with her soft, gentle hands. "Getting rid of him is the price he will have to pay for our freedom."

The logic was peculiar. But somehow Parker understood.

"You mean the money," he said.

"Yes. It is about the money. Anyone who says otherwise is an idiot and a liar. I can't tolerate either of those, can you?"

"No," he said.

"You will need to be the shooter," she said. "I can't risk it."

"I thought you said there was no risk."

"Parker, there's always a risk. Making love to you just now was a risk. A cop could have come by. Some do-gooder with an overactive moral compass could see us and turn me in for stealing your youth. That is, if they could tell that I was older than you. You look so mature."

She kissed him and he felt that tingling feeling run through his body.

"Do you want me to go over the plan again?"

She let her tongue slip between his lips. They kissed again, this time with more passion.

"I just want you inside of me again. I want us to be able to be together forever. I want us to enjoy each other whenever we want."

"I want that, too."

"As far as the plan goes, no need to cover that again. You know what to do."

Parker had never seen Tori look like that before. Her eyes were cold, almost devoid of life. She stood next to his bed in the guest room and spoke in a scary, quiet whisper.

"You little shit," she said. "You are backing out on me?"

He sat there mute for a moment, before finally speaking. "I'm sorry."

Her eyes blazed. "Sorry? Goddamn you, Parker. We agreed to this. You promised me. You said you loved me and would do anything for us to be together."

"I want to kill him. I want to."

"I want things, too. Wanting you to live up to your promises was at the top of my list. But you've really let me down. You're like every other man I've ever fallen for. They want what I have, they take it, and then when I want something in return, they shove me aside. I expected better of you, Parker."

He stood up. The teenager was taller than she was, but somehow he shrank in her presence.

The carriage house adjacent to the Victorian held the updated mechanical plant that supported the house, including the water heater, the AC unit, and the redone electrical panel. Huddled on a sleeping bag behind the Lexus and a disconnected coal-fired kitchen stove—a relic from two or three remodels ago—was the shaking frame of a teenage boy.

He held a gun stolen from the house across the street.

Tori's voice came at Parker with the sweetness of honey. "Baby, you have to pull yourself together."

"I can't do this, Tori."

"You can and you will. You have to do this. It is the only way we can be together."

He'd been crying and he detested that she knew it, but he looked directly at her.

"You mean, it is the only way we can get the money. If it was just about being together, we could just run off. You and me. Away from here."

She dropped to her knees. She was wearing nothing but a nightgown and the icy air hardened her nipples to eraser points poking at his face.

"Look, I can't stay here and try to build you up," she said. "Try to convince you. You need to pull yourself together."

Her voice began to carry an edge, and she recognized it. She modulated her words.

"How can you do this to us?" she asked.

"I thought I could."

"Give it to me. Give me the gun. True love," she said, "means doing the right thing."

He handed her the weapon.

"Do you still love me?"

"You're not making it easy, but, yes, baby. I do."

When it came time to do what they'd agreed to do, Tori stood there naked, her young lover behind her. He was dressed. He was supposed to be the shooter, but he was unable to do what needed to be done. The smell of gunfire filled the living room. Blood had blown back on her breasts. A piece of her dead husband's brain stuck on her neck, and she flicked it off.

Her eyes were ice. "Fire it."

Parker looked at his father's body. "He's already dead."

She poked the gun in his direction. "Are you serious? So what? You have to be a part of this. I'm not carrying this burden alone."

"Tori," he said. No other words came.

"You've got two seconds. Now you've got one second."

Parker stepped closer to his father and pointed the gun. His hands were shaking.

"Steady or you'll hurt someone," she said.

The gun went off, and Tori took it. She immediately pointed it at her thigh and fired. She didn't even wince.

"Get out now," she said.

Parker didn't know that she'd made sure that his fingerprints were on the gun. She thought of it as her "insurance policy."

Or one of them, anyway.

CHAPTER TWENTY-SIX

Tacoma

The note that appeared at the front desk stared at her, and Kendall Stark stared back. It was like looking at the face of a cobra, ready to lift its head and strike. It was a shark with its jaws wide open and a ladder lodged in it so that all a person had to do was climb down to die.

So easy. Just come on inside.

STOP AND THINK. JASON TOLD ME. I KNOW. YOU NEED TO BACK OFF.

Kendall swiveled out of her chair and shut her office door. She turned to face the portrait of her family and the dying fern on her desk. She pressed her back against the door not because she was tired, but because she could barely stand. Her lungs were devoid of oxygen. She felt as if her knees would fail her, like a wooden peg doll that had its pins removed by a terrorizing child.

She felt such fear, and she knew that the sender had declared war on her weeks ago.

I know you sent this, Tori. I know you are the one.

She heard a knock on the door and she spun around.

"Kendall?"

The voice belonged to Josh.

Now isn't a good time, she thought.

"On the phone with my mom's doctor," she said. "Be a minute."

She let herself slide to the floor.

The voice on the other end of the line was toffee—sweet, but with sharp, dangerous edges. The conversation between Parker and Tori was spoken in the kind of hushed tones reserved for those who do not want others to hear.

"What is it that you want now?"

"You. I'm waiting for *you*."

"Hold on a bit longer."

"Waiting for you is hard."

"Really? I like that."

"Not that. You know, I miss you."

"You miss making love to me."

"Yes. I miss everything about you. I want to hold you. Taste you. Be inside of you."

"Patience."

"You said it wouldn't be much longer."

"Mmm. Longer. I like that, too."

"Knock it off. I'm going crazy here."

"Come to me."

"Where? When?"

"I'll make a plan."

"You're good at that."

"Yes, I am."

The bedroom door swung open and another voice cut into the conversation. It was Parker Connelly's mother, Laura. He set the phone down.

"Hey, don't you knock?" he said, his eyes blazing annoyance.

She noticed the phone in his hand. "Who were you talking to?"

"Were you listening? A friend."

"A girlfriend?"

"Mom, that's none of your business."

"All right, Parker. You're right. None of my business. But you can't blame me for wanting to know what's going on with you. Come on, get up. Let's make a run to Costco."

Parker didn't move. Noticing the placement of his hands under the covers and the redness of his face, the first Mrs. Connelly knew why. She averted her eyes and backed out toward the door.

"I'll be in the kitchen," she said, shutting the door.

"Okay, Mom. Next time you come in my room, knock first."

He put his phone back to his ear.

"Sorry about that," he said.

"Your mother's a control freak. If she finds out about us, you can expect nothing but trouble," the toffee voice said.

"I love you, Tori."

"I love you more, Parker."

Parker turned off his phone. A quick cleanup and he'd be ready to go to Costco.

Laura Connelly reached for the knob of her kitchen TV and turned the sound up slightly. Her stomach started to knot. The news was playing a segment about a memorial service for a minister who'd been murdered at his church in North Kitsap. The name of the church scared her: Lord's Grace.

She's seen that name before and she knew where.

"Ready to go?"

She turned to see her son.

"You look like crap, Mom."

"I'll be okay," she said.

God, I hope we'll all be okay.

Tori Connelly's face fell like a chocolate soufflé four minutes after serving. The summer before she made her plans, she opened the Blue Chip Benefits envelope addressed to her husband. *What?* It was as if a lightning bolt had struck her in the heart. The words were direct, incontrovertible.

"Pursuant to your request, the change in beneficiary is complete. Sole beneficiary is Parker Adam Connelly."

She carefully folded the insurance company's missive and returned it to the envelope. She considered attempting to reseal it, but thought better of that plan. She'd torn it when she passed a silver letter opener along the seam across the top. Instead, the only solution was to destroy it and pretend it never arrived. Quietly, she walked into her husband's office and turned on the shredder.

In a second the letter had been turned into confetti.

Confetti she would use to sprinkle over his grave.

Tori knew what was coming next. Alex would leave her for that bitch he worked with downtown. He'd make up some lie and try to wriggle out of everything he'd promised her. Like her mother had. Like Jason. Like Zach. Like all of them. Her heart was racing, pounding like a broken drum inside her chest.

Damn him. Damn all of them. I will not be set aside by anyone!

Tori drew a deep breath and made her way back to the master bathroom. *Never again!* She turned on the cold water faucet, filling the white basin of the vintage pedestal sink. *Never!* She splashed the water against her face. Over and over. Water puddled all around her, but she didn't care. She was fighting for control, for reason, for what she would do next. *I can do this!* She was trying to pull herself together.

She didn't cry. She didn't want to open her emotions for the world to see. She'd been good at hiding them before. Tori had been adept at going with the flow.

Tori knew that her answer was the teenage boy playing World of Warcraft in the bedroom down the hallway. She'd seen the way he'd looked at her. She could think of at least two million reasons why she was going to do what she must do. She thought of it as a test, a challenge to determine if she could still get the job done. She stripped off all her clothes and stood in her closet, facing a row of dresses. The black wouldn't do. Neither would the white. But the red one, that one seemed perfect. Like the other two she considered, it was strapless. She slipped into the red dress, holding it close to her body as she walked into his room.

"Parker, will you zip me?"

He looked up at her.

"Sure, hang on. I'm almost done."

She let her hand slip just a little so that from the boy's vantage point on the bed he'd get a glimpse of her breast. It was a move that at once was both deliberate and devious.

"I don't mind waiting," she said, her voice soft. "You're so good at what you do. Keep playing, Parker."

By then, he'd stopped, of course. His eyes were fastened exactly where she wanted him to look. She didn't say another word. She didn't have to.

The beginning was messy, awkward, and unfulfilling. But she never said so. That would ruin everything.

CHAPTER TWENTY-SEVEN

Seattle

Penny Salazar and Adam Canfield had been assigned the task of managing the incoming items for the Class of '95's Fifteen Minutes of Fame Auction. Adam knew that meant Penny would stake her claim as the "chairperson" of the event and "solely responsible" for making it a success.

He was fine with that.

It's a bunch of crap anyway, he thought, as he surveyed the contents assembled in the hospitality manager's office at the Gold Mountain Golf Club, the staging area for auction items.

"Awesome," Penny said, pointing to a lacquered black box with a trio of white herons painted on its gleaming surface. "This is going to bring in beaucoup bucks."

Adam pretended to agree, but he said softly, "If you have bad taste and twenty bucks, maybe."

"Huh?"

"Love it, Penny," he said. "Love it."

She looked at him, not sure if he actually did love it. Adam was so hard for Penny to read.

Adam knelt down to inspect the single item that caught his interest. It was a Victorian dollhouse that looked hand-crafted in the way that suggested it could be pawned off as a piece of folk art. Folk art, the kitschier the better, appealed to Adam.

"I might bid on this myself," he said.

"I didn't know you still played with dolls."

He refused to take the bait. "You'd be surprised, honey."

Penny shrugged and looked over a set of carnival-glass cat figurines that she thought she might bid on.

Adam bent down and lifted the house. "Wonder if there is a label here or if this thing is completely handmade."

When he scanned under the front porch he noticed the writing. It was written in red-brown.

"I know who killed Jason Reed."

"Jesus, Penny, check this out." He scratched it with the edge of a dime. "It isn't a red crayon. Something else."

Penny set down the glass cat and went over.

"That's freaky," she said, bending close to take a better look.

Adam's eyes met hers. "I agree. But it's more than that."

Penny stood. "Just some kid saying something stupid. Mad at someone."

He shook his head and reached for his phone.

"I'm calling Kendall," he said. "She needs to see this."

Penny put her hand out and gently pushed the phone away from Adam's ear. "Wait a minute," Penny said. "We need the money for the auction. I overspent. We can't have the cops involved here. They might confiscate this or something."

Adam ignored Penny and dialed Kendall. Of course she overspent. She ran the committee like she ran her life. Right into the ground.

Fifteen Minutes of Lame, indeed.

* * *

Kendall Stark was running on fumes as she and Josh Anderson hovered over the dollhouse collected from the class reunion committee's Adam and Penny. A phone call to the woman who'd donated the dollhouse for the fund-raiser revealed its chilling origin.

"My kids outgrew it, and we're moving to a condo," the woman said. "I know that it was made by the prisoners at the reformatory. I never saw any writing on it."

"Tori was there," Kendall said as they turned the house on its side on the counter in the Kitsap County crime lab.

"Maybe she blabbed to someone there," Josh said.

Kendall prepared to swab the first letter of the message with leucomalachite green.

"We'll have to send it out to the state crime lab for DNA testing," she said.

"If it is blood," Josh said.

Almost instantaneously, the LMG turned the tip of the swab a pale green hue.

"It's blood, all right," she said, putting the swab into a tube and sealing it in a plastic bag.

Next, she took photos of the text.

I KNOW WHO KILLED JASON REED.

"Written by a lefty," he said, noting the smear and slant that came with each letter.

Kendall nodded. "The question is not only who wrote this, but when?"

"And why?" he asked.

Kendall put the packet with the swab into an envelope and logged the date, her initials, and the case number for Jason Reed.

"Yes, why would someone write a message like this in the first place? Seems like a heavy burden," she said, not wanting to say what was really on her mind. Not to Josh. Not to anyone.

It was as if Jason were calling out to her.

Actually, it wasn't fun to dream. Not when the dreams came at her like the most cunning stalker, through the darkness that swallowed every trace of their invasion before finding her under the covers. At first, Lainie O'Neal had begun to see insomnia as a gift, a respite from the dark dreams that ice-picked at her when sleep finally came. Doctors told her that her insomnia was something that she used as a defense mechanism, a response to real or perceived trauma.

In one dream, the house in Port Orchard was very, very quiet. In her mind, Lainie thought that she and her sister would both select the phrase "quiet like a tomb." That was when they still could joke about such things.

The way that children sometimes do.

"Black makes you look thinner, you know," Lainie said to Tori.

"Funny. I thought you were the fat twin."

Lainie spun around and looked in the mirror, her hand on her hip. She caught Tori's gaze and flat lined her expression. Neither girl was fat. Both were lithe, blond, blue eyed, fine boned. They were petite for their age—fifteen—but there was nothing particularly fragile about them. The same could not be said for their mother—the reason they were dressing in black that morning.

Vonnie O'Neal was an exceedingly tragic woman who'd suffered postpartum depression with the twins to such a severity, she never seemed to pull herself out of it. Having the twins was too much at once. More than she could bear. She once confided to a friend that her girls took her figure, stole her husband's attention, and made her into "someone's mother, nothing more." She telegraphed her less-than-joyful take on motherhood with everything she did.

No love was doled out without at least a sprinkling of resentment.

For as long as they could remember, their mother had done nothing to give them much of a reason to love her. She slept most of the time. She abdicated most of the child-rearing duties to a series of nannies and babysitters. She let her husband do all of the nurturing.

Lainie put on a jacket for the ride to the memorial.

"Are you going to miss her?" she asked.

"A little," Tori said, opening the bedroom door.

They found their father at the kitchen table. His callused hands cradled his handsome face. Despite what she'd done and all he'd been through, it was obvious that Dex loved his wife.

"She was a fighter, girls, wasn't she?" Dex said.

Tori nodded. "Yes, Daddy, she was. We were lucky to have her as long as we did."

Tori used the term "Daddy" as a way to endear her father to her. It was completely at odds with the way she talked about him behind his back. According to her, he was weak. He was not ambitious. He let a depressed woman chart the course of his life.

He held his forefinger to his lips. "We can't tell anyone how she died," he said.

And there he was, protecting her once more.

"I can keep a secret, Dad," Lainie said, the tears flowing.

Tori nodded. "I can, too."

Dex reached out for the girls and pulled them close against his chest. Lainie started to cry, feeling her tears absorbed by the lightly starched cotton of his laundered and pressed shirt.

Only one of the girls knew the true depth of the secret, a secret she'd never tell.

Their mother's death was classified by the coroner's office as "accidental," but those closest to her knew that ruling was a gift that allowed her survivors to carry on without the specter of a suicide and the implications such deaths frequently bring to those left behind.

Vonnie had taken a fistful of pills for depression and anxiety and went to sleep. No one saw her take them, but when her stomach was pumped the night she slipped into a coma, the doctors recovered more than ten that had not yet dissolved. It was a party mix of pills for a party that never took place. Vonnie did not leave a note. She merely said "good night" and went down the hallway to bed.

As she had when the family cat had died, Tori seemed to hold up better than her sister or father. She cried when there was someone there to see it—if the person was the type to pass judgment on her emotions.

One time she told Lainie that "tears are for the weak or those who pretend to be so that others won't judge them."

It was easy for Lainie to know which category Tori fell into. She was that consistent.

Lainie, on the other hand, could barely get over the very idea their mother was gone. Her own depression sent her farther and farther down a path that sometimes made her question her own stability.

I don't want to be like her. I don't want to end up like her, *she thought.*

Of course, she wouldn't. Unlike her mother, Lainie was a survivor. Both O'Neal twins were. Just in very different ways.

CHAPTER TWENTY-EIGHT

Tacoma

Darius Fulton lawyered up lickety-split, which certainly was no surprise to anyone. He protested that what made him look most guilty was nothing more than an error in judgment, not a clue to his culpability or complicity in a crime. He'd never once harmed anyone. Plus, he said there was no proof. Because there couldn't be.

Oh, really, Detective Kaminski thought as he prepared for a meeting between the person of interest and his lawyer.

The crime lab determined that the partial print on the murder weapon matched a latent one recovered from the Dasani water bottle that Kaminski carried from the interview room with a Bic pen inserted into its neck after the meeting in which Darius Fulton confessed his indiscretion with Tori Connelly.

It was true, as Darius insisted; all of that could easily be explained. It was *his* gun. His fingerprints *should* be on it.

But an e-mail to the police department's community web page sent by an anonymous tipster had changed things. There was something else suggesting that Fulton had done more than covet his neighbor's wife. The e-mail came in from a Kinko's rent-by-the-hour PC, and plainly indicated that Fulton was obsessed with Tori.

"Get his computer," the tipster wrote. *"You'll see."*

Later that afternoon, Darius's lawyer, Maddie Crane, a glossy-haired woman with an expressionless Botoxed face and a penchant for seeking out the red RECORD light of a TV camera, made a succinct statement to the media in the lobby of her Tacoma law firm offices.

"Yes, my client had a relationship with the deceased's wife. We don't deny that. But that's the sum of his involvement here."

A young man from KING-TV in Seattle was the only one to get a question out before she ended the press conference.

"Wasn't he stalking her? Didn't he bombard her with phone calls and e-mails?"

Ms. Botox's fluttering eyelids were her only indicator of a reaction. She almost bent the folds of her face, but the 'tox had done its job.

"Statement over," she said curtly.

The KING reporter winked at a newsroom associate, a woman he'd been flirting with for six weeks.

"See what I mean," she said. "It's all about the tips."

"You going to tell me how you knew?" the young reporter asked.

He put his hand on her shoulder, a touch that sent a chill down her spine and reminded her why her father hadn't wanted her to go into TV in the first place.

"Nope. Just a call. Just knowing the right people."

In actuality, he, too, had received an anonymous e-mail.

Eddie Kaminski and four uniformed officers served a search warrant on Darius Fulton's residence. His computers— a desktop and a laptop—were confiscated, as was a stack of

DVDs and CD-ROMs. Among the electronic equipment was a video cam feed that emanated from the Connelly home across the street. The camera had been placed behind a Thomas Kinkade painting.

"Guy was a major stalker," a cop told Kaminski.

"A regular Steve Jobs with all this electronic surveillance crap. Probably has an app on his iPhone that allowed him to keep an eye on her no matter where he was."

"Sick, twisted piece of crap."

Kaminski nodded.

"Yeah. He's as good as going down for this."

Kaminski recovered another item tucked into the cushions of the sofa—a black ski mask.

"Looky here at what I've found," the detective said, holding it up with the tip of a pen.

Forensic specialist Cal Herzog grinned at the discovery.

"Boom! This guy's done," he said.

The camera used to feed images from the Connelly place to Darius Fulton's residence was a wireless model manufactured by Lorex. Eddie Kaminski told the lab guys that he'd chase down the model number with the idea of determining just where it had been purchased. None of the credit card receipts thus far indicated that Darius had purchased a unit.

Stalkers are more paranoid than their victims, he thought as he scrolled through the database display of suppliers on his computer.

A box of pizza with congealed cheese and pepperoni beckoned from the corner of his desk, but Eddie Kaminski was working as hard on his case as he was on his waistline.

I will not eat another bite, because it is too damn wet outside to go running.

The model number in question was sold in only Best Buy and Radio Shack, which ordinarily would be good news for a detective trying to determine who had purchased the camera. However, the fact that their Internet sites also sold the cameras made it a lot harder to determine their point of sale. Any thought of heading over to the Tacoma Mall and presenting a photo display of cops and a suspected killer was dashed.

It was possible that the cam was purchased online, but the techs examining Darius Fulton's computer had revealed no such transactions. In fact, apart from the e-mails they'd easily discovered at the first examination, there was nothing else to tie the neighbor to his victims.

In his pristine lab on the second floor, Cal Herzog cataloged the ski mask recovered from the Fulton residence. It was black with three holes for the eyes and mouth. REI manufactured the item of wool poly-blend yarn. It was of the type that could be purchased online or at any of the recreational company's retail stores.

As he worked through the process of examining the mask, two things were remarkable and Cal made note of both of them.

First, he noted that there were absolutely no biologicals around the mouth or eyeholes. No saliva as would be expected. It wasn't out of the realm of possibilities—he'd once examined a woman's blouse on a rape case that was clean as a shirt off the rack at Macy's. Blood from both Alex and Tori Connelly was found, though a greater amount of her blood was present than his.

Of the three hairs recovered, two had intact follicles, making them candidates for nuclear DNA testing. One was too damaged, but the other was in good shape. The third hair was shorter, darker, and without the benefit of a follicle. It would require the more comprehensive mitochondrial DNA testing.

Later, when the tests were complete, only one person's name was on the report: *Darius Fulton*. The third hair? *Unknown*.

Tori's words resonated in his ear. Tori knew that the right delivery ensured the prize—no matter what it was that she was after.

"Use cash for everything, babe. I'll make sure you have the money. Never, ever use a debit card."

"Only people over forty carry cash now," he said.

"Yes. Only an old fool would carry money in his wallet. Plastic is so much cleaner."

He played the conversation over dodging raindrops as he left his hand-me-down Camry, a crappy gift from his father. He loathed his dad for being an ass, first to his mother, then to Tori. Doing what he needed to do was getting easier with every step. His heart rate escalated as he entered the west end of the Tacoma Mall. The place smelled of popcorn and damp clothing.

He noticed the pimply-faced clerk, probably his age, as he went inside Radio Shack. There was no one else in the store.

"Hey," the clerk said, sauntering over to the video cameras where Parker stood, his shoulders hunched and his hands stuffed inside his dark-dyed jeans. "You looking or buying?"

Parker glanced at him. "Buying."

"Excellent. We've got a sweet sale. Do you know what you want?"

Parker shook his head, though he already knew what he wanted.

Tori had been specific. She always was specific. Her clear-cut instructions would make it easier when the time came.

"How do those Lorex cams work?" he asked.

"Like Jason Bourne," the clerk said, "on a road trip."

"Awesome. I'll take one."

The day before the intruder killed her ex-husband, Laura Connelly and Parker had a fight that left her to contemplate the difficulties of motherhood with half a bottle of Riesling and a tub of Dreyer's vanilla frozen yogurt. He'd been moody since his most recent visit with his father. It wasn't that he ruminated about what a jerk his dad was; it was how much he wanted to return to North Junett.

"I want to live with Dad again," he said.

"We've been over that. You've made a commitment and you have to live up to it, Parker. That's the way life is."

"I hate it when you say such bullshit."

Laura winced. "Parker, I don't think you should talk to me like that."

"Why not?" Parker asked, now standing close to her. "I can talk to you any way I want. I'm not some little kid who can be shuffled around by you or Dad or anyone. You know, I'm not going to be pushed around by someone like you. The day I turn eighteen, I'm out of here."

"I've never ignored you," she said, backing away.

"More bullshit."

"Parker, please."

He turned away. "I'm going to spend the night at Drew's."

"I didn't say you could," she said, raising her voice a little for the urgency.

Parker's eyes flashed at his mother. "Are you serious? Are you really trying to control me? Give it up, Mom. You lost that ability a long time ago. I'm doing what I want to do, for the reasons that make me happy."

"I've made dinner."

"You're a shitty cook, Mom," he said.

The door slammed and Laura turned off the oven. The lasagna that was one of her son's favorites wasn't going to be served that evening. The little boy whom she had loved was lost to her. She knew it. She knew it the way that a mother does when her child no longer looks up with adoring eyes, but eyes that see the truth.

I pushed him. I pushed him too hard. Why did I do that?

Laura poured herself some wine and went into his room. A Ghostbusters *poster, a reminder of her boy's favorite movie, hovered over his bed. Laura sat down and looked around the room. On his desk was a cutting board and spools of colored duct tape. He'd once spent hours there making duct-tape wallets that he and his best friend, Drew, thought they could sell door-to-door. It seemed so long ago. It seemed like he was a different boy. She wondered when he'd grow out of his moodiness. She hadn't been a perfect mother, but she did the best that she could. Like her mother, probably. And her mother's mother before her. There was no owner's manual dispensed with each hospital birth.*

She noticed the packaging for a webcam and she wondered what that was all about.

I really don't understand all this social networking stuff, *she thought.*

In his car, Parker called his buddy, Drew Cooper, and explained that he wanted to lie low and that he'd told his mother he was staying with him. He didn't have a hands-free device, so he hunched a little as he passed a Washington State patrol vehicle parked by the Puyallup River Bridge exit. The last thing he needed was to be noticed.

"When are you going to tell me about the chick you're boning?" Drew said.

Parker laughed. "Soon enough, bro."

He and Drew were no longer close, and he'd never tell

that doofus about Tori. Drew had a big mouth and a judgmental mother. Confiding in him was as good as posting it on his Facebook wall. In two minutes' time, the information would be shared by everyone he knew.

"You staying with her?" Drew asked.

"Yeah. For a day or two. Watch my back, all right?"

"Sure. Her parents gone?"

"Something like that."

"Why can't I be so lucky? What do I have to do to get a girl to put out?"

Don't go for a girl, go for a woman.

"Don't have an answer for you, bro," Parker said. "Just be patient. The right one will come along."

That was a lie, too. Parker Connelly knew that soul mates almost never really found each other. Drew was a loser like the rest of the people he knew. Like his dad. His mother. They couldn't conceive of the power and deep satisfaction that comes from finding the other half of one's self.

For always like swans.

Parker hung up and turned on the radio and listened to the news. Tori liked him for his body and his brain. He wasn't like anyone she'd ever met. He was handsome, strong. Smart.

He parked and made his way to the airport ticket kiosk. It was the one tricky element of their plan, a ticket to the Caribbean so they could start their life together. They talked about the danger of leaving a trail of any kind, even though there was absolutely no way they'd be caught. He didn't even buy the ticket under his own name. Tori thought of everything. He wore a down vest under his dark blue hoodie and kept his head down.

"I wish we could buy a ticket with cash," Tori had said as they snuggled in bed, making their plans. "But those terrorists have screwed up everything for everyone."

"Yeah, you're right."

"Cash in your father's frequent flier points," she said.

"Got it handled, Tori."

"Then make love to me."

"So the money will be transferred at midnight?" Tori asked.

"Midnight their time, but yes, that's right."

"We do not have to take any action to have the money go directly into the offshore account?"

"Nope," the lawyer said. "Nothing. All set up."

"Wonderful," Tori said.

"Two million dollars, that's some birthday present," she said.

Tori felt a surge of excitement, like the first few minutes of really good sex.

"Yes, it is. He's a very lucky boy."

Kendall crawled under the covers and nuzzled Steven. He was asleep, snoring softly in the manner she found more charming than irritating. The regular rhythm of his slumber was something that she could always count on and it comforted her just then. She found herself thinking of how her life might have gone if they'd stayed apart. She remembered how lost she'd been those lonely, dark days.

Jason Reed's voice reverberated in her memory.

"Kendall, I don't know what to say."

"I don't, either," she said. *"We need to do what's right."*

"I need more time to sort out some things."

"I'm begging you," she said. *"Please."*

That was the last time that they really spoke. She was seventeen, ashamed, and feeling as if the world was going to come to an end. She talked things over with her mother. She prayed to God. She'd done what every other teenage girl who became pregnant since the world made such things shameful did. She hid it from everyone.

But the baby's father.

As she lay there next to Steven, she thought of how much the world had changed in the past fifteen years. Celebrities had babies without marriage every day. They even posed for magazine covers as if there was nothing wrong. The stigma had been washed away. Even in conservative Port Orchard, people had changed their thinking.

And yet, Kendall *had* kept it a secret. She didn't tell Steven, though there were many times when she could have. It was private and she wanted it to stay that way. As time progressed, she was able to set aside some of the emotion that came with her decision.

I did what I had to do, she thought. *I did what was the right thing at the time. Not the right thing for who I am today, but who I was back then.*

When Cody was diagnosed with autism, Kendall blamed herself. She felt that it was payback from God for the choice that she made.

How many times can I say I'm sorry? she asked.

She wrote a letter to Steven that she'd intended to give him, but never did.

> *When I dreamed of falling in love, I dreamed of you. I don't know if you'll ever understand, but I'm begging you to try. For the rest of my life, I'll live with the shame of knowing that the mistake I made was only compounded by the lies that I've told, the past that I've swept away.*

Years later, when cleaning out the bedroom closet of their Harper house, Kendall found a cache of letters in a cigar box that had belonged to her father. There were postcards, too, from trips she and Steven had taken before Cody was born.

Paris. The Grand Canyon. Vancouver Island. Among the items was the "I'm sorry" note. She picked at it, not sure if she wanted to unfold it. The letters bled through the stationery like a ghost from a bad dream. She could make out some of the words, and her heart sank. *So much to remember. So much to save.* No review was needed, of course. Every word from that time had been etched in her memory. She unfolded it slowly, feeling the texture of the slightly rippled paper. She remembered she'd cried when she wrote it.

The final words lay on the page like the message on a tombstone, destined to be forever.

Forgive me, so I can forgive myself.

CHAPTER TWENTY-NINE

Tacoma

If anyone passed him on the trail along the Thea Foss Waterway that morning, Eddie Kaminski would have conjured the image of an old steam locomotive. He ran through the chilly air, streams of warm breath following him step by step. *Puff. Puff. Puff.* His running was on autopilot because his mind was so wrapped up in his thoughts of what had transpired over the past few days. There was no denying that there had been some anomalies in the Alex Connelly case that made it of the twisty sort that detectives mull over. Sometimes obsessively so. Out running, in the car, or with his daughter as they shared a couple of calzones at a restaurant in Spanaway—any time, all times. Wealthy husband shot to death and a stunningly beautiful woman who seemed less concerned about her husband than the appearance of her own culpability. It was apparent to the investigative team that Darius Fulton had been obsessed with his neighbor and more than likely had been the triggerman.

But had he acted alone? It was a question they were asking back at the Tacoma Police Department. In fact, a lot of questions were being asked. Nothing got cops talking like a beautiful and bloody blonde. The Connelly case was a far cry from a drug- or gangland-related murder, by far the most common in gritty Tacoma.

A little digging by Cal Herzog had turned up one little nugget that suggested Alex Connelly might have had a girlfriend, possibly someone at work. And that affair, if true, had occurred *before* Tori slept with Darius Fulton. Had she done so to get back at her husband? The scenario was familiar.

Kaminski stopped to catch his breath and rested his hands on his knees. Ten more pounds off the middle and a final run up and down the Spanish Steps downtown would be easier. He slowed his breathing a little and acted as if he was doing just fine when a young woman jogging with her Rottweiler ran by, the gravel crunching under the dog's heavy black paws. As she disappeared around a corner, he resumed his labored breathing. Sweat streaked his back and the space between what he imagined should be well-defined pecs, but weren't quite there yet.

A moment later, composed, lungs no longer contracting, he went back to the office, showered, and dressed. He had an appointment at Alex Connelly's office. The president of Pacific Investments had made the call himself.

When the elevator doors opened to the seventh floor of the Tacoma office building that was Alex Connelly's place of employment, it was like the scene in *The Wizard of Oz* in which Dorothy opened the door of the tornado-hurtled Kansas farmhouse to reveal the shiny, colorful world of Munchkinland. Pacific Investments was an opulent place of white leather couches, a tsunami of colorful artwork splashed on the walls. Eddie Kaminski was duly impressed—as would any visitor to a floor accessible only by invitation.

Or by detective's shield.

"Detective Kaminski?"

He turned around from a painting that held his attention.

A young woman in stilettos and a dark blue suit had crept up behind him.

She was pretty, so he smiled. "Yes. That's me."

"I'm Daphnia. Mr. Johnstone and the rest of Alex's team are in the boardroom. Follow me."

She led the way, Kaminski's eyes embarrassingly, but unavoidably, riveted to her backside as they made their way past a row of rosewood desks and Eames chairs. She pressed a burnished nickel-plated button and a pair of frosted-glass double doors slowly opened.

Three people—two men and a woman—occupied a conference room large enough to play a volleyball match. A Chihuly hung like a sheaf of glass bananas from the ceiling.

The firm spared no expense.

Eli Johnstone was a physically fit man of about sixty, with light gray eyes, a shaved head, and a tuft of white hair protruding from the front of his collar. The firm that his father had built from nothing was impressive—a multimillion-dollar portfolio that had made it through the junk bond years and the scandals that defined Wall Street in the first years of the new millennium. Johnstone was no Bernie Madoff. Eli sat at the head of a black walnut table in a conference room that looked out to the cold waters of Commencement Bay. At his right was a woman of considerable beauty. She had faded blue eyes and a short blond haircut that looked still damp from the shower. She seemed cold and indifferent—almost as if she had better things to do and couldn't wait to get back to them. Next to her was a young man with the kind of eager-beaver attitude that Kaminski knew might come in handy.

Overly helpful is always a plus, he thought.

"I'm sorry for the loss of your friend and colleague," Kaminski said as he approached the group.

Johnstone put out his hand and shook the detective's like he meant to choke the life out of him. "Thank you," he said. "Alex was an important member of our team here." He motioned for Kaminski to sit as he introduced his colleagues: Lissa March was the ice-princess vice president of Human Resources, and Hank Wooten was Alex Connelly's assistant, a trainee that he'd mentored for the past year.

"Thanks for seeing me."

"Alex was very important here. Important to all of us."

Kaminski looked at the others, but none seemed broken up at all. They were young professionals on autopilot with their emotions.

"You said you had some information that might be helpful in the investigation of his murder," Kaminski said.

The company president acknowledged the remark with a quick nod. "That'll be your job to determine."

Neither of the other two said a word, though the younger man appeared to bobble-head with great enthusiasm.

"Ms. March advised me of a turn of events that we thought you might find of interest." He turned slightly in Lissa's direction and she immediately produced a black file folder.

Kaminski looked at the folder. "What do we have here?"

"Last year Mr. Connelly made a change to his life insurance policy," Lissa said, her voice softer than her standoffish body language might have suggested it would be. Kaminski caught a faint accent, maybe North Carolina.

Maybe Lissa wasn't as tough as she wanted the world to believe she was.

"What kind of a change?" he asked.

"An interesting one," she said, her tougher façade back in full force, "especially considering the recent tragic turn of events. Alex removed his wife as a beneficiary and left the sum of the policy's payout to his son, Parker."

It was an interesting change, indeed.

"I see," Kaminski said, reaching for the document that Lissa had excised from the black folder and slid across the high gloss table. "Shouldn't the beneficiary be his wife?"

"Ordinarily, yes," Johnstone said. "In fact, she called here not wanting it that way at all. She said it wasn't about the money, but what was best for Parker. Tori thought that setting up a trust for Parker would be best for the boy, too."

Kaminski directed his attention to Hank.

"Were there any problems between the Connellys?"

The younger man drank some water before answering.

"Well, not that I know about. I mean—"

"—everyone has problems," Johnstone said, effectively cutting short Hank's comment.

"Tell me," Kaminski said, in part, a comment about his own life and dusted-up marriage, but also, he wanted to know more. "This is a murder investigation."

"We work in black-and-white here. We don't delve into pie-in-the-sky theories or gossip."

"Understood," Kaminski said, "but was there trouble in the marriage?"

Pacific Investments President Johnstone's eyes flashed and he glanced in the direction of the comely human resources executive.

"This doesn't leave this office," he said.

Kaminski shook his head. "I can't promise that."

"It has nothing to do with any of this."

"I'm sorry, Mr. Johnstone, but you can't be the decision

maker on that. That'll be up to me, then the Prosecutor's Office. What are you holding back?"

He looked at Lissa and she shifted nervously in her chair. All of a sudden she looked more frightened than sophisticated. Kaminski had seen it before, many times. Fear had a way of dissolving all traces of beauty.

"I had a brief affair with Alex," she said. "Tori knew about it." Tears started to roll down her cheeks and she turned away to wipe them. She dabbed gently at her skin as if she didn't want the humiliation of her disclosure made worse by the smudging of her makeup.

Eli Johnstone handed her a second tissue.

Kaminski would never have thought the woman in the pencil skirt would have been a crier.

"The affair was brief. Very brief. Lissa came to me and disclosed the indiscretion—which was against company policy. Since she reported it to me, I agreed to keep her on." He looked in Lissa's direction. She was dabbing her eyes. "Alex was reprimanded, too."

"I see. When was this?"

"Last year," she said. "It was a couple of dates following our Christmas party. We broke it off amicably."

If it was so amicable, why was she crying about it still? he wondered.

"How do you know his wife knew?"

"She confronted me and I broke it off the next day. There was a lot of drama, but it was really over after a week or two."

Kaminski pushed the button to the elevator and got inside. Just as the doors inched closed, Lissa March slipped between the panels. Her eyes were red and her makeup was smeared. She caught a glimpse of herself on the polished chrome-plated doors.

"I look like hell."

"Going down?"

"I'm already down. But, no." She reached over and pushed the STOP button. "I just wanted to tell you that Tori Connelly scared me."

"How so?"

"Look, I know I shouldn't have messed with Alex. I can't even say it wasn't my idea, you know, to make me look like a better person. And I wouldn't lie about a dead man. She came to my condo after she found out. She's a pretty woman, but she wasn't pretty that day."

Lissa took a breath. She was beautiful, smart. She'd made a big mistake and it was clear that she'd been paying for it.

"Tell me what happened," he said.

"All right," she said.

"From the beginning."

Lissa March was sweaty from a workout on the elliptical machine in the living room of her top-floor Stadium District condo overlooking Commencement Bay. It was a Sunday afternoon and she relished the respite from Pacific Investments. While others were at church or with families on Sundays, she was usually at the office catching up on paperwork. Her job was her life. Lissa wrapped a towel around her neck, put on some smooth jazz, and poured herself some Evian with a slice of lime and looked out at the water. Things were good just then.

The mezzanine doorman buzzed to tell her that a woman was there with a delivery—a large bouquet of white lilies.

"Can she leave them?"

"She wants to come up. Says she knows you."

Lissa wasn't expecting a visitor, much less flowers. Fleetingly, she allowed herself to believe that Alex had sent them as a peace offering.

"Oh. Who is she?"

"Name's Tori Connelly."

Lissa could feel the air go out of the room. It wasn't Alex, after all, but his wife. *Lissa felt a wave of nausea. She never wanted to be the ugly part of a triangle. It was certainly nothing her Southern upbringing had ever considered even the remotest of possibilities. Her mom always said, "The other woman is always a tramp. Tramps always end up with nothing but a swim in a pool of shame."*

In that instance of guilt and introspection, Lissa felt she had no choice but take her lumps and steep in the shame of what she'd done.

"All right, send her up," Lissa said. She patted her face with the towel, ran her fingers through her hair, and made the best of her attire by smoothing out the black T-shirt she wore over a pair of black workout shorts. She didn't look good.

I don't deserve to look good.

A knock on the door, and she opened it. Tori Connelly stood outside, poking the bouquet of overly perfumed lilies at Lissa.

"Are you alone?" she asked, her blue eyes sparking disgust as she ran the length of Lissa's body.

Lissa's face tightened, but she nodded. "Yes. I'm alone." She knew that the comment was a dig, a suggestion that she'd pulled herself away from a horny suitor just then.

"You look so damp, I just thought . . ."

"What do you want?"

"I want you to get out of our lives."

Lissa took a step backward. "I'm out. It's over."

"Really? I know women like you never give up on what

*you want. I brought these for you," she said, shoving the
white flowers at Lissa as if they were a weapon. "When my
mom died we buried her with these, her favorite flower."*

*Reflexively, Lissa took the bouquet thrust at her. "I don't
want any drama, Tori. I made a mistake. I'm working through
it."*

"Poor you."

*Tori looked around the condo, her eyes taking in the
expensive furnishings, the original artwork over the fireplace.*

*"You have expensive taste, Lissa. Uninteresting, but ex-
pensive. You can't have my husband."*

*A chill ran down Lissa's spine. "I don't want him. Will you
go now?"*

*"I'm leaving. I just wanted to make my point. If I can't
have Alex, no one can. You see, he's boring and rich. That's
enough for me. At least the rich part is. You'll be sorry—he'll
be very, very sorry—if you cross me."*

The elevator holding Lissa and Kaminski started to move
and the female executive quickly pushed the button to the
next floor with her perfectly squared-off French-manicured
nails.

"I'm getting out here," she said. "I just wanted you to
know that Tori Connelly was a total bitch. I might have deserved what she said, but I want you to know I felt that she
making a serious threat. She looked at me with those ice-
cube eyes of hers and told me basically that it wasn't beyond
her to make sure that no one got in her way."

Lissa stepped across the threshold of the elevator. She
was more composed than she had been. It was as if getting
the story out had eased her mind.

And maybe her conscience.

"If she couldn't have him, no one could," Kaminski repeated.

"That's right."

"Did you think she was threatening to kill you?"

"No. Not at all. I think she was going to kill *him*."

CHAPTER THIRTY

Tacoma
The previous summer

Tori Connelly looked out the front window, the sun falling in patches over the precision-mowed lawn onto the street and into Darius Fulton's front yard. She sipped a diet soda through a long red plastic straw. She'd bleached her teeth to an icy white and didn't want to stain them. She was dressed in a filmy sleeveless blouse and capri pants. A strand of liquid silver coiled around her spray-tanned neck.

There was a lot to think about. The summer was edging toward fall. Alex had been more distant than ever, and Tori wasn't exactly sure why. She'd been so very careful, covering her tracks.

Taking a lover right under their own roof had seemed reckless at first, but it had proved to be the cleverest solution to a problem that needed solving.

Parker came down the stairs, showered and with a tiny piece of tissue red-glued onto his chin. He'd shaved, though he barely had to.

"Plans for the day?" she asked. "We're having dinner tonight with your dad at Indochine."

"I hate Thai food," he said.

"Oh, really? I thought you liked a little spice, now and then."

The teenager smiled, catching the sexy undercurrent of her words. He felt himself get hard. All she had to do was look at him in a certain way, turn her head, laugh, talk. Just about anything excited him to the point where he had no control over his body.

At least what was below his belt buckle, anyway.

"You're going to have to learn how to tame that," she said, looking at his obvious arousal.

He moved closer and touched her. She pulled back.

"What up?" he asked.

"I've been thinking," she said. "You might want to try using your other head." She was irritated, but she hadn't meant to hurt him. The look on his face told her she'd gone too far.

"That's harsh," he said.

"What I meant is that we need to figure a way out of this, and that will take two of us. I can't be expected to do everything, Parker."

"Just leave him. We can go away."

"I've explained that to you. Maybe you just can't grasp what I need you to."

"I know what I want you to grasp," he said.

"Knock it off, Parker." She looked out the window again. She could see Darius Fulton move about the space of his open carriage-house garage. He was clearly organizing the things that his ex-wife had left behind.

"I'm going to wash the Lexus," she said.

"I can do that for you," Parker said.

Tori shook her head and went toward the staircase. "Why don't you play a video game or something?"

"You can be such a bitch," he said, softly, in the quiet voice that is still meant to be heard.

"I guess I can be," she said.

A few minutes later, she passed by Parker's bedroom. She was wearing short shorts and a tank top sans bra.

"I hope I don't get my top wet," she said.

He watched her from the window, as she lathered up the car, allowing the spray to fall over her. Darius Fulton was watching, too.

They always did.

Later that night after the strained dinner with Alex, Tori arched her back and Parker's eyes landed on the scars under each of her breasts. They were thin, faint, but unmistakable reminders of the surgery that had made her look the trophy wife that his father had wanted. She had once told him that his father had always wanted triple Bs.

"Huh?" Parker had never heard of the size.

"Boobs, blond, and brainless," she said.

"That makes me sick. I think you were probably perfect before," he said.

She wrapped her arms around her breasts and shook her head.

"I don't like talking about it."

"I'm sorry. I just think, well, that I would love you no matter what. You're more than a beautiful body," he said.

"Your father didn't think so."

"He's an asshole."

He reached over and loosened her arms, to expose all that she was.

"He's just wired like a lot of men, Parker. You're not that way. You're deeper, more evolved than those typical guys. That's one of the reasons you fascinate me so."

Her words pleased him and he wanted to know more. It was as if whatever Tori had to say was like a giant candy bar; he'd always want another bite.

"I fascinate you?" he said.

Tori smiled slightly, the kind of smirk that promised some kind of conspiratorial disclosure. "Of course you do."

Parker kissed her. "You really love me, don't you?"

"I love you more than you will ever know," she said, embracing him with a forceful hug. "We are like those swans. We are forever."

Down the hall in the master bedroom, Alex Connelly woke up and turned to the empty place in his bed. He felt around, but nothing.

Where is Tori? he thought.

It took him a moment to compute that it was a sound, not spicy Thai food, that had awakened him in the first place. A thumping and voices. It was coming down the hall from the room where Parker was staying.

The dark wood of the hallway floor made it difficult to navigate in the night, so he flipped on the lights. The noise stopped instantly.

He turned the knob on his son's door.

Tori was sitting on the edge of the bed. Parker was under the covers, his face turned away.

"What's going on?"

Tori turned around and faced her husband. "Oh, you startled me."

"What's happening here?" he said a second time.

"Did you know Parker has night terrors?" Tori patted the teen on the shoulder.

Alex took a couple of steps closer. He noticed a candle was lit on the nightstand. A damp washcloth was folded next to it. *Did the boy have a fever?* The bed was so completely thrashed that it was clear that Parker had been in some kind of sleepless torment.

"Son, are you all right?"

Parker seemed out of breath, but he answered. "I'm okay."

Tori looked at her husband and then over at her stepson.

"I'm so glad I could be here for you, Parker. Let me know if you need anything more."

Parker lifted his head slightly from the pillow. "Thanks, Tori. You really helped me a lot."

Tori and Alex backed out of the bedroom and returned to their own.

"I don't think you should dress that way around Parker," Alex said, indicating the short, thin nightgown. Underneath she wore no panties.

"Honestly," Tori said, "how I dressed when I went to help him was the last thing on my mind. The boy needed me. Needed someone, for God's sake. You wouldn't know much about that, would you? You seem too wrapped up in work. Too wrapped up with that bitch Lissa in the office."

"Let's not go there. I was just saying . . ."

"Good night, Alex. You don't have a clue how to be a decent person. Not to me. Not to your son."

Parker lifted the top sheet and comforter that he and Tori hastily pulled over his naked torso when the hallway light went on. It was a close call. Somehow the fact that he and his stepmother-lover had almost been caught red-handed excited him. He reached for the washcloth and wiped up the semen.

Tori had been there for him that night.

Oh yes, she had.

CHAPTER THIRTY-ONE

Tacoma

The interrogation room at the Tacoma Police Department was windowless. The only break in the pale gray drywall was the grate for the heating duct that filled the room with stifling warmth on a cold winter's day and so much cold air during the summer that a pair of gangbangers actually asked for—*and got*—a couple of blankets.

"Trying to do something about the AC," Eddie Kaminski said as he led Maddie Crane and client Darius Fulton to a pair of plastic molded chairs that would be more appropriate for a campus dining hall.

Maddie dropped her coat onto the table to demonstrate that she was bored and irritated. It was a couture label, but so convoluted in its design that one had to know it by sight and not read it.

To be sure, Kaminski didn't care about those things. There was a good bet that the man sitting across from him was exactly who he was looking for.

Maddie was as high priced as she was shrewd. She wasn't

about to show up with her client if she didn't think she could persuade the police to back off and look somewhere else.

"What you have so far is annoyingly circumstantial," she said, her flinty eyes bearing down on Kaminski.

"The gun was his," he said, glancing at Darius before returning his gaze to the lawyer with the great coat and imperious demeanor.

"So? It was stolen."

"Wasn't reported."

"He didn't know that."

"Are you kidding me?" He glanced at Darius, who looked passively in the direction of the vent as it funneled hot air right at his face. "Look, everything about your client suggests that he runs a tight ship. He knows where everything is."

The lawyer had quick answer. "He's had some personal problems as of late. He's recently divorced. His wife took things from the house and he wasn't exactly sure what she pilfered. She absconded with his stamp collection, for crying out loud."

"And my dad's antique decoys," Darius said.

Maddie shot him a look. "You'll talk when I say so."

Kaminski almost felt a blush of embarrassment for the guy just then. His wife took his stamp collection and his lawyer had snipped him of his manhood.

"All right. That's your explanation for the whereabouts of the gun—that, by the way, conveniently turned up in a murder across the street."

"Yes, Detective," she said. "That really is an interesting coincidence."

"All right, then," Kaminski said, reaching for a file folder that both the person of interest and the lawyer had been keeping an eye on like it was some scorpion sitting on the table in front of them. "What can you tell me about the e-mails?"

Darius seemed confused. "What e-mails?"

Maddie leaned across the table. "I'm talking here. What e-mails?"

Kaminski pulled out a sheet of paper, making sure that it was obvious that there were many, many others inside.

I want you. I need you. You are everything to me.

Darius shook his head. "I didn't write that. I didn't even know her e-mail address."

Maddie touched his shoulder with the tip of her index finger. It was not a gesture meant to calm and show support, but to pointedly get him to zip it.

"Please, I'll handle this," she said.

Darius wasn't having any of that. He was flustered. "Handle this? This thing is beginning to spin out of control. This damn *handling* you've been doing is going to send me to Walla Walla with a needle in my arm. I didn't write to her. I had sex with her once—and I admitted that. I didn't even fantasize that there would be any other encounters. Not seriously, anyway."

He slumped back down in his chair and put his hands on his forehead. He started to rub the beading sweat from his eyes. He looked puffy and red.

A heart attack waiting to happen.

"Can we turn down that goddamn heater?" he said, loud enough for the investigator on the other side of the mirror to hear without the benefit of a microphone.

"Sorry. We'll get you out of here in a minute."

"We're going now," Maddie said. She snatched up her coat and moved toward the door, motioning for her client to follow.

Kaminski went in for the kill just then. He didn't want

Darius Fulton to drop dead, but he was all but certain this was the last chance they'd be able to speak unencumbered by a legal process that would send up walls to keep them apart.

"Your hair was in a ski mask hidden between the cushions on your sofa. Tori Connelly confirms that it was the mask that the intruder wore the night she and her husband were shot. Will you stop lying just for a second?"

Darius looked like he was going to have a heart attack. His eyes popped like a hermit crab.

"I'm not lying," he said.

Maddie shook her head at Kaminski. "This interview is over. Mr. Fulton wanted to be helpful—against my advice."

"Fine," he said. "Just one more."

Darius looked at the bottled water but didn't touch it. He'd crawl on his hands and knees through Death Valley before he'd fall for that ruse a second time.

"Drink it. We don't need your prints again," Kaminski said.

"I'm fine."

"You don't look fine," Maddie said, still hovering with her coat.

He took the bottle and guzzled.

"You really want me to believe that you've been set up by Tori Connelly? That she screwed you one time to spin a web around you and make you the fall guy? Why in the world should I believe that? You haven't given me any reason to make that seem one bit plausible."

Darius blinked hard. "I wish I had some answer that would satisfy you, Detective. I wish that I hadn't been a big, dumb, old fool."

"Did you think that the plan to kill Alex would allow you to step right in?"

The lawyer glanced at her client, telegraphing with a finger to her glossed lips for him to remain mute.

"We've already told you, Detective," she said. "Mr. Fulton

had absolutely nothing to do with the murder—the planning, the execution of it. None of it. If I were you, I'd focus on the merry widow. We're done here."

When she opened the door, the air felt like a blast from a freezer as it met the Panama heat of the interrogation room.

Darius lingered. "I didn't hurt anyone. I would never shoot anyone."

"Shut up, Darius. We're leaving."

His eyes were pleading.

"Now!" she said, snapping him to attention the way his wife had done throughout their whole marriage. Darius jumped to his feet.

Their father had always said that one had to "break some eggs to make an omelet," but Tori Connelly highly doubted that he was referring to murdering people in order to get one's heart's desire. Yet the thought circled through her brain. She would not always be beautiful. She might not always be rich, but she was willing to do what she had to do to try to get that way.

She owed it to herself.

Tori looked at the date on her phone. In just a few days, Parker would turn eighteen. Her sister would be dead. She'd be rich.

Life would be so, so good.

CHAPTER THIRTY-TWO

Tacoma

Instead of meeting a stone wall, Eddie Kaminski was greeted with the offer of coffee or a drink when he knocked on Tori Connelly's front door to relay the latest updates to the case, though some details had already been on the news.

"Chilly out there, maybe you'd like something that would really warm you up," Tori said as she led the detective into the living room where her sister was sitting with an open laptop.

"A break in the case," she said. "I've offered him a drink, but he's on duty."

"Just like on TV," Lainie said. She'd grown weary of her sister's antics with men. She could see how Tori used her body to call attention to herself. That day she wore a fuchsia-colored scoop-neck sweater that left very little to the imagination.

"If you've got it, flaunt it" was one of Tori's catchphrases from high school.

"Been a lot of activity across the street," Lainie said.

"Nothing on the news, though." She looked at her laptop and shut the lid with a snap.

He took a seat on the end of the sofa. Tori brushed against him as she bent close to take his coat from his lap.

"Let me hang that up for you," she said.

"Oh, thanks," he said.

Lainie watched as the detective's eyes followed Tori. If her sister had hooked a worm and dropped it into Puget Sound, Eddie Kaminski had his mouth open, ready to take the bait. The moment was uncomfortable and familiar.

"What's been going on?" she asked again.

Tori slithered back into the space next to the detective.

Kaminski breathed her in, deeply. *Maybe too deeply*. She smelled of wild honey and flowers. He glanced at the wall, the vacant spot where the tacky painting had hung before the forensic team came and confiscated it.

"My husband loved that painting," she had said as they carried it away. "It makes me sick that it was used in such an evil way. Used against me by that awful man next door."

"Mrs. Connelly—" he started to say.

"Tori," she said.

"All right then, *Tori*. I have a few questions. I'm hoping you can help."

Lainie watched as her sister inched a little closer to the detective.

"I have nothing to hide."

"What can you tell me about your affair?"

She shifted a little and crossed her feet at the ankles. "Oh, that. It all comes back to that."

"I'm sorry. I know it is painful to recall all of that."

"He practically raped me."

Kaminski was surprised, but he didn't show it. "Mr. Fulton?"

Tori looked right at him, with those drilling-deep-as-possible blue eyes. "Who else?"

"But you've never indicated it was a rape. I thought it was consensual, an affair."

Her eyes started to flicker.

The tears are coming, Lainie thought.

And they did.

"I didn't put up a fight; there wasn't a struggle. But I told him I didn't want to do it. He just kept pushing and we drank too much. It was not an affair."

The remark was curious. Kaminski looked at the e-mails recovered from Fulton's computer. He could quote them almost verbatim, though he didn't just then. Instead, they ran through his mind like the juvenile prose from a lovesick middle-aged man.

You're the most beautiful woman in the world.

You make me feel so good. Too good. I can't take it.

I saw you today in the yard. I love the way the sunlight spins your hair into gold.

When can I see you? When will he be gone?

Maybe I'll just have to make him gone.

"I feel completely violated," Tori said.

"I'm sure you do. You have every reason to feel that way."

Lainie said nothing. Her sister was fascinating as always, and this man, this detective in their midst, seemed to play her in a way that she hadn't seen before. It was unclear if he was buying all that she had to sell.

"One thing the team wonders about," he finally said, "is how it was that you didn't recognize him when he was in your house the night your husband was gunned down. It was in this room, right?"

All three of them knew full well that it had been.

"Yes," Tori said. "Right here." She reached for her glass.

Ice water? Vodka?

"So how was it that you didn't know it was him?"

"I told you. He wore a mask."

"Yes, you did say that. But didn't he seem at all familiar? His voice?"

"Not really. I was too upset. I was in shock."

"Of course you were."

Lainie thought of jumping in to defend her sister, but she thought better of it. Tori was a big girl and if she'd gotten herself into trouble, she alone was the one to extract herself from the mess. No one could wriggle out of a conflict better than she.

Tori set down her glass, aiming for the ring of condensation on the coaster. She liked things to be just so.

When she stayed mute, Kaminski asked once more. "I mean, you knew him pretty well."

"He had his pants on, if that's what you're getting at." She looked at him, then at her sister. "I'm sorry. I didn't mean to be rude. I know you are doing your job."

"Yes, I am. So, please, how was it that you couldn't place the intruder as someone whom you'd slept with?"

She tilted her head and looked at him, once more, dead-eyed. "It's hard to keep track of my lovers, detective."

"I wasn't suggesting anything like that," he said.

"Really?"

"I'm sorry if I offended you."

"I'll add it to the list of things I'm trying to get over. It'll be somewhere at the bottom on a list topped by the fact that the Tacoma Police treat crime victims like criminals."

She stood. "I'm glad that you've got that creep, detective. I am happy to help with the investigation in any way that I can, but I will not have you come in here and treat me like trash for an error that I made."

Kaminski got up and thanked the women for their time. His eyes lingered on Lainie, who said nothing more.

* * *

A good night's sleep was so needed. The endless drama with Tori had tied her stomach in knots. Lainie O'Neal looked up at the gauzy canopy and stared. There were no tiles to count and her eyes were too tired to try to discern something in the weave of the fabric to hold her interest and work her brain into slumber. She slipped out of bed and put on a robe that Tori had hung on an antique hook by the doorway. She wasn't really thirsty, but a glass of milk seemed like a good idea.

As she walked down the hallway, she noticed a sliver of light coming from under her sister's doorway.

Maybe she can't sleep, either.

She was about to knock when she heard Tori's voice.

"All right," she said. "That sounds good. But be careful."

Silence.

"Look, for this to work you have to use the phone I gave you."

The phrase was odd. Lainie pushed closer to the door frame and turned the knob, cracking it open a bit more so she could hear exactly what her sister was saying.

". . . soon. I love you. I need you."

Lainie felt the muscles in her legs weaken some. Who was her sister talking to at that hour? Who in the world did she love? Her husband was dead.

She let go of the knob and took a step backward, turned around, and started toward her room.

"Lainie!"

The voice was loud, jarringly so for the stillness of the night.

She turned around. Tori stood right behind her.

"What are you doing up?"

Lainie stood still before slowly folding her arms. She was unsure of how that hallway meeting would go. Argue? Confront?

"Just can't sleep," she finally said.

Confrontation never worked.

Tori studied Lainie's face, looking for something.

"I have some pills I can give you," she said. "To help you sleep."

Lainie shook her head. "No, thanks, Tori. I think I'm just going to lie down and try it again." She had another thought on her mind and she knew right then she'd never voice it. She couldn't help but wonder just what pills her sister would give her.

To help her sleep . . . like in the dream of their mother's death.

Tori had scattered three dresses on her bed. They were expensive with fine embellishments that caught the light, organza overlays that undulated in the crisp air from a cracked-open bedroom window. Oversize tags hung from the bodice of each, reminding the purchaser that "special occasion" dresses could not be returned without the tag intact.

Lainie peered over Tori's shoulder and offered her assessment of the dresses that they'd looked at the week before when they were doing a reconnaissance shopping expedition at a downtown Seattle department store.

"I thought you only got the blue one," she said.

Tori offered up a slight and knowing smile. "I went back for the yellow and the lilac."

"I didn't realize you had so much money," Lainie said. "I could barely afford one.*"*

Her sister smoothed the fabric on the lilac dress. "Who says I paid for them?"

"Seriously, Tori. You're bad, but not that bad."

Tori sat down on the bed and faced Lainie. "I guess you

don't really know me." She grinned as though she'd revealed some big secret.

Lainie refused the obvious bait. She'd been there before a thousand times. Tori liked to challenge her, provoke her. Push her. That afternoon she was having none of that. She was in too good of a mood. She was excited about the dance, her date, the evening out of the house. Lainie pointed to the blue dress. It was the shortest of the three with a sweetheart neckline that she knew Tori would like.

She always liked to shove what little cleavage she had into the faces of her admirers.

"I like that one," Lainie finally said.

Tori made a face. "I hate that one," she said. "Boring. I like the yellow."

Lainie let out an exaggerated sigh. "Then why did you ask me?"

"Because I know you'll pick the worst one. You always do."

Lainie resisted the urge to offer up an insult of her own. She could do it, of course. But not right then. "Guess you know what not to wear, then."

Tori thrust the yellow dress at Lainie.

"I want you to put this one on," she said.

Lainie shook her head. "I have a dress."

"I know, stupid. I want you to put it on so I can see how I'll look in it. You know, to decide."

Lainie knew there was no arguing with her sister. The only thing that made her truly happy about the approaching South Kitsap dance was that it was the beginning of the end, the constant sharing. The car. Classes. Their father's house. Soon, they'd go off their separate ways to different colleges and different lives. Their twinship would bind them forever, of course, but the pressure to be close would abate.

At least that's what she told herself.

She stripped down to her underwear and stepped into the dress. She didn't ask Tori to zip it; instead, she struggled on her own, reaching awkwardly around her back and pulling up the zipper. Dress on, she faced her sister.

"I don't expect you to stomp it out on the catwalk, but can you at least stand up straight? I would never stand like that. Maybe hold your pooch in a little."

"I don't have a pooch, Tori." She was getting angry then, but anger never seemed to get anywhere with Tori. In fact, it made matters worse. It was almost always better to just give in.

"Whatever," Tori said. "Turn around."

Slowly, and without any joy, Lainie spun in a single rotation. No trace of a smile on her face. Just the look of a teenager who wished she'd never said yes to the request.

"I'll stick with the blue," Tori said. "You can have that one. Cute on the hanger, but ugly on us. Or maybe it's just ugly on you."

The *Tacoma News Tribune* missed the news cycle of the arrest in the Tacoma murder case, leaving KING-TV the scoop on its broadcast and updated website:

Fulton Arrested for Connelly Murder and Assault

Darius Fulton was arrested by Tacoma Police in his home across the street from the shooting that took the life of Alex Connelly and left his wife hospitalized on May 5.

Police say that Fulton, 55, had been stalking Tori Connelly for several months.

"His advances were unwanted and relentless," lead investigator Edmund Kaminski said, though he refused to elaborate.

"Although we're devastated by the news of the arrest," said Charla Maxwell of the North End Neighbors' group, "we're glad to know that our quiet street is safe once more."

Police had originally suggested that the killing was a home invasion gone wrong.

If Darius Fulton had thought even for a nanosecond that his life couldn't get any worse up until that moment—arrested, handcuffed, and dispatched to the Pierce County Jail like a common criminal—he was sadly mistaken. He was herded into a holding pen with three dozen other men, drug dealers, violent felons, guys who knew their way around the system.

Or at least knew there was no way around it whatsoever.

"Dude, you like this?" a shirtless man called over from the other line.

Darius looked away.

"Like cattle in here. You'll get used to it."

He shrugged, thinking that some reaction might be more prudent than completely ignoring the guy.

An officer took an orange marking pen and drew an ID number on Darius's upper arm.

"Branded, dude! You've been branded!"

As he sat there wondering how an afternoon with a beautiful woman could have gone so wrong, Darius Fulton said a silent prayer. He prayed he'd live long enough to get out of there in one piece. His frame of reference for prison life was an old HBO television series, and he was sure that even though it was on cable, it was sugarcoated. He wasn't with a gang and there was no one to protect him. He'd called his lawyer and she was on her way.

Carrying his meal—a cellophane bag containing a slice of bologna, two pieces of bread, and a yellow mustard pack— Darius was led with a half dozen other men to another holding cell. Whether it was shame or self-preservation, he couldn't be sure. He kept his head down low. As the linked-up badasses passed the metal detector, he looked up. He heard a familiar voice. It was Eddie Kaminski talking with a corrections officer.

There to see him suffer, maybe?

"Kaminski!"

The detective turned toward the sound of his name.

Fulton jerked on the chain to slow down the stream of men.

"I didn't do this! I would never hurt anyone. I liked Tori Connelly. I know she didn't like me."

"Shouldn't talk to anyone but your lawyer, Fulton."

The prisoner next to Darius looked back at the disheveled businessman.

"He's right. Shut the fuck up."

After he passed by, the detective walked in the direction of a couple of prisoners yakking it up on payphones.

Kaminski picked up the phone, dropped in some coins, and dialed.

"These phones are for inmates only," said a young man with a spiderweb tattoo over his neck. "Use your own phone."

"Screw you," Kaminski said, flashing his badge. "I'll use whatever goddamn phone I want."

Maddie Crane could not have been angrier at her client. They sat in a private cell set aside for lawyers and clients. If its walls could talk, they'd likely scream. Wife murderers. Child killers. Boys and men who'd killed for the fun of it. All types of evil had been housed in that jail, and they had crawled around the slab floors like the vermin they were. Maddie, relieved of her purse and luxurious coat, sat like a chorus girl in search of a date as she nervously waited for Darius to come down the corridor. She stiffened a little when she heard the rattle of chains and the sound of voices. A beat later, Darius appeared in the doorway to the holding cell. He wore a county-issue jumpsuit and flip-flops. The marking on his forearm was still visible. He'd come a long way from his cozy life in North Tacoma.

A very long way, indeed.

"Do you realize that you've got to get it together?" she asked as he sat across from her.

"I'm doing the best I can, Maddie. This is more concentration camp than boutique hotel."

"Yes, I know, but that's not what I'm talking about."

"What *are* you talking about?"

Nervously, Maddie looked up at the guard who was pretending to ignore them.

"The last thing we need to do is get the likes of someone like him to testify against you."

"Why would he?"

"Look," she said. "No more phone calls, okay? You have no idea what these places are like."

Darius was unsure of what she meant.

"I didn't call anyone," he said. "This is a setup. That bitch across the street set me up."

She looked hard at him. "Look, I understand how you feel. I'm going to get you out of this mess. We have to work through the system."

Darius was sure he was going to have a heart attack.

"Trust me," he said, almost laughing at the words that just came from his lips. "I'm getting a very good idea about how things work around here. An hour ago I saw two guys beat the shit out of each other for a deflated bag of potato chips."

Maddie drummed her nails on the table.

"I'm not going to spell it out," she repeated. "Just trust me. Call *only* me."

CHAPTER THIRTY-THREE

Tacoma

Tori Connelly stood impatiently in the reception area at the Tacoma Police Department. Her blond hair was a halo. Her blue eyes caught the light in a way that seemed almost unearthly, so sparkly, so capable of drawing someone in. Eddie Kaminski almost blinked when he met her to go upstairs to an interview room, where Cal Herzog was waiting.

"You've met Cal," he said, introducing the forensic specialist on the Connelly investigation team.

"Yes, Cal," she said.

"How's your leg?" Cal asked, as she sat down in the interview room. "You look like you're doing better. No limp."

"Are you flirting with me?" she asked.

"I didn't mean anything personal, just asking."

She pretended to be a little disappointed. "I'm better, thank you."

"What can we do for you?" Kaminski asked. "We've arrested your shooter, your husband's killer."

"I'm grateful for the attention you're giving my husband's case. My case. That's why I'm here."

"You're welcome," Kaminski said. "Anything else, Mrs. Connelly? Anything else on your mind?"

"Tori. Please."

"All right then, Tori, anything else? I mean, if you're here for a status update on the case, I can't tell you anything more than I already have."

Tori nodded. "I didn't come here for anything other than to thank you."

"Now that you're here," Cal said. "I guess we can go over a few things that I've been wondering about."

She looked surprised. "Loose ends?"

"Something along those lines," he said, looking for his notes.

"All right, shoot," she said, then corrected herself. "Guess that's not the best expression to use under these circumstances."

Kaminski shook off Tori's attempt at disarming him with a little humor.

"About the insurance," he said. "You didn't know that Parker was the beneficiary, did you?"

"My husband left me well provided for. If his wish was to take care of his son, then fine. I'm grateful to be alive."

Cal took the next question. "You weren't devastated by his office affair?"

Tori's eyes stayed fixed firmly on his. "You know I was. But I've made my peace with that. I forgave Alex. Water, detective, under the bridge."

"Right," he said.

"You don't believe me. That's because you don't know me. I have been through a lot in my life. I can be very forgiving."

This time Cal pushed a little harder. It wasn't good cop, bad cop. Just Cal on overdrive. "Are you referring to your incarceration? Or the death of your first husband?"

Once again, Tori did not flinch.

"I came here to thank you. You're treating me like a suspect."

"Just looking for some answers . . . Tori," Kaminski said.

"My record was expunged. I'm guessing someone from Port Orchard told you. Small-town people never forget things like that, though they should. I served my time. I went on with my life, and, above all, Jason Reed's death was a terrible, tragic accident," she said. She reached for a tissue as if she were about to cry, but there was no evidence of tears.

"I've talked with the Sheriff's Department," he said.

"Detective Stark?"

"Yes."

"She's a very good friend of mine," she said. "She knows what I've gone through."

"What about Zach Campbell?"

"What about him?"

"His death."

Tori indicated a water bottle and Cal handed it to her. "An accident. I told you."

"But it made you rich."

Her face tightened a little. Loveliness turned to menace.

"I loved him. Do you really think for one second that I'd have wanted his money over his life?"

"You tell us, Tori."

"You know I came here to say thank you. I came here because I was going away for a few days and I wanted you to know how to reach me. In case you needed any help. Talk about blaming the victim. If this rinky-dink police department had a victims' advocate, I'd go to his or her office right now and read him the riot act."

Kaminski stood and held his hands out, as if to push down the diatribe. "Hey, calm down. Those questions had to be asked. And they will be asked. At trial, Fulton's people will make sure that they tie you up and run the bus over you back and forth, every which way they can. They'll make you out to be a total bitch."

Cal wanted to interject, "Which is exactly what you are," but he refrained from doing so.

"I understand that, Eddie," she said. "But you have no idea what I've been going through."

"Please, call me Detective Kaminski," he said, looking over at Cal. "And yes, I have an idea. A pretty good one."

After Kaminski walked her to the elevators and down to reception, he returned to find Cal hovering by his cubicle.

"Jesus," Cal said, scratching his head. "What a piece of work that one is."

"No kidding."

"Only one thing I got out of that."

"What was that?"

"She likes you. I'd watch out."

They both laughed.

"Why do you think I've taken up running? To get away from women like her."

Kendall Stark stood on the Harper Dock while Steven and Cody pulled in the yellow nylon rope tethered to a crab pot they'd baited and dropped earlier that day. She held her phone to her ear and listened as Eddie Kaminski called back about the condom wrapper Lainie had found in the guest room.

"Anyway, can you cut us some slack on this? This isn't your case and, besides, Darius Fulton's our guy."

"I guess so," Kendall said, not believing her own words. The air was cool and the wind had started to blow across the water. She closed her phone.

"Catch anything?" she asked as Steven and Cody teamed up to draw in the line, hand over hand.

"I should ask you the same question," Steven said.

Kendall smiled at her husband. Steven was supportive and patient. He knew the importance of catching the bad guy, or in that particular case, the bad *girl*.

"Working on it," she said.

The crab pot broke the surface of the silvery water of the Sound. Inside, a large Dungeness crab clamped onto the punctured cat food tin the Starks used for bait.

"Look, Mommy!" Cody said. "Watch out. Sharp!"

The pot on the dock, Steven stooped down and opened the lid to the trap. "Damn!" he said. "It's a female! Got to throw her back. Don't let her get you."

Kendall thought the same warning might have been good one for the men involved with Tori O'Neal Campbell Connelly.

Don't let her get you.

CHAPTER THIRTY-FOUR

Port Orchard
Fifteen years ago

It didn't matter if the twins were in the same room or a thousand miles away from each other. Key moments in their lives often percolated in their thoughts at the same time. The big moments, the ones that shaped each girl into the woman she became. And while they thought of the same things, they didn't always share matching perspectives. Lainie tossed and turned in the loneliness of a bed that she never shared with anyone more than a few nights at a time. Alternately, Tori curled up next to a man and did what she could to keep him interested in her, even if she wasn't truly paying attention to him.

And yet they thought of Port Orchard, what happened that night on Banner Road, and in the months that followed.

Both had reasons to keep it all secret.

The visiting room at the Secure Crisis Residential Center was outfitted with sofas, tables, and bolted-down end tables and lamps. It was either the milieu of Motel Hell or the sitting room of a paranoid miser who wanted to ensure that nothing left the premises. Handwritten signs indicated that visitors and residents would be searched after the conclusion of their time together. Visitors got a simple, unobtrusive pat-down by a pleasant-faced person of their own gender. Though it wasn't always the case—because it depended on who was on duty—residents were strip-searched. Women were examined by a rubber-gloved female officer, of course, but for safety and security reasons, an observer would be present, too. Often it was a male. And while they purported that they were there only for the benefit of the person doing the search, some were there because, like all creeps, they liked to watch.

Daniel Hector was one of those. A thirty-five-year-old who became a corrections officer because he liked the control, the gatekeeper's power, and the kind of personal proclamation that came with the duty. He was a short man with dark dead eyes, hairy knuckles, and a Fu Manchu mustache. The difference between his ID badge and the inmates' badges was solely based on the better lighting afforded staff members. Indeed, if a photo ID was set before anyone with an array of inmate and corrections officers and someone was asked to pick out who was who, Hector would be the first pick for the criminal.

And, considering what he did, they'd be right.

"You're a pretty little thing," he told Tori a few days after her incarceration. She had come out of the shower room, her flip-flops and robe on.

"You're pretty gross," she said.

"You have pretty titties. I'd like to see them."

"You would? What's in it for me?"

"I don't know," he said, stepping closer. "Maybe you'd like a cigarette?"

"I don't smoke."

"Candy bar? Magazine? I can get you whatever you want."

"Not interested," she said.

"You're not a chick with a dick, are you, Tori?"

"Funny. Like you haven't checked me out already, you freak."

He grinned. "Yeah, I've checked you out. Like to get another look at you."

She had no idea what it would get her, but she agreed. She opened her robe.

He put his hand against his crotch and stepped away, out of the sightline of the video cameras and their unblinking eyes.

"Nice," he said.

"Want me to do anything?" she said, aware that she hadn't set a price.

"Yeah," Hector said, "I want you to move around a little. Dance a little for me."

Tori almost said she was a good dancer, but she didn't bother. She didn't know why it was that she was performing for him the way she was, but she could see the twisted pleasure that he was getting from what she was doing.

"Slower," she said to him.

He complied.

She was the captive one, of course. Yet she held some kind of odd power over him. He was a piece of garbage, but he was a man nevertheless.

She was in control. She liked it that way. That was better than a candy bar any day of the week.

The visits between Tori, Lainie, and Dex O'Neal in juvenile detention were always fraught with emotion. Tori cried. Lainie cried. Dex wanted to cry, too, but he felt that someone had to be strong in the situation that had heaped on more heartache than their little family ought to bear. Vonnie was dead. Tori was in jail.

* * *

CORRECTION CENTER *flashed on the caller ID. Lainie was getting ready to go out with some friends from school and she almost decided to pretend that she didn't hear the phone. Her father was painting a chair in the garage. He wouldn't hear it ring.*

She picked up and waited for the message that warned her where the call was coming from and how she should immediately hang up if she didn't know who might be calling.

"Hang up immediately!" A robotic-sounding woman's voice intoned.

Lainie answered.

"Hi, Tori," she said.

Silence.

"Tori?"

Then she heard some sobbing.

"Tori, is that you? Are you okay?"

"No, I'm not okay. I need to see you. I can't take it anymore."

"You only have a few months to go. I know you are getting out soon."

"You don't understand. I'm going crazy in here."

Lainie thought she heard someone else talking.

"Who is that?"

"Just some bitch that wants to use the phone. I'll get rid of her." She set down the phone. A moment later she picked it up and spoke.

"I need you to come on Saturday."

"Dad is working. We can't come until the Sunday visit."

"You can come. I need you, Lainie."

"I can't get in without Dad."

"You can. I arranged it. I have special privileges here now. Good behavior."

Lainie noticed that Tori was no longer crying.

"*Okay. I'll be there at eleven.*"

"*Come at ten. We can have a special visit.*"

Special visit *was code for something Tori had planned for her sister. Something, she was sure, she'd never forget.*

CHAPTER THIRTY-FIVE

Tacoma
The previous summer

Naked and tangled in the damp white sheets under the canopy bed, Tori Connelly pressed her breasts against her stepson's back and whispered in his ear. She did so with a gentle puff of each breath so he would not only hear her words, but *feel* the desire that came with each one.

"You want to play again, Parker?"

It was late in the evening and, save for the creaking that comes with an old house, it was quiet, so very still. It was as if at that very moment there were no others in the world. No husband to control her. No mother to tell him what to do. No one.

Just the two of them.

The teenager grinned and rolled over to face his lover. The light from the bedside lamp was low and golden. She was beyond beautiful. A dream. A very sexy dream. Even in the dimly lit room her hair glowed. Her lips shined with gloss and the moisture from their lovemaking.

"I like it when you call me that," he said.

She smiled. "It's *your* name."

"I know. I guess it's the way you say it."

She brushed her fingers down his hairless chest, stopping at his stomach for a teasing moment before moving lower.

"You've gotten bigger, haven't you?" she said playfully.

Parker tried to suppress a proud smile, but it was impossible.

"Shut up," he said, not meaning it. "That's embarrassing. But I'm glad you noticed." He kissed her again, his tongue exploring the warmth of her mouth. "I've grown up a lot since last summer."

"You have," she said, proffering a condom from the bed stand. She rolled the wrapper in her fingertips. "Want me to put it on?" she asked, pulling away from his embrace.

Parker shook his head. "I don't want to wear one. I want to feel you."

"You can feel me just fine. I don't want to get pregnant."

"Would it be so lame if you did?"

"Let's ask your father that question, Parker, when he gets home from New York." She put away the condom for a moment and concentrated on pleasing him with her hands.

Parker stretched out on the bed and looked up at the gauzy canopy. "You could lie to him. You know, tell him that it's his baby. That would be kind of funny."

"That wouldn't fly at all. He's had a vasectomy. I thought you knew that."

Parker shook his head. "Figures. The asshole didn't want to have any more kids. Never wanted the one he had."

Tori put the condom on Parker and they kissed, first slowly, then a little faster. She pushed his shoulder back and crawled on top of him.

"I'm going to make you scream," she said. "And you can't stop me."

"No," he said, bracing himself as she moved onto him. "No, no. Don't ever stop."

"I want this forever," she said. "I want you forever. We are soul mates."

Parker's body started to shudder, his legs tightened, and his eyes nearly rolled backward. She felt so good. She was so beautiful. And she loved him so much. There could never be a better woman for him. Nowhere on earth.

"We are soul mates," he said.

"Yes, baby, we are."

"I want us to be together, too. For real."

"I know. I know. But, you know, that can't happen."

Parker indicated for her to stop. "Because I'm younger?"

"Age is a number. Don't even go there. You are more of a man now than anyone I've ever known."

"More than my father?"

"Parker," she said, leaning over him.

"More than my dad?" he asked again.

"Yes, baby, you are. You're nothing like him," she said, grabbing his hard penis again. "You're so much more."

Parker closed his eyes, allowing her to play with him.

"I wish we could be together like this forever," she said once more.

"I wish he was gone," Parker said, his eyes open a slit.

"You might not understand," she said. "But there's more to the world than our love."

"No there isn't."

"Trust me. There is."

"What are you getting at, Tori?"

"I signed a prenup. If I leave your dad, I'll have nothing."

"Do you care about money or do you care about me?"

"Don't be silly," she said. "I care about both."

Parker pushed back, turned away, and sat on the edge of the bed, his back to Tori.

"Look," he said. "I will do whatever it takes to have you."

Tori moved across the bed and put her arms around Parker's shoulders.

"I'll think of something," she said. "I promise."

Tori poured red wine into two glasses and handed one to Parker as they sat in the living room and snuggled on the couch. They had made love for the last time before Alex would return from his business trip. All evidence of what they'd been doing that long weekend had been erased. They'd showered. The sheets in the guest room had been laundered and the used condoms had been wrapped into paper towels, tucked inside a plastic bag, and shoved into an empty pickle jar before being deposited into the trash.

"A pickle jar, nice," Parker had said.

Tori smiled. "I thought so. It works on so many levels."

As the clock ticked toward Alex's arrival time, the joy of their tryst faded. Reality was a car ride away. A tear rolled down her cheek and she looked away toward the TV, the news flickering on mute.

"Tori," he said. "What is it?"

She faced him. "Parker, I've been thinking about us. I just don't think we're ready. This thing is going out of bounds."

"You mean that I'm not ready, don't you?" His face was contorted in anger, not scarily so, but his eyes popped and the veins on his neck filled with blood. "That I'm not mature enough."

Tori shook her head slowly, deliberately. "No, I didn't mean that. I mean that the world won't understand our kind of love. It doesn't fit into the way things should be."

"Just because you're older doesn't mean a thing. I've looked it up. We could go to France or some other country where we could live in peace, where people understand that love has no limits, no boundaries. Mexico maybe."

"You are so young, Parker. I don't want to hurt you. But there's no way we can live on love alone." She took a sip of her wine, swirling the red liquid in her glass. Her hands trembling just a little.

Just enough.

"I think you judge *me* more than the rest of the world would judge *us*. Sometimes, Tori, you can be a real bitch, you know."

She wiped her tears and forced a smile. "I like it when you get a little mad. It shows me that you care."

"I'm more than mad. I'm pissed off. I want you and me to be together."

"Look," she said, "this is very complicated. I know we are not related by blood, but people would judge us harshly. I don't need a Woody Allen/Soon-Yi drama here."

He didn't get the reference. He'd never heard of Woody Allen or Soon-Yi.

"We have that little problem beyond all of that. It is legal and it is real."

"I've thought of it," he said. Resolve had replaced anger on his face. "I know what we can do."

"What's that, Parker? I'm not seventeen. I just can't throw my things into a backpack and leave for Europe or Mexico or wherever. I can't live that way."

Parker grabbed her by the shoulders. "Let's get rid of him," he said.

"How do you mean?" Her eyes were wide, but not overly so.

She knew the answer, of course.

"Kill him."

Tori leaned closer and planted a kiss on his lips. Parker could taste the salt on her skin and he set down his glass. Next, she put her hand on his crotch and loosened the buckle on his belt.

"I love you," she said. "You would do that for me?"

"I would do it for *us*," he said.

"Do you know what you're saying, Parker?"

Parker leaned back while she brought him to climax.

"Yeah," he said, barely able to get out the word. "I do."

"Good," she said. "I have some news and I needed to know the depth of your commitment to me."

"What?" he asked.

She touched her abdomen. "I'm pregnant. You're going to be a father, Parker."

CHAPTER THIRTY-SIX

Tacoma

No one who was not a twin would ever comprehend the connection shared between the two halves of a whole. It is Hells Canyon deep and Mount Rainier high. It is both unbendable and unbreakable. From the womb to the sandbox to college graduation, events were more complicated when they came in twos. Lainie and Tori were always competitors and supporters, both jealous of and comforting to each other. They came home from the hospital as a cherub-faced pair in matching lavender infant sleepers. The only thing to differentiate them was the color of ribbon looped around their pink wrists. When one cried, the other chimed in. It took Dex and Vonnie a week or two to tell them apart, but even though they could do so, the girls were considered a unit. Close, combined, and with a bond that could never be denied by those outside their private little world. And yet, as close as two people can be, there was always a flip side.

A dark, disturbing flip side, indeed.

When Tori indicated she was going to visit her lawyer in

downtown Tacoma, Lainie said she didn't mind being left alone.

"Unless, of course, you need me," she said, although other plans she'd made kept her from being persistent.

"Oh, it might be fun to have you along. But I can manage. I always have," Tori said, calling from the top of the stairs as she made her way to the landing where Lainie waited.

Her sister, as always, was a sight.

Tori was dressed to the nines in a charcoal suit and black boots that bent at the knees. She had a black handbag that Lainie figured would take two months to pay for with her web content work. Her makeup, once more, was a little more evening than daytime. Lainie was unsure if it was a Tacoma society thing or the remnants of her sister's short-lived career as a singer. In general, Pacific Northwest women favored a less glamorous, less fussy appearance.

"I'll be fine," Lainie said. "I'll catch up on e-mail. Maybe watch some TV." She paused for a beat, resisting the expected compliment that Tori always courted from onlookers as she made her grand entrance. "What are you talking to the lawyer about?"

"The estate, the investigation, whatever," Tori said, hearing the town car pull up. "You know, I don't really have a head for legal matters despite my unfortunate background."

Her tone was cool and the remark was meant as a little dig.

Lainie pretended not to notice. Giving her sister any ammunition for an argument or challenge was to be on the losing end of a proposition. Tori always won. Though neither twin would concede the matter, Tori had won even the one time when she'd lost her freedom.

Lainie locked the front door and dialed Kendall on her crappy replacement phone and huddled by the doorway, making sure that her sister was really gone.

"She just left," she said.

"Finally," Kendall said. "What are you going to do?"

"I'm going to find out what I can. Anything that points to her being the liar that we both know she is."

"You are not doing this as an agent of the Kitsap County Sheriff's Office," Kendall said. "You understand that?"

"I get that, Kendall. I'm doing this because I'm scared. I don't trust her. She's planning something and she has to be stopped."

"Be careful," Kendall said.

"You can bet on that. Later."

Lainie had already gone through the medicine cabinet the first night there—the kind of thing that many overly curious houseguests probably engage in, but never admit to. Other than of a few prescriptions for antidepressants for Alex and a script for codeine for Tori—apparently for the residual pain for her gunshot wound—there was little to pique Lainie's interest. A few things merely confirmed what she already knew—everything Lainie had was the best that money could buy. Her makeup was Chanel, her perfume was French.

If you can't pronounce it, you can't afford it, she could hear her sister say.

She moved quickly to the first-floor study and the immense mahogany desk, library bookshelves running the length of the room, floor to ceiling. She wasn't sure what she was trying to find out. She told herself as she neatly put back each envelope and folder that she was only curious.

Tori is a mystery to me and she shouldn't be. Her affect about her dead husband is off. She is too cool. Tori cool.

Most of the paperwork in a folder on top of the desk was related to Alex's business affairs. As she flipped through the mix of originals and photocopies, she found that her dead brother-in-law had a sizable, though dwindling, stock portfolio.

Like my lousy 401K from the paper, she thought. *We're all going down the drain. Some people like Tori and Alex simply have a bigger reserve.*

Next, she went upstairs to the master bedroom. In her time as a houseguest she barely set foot inside. Her sister, possibly rightly so, considered it her private sanctuary. The door was unlocked and she went into the room. The white linens and pillowy duvet cover made the large antique Rice bed look like it was topped by a cloud. A painting of Tori hung over the bed, which signaled in no uncertain terms who was the most important person in that room. Apart from a crystal dish that held two pairs of cufflinks, there was nothing in the room that remotely suggested a man had lived there after her sister's discharge. It was all perfume bottles, sachets, and an étagère that displayed pink art glass.

You can take a girl out of Port Orchard . . . Lainie thought.

Lainie moved quickly to the dresser and started to prod through Tori's belongings. It was wrong and she knew it, but she couldn't stop herself. The compulsion to find out whatever it was that she was looking for was too great. She gingerly lifted her sister's lingerie, all beautiful, white and ivory silk. Nothing trashy. Everything was tasteful and expensive—the kind of undergarments a woman buys for her lover, not because she needs them for herself.

Under a set of cranberry-colored satin sheets, which seemed so '80s that it gave Lainie some temporary relief from her jealousy of her sister's lavish life, she unearthed a battered manila envelope. It was clasped shut but not sealed, making it fair game for an interloper. She went over to the bed and sat down, fanning out photographs and papers inside. Among them were images of the sisters, their father, their mother. It nearly brought tears to her eyes to think that Tori cared enough about any of them that she'd keep the photographs.

Lainie soaked in each image. There was proof in the faded snapshots that indeed there had been happy times in the O'Neal household. Their mother sat on the old camel-back sofa with her babies in each arm, their Siamese cat Ling-Ling at her feet. One photo showed their father with Tori . . . or was it Lainie? . . . at the seagull-calling contest in Port Orchard. Several pictures revealed the family as they opened Christmas presents under an obviously fake Christmas tree.

Dad hated that tree, but Mom insisted it was wrong to cut down a living tree for the holidays, Lainie thought.

Her blue eyes pooled with tears. Vonnie O'Neal had her moments. She was not always the tragic figure that she later became. For a time, she did love life. She loved her husband and her girls. She loved the family cat. She made chocolate chip cookies for the twins and never failed to put extra chips on the top of each cookie—"because you can never have too much of a good thing, girls."

Under the last photo Lainie found an envelope marked "Hawaii." She instantly knew the connection her sister had with the Aloha State and her heartbeat quickened a little. It was a part of her sister's life about which she knew very, very little. She pulled out the contents of the envelope— photocopies of a police report, a couple of photographs of her sister, and some other notes related to the accident that took Zach Campbell's life. His photo, the Washington state driver's license image, brought few memories. She'd seen him only once or twice before her sister called and said she'd married him.

"He's handsome, has some money, and wants to have a family," Tori had said.

"I'm happy for you," Lainie said, though she really wanted to say, *"Since when did you want kids?"*

As she flipped through the pages she noticed a couple of other photos—a young man and a car. As she wondered about their inclusion in the packet, the security alarm sounded its quiet chime that someone was coming up the steps.

Lainie turned toward the sound and crept toward the hallway to the staircase. She heard footsteps coming up the walk. It was the smacking of heels. Expensive boots against the pavement.

Tori was back.

As quickly as she could, Lainie hurried back to the bedroom. She shut the drawers, fluffed up the spot on the bed, and ran down the hallway to her bedroom. She went into the bathroom and locked the door. Her heart was pounding and sweat collected under her arms.

What to do? How to explain what she was up to?

"Lainie, I'm here! Forgot some paperwork," Tori said, calling up the staircase.

Lainie splashed water on her face and patted herself dry. She waited a beat and flushed the toilet, as if she'd been using it. She ran the water, taking another moment to eat up some time. She wanted the redness from her face to fade. She realized she'd taken the Hawaii envelope with her. Whatever panic had seized her when she heard her sister return was ratcheted up tenfold.

Where to put it?

She lifted the toilet seat cover and put the envelope on top before setting the lid back down.

When she opened the bathroom door, Tori was right outside in her black boots and charcoal suit, with a wary expression on her face.

"I'm not feeling well," Lainie said, pressing her hand gently against her abdomen. "Must be something I ate."

Tori studied her sister. "We had the same thing," she said. "I feel fine."

"I don't feel good," Lainie repeated, which was the truth, though not for the stated reason. It was more about what she'd been doing and what she saw. She lingered in the doorway.

Tori looked past Lainie. "Oh, I see," she said. "There are some antacids in my bathroom. I'll get you some."

"No," Lainie said, a little too forcefully. She didn't want her sister to go into the bedroom. In her haste to put things back, there was room for error. "I just took some."

Tori studied her sister. She could always see when she was hiding something.

"All right. I'll be back at four or so."

"I'm sure I'll feel better then."

"Good, because I want to take you out for a nice dinner to celebrate our reconnection, our sisterhood."

Lainie smiled and nodded as she watched her sister leave, hesitate for a moment, then head back to her bedroom before going down the staircase to the waiting car and driver.

That was odd, Lainie thought, *Tori didn't pick up any paperwork.*

Lainie O'Neal had no idea that the whole time she was rifling her sister's belongings in search of God-knows-what, the eye of a webcam was on her. On the other side of Tacoma, in his bedroom in Fircrest, Parker Connelly watched the goings-on in the master bedroom that had once belonged to his father and stepmother.

But now, in some strange way, he felt it belonged to him.

Tori had told him so.

"All of this will be ours," she said, not long after they first started making love in that very bed. "Yours and mine."

Tori had kept the two-way webcam on for his pleasure.

"I have no secrets, baby," she said. "I want you to see me, as I am."

Sometimes she would linger a little as she undressed, teasing him with the beauty of her body. One time, she turned to the camera and fondled her breasts.

"When I was your age, I was told I had nice titties," she said. "I still do, don't I?"

"I want to touch them," he said. "No fair."

"Soon, baby."

They had talked the morning before she was to go to her lawyer's to discuss the estate. Tori showed Parker different outfits, and he selected the black boots and the charcoal suit.

"Makes your hair look really sexy," he said of the color he chose over a dark blue dress. "And your legs, the boots make your legs look hot."

A few minutes after she left, he saw Lainie go into the bedroom.

What's she doing in there? he thought. He picked up his phone and texted Tori.

YR bitch sister is in YR RM.

Tori texted back: What is she doing?

looking where she shouldnt.

Ill take care of it, she texted. Ill give her a surprise. LOL.

Fifteen minutes later, Tori appeared in her bedroom and faced the webcam. She mouthed the words "Stupid bitch," indicating her sister.

Next, she blew a kiss at the webcam and whispered, "I love you."

A teenager with barely noticeable stubble on his chin was likely smiling back. She couldn't see Parker, but she knew the power she held over him. It felt very, very good.

The shower in the guest bath was running and the door was shut. Tori Connelly set down her coffee cup and walked over to the bureau next to the canopy bed. Her sister's purse was sitting on top, slumped over like it was just waiting for her to reach inside. She shifted its contents until she found Lainie's cell phone. The water turned off and she heard her sister get out of the shower. With the precision and speed of a kid at a mobile phone kiosk, she opened the back of the phone and removed the SIM card. She inserted another, closed it up, put it back into the purse.

Too bad Lainie doesn't have enough money for anything better than a Coach, she thought.

When Lainie emerged from the bathroom, she noticed that her sister had brought her some coffee. It wasn't hot and it wasn't a full cup, but Tori was never the "hostess with the mostest," so it wasn't a bad effort.

She's not all bad. She just can't be, she thought.

"Don't you think it's odd that neither one of us had any kids?"

Tori looked at her sister as they stood in the foyer of the grand Victorian.

"How do you mean, odd?" she asked.

Lainie watched the street for the taxi. She wondered if the same driver would pick her up for the ride back to Seattle.

"I wanted to," she said. "But Alex didn't. He said that Parker was enough and that he was getting too old."

"He wasn't that old. At least not by today's standards. Look at Larry King."

"I'd rather not. But, really, the point was pretty moot," Tori said. "He'd had a vasectomy years ago. I didn't push it. I might have enjoyed being a mother, but honestly, I didn't really want to ruin my body."

"No, not when you've put so much money into it."

The remark was a dig and Lainie wished she hadn't said it. Tori didn't seem to care. It might have been that she was just as glad that the O'Neal sisters' reunion was over. Lainie had come to Tacoma to help her sister get through a very rough patch. She was uncertain if she'd been asked out of love or because there was no one else who her twin would be able to call.

"How many years this time?"

"Excuse me?"

"How many years will pass before I see you again?"

"You'll see me soon. I'm thinking of coming out to the class reunion. I'd like to show those losers that no matter what life has handed me, I'm still smarter, better looking, and, yes, richer than any of them."

The taxi parked and a driver started up the walk.

Lainie turned to hug her sister good-bye. The past few days had been full of drama, resentment, bitterness. Except for the murder, it seemed like old times.

Or maybe it was because of that.

"See you soon. Call me," she said, as she walked out the door.

Lainie smiled warily at the cab driver as he lifted the door handle to let her inside.

"Heading home. Stayed with my sister."

"Nice visit, I hope," he said.

"I guess so," she said. "I stayed about as long as I could, as I was needed."

"I've got a sister like that, too," he said.

Oh, no you don't, Lainie thought. She got into the backseat and reached for her phone. The screen was dead.

"Damn," she said.

The driver looked over his shoulder at Lainie before pulling away from the Connelly house.

"What's the trouble?"

She held out the phone. "I recharged it, but it isn't working. Says that the SIM card is corrupted."

"That sucks," the man said. "That happened to me one time. You'll have to start over."

Lainie didn't say anything, but she agreed. She would have to start over. Seeing her sister brought back so many memories that needed to be laid to rest. Once and for all.

Kendall walked across the plaza toward the sheriff's office. She looked down at her ringing phone.

It was Lainie.

"How are things? How are *you*?"

"A nightmare. But you could have guessed that."

"It wouldn't take a detective to figure that out. You're right," Kendall said. "How's Tori?"

"She's mad because the police want to question her. Again."

"Tell her to get a lawyer," Kendall said, stopping by a parked car and squinting up at the damp May sky, hoping no more drops would rain down. It had been the soggiest spring in recent memory and she had to fight the urge to wring out her shoes.

"I'm surprised you'd offer up that kind of advice."

"Look, it's the right thing to do. How long are you going to stay?"

"I'm about ready to leave."

"Funeral this week?"

"Get this . . . no funeral. She says she's too upset. Or something."

"Sounds like the Tori I remember."

"You'd be surprised. She hasn't changed a bit. Except for a boob job. She's about the same."

"Really?"

"Really," Lainie said before switching the subject. "What's going on with the Jason investigation?"

Kendall sighed. "You know I can't talk about that. But not much. I guess you are caught up in the Mike Walsh murder."

"You know he was there the night of the accident?"

"Yes, I do. But that's all I can say. You know that."

"I guess so. I hope you catch his killer. Sad to think of a man who'd pulled his life around only to get murdered."

"All murders are tragic," Kendall said. "But, yes, this one is very sad."

"Tori doesn't remember Mikey, but I do. Tori doesn't remember anything that doesn't move her ahead in any game that she's playing."

They talked a bit more, about Tori, about the committee and the reunion, before saying good-bye. Kendall slipped the phone into the pocket of her purse. She wondered what it was like to have a sister like Tori. She was always a drama queen, the center of attention, the kind of person who truly believed that any attention was better than none at all. She'd wanted to be a singer, an actress, something that would get her noticed by everyone.

Ahead in any game she was playing. That was Tori to a T.

After hanging up the phone in her Tacoma bedroom, Tori rolled closer to snuggle her lover.

"That went pretty well," she said. "She thought I was Lainie. People are so stupid."

"It was genius to dog yourself over the boob job," he said.

"Genius. That's me. A very naughty genius."

"Let's make love again," he said.

She smiled. "Fast, okay? We've got things to do."

CHAPTER THIRTY-SEVEN

Tacoma

The hospital cafeteria at St. Joseph Medical Center was having a special on salmon in a creamy dill sauce, and the entire space smelled like a fish and fry shack. While waiting for the two nurses to join her, Kendall Stark stupidly selected the salmon. It was a light gray with a swath of green sauce that was anything but appealing. Ultimately, she wasn't hungry. Not really. She was way out of her jurisdiction and she hadn't bothered to notify Eddie Kaminski that she was going to talk to his witnesses. It was a lapse in protocol, but she thought it was worth the ethical misstep. No one could understand Tori O'Neal like those who knew her.

To know her was to distrust her.

She'd told Josh that she was running an errand. He didn't seem to understand her preoccupation with Tori, either, and it was just as well. Steven, however, was another matter. He deserved to know what she was thinking. But she wasn't ready for that.

It was around 1:00 P.M. and the cafeteria was busy. Kendall shuffled her tray along the steel shelf to the cash register. A young man with heavy-lidded eyes and a soul patch that was so overgrown it might have required a hairnet if he'd been on the food-serving side of the operation took her money and told her that refills were free.

"Hopefully, you aren't an iced tea drinker," he said. "That spigot's dry."

Kendall took a seat next to the window. It had rained most of the day and the parking lot glistened. If there was any-place she hated more than a hospital cafeteria, it was proba-bly the visiting room at a mortuary. *Slumber room*, as the mortuary staff had called it, in the euphemistic vernacular of an industry that sought to make death seem transitory, rather than permanent.

Corazón White and Diana Lowell caught her attention from across the cafeteria as they ambled over with their trays of assorted lunch items.

"Salmon's good," Corazón said.

"Good for you, I guess. But not so good here," Diana said.

"I'm glad that you could see me," Kendall said.

She waited for them to sit before she gave her spiel that the Connelly murder investigation was ongoing and that she'd need them to sign statements later if she thought what they had to say was important to the investigation.

"Administrator says we can cooperate," Diana said. "They like to help the police—"

"—when the death isn't on our watch," Corazón said, in-terrupting her.

Diana gave the younger woman a cool look. "You didn't hear that from me."

Kendall drank her mocha, a regular, not the Tuxedo from Starbucks that she favored. It gave her one more reason to hate hospitals. As if she needed one.

"Of course not. What I did hear from you," she said, look-ing at Diana, "is that you and Corazón observed a few things that bothered you a little during Ms. Connelly's brief stay here."

Corazón pierced a limp lettuce leaf with her fork before dipping it in a small container of low-cal Thousand Island dressing. "That's right. She was arguing with someone on the phone. Telling someone that she didn't want him to call the hospital."

"A *he*?"

Corazón shook her head. "No. She said it was her sister. But she talked to the person like he was a man, maybe a boyfriend. I don't know. Thought you'd want to know."

Kendall was interested, but she kept her affect flat. "What specifically did she say?"

" 'Don't call here.' That kind of thing."

"How about you," she said, this time to Diana, the older of the pair of nurses.

"About the same thing. I distinctly remember her saying, 'Don't ever call me here again.' She told me it was her sister from Seattle or Portland and that she was coming. She was all sweetness when talking to me. But she was full-bitch when she was talking to her 'sister' or whoever it was."

"You going to eat that?" Corazón pointed to Kendall's Dutch apple pie.

"Nah. You can have it."

Corazón smiled broadly. "Thanks."

Diana lowered her glasses to get a better look at her barely toasted BLT. She didn't say a word. And for a woman like Diana Lowell that was not an easy thing to do.

On her way back across the Narrows Bridge to the office, Kendall wondered about the tenacity of a caller such as the one who'd been dialing Tori Connelly's room.

Someone she didn't want to talk to. Someone who wouldn't take no for answer, she thought.

Once behind her desk, she rifled the furthest reaches of her desk drawer for an antacid. Her stomach was a sour mess and she needed something to calm it. It had to be the salmon she had for lunch.

Josh Anderson flopped himself down in her visitor's chair.

"Where'd you go for lunch? Amy's?"

She shook her head.

"I wish I did." She patted her stomach. "I grabbed a bite at a drive-through and now I'm paying for it."

"Biting you back, huh?"

"You could say that." Kendall paused for a moment, weighing her options. "You might need to run things around here for a few days. A family emergency has come up and I might have to leave town."

She hoped he wouldn't ask where she was going. She'd already lied to him too many times. Lying, she was sure, didn't get easier with practice.

"Anything serious?"

"Just family stuff."

CHAPTER THIRTY-EIGHT

Kitsap County
Fifteen years ago

The parking lot of the Secure Crisis Residential Center was mostly empty, though Lainie knew that there would be fifty cars shoehorned into the lot by the time she departed after seeing her sister. She parked her hideous green Toyota Corolla ("Nagasaki's revenge," she frequently said, making a dark joke of the car's unfortunate paint color) and went inside. Daniel Hector was the only guard on duty and he signed her in. He led her to the craft room where Tori was sitting next to a Victorian dollhouse. She stood.

"I knew you would come. I knew I could count on you, Lainie."

Lainie embraced her sister; this time she felt a slight hug in return.

"I love you, Tori."

"I know you do," she said, tears coming to her eyes. Coming, but not falling. "I need you to do something for me."

"What? What can I do?"

"I can't take it anymore. I'm going crazy. I'm going to die. I need to get out of here."

"You will get out. You're almost there."

"I want out today."

"Of course you do. I want you out."

"I want you to take my place."

"What are you talking about?"

"You heard me. You owe me."

"I don't owe you that."

"You do."

"I'm leaving now."

"I'll tell."

"No one will believe you."

"Is that what this has come to? That you think no one will believe me because I'm the bad twin? You're so effing perfect?"

"I never said that."

"You don't have to. Everyone else does. I'm sick of it. I'm sick of you, Dad, prison, Port Orchard."

"Look, I know you are hurting. I wish none of this ever happened."

"Wishing something doesn't make it so. Just one day, Lainie. Can't you give me one freaking day?"

She looked at a pair of scissors. "Cut my hair like yours."

"I won't," Lainie said.

"You really want to go there? You were driving that night. It was your idea to take the car, not mine." An intensity came to Tori's eyes, replacing anguish. *"I'll tell. Don't think I won't. Don't think for one second that I won't do whatever it takes to get what I want."*

Lainie could feel her heart pound. She didn't know what to do. Should she get up and run, or should she stay and reason with her twin?

"You made an agreement."

"I lied," Tori said.

Lainie pushed back on her chair. She could feel her legs wanted to rise up and lift her, but they didn't. For some reason, she stayed. "Are you lying now?"

"I get that it's a risk, but you're going to have to take a chance. Or I'll ruin your life. Goody-goody Lainie's not so good after all."

"Just one night?"

Tori picked up the scissors and slid them across the table-top. "Here, cut." She swiveled in her chair, her back now facing her sister.

Reluctantly, Lainie reached for the scissors. "I didn't think they could have sharp objects in a place like this."

"Start cutting," Tori said. "You'd be surprised what goes on in here."

Wearing Lainie's clothes, blue jeans, and sweater over a long-sleeved T-shirt, Tori O'Neal spun around in a circle as she and Daniel Hector left 7-Pod and her sister. It was part fashion show, part makeover, and a celebration of freedom. Hector nodded approvingly.

"She'll never tell," Tori said. "Do whatever you want with her."

The corrections officer smiled, his uneven teeth stained by chewing tobacco. "Wish I could have you both at once."

"You can pretend," she said.

He handed her Lainie's purse and car keys from a storage locker behind the counter.

"She did a nice job on the cut, Tori," he said, as she started toward the door. "I know you were worried about that."

"Lainie, officer. I'm Lainie."

"Right." He reached down and turned on the video cam-

era mounted in the craft room above a painting of an Old English cottage.

Mikey Walsh's trailer wasn't hard to find. Tori went down to the boat launch across from Al's Grocery on Olalla Bay and asked around. She didn't say she wanted to score some speed, but a man on a chopper figured that's what the pretty blonde with the ugly car wanted. She pulled into his long wooded driveway, to the mobile home that was one or two winter seasons away from falling into the soggy soil of South Kitsap.

She let herself inside and found Mikey on a ratty sofa watching CNN.

"I didn't take you for a news buff," she said.

Startled, he looked up. "What the fuck are you doing in here?"

"I'm here to talk to you."

"I don't have nothing to say to you. Get out of my house."

"This isn't much of a house and you don't have anything to say," she said. "I'm going to do the talking."

"What do you want?" Mikey stood. He wore ratty Levi cutoffs, a tank top, and athletic socks. He smelled of beer and body odor.

"I'm here to make you a promise," she said.

"I don't want anything from you. Your sister is in jail and we're done."

Tori didn't correct him. She was Lainie.

"You think my sister is trash, don't you?"

"She is trash. She's a freak."

"Like I said, I'm here to make a promise."

"What kind of a promise?"

"I promise that you're a dead man if you ever, ever, ever talk about what you saw."

His eyes flashed defiance. "You mean how she killed that kid?"

She took a step closer. Tori refused to give an inch of ground to that piece of garbage standing in front of her.

"You want to die, too?"

"You're some stupid girl. I'm not afraid of you," he said, backing off a little.

There was a coldness in her eyes that was like a bucket of ice water in his face.

The girl wasn't kidding around.

"You think my sister's a piece of work?" she asked, again with a simmering rage behind each word. "Don't even think about trying to mess with me, Mikey."

"Look," he said, "I have no intention of saying anything. Who would believe an addict like me, anyway?"

"That's what I was thinking, too," she said. "Don't blow it, Mikey. Don't ever blow it or I'll hunt you down and slit your scrawny neck ear to ear."

Mikey slumped back onto the couch. Besides the rage behind the threat, something didn't seem right.

"You're not the nice twin, are you?" he asked.

"No one's nice, Mikey," she said as she turned to leave. "As much as I love a challenge, don't make me come back and prove it to you."

Switching the part in her hair was easy, though such a small change hurt like hell as follicles were shifted in a new direction. As mirror twins, it had to be done. Tori never thought her father paid that much attention to the girls, not enough anyway. She bought a latte at an espresso stand in downtown Port Orchard and walked along the waterfront. It was late afternoon by the time she pulled in front of the house behind her dad's car. The old pear tree was in full bloom, a cascade of blossoms stuck to the pavement.

"Dad?" she called out.

No reply.

Typical. No one is ever here for me, *she thought.*

The house was the same. Smelled the same. The furniture in the living room was placed as it had been before Tori went to serve her sentence. Tori was unsure what she'd expected. She had that strange feeling as if she had been away on vacation and expected the world to be turned upside down in her absence. But there wasn't anything different about the O'Neal home.

Dex was washing his hands in the kitchen. With the tap gushing into the sink, he hadn't heard her come in. He turned and smiled at the sight of her.

"How was your run this A.M.? You got out of here like a bat out of hell."

"Fine." She slid in to a seat at the kitchen table. "Tired. Long day. Ran a few errands."

"Good. Sit down and I'll make dinner." He swung open the refrigerator door and brought out two cans of iced tea. Tori hated that canned tea, but she was Lainie just then.

"Thanks, Dad," she said, pulling open the top.

The relationship between her father and sister was closer than her own with either. Tori wondered about that. Was it because she'd hated or resented him and he was merely reflecting her emotions in their relationship? He wasn't unkind. He was cool. But not now, not to Lainie.

She decided to bring it up.

"Tomorrow will be a long day," she said. "Not looking forward to it."

"Your sister? That place?"

"Probably both." She decided to gamble with her next statement. "We've talked about it before," she said. "I don't like seeing her."

"We're obligated. We're a family."

Obligated.

"She doesn't even appreciate us."

"Don't get me started. You know where I fall in that argument."

Tori felt a surge of hope. *"Yeah, she's not so bad."*

Dex O'Neal let out a laugh. It was the kind of chortle that cuts to the bone if one is the target of the rub. *"Honestly, Lainie, your sister scares me sometimes."*

Tori could have probed a little. She could have pushed her father's buttons, but she chose to keep her mouth shut. She'd sit there, play nice, and seethe quietly.

She always knew where she stood in that family.

It had rained all night. Tiny bullets of water glanced off the window of 7-Pod. Lainie O'Neal curled as tight as a hermit crab in the scratchy military-issue blankets that outfitted her sister's bottom bunk. There were only three girls in the pod. None of them seemed to care one whit about anything but themselves and their own misery. Lainie put the girl named Tara at about sixteen. She was a sullen-faced biracial girl who had almond eyes that illuminated nothing of her soul. She was on the bunk above Tori's. The other girl was named something like Gigi or maybe G.G. It was hard for Lainie to determine her story at all. She barely said two words. Officer Hector told her where she was sleeping and that the girls wouldn't engage with her if she ignored them.

"The less you say, the better," he said.

"I want to go home."

"Like I haven't heard that before," he said.

Lainie spent the day and the early evening on a filthy red beanbag chair in the juvenile correction center's lounge watching MTV and wishing she could be home with her father. For dinner, she ate a rubbery chicken wing and some mashed potatoes. She pretended to be angry about something.

"Act mad. People will leave you alone," Tori had advised.

That her sister had been living like this for months crushed Lainie.

"It was a damn accident," she said. *"Nothing more, just a sad, stupid accident."*

The rain continued to streak the window above her bunk bed. It was dark, desolate. The door to the pod was locked. A toilet and washbasin in the corner was there in case any of the girls needed to use a bathroom during the lockdown hours. The idea was disgusting to Lainie. She'd rather hold it for eight hours and writhe in pain than suffer the indignity of using a communal privy. Tara didn't seem to mind at all.

A half hour into the darkness of the pod, Lainie heard footsteps, the sound of a key inserted into the lock. She turned in her bed as a hand went over her face.

She couldn't breathe.

What is happening to me?

The smell of chewing tobacco came at her.

"Shut up. You're mine."

Lainie rolled onto her back, twisted her frame to try to get some leverage. She wanted out of there. She clawed into the darkness. The sticky hand over her mouth pushed harder. She couldn't breathe. She was a virgin, but she knew what was happening. She knew what that man was trying to do to her.

Please, God, don't let him rape me!

"Stop it, you little bitch. You're ruining my game here," Hector said. *"I like a good dust-up in the sack, but you still have to get the job done."*

Why isn't Tara or G.G. or whatever her name is doing anything?

Lainie was unsure how it happened, but he was on top of her. Somehow he had slithered under the blanket. She could feel his body and she started to cough, then vomit. Vomit of chicken wings and mashed potatoes spewed over the bed, onto the officer, over the surface of the scratchy blanket.

"You fucking dirty little bitch!"

She was choking on her own vomit. She couldn't breathe. She fought, and she fought hard. There wasn't a moment in which she wouldn't have begged for her life, even if he'd loosened his grip enough so that she could. No one who'd been pinned down, held tight with the hot breath of an assailant all over her, would deny the feelings that spun through her terrified mind. He put his hand on her breasts and pushed before he bent down, panting, and whispered in her ear.

"I know what you did," he said. "Don't piss me off. You did a real number on your sister, you little privileged bitch. You mess with me by saying anything and I'll kill your sister and your dad. After I feed them to the sharks in Puget Sound, I'll go out and have waffles and eggs for breakfast. And then, I'll come looking for you."

He released her. A sliver of light fell over the room. The door shut.

Lainie was crying, coughing, choking. Tara climbed down and took her over to the toilet. She handed her a towel.

"Get a grip. Pull yourself together," she said. "What the hell was all that drama tonight, Tori?"

"Drama?" It was a single word, but the only thing that could come to her lips.

Tara started for their bed. "Whatever. Your puke really stinks. I don't know how I'm supposed to sleep around here. Thanks for nothing. God, I hate this place."

The dreams started then. The nightmares. Whatever they were. Tori didn't come back the next morning. In fact, she never did. Tori told her father that she just couldn't go back to "that place," that it "hurt too much" to see her sister that way.

Tori let Lainie serve out her sentence.

Dex O'Neal had no idea what had happened, that the switch had been made. When he saw his daughter in the correctional facility later, he remarked about her new look.

"You cut your hair like your sister," he said.

"Yeah, it was getting too long," Lainie said.

"I love it."

The sisters never talked about what had transpired the last time they ever switched places as twins.

Tori ran across Daniel Hector at the Safeway on Bethel Avenue one time, and he approached her.

"Your sister was a total bitch," he said. "You said she was going to be hot stuff. Fun stuff. That she was into a sexy, fun scene."

"Didn't you have fun?"

"She practically threw me on to the floor."

"She's a fighter."

"She was a bitch. I'm glad I've got you to mess around with."

She smiled. It wasn't a real smile, but he was too stupid to know. "Those were good times. Freaky, but good."

When Daniel Hector was arrested for molesting a ten-year-old girl three years later, it opened a Pandora's box of other accusations. There were some suspicions from the staff at the Secure Crisis Residential Center in Port Orchard, but no one really had anything conclusive. The girls in 7-Pod had turned over to a new group three times since Lainie as Tori O'Neal walked free.

Lainie was in college studying journalism when she saw the item in the paper, but she resisted the urge to dial the Kitsap County Prosecutor's Office. While it was true that she didn't want to be thought of as a victim, neither did she want anyone to know that she'd been duped by her sister. She was damaged goods. Raped. Abused.

Tori had faded away after her release and the time between visits with what was left of their family lengthened.

The only time she saw her sister was in her dreams.

CHAPTER THIRTY-NINE

Tacoma

Tori Connelly paced the house, starting in the master bedroom, then the guest room, down the hall, and to the stairs. Everything in that old Victorian was perfection. On the first floor she lingered in the kitchen looking at all the things she had amassed. The best appliances. An antique paella pan from Spain that hung on the wall cost more than two thousand dollars. She didn't even cook and never intended to learn. She was going to have to leave all of what she'd fought so hard to get. She was going to have to pray that her sister and Kendall Stark didn't talk.

Kendall was digging into her affairs. Lainie was poking around in things that she should leave alone. And Parker had been a fool.

I've been through more than any of those idiots can imagine. If they knew what I'd faced, they would back off and give me some space, she thought. *I don't deserve this.*

She went back upstairs to her phone. Her heart was racing a little, a feeling that she did not appreciate at all. She dialed Parker's number. It went to voice mail.

"Baby, I was just thinking about you. About *us*," she began. "We have to go *now*."

She hung up and continued to review the house that would never again be her home. She went into the living room where she'd pointed the gun at the back of Alex's head and kick-started the series of incidents that was the middle of her plan. Not the beginning. She smiled. She knew that she'd never come back to the old Victorian that she had been her dream. It had reminded her of the dollhouse that she, her sister, and the other girls in juvy had worked on, and owning it was a big F-U to all of those who'd hurt her.

Her mother.
Her father.
Her sister.
Her husbands.

She examined herself in the mirror. She looked pretty in an ordinary way. Her hair no longer golden, but some color that approximated averageness, something she never wanted to be. Inside her purse, she'd packed plane tickets, five grand, and the code to her Bahamian bank account.

She drew a deep breath and reminded herself that the best plans in the world had to be fluid. She knew that, but taking that deep inside once more was necessary. She understood the power of adapting and changing. *Steady, Tori.* The only person who should know someone's next move is the one holding the cards. She set a single overnight bag on the front step and turned the key in the deadbolt.

Tori went inside the carriage house and shut the door. She could hear Alex's voice as he told her that he no longer loved her, that he wanted out of their marriage. She'd begged him to reconsider, though she really was only buying time.

She climbed into the deep, dark leather seats of her Lexus and shut the door.

Then she screamed as loudly as she could.

*   *   *

As she dealt with another sleepless night, Lainie's thoughts fell to her sketchy memories of Zach Campbell. She'd remembered how excited her sister had been when she announced that she was going to marry the former navy officer based in Bremerton. Tori had met him when she was a casino singer at the Clearwater in Suquamish. He was handsome, almost two decades older. His chiseled good looks had softened with age a little, but with brown eyes and a full head of sandy hair—so full that some wondered if it had been a toupee, which it *wasn't*—he was a charmer.

"Aren't you worried that he's a little, you know, old?" Lainie asked when her sister met her at a Port Orchard coffee shop on Bay Street. They were barely in their twenties and their relationship had slowly ebbed since high school. Lainie had gone to Western Washington University in the northern part of the state. Though Tori was given her high school diploma, it came with the tarnish of having finished her education in juvenile detention. Neither had ever acknowledged it was Tori who walked at graduation as Lainie. So much had never been discussed. The crash. The prison. The switch.

All had turned them into friendly adversaries, not sisters.

"I was a little concerned, at first," Tori said, of Zach's age. "But he told me that age is nothing but a number. Besides he's financially secure and that matters. I don't have a career like someone I know."

"Just so you know, reporters make less than teachers," Lainie said.

Tori shrugged. "Casino singers make less than just about anyone, Lainie."

"Very funny. Don't you want a family someday?"

"He's old, not dead, Lainie. And maybe a baby sometime. I'm not in a hurry."

"What about the wedding? When and where?"

Tori held up her ring finger. Set in a thin platinum band was a one-carat square-cut diamond that sparkled like a midnight star. It was an ostentatious stone that was meant to draw gasps and envy. And it did.

"We were married last weekend in Las Vegas."

"Oh . . . congratulations."

"We'd always planned on being maids of honor for each other. We'd talked of a double wedding. Remember how the other would wait for her sister?"

"That was before," *Tori said. "Before the accident. Before Mom died. I just want to get out of Kitsap as fast as I can. Zach is my ticket out."*

"That sounds lovey-dovey."

"You can think whatever you want to think, Lainie. Just remember that when I'm gone, no one will look at you and think that you're me. The scorn or pity or whatever it is that is passed in your direction by mistake will vanish."

Lainie thought a moment, choosing her words carefully.

"Because you're *going to vanish."*

Tori let out a breath.

"Something like that," she said.

CHAPTER FORTY

Port Orchard

The phone at the Kitsap County Sheriff's Office had rung nonstop with calls from congregants of the Lord's Grace Church. Most callers were exceedingly polite, offering prayers and volunteering to do whatever they could to help with the investigation. Although Josh was designated lead on the Mike Walsh homicide, both he and Kendall took turns fielding those who wanted to help in one way or another.

Kendall told each they were in the middle of the investigation. She never offered specifics. She knew better from seeing other cops get burned when they made promises of solving a case.

An obvious murder like Pastor Walsh's, with bloody footprints and sadistic binding of the victims' wrists, could languish until such time as the killer struck again.

If, indeed, the killer was prone to do so. Josh was convinced it was payback for sexual abuse because of the repeated and unnecessary stabbing. Kendall was of another mind.

There was a connection and a very real one with Jason Reed.

One call from a prepaid cell phone, however, was nothing like the others. Kendall took the call. It was a woman's voice.

"You really messed up on this one. We'll never know what happened to Jason Reed now. Thanks for nothing."

"Who is this?" Kendall asked, her adrenalin pumping.

"It doesn't matter.

"It does to me."

The line went dead.

Under the green glow of her desk's banker's lamp, Kendall Stark spread out copies of the case file from the Connelly homicide investigation. She was on thin ice and she knew it. The material was given to her as a courtesy because of her reinvestigation of Jason Reed's death and Tori's connection with the cases. She'd already overstepped some boundaries by talking with the nurses at the hospital. She doubted Kaminski would appreciate her doing anything more—and she knew she'd resent any cop who'd insert him or herself into one of her active investigations.

But this was different. *It was personal*. It was something she simply had to do.

She found herself flipping back and forth between the reports made at the scene and the interview notes for both Darius Fulton and Tori Connelly.

Tori claimed she'd been in bed when she heard the gunfire. She went downstairs and the masked intruder shot her as he ran out of the house.

Darius claimed he knew nothing of that, of course. But his statement had one detail that seemed puzzling.

". . . Mrs. Connelly arrived in a nightgown . . . bleeding . . . her hair was wet."

Kendall poured herself a diet cola and returned her attention to the notation made by Kaminski:

"... *The master shower had been wet.*"

It was easy to surmise that Tori Connelly had taken a shower that evening. No crime there. What troubled Kendall was the idea of a woman going to bed with a sopping wet head. She never would have done that. In fact, Kendall, like many women, took her showers in the morning precisely so she could blow-dry her hair to perfection before work.

Tori Connelly's hair had been soaking wet.

She looked at the photos of the master bedroom. The image showing the Rice bed revealed that while it had been turned down for the night, no one had been inside it. The duvet was smooth. There was no indentation where Tori Connelly's head might have rested.

And certainly, there was no indication that there was any dampness on the pillow.

If Tori wasn't in bed, as she had said, what was she doing?

Kendall felt that the condom wrapper found in the guest room was also problematic. It hadn't been seen by Kaminski or the others who'd processed the scene for the Tacoma Police Department. She conceded that the first floor of the house on Junett would have been the most crucial for processing. But the master bath, master bedroom, and the guest rooms upstairs were also relevant. Certainly what transpired May 5 was not a sex crime, so there would have been little reason to consider it of any evidentiary value. Yet, why was it there?

It didn't make sense. Something, she was sure, was amiss.

Kendall left her office and found Josh Anderson behind his desk surfing Match.com. She lingered a moment, kind of happy to see that he was working out of his personal funk. She no longer saw Internet dating as pathetic, but necessary.

Especially for Josh.

"Making a connection?" Her tone was kind, not snide.

Flustered, Josh looked up and clicked his mouse to shut the window. His face went red. "How did you—"

Kendall pointed. "Behind you. The glass on the watercolor reflects your screen."

"Thanks. I didn't know."

"Of course you didn't," she said.

"What's up," he said. "You're obviously not here to critique the state of my love life."

Kendall smiled briefly. "No, not this time," she said, holding out the Tacoma Police report and pointing out what Lainie told her about the condom wrapper.

"She found the wrapper. Practically in plain sight."

He pushed the paperwork back. "Two things," he said. "One, what does Kaminski say? And two, why in the F are you working their case when we have our own here?"

"He doesn't say. He's probably embarrassed that his tech missed it. I know I would be." The muscles in Kendall's neck tightened, like they always did when she felt backed into a corner. "As for your second point, I can't give a clear answer. I think—and it's a gut feeling that I'm sure you'd dismiss as woman's intuition or something of the like—that Tori is responsible for her husband's murder. Not the sap they've arrested."

"I won't denigrate your intuition, Kendall. You know I don't put much stock in things that aren't black-and-white. And that's the way I've lived my life and do my job."

Kendall held her tongue. She could have said something cruel back, something along the lines of how lousy his life had turned out, but she didn't. Being overly defensive wouldn't get her anywhere.

"Thanks. I just know that Tori killed Alex, Zach, and, yes, Jason."

"Good luck with that, Kendall," he said. "You're on dangerous ground."

"Fine," she said. "Thanks for listening."

Kendall retreated to her office, angry at Josh, but knowing that her compulsion to figure things out was greater than any admonishment she'd get from her partner, her husband, or the sheriff.

If it came to that.

She called Darius Fulton's lawyer Maddie Crane's office. Her paralegal Chad told her that Ms. Crane was out to lunch.

"She doesn't take calls during her lunchtime, but if you're nearby, you can bug her in person. I don't care."

Kendall knew where Maddie and all the lawyers congregated in Tacoma. Only two blocks from the Pierce County Courthouse, an Italian restaurant called Mama's was the scene of more one-upmanship than a fight club in a dank warehouse downtown. Lawyers were showy competitors. That meant they liked to be seen.

"I'm going on an errand," she said, barely stopping by Josh's office as she made her way down the hallway—a place that had been remodeled too many times without consideration for function.

"Your mom?"

"Yes, Mama's," she said, relieved that it really wasn't a lie.

When her phone rang, it was Laura Connelly.

"I don't want to say anything over the phone," she said. "I need to see you."

"Are you all right? Can you tell me what it's about?"

"Parker," she said, her voice catching a little in her throat. "It has to do with my son. Meet me at Shari's on Union. I'll be there at three."

"Can you make it earlier? I'm planning on heading over to Tacoma around lunchtime."

"All right. How about one-thirty?"

"Perfect."

She hung up, wondering what was up with Laura, though she had an idea.

Kendall Stark was greeted by a wave of garlic as she swung open the big brass doors of Mama's Ristorante. Finding Maddie wouldn't be hard. Everyone in the Northwest knew Maddie Crane. Kendall and the lawyer had actually met a time or two before. Maddie got around. Kendall passed through the restaurant and went into the dimly lit bar, where she immediately caught the attention of Maddie's horde, two women and a man in dark, expensive suits and spray-on tans. She nodded at the defense lawyer. Maddie made a face and got up to greet her.

"You wouldn't be unlucky enough just to stumble on this place," she asked. "What is it?"

The place was warm, so the detective unbuttoned her jacket.

"It might not be anything," she said. "Can we sit?"

Maddie seemed irritated. "Make it fast. I'm with friends."

"I see that. Looks like a fun crowd."

They found an empty booth by the kitchen door. "What is it?" she repeated.

"Like I said, it might not be anything. Tacoma PD missed a potential piece of evidence. Or maybe not. I don't know."

Kendall chose her words carefully, but in doing so, she made the scenario appear worse than it was. She was, as Josh said, on shaky ground. While she was technically working her own case involving Tori Connelly, she was stepping on the toes of Tacoma Police and that was never a good idea.

"I'm working my own case," she said. "But it could be related to yours. Hear me out."

Maddie was devoid of facial expression, which spoke more of her ability to hide her feelings than of Botox. It didn't matter to her if she believed her client or not, but a mistake by the police was always a good thing.

"Go on. All ears here."

"Lainie says there was a condom wrapper in the guest room. The deceased had a vasectomy."

Maddie's eyes were flinty. Again, cool. "All right."

"What about your client?"

"That's extremely personal."

Kendall fidgeted a little in her chair. "Well, sure it is," she said. "But we can't figure out why there would be a condom wrapper in that bedroom."

The lawyer tapped her long nails against the dark walnut surface of the tabletop. "So what you might be saying—and what Kaminski probably would not like brought up at trial—is that there might be another man involved with the charming Mrs. Connelly."

"Something like that," Kendall said.

Maddie got up and started for her table.

"I'll get back to you," she said.

CHAPTER FORTY-ONE

Tacoma

It was 1:40 P.M. Ten minutes after Kendall's appointed meeting with Laura Connelly. Kendall slumped into a booth in the back, but facing the front door at Shari's Restaurant off Union Avenue in Tacoma, just past the Target store.

"I don't want to say anything over the phone," Laura had said.

"Are you all right? Can you tell me what it's about?"

"Parker," she said, her voice catching a little in her throat. "It has to do with my son."

Despite the waitress's chirpy delivery of the "Strawberry Fields" promotion ("pie, sundaes, pancakes, smoothies, shakes—just about anything you can freckle with strawberries, we're doing it this month"), Kendall ordered only coffee. As she waited, she wondered if Laura had backed out. She texted a message to Steven, letting him know that Laura was late, and that meant she might be, too.

"Over here," she mouthed as Laura came into the restaurant. She was wearing black jeans, a black sweater, and a rope of silver chains around her neck.

"I thought it would be more private here," Kendall said.

"After I talk to you, what difference will privacy make?" There was a coolness, a directness, to Laura's words, and Kendall nodded understandingly.

"It depends on what you have to tell me."

Laura barely blinked. "I guess so. Believe me, I thought about not coming inside. I sat in my car for fifteen minutes. I saw you go in and thought about just driving away."

"But you didn't," Kendall said.

Laura nodded at the busboy, but kept silent as he poured her a cup of coffee. "No, I didn't. But that doesn't mean I'm crazy about this."

"I understand."

The waitress scurried over with a thermal coffeepot. "Coffee? Something to eat?"

"Coffee's fine," Laura said. "Nothing else for me."

"Strawberry Fields going on now," the waitress said.

"I'll fill her in," Kendall said, somewhat sharply.

The waitress shrugged and went back to the counter across the room, where a man had been complaining loudly that his popcorn shrimp was heavy on the batter and low on actual shrimp.

"I'm worried about my son," she said.

Kendall nodded. "Yes, I know you are."

Laura ran her fingers through her hair, pulling it away from her face.

"I don't think I can talk about it. This was a mistake."

"What was a mistake, Laura?"

"Talking to you."

"I don't understand."

"My son. He's all I have."

"Yes, I love my son, too."

"I think my son is mixed up in something."

Kendall had seen that look, heard those words, felt the palpable fear that came with a mother trying to save her boy.

She prayed that she'd never be the woman telling the story. God knew that she had her own challenges with Cody, but he was inherently sweet. It was possible that he could be victimized by someone, but she could never imagine him doing something that would harm someone. Laura Connelly clearly thought something was up with Parker.

The waitress approached and Kendall waved her away. *Not now. Couldn't she see that moment was not made for a slice of berry pie?*

"Talk to me, Laura."

The tears welled up in Laura's eyes and she steadied herself by holding the coffee up in both hands, her elbows planted on the table's oak trim.

"I read about that minister. The one who was killed."

Kendall had no idea where that the woman was going.

"Yes, that was a terrible tragedy. Go on."

"Well, I found something in his room. Something from that church."

"What did you find?"

"I brought it with me."

She reached into her purse and pulled out the money pouch emblazoned with the name of the dead minister's church. She slid it across the table.

Kendall didn't touch it. Though she could readily ascertain that Laura Connelly had her fingers all over the pouch, she didn't want to degrade any potential evidence. She knew of one case in which a positive DNA match was made to a hairbrush that had been used by other family members two years after a murder victim had been dumped and found. It was not a familial match, but dead-on to the individual.

"Did you ask him about it?"

Laura nodded and awkwardly slid her elbows close to her sides. "Yes, a couple of days ago," she said. "I know I should have told you sooner. I don't think he had a thing to do with the murder. He's not a violent kid. I just think he must know something."

Laura started to cry, loudly enough to get the attention of diners adjacent to them.

"Tell me what happened," Kendall said.

"I know you'll help me, mother to mother," she said.

Laura Connelly had wrestled with the discovery of the deposit pouch to the point where she couldn't think about anything else. While it was true that her relationship with Parker had worsened since his father's death, she could see that the disintegration had been coming for quite some time. He'd been evasive, indifferent, and on occasion, almost threatening. There was no "you and me against the world" banter. No more promises to "take care of you when you're an old lady, Mom."

Parker was sullen, agitated, and counting the days to his eighteenth birthday.

Her heart thumped hard inside her chest as she knocked on the door of his bedroom. It was never open when he was home anymore. In fact, she only knew he was home when he'd come out, get something to eat, and scurry back to whatever it was he was doing. She'd allowed that pattern to take root and she regretted it. The isolation between mother and son had likely allowed something very dark to fester.

"Honey, we need to talk," she said, poking her head into his room.

Parker was on his computer. He snapped his laptop shut.

"Do you mind?" he asked.

"I'm sorry," she said, not knowing why she felt a need to apologize. She'd seen something that could be tied to a murder case near Kingston. She never thought for one second that he'd been involved in anything, but maybe his friends had? Drew's mother had complained to her when they ran into each other at Top Foods that her son was "practically incorrigible."

"We need to talk."

"You're talking, Mom. I'm busy. What is it?"

"Can I come in?"

"You're in. Fine. What?"

"I didn't mean to, but I saw something of yours that concerned me."

She was sugarcoating it and she knew it. She wondered how she got to the point of being so weak around her son. It was as if the stronger he got, the more belligerent he became, the weaker she grew. It was like when she discovered that Alex was cheating on her and she thought of every reason why it was her fault, not his.

Parker stepped away from this laptop and sat on the bed. "Mom, I have stuff to do."

"Parker, I found the money pouch from the church." Her hands shook a little, but she tried to steady them.

Calm. Be as calm as you can.

He didn't allow any expression to cross his face. "Were you going through my stuff?"

She shook her head slowly. "I didn't do that. I wouldn't do that."

"I can't believe you, Mom. You are so full of crap."

She sucked in some courage. The issue here wasn't how she saw what she saw, it was that a relic from a murder scene was in their house.

"Where did you get that pouch, Parker?"

"I found it."

"Where?"

"I don't remember. Just somewhere."

"You were gone the day that minister was killed. I remember that we fought."

"We always fight, Mom. I said I found it; I can't even believe for one second that you would think that I would ever lie to you about anything."

Parker didn't state the obvious and it crushed his mother. He didn't say, "What minister?"

Laura didn't want to give voice to the truth just then. The truth was ugly. She had caught him in many, many lies. After his last summer visit with his father, Parker had become a frequent and facile liar.

"We need to give this pouch to the police. You need to tell them where you found it."

"At the skate park. That's where I found it, Mom."

Kendall listened to the anguished mother sitting in front of her. She watched her slide lower in the booth. She was all but disappearing. She handed her a tissue from the packet she kept in her purse for such occasions. She didn't want to tell Laura Connelly about one little flaw in her son's story.

There was no skate park in Port Orchard.

"I'll need to talk to your son, Laura," she said.

Laura nodded. "He's at home."

"I'm going to call my partner and have him meet me there. You go on ahead. We'll be there as soon as we can."

"There's one more thing. I think that he's involved with Tori."

"Involved? How so?"

"She's all he talks about. They're too close. Something's going on."

Kendall set down her coffee and waved away the waitress and her pot.

"Something inappropriate?" she asked.

Laura shook her head. "I'm not sure. I mean, I don't really know. She's his stepmother."

"But you think he's involved," Kendall said, pushing a little. "You used that word, *involved*. What do you mean by that? I want to understand."

Laura stood up to leave and reached for her purse. "I thought he had a girlfriend, but, well, I really do think that he's sleeping with her. There, I said it."

"She's always been a manipulator, Laura. If she's been using your son for whatever reason, it's just what she does."

"You aren't going to arrest him, are you, Kendall?"

The Kitsap detective shook her head, though she really wasn't sure. She didn't want to lie, so she just left it at that.

They met in the TV room of the spotless Fircrest home Laura Connelly purchased with the proceeds from her divorce from Alex. Laura was still unsure if she should call Alex an ex or a late husband. After the shooting, she knew she still loved him a little. When the Kitsap detectives arrived, Parker begrudgingly emerged from his bedroom to talk with them. He wore blue jeans and a black hoodie and an impatient look on his face. His pants were slung low, low enough to show the top two inches of the waistband of his underwear. *Emporio Armani, no less.* Kendall and Josh conferred on the phone before meeting there that the Lord's Grace money pouch alone was not enough for an arrest warrant. It was a start, though. While there were bloody footprints at the Kingston crime scene, they were smeared and not much evidentiary value.

The shoes themselves would be good, but they'd have to be in plain sight in order for the detectives to pick them up without a warrant. The other key piece of evidence was the red tape. Kendall and Josh scoured the Connelly residence in as casual a manner as possible—without opening doors, drawers, or closets.

Nothing.

"Son," Josh said, "you need to tell us what you know."

Parker looked away at the TV. "Why does everyone call me 'son' all of a sudden?"

Laura got up and turned it off.

"I was watching that, Mom."

"You need to talk to the detectives here."

Kendall pulled a bench a little closer to where Parker was sitting. Josh stood. It was a show of domination that wouldn't have gone unnoticed by a police cadet.

Or a teenager.

"You don't intimidate me," Parker said.

Josh leaned closer. "Look, I'm not here to do anything but help you."

"Whatever. I don't give a shit about what you're here to do. And my mom's a stupid bitch for asking you to come over."

Laura was at the breaking point and his name-calling didn't exactly do her fragile psyche any good. She looked like she was going to crumble.

"Parker," she said. "Please don't."

Kendall took over. "You need to trust us," she said to the teen.

"I didn't do nothing wrong," he said, his eyes still riveted to the black TV screen.

"*Anything* is the word," Josh said. "You didn't do *anything* wrong but miss English class."

"You're funnier than Letterman. About as old as him, too."

Kendall shot a bruising glance at Josh that was meant to have him dial things down.

"Ms. Connelly, what do you say you get us some coffee?"

Laura didn't mind leaving the room. She had dissolved in tears twice that evening already. She had called on Kendall and her partner because she wanted to extricate her son from something that might ruin his life. Tori, she felt, was somehow involved in all this.

"Your mom said you found the money pouch," Kendall said.

"Yeah, so what?"

"Do you know that the minister of that church was murdered this week?"

"I'm sure he's in heaven, then."

Kendall ignored the sarcasm. She knew that making a point of calling him out on it would only antagonize him.

Josh Anderson, however, had no ability to show restraint.

"You boning the old girl?"

Kendall resented both the term *boning* and that Josh called Tori "old girl," because they were the same age. Before she could rephrase, Parker answered.

"She's hot," he said.

Josh nodded. "Yeah, she is. Nice rack."

"Are you involved with Tori, Parker?" Kendall asked.

"You mean, am I screwing her?"

"I guess if you want to put it that way."

"It isn't like that. And even if it was, it's none of your business."

"Tell us," Kendall said, gently. "We want to understand."

"You could never understand."

For a second, Josh seemed to warm up to Kendall's soft touch. "Try us."

"Have you ever really been loved? Do you know what it is to find your soul mate?" He looked at Josh. "You've been around. Bet you haven't got a clue. All tough, you are."

Josh suppressed a grin. "I've married three of my soul mates," he said, as dispassionately as possible. "Am looking for my fourth."

"I knew you wouldn't get it." He turned his attention to Kendall. "How about you, Detective Stark?"

"We're here to talk about you, Parker," she said. "Not whether or not we have found our soul mates."

"Am I under arrest?"

"No, Parker, you're not."

Parker got up. "Mom, I don't want to talk to them anymore. I want a lawyer. I want them out of our house."

Kendall noticed a flash of red on the boy's wallet as it peeked from his hip pocket. She looked over at Parker, then back at Josh. The two detectives excused themselves and went into the kitchen.

"We need a warrant," Kendall said. "Call it in."

Josh retrieved his phone and started for the door to make the call in private.

"Calling now," he said.

CHAPTER FORTY-TWO

Port Orchard

"Look, Josh. She's a black widow," Kendall said as the two Kitsap County detectives huddled in her office, waiting on the search warrant for the Connelly place. Josh opened his mouth wide and tipped back the bag of Bugles he'd bought from the vending machine in the break room. Apparently, he didn't want to miss one crumb.

"She's killed two husbands and a boyfriend," she said.

He wadded the bag and tossed it into the trash behind Kendall.

"Nothing but net," he said.

"Are you listening to me?"

"Yeah. But I'm not hearing anything new. Although, if she's anything like her photo in the paper, Tori Connelly is the best-looking femme fatale to come around since Kathleen Turner in *Body Heat*."

"I'm not kidding," Kendall said, getting up from her desk. Even in the tight confines of her office, she found space to pace in front of her partner.

"Think about it. Jason, Alex, and Zach are all dead. The last one to see each of those men alive was Tori."

Josh backed off toward the doorway. "They've nailed Darius What's-His-Name for the Connelly shooting."

"I know," Kendall said, tensing a little. "I don't know why they don't look at the obvious. The totality of her life and what she's done. She's not a nice person. She never has been."

Josh held his hand out as if to calm her. "This is beginning to sound personal, Kendall. Personal never works and you know that."

Kendall knew what he was saying was right, but there was more to this.

"Hear me out one more time."

"Okay, go."

"Tori is a user. She's a master manipulator. She always has been. She likely killed Jason herself—she was the one with the opportunity."

"Motive?"

"I have some ideas, but consider the idea that she's amazingly adept at making people—men, specifically—to do her dirty work."

"Like the Connelly kid."

"Yes, like Parker. Did you see the way he defended her? He is in love with her. He'd probably do anything to please her."

"So you like him for the killer of his own father? Darius Fulton's been arrested for that."

"Yes, and he's probably the killer, put up to it by Tori."

"So you think the kid killed the preacher?"

"I do."

"Why?"

"The reason I think he's the killer or that she put him up to it?"

"Either or both."

Kendall nodded. "She wanted Mikey silenced for what he saw on Banner. He probably saw her kill Jason. We might not ever know that for sure. But with all the publicity, it was only a matter of time until Mikey, now a minister, did the right thing."

"Maybe. What else?"

"Remember the red tape?"

"Sure. It's our biggest traceable piece of evidence."

"Parker had a duct-tape wallet."

"A what?"

"Kids make wallets, clothes, belts—all sorts of stuff—out of duct tape."

"Sounds dumb."

Kendall shrugged. "Dumb, maybe. But Parker's wallet was a duct-tape wallet. I saw it tonight. It was trimmed in red tape."

"Interesting," he said, "but just interesting. Nothing concrete."

"What about the dead guy in Hawaii?"

"She must have had help there, too. They just missed it."

"Sounds like you really dislike her and you want to nail her for personal reasons. You don't care what I think, but that's how I feel, Kendall."

After Josh left, Kendall closed her office door. It *was* personal, but not for the reasons he'd presumed. Kendall wanted the truth. She felt that Mary Reed deserved it. Lainie did. *They all did.*

She sat down and looked at the bulletin board in her windowless office.

The answer was staring her in the face. A postcard Barbara in Records had sent to Kendall from her vacation to Hawaii.

The answer was in Hawaii.

Kendall got online and booked a flight on Alaska Airlines using 45,000 frequent flier miles she and Steven had saved for the past six years. She'd call in sick, lie to her husband about where she was going, and pray to God that whatever she found out would set them all free.

Kendall returned home and packed a single carry-on bag. The one she always took whenever she went on a business trip. She pulled off the tag for SFO, the remnant of her last forensics conference the previous fall.

"Conference came up out of the blue," Steven said, sitting on the edge of the bed.

Kendall didn't look at him. *She just couldn't.* "I guess. When the other investigator couldn't make it, I volunteered. Budgets are so tight these days, we're lucky that we didn't take a bath on the entire conference."

"Yeah, that's good."

Her clothes were all lightweight and Steven noticed.

"Hot weather in L.A., I gather."

She nodded. "Scorching."

"Sure you don't want us to take you to the airport?"

"Too late, babe. I'll park at Thrifty and take the shuttle."

Kendall hated lying to Steven. She wanted to grab him by the shoulders and tell him just why she was going, where she was going, and that she just couldn't let Tori get away with murder.

Not again.

She got out of her car on the Southworth ferry for the crossing to West Seattle, and went upstairs to the passenger deck. She let the wind wash over her, blowing her hair, caressing her like the love of a lifetime ago.

I'm sorry, Steven. I'm sorry that I couldn't tell you everything.

* * *

The telephone conversation didn't go well but Parker Connelly could have guessed that would be the case. He knew by his mother's overwrought, and *judgmental*, reaction that he'd screwed up big-time. Murder was big, indeed. Pour a big heap of suspicion coming from the Kitsap detectives on top of that and he knew he was in deep trouble.

"You did *what*?" Tori repeated.

"It was a packet of money and I took it."

"Are you stupid because you're young or just plain stupid?"

"Don't treat me like this," he said, his voice low because he didn't want his mom to hear him arguing with his lover.

His stepmother.

There was silence on the line and Parker pleaded a second time.

"I'm sorry," he said.

"What did Kendall and her partner say?"

"They thought we were sleeping together, but I convinced them otherwise. They are going to get a warrant or something, at least that's what Mom thinks."

She seethed on the other end of the line, doing her best to maintain control.

Finally, Tori spoke. "We're going to have to speed up our plans," she said. "Use the ID I gave you and check in to a motel in South Tacoma. A rat hole. A place where no one is going to pay attention to you. I'll come and get you," she said, hanging up.

Parker grabbed his car keys, his laptop, and a jacket and climbed out the window. He was gone.

Tori rolled over and raked her fingernails down the chest of her lover.

"You have been working out," she said.

"Yeah, I have," he said.

"We have a problem," she said.

"So I heard."

She scooted closer. "Nothing we can't handle."

CHAPTER FORTY-THREE

Honolulu

As Kendall Stark sat on the overnight flight for Honolulu, she knew she was an anomaly among the other travelers. She wasn't going to Hawaii to celebrate a wedding anniversary, a birthday, a honeymoon. She was going there to find out what, if anything, had been missed when Tori Connelly's first husband died there. Of course, there'd been an investigation.

A cursory investigation at best, Kendall thought.

A retired Honolulu detective named Rikki Tyler had sent her a portion of a minuscule case file as a courtesy. It consisted of two witness statements. One was from a bystander who'd come across Tori on the beach as she screamed that something was wrong. It was to the point.

"The woman in pink was on her knees yelling about her husband. I saw the body in the surf and I pulled it ashore. I don't know CPR. The lady was too upset to do anything. I think the man was already dead. I don't know what happened. I am very sorry that the man died."

Tori's own statement was a little longer and it pretty much

echoed what she'd told her sister when she called the evening of the accident. Lainie told Kendall how she was at the *P-I* working on an article about incorporating vegetables in the Northwest landscape—a very Seattle kind of story. The kind she never wanted to write in the first place. The kind she would kill to write if only the paper had not gone under and left her jobless and now consumed by what her sister might have done. Lainie told Kendall how the newsroom seemed to go silent and how the air thickened when her sister told her.

"Zach is dead! He died in an accident! I'm coming home."

"Oh my God, Tori. What happened?"

Tori sobbed a story into the phone and, despite her being a reporter, Lainie asked no questions. It was so much of a shock that she could barely catch her breath and tell Tori that she'd be all right. Everything would be okay. She wrote down the flight number for Tori's return the next day.

"I'll pick you up," Lainie said.

"I have to go now," Tori said. "I have to make arrangements for Zach."

Lainie wanted to ask if that meant she was shipping the body back, but it seemed too touchy, too painful a thing to bring up.

Yet Tori answered the question before her sister asked it.

"I'm having him cremated and his ashes spread over here. He loved Hawaii. I don't want him to ever have to leave."

The scenario played in her mind those many years later. This was a second dead husband and a second rush to the crematory.

Why the hurry? she wondered.

As the jet engines droned outside her window, Kendall finished her complimentary mai tai and looked down at Tori's statement, given the day of the accident. A few things leaped off the pages.

"I told him that the surf was too rough. You'd think he'd listen to me. I'm an expert swimmer. I could have been on the Olympic team if I'd put my mind to it."

It was true. Tori was a great swimmer. Maybe not Olympic material, but knowing Tori as Kendall did, there was nothing she couldn't excel at—swimming included. She recalled how Lainie told her that she didn't even try to compete in swimming at South Kitsap. She didn't have Tori's speed, but she was a better diver. That rankled her sister a little and she appeared to love it. It was always hard to get the best of her if she decided she was going to do something. Piano. Cooking. Public speaking. Kendall knew Tori as the one who showed the instructors how things were done. She didn't care if they hated her for it. She never cared what anyone thought.

"We'd taken the boogie boards out after lunch. It was about 2 P.M. My husband was an experienced surfer, having summered with his grandmother in Huntington Beach, California. I'd been on a board a time or two myself. . . ."

Kendall wondered what "time or two" she was referring to? When she was younger?

Always bragging about something. So very Tori.

Also, Tori seemed to speak in a vocabulary that suggested the O'Neals were blue bloods from the East Coast. *Summered? Did she really say that?*

Kendall turned her attention back to the report.

"My husband proceeded to swim out about a quarter of a mile from the shore. It might not have been that far. The sun was bright in my eyes and I lost track of him. I was paddling around when out of the corner of my eye I caught a glimpse of an enormous rogue wave. It must have been twenty feet or maybe thirty. It is hard to tell with any certainty. It happened so fast. When the wave got to me, I hung on to my board for dear life. I didn't see what happened to Zach. I found him ten minutes later on the shore."

That was her statement. The case was closed. The Hawaiian authorities wrote it off as a tragic accident. Detective Tyler, who'd agreed to meet with her on the island, had included a truncated version of the coroner's findings: "*Victim died from blunt force trauma to the head while surfing.*"

There were four photos in the file. Only four, which in itself was surprising. There was a shot of the beach, the color of raw sugarcane, with barely a footprint to mar its smooth, broad nothingness. Off to one side of the image, she saw a paddle and a pair of sunglasses. Across the bottom of the scan was a notation that the photo had been taken at 4 P.M., "*near the location of the accident.*"

Two others came without any notation. One was the image of young man, Asian or Hawaiian. He wasn't posing, but it was clear the image was taken near the beach. Coconut palms were visible in the background. The next also included the young man, this time in front of a car with a Hawaiian plate.

What does this have to do with Zach?

The final photo was a picture of Tori, her blue eyes caught in a frightened, *terrified* gaze. The shiny glaze of her tears streaked her lightly tanned face. It wasn't a face that Kendall would have ascribed to Tori. The woman in the photograph was in complete anguish.

There was no way of faking that look.

Kendall finished her drink. She was tired but too stressed to sleep. She only had two appointments—the owner of the house where Zach had last been seen alive and the retired cop. It wasn't much, she knew, but if there had been a pattern of murder, Zach Campbell had been in the middle of it. Women serial killers often killed for profit, for greed.

Greedy was Tori to a T.

Female serial killers often employed poison. They liked killing in a way that left their hands clean. A stabbing was too up close and personal.

Kendall knew that if Tori had killed Zach, she probably had help.

Just as she probably did back in Tacoma.

People are supposed to love the weather of the Hawaiian Islands. Kendall figured she'd love it, too, if her body temperature didn't rise when she was stressed over something. From the moment she landed in Honolulu, she felt the characteristic blooms of sweat coming from her armpits and lower back. She stopped to pull the fabric of her too-tight shirt and knew why her mother had always sworn by the properties of natural fabrics. Her shirt, a light blue cotton-poly blend looked better on the hanger than it did after a five-hour flight from Seattle. She'd gone with the poly blend because she knew that she would never have to send it out to be cleaned and pressed. She liked saving time—and, given that this was not a Kitsap County junket—saving money.

She grabbed her ribbon-handled bag from the conveyor belt at the baggage claim as a group of tourists dove for their unfortunately identical black bags, the kind stewardesses used in the day when people still called them that. Now they were flight attendants, of course.

Kendall caught a shuttle bus to the car rental lot to pick up a Jeep for the short drive up to the North Shore town of Haleiwa. A Jeep sounded like fun, but it was noisy and rough driving. She wished she'd settled for a Honda Accord. She arrived at 11:30 A.M.—characteristically a little early. Early, she knew, was almost always a good thing. The address was a mile out of town, a secluded place with a large, heavy gate decorated with a family of sea turtles in bronze. They'd gone verdigris in the hot humid weather, making them look nearly lifelike in the way that metal sculpture artists can do. They know that the passage of time reveals new truths in their work.

She was hoping for the same thing.

Kiwana Morimoto met her outside on the driveway. She was an attractive woman, a fifth-generation islander with silver-streaked black hair, a broad freckled nose, and hands so tiny they'd have suited a child better than a grown woman of more than sixty.

She held out her hand and smiled warmly.

"I hope you didn't have much of a problem finding Bali House."

Kendall returned the smile. "No, no worries," she said.

"Mai tai?"

"Too early," she said. "Iced tea?"

"Sure. Follow me."

Kiwana led Kendall around the house, an '80s abode with a low roofline and a seamless bank of windows overlooking the basalt-studded shoreline. A fisherman with a pole that must have been fifteen feet long worked the current in hopes of a suppertime catch. Kendall had no idea what one would pull from those pristine waters, but with a pole like that, she expected it to be big. *Really big.*

They sat on a pair of bright blue lounge chairs under an almond tree that dropped green nuts and tangerine-colored leaves onto the brick patio.

A giant green sea turtle basked in the sun.

"I've never seen one," Kendall said.

"Yesterday," Kiwana said, "we counted eighty-seven here on the beach."

"They bring good luck, right?" Kendall said. She already knew that they did because she'd flipped through the in-flight magazine before takeoff.

"Yes, Bali House for the most part has been a blessed place."

Kendall knew that when the hostess said "for the most part," she was referring to the reason she'd come across the Pacific Ocean.

Tori O'Neal Campbell Connelly.

Kiwana disappeared into the house and Kendall watched the fisherman and the waves. When the homeowner returned, she carried a rattan tray of macadamia nut cookies and a pitcher of the pinkest iced tea the detective had ever seen.

"Guava syrup," she said, catching Kendall's eye on the pink drink.

Kendall sipped. "It's good," she said, stifling the gag reflex that kicked in as she swallowed the liquid cotton candy. "Let's talk a little," she said, swallowing hard. "Then maybe you can show me around the house."

Kiwana looked out at the water, then at her glass before answering.

"As I told you," she said, her black eyes suddenly flinty, "I've covered this ground a time or two with the police."

"I know it must be boring for you to talk about it again. I'm sorry."

The older woman let out a sigh. "It's all right. I don't have guests coming to the house until tomorrow. I have to warn you about something, however."

Kendall rotated her glass, catching shards of the sparkle of the lowering sun. "What's that?"

"There aren't many people that I've met in my life—a pretty long one at that—whom I cannot stand. Your friend's sister probably stands alone on the list, when I think about it." Her words trailed off. It was clear that this woman, this host to strangers in her North Shore ocean home, didn't like to speak ill of anyone.

"I can see that, but I still need you to help." Kendall wiped the condensation from the tall glass onto her pant leg. She wished she'd worn shorts. "I understand."

"Fine then. I couldn't stand her. I've been renting out Bali House for twenty-seven years. I've never met anyone like her."

Kendall urged Kiwana to continue without saying so. Truth be told, nothing could stop her, reticent or not. Tori had made an impression.

She always did.

Only one time did Lainie O'Neal find the courage to broach the subject of what had happened to her in juvenile detention when she switched places with Tori. It wasn't that the images of that night in 7-Pod had faded completely from view. But it was not her experiences that haunted her. It was what she imagined her sister had gone through the months of her incarceration following the accident on Banner Road. She was working as an intern at the *Whatcom Weekly* during her senior year in college. The story she'd been assigned was what she considered an easy A as far as the instructors at the university were concerned. Students in her journalism major knew that their professors could never fault a story that touched on incest, rape, or child molestation.

"Pick one of those subjects and you've got yourself a guaranteed award winner."

She dug into a story at the *Whatcom Weekly* that fit those parameters. It centered on a young woman who had been raped by a guard at the Washington Corrections Center for Women in Purdy. The woman known in the media as "Inmate Nicola B" had filed a civil claim against the state—and it was clear that the state would have to pay. Her proof was the guard's DNA match to her baby girl. After several weeks of constant but respectful requests, Lainie scored an interview with the former prisoner. It was more than the basis for a story; the meeting between the young reporter and the rape victim was life changing. Nicola, a small woman with penetrating brown eyes and a surprisingly sweet demeanor, said something that Lainie underlined four times after the interview as she built her courage to talk to Tori.

"I honestly felt that the guard owned me. I felt that I was powerless and to try to stop him from the rape was to say that my life was worth nothing. I knew that he would kill me. For the longest time, I thought that all that I'd done in life had brought me to that moment, like some sick payback from God or maybe the devil."

A few days after the interview, Lainie drove I-5 to Seattle and took the ferry to Bremerton. Tori was living in a cheap apartment close to downtown with a peekaboo view of the Manette Bridge. It wasn't a great place—ratty, dirty. A man was urinating around the corner as Lainie parked. She felt that her sister lived there because that was how she saw herself. She couldn't shake what the guard had done to her. Tori was singing at the casino then. The only suggestion that her life had any promise was the sparkle of the sequins on the costumes that hung in her closet.

"Pretty," Lainie said as Tori showed her a red sequined dress she planned on wearing that night.

"Better be, for what it costs."

"I'd like to hear you sing sometime," she said. "Dad would, too."

"I'd be too nervous to have you two there. You understand, right?"

Lainie didn't, not really. "I guess so."

Tori mentioned she was dating someone, a fellow named Zach. He was older, had a good job, and drove a nice car.

"Serious?"

"Hell no. I'm never going to be serious."

Lainie mentioned that she had been working on the prison rape story. She unveiled the case slowly, watching her sister's reaction.

But there wasn't one. At least not one that Lainie could see.

"Did anything like that go on when you were in juvy?"

Tori went into the kitchen and opened the fridge. She pulled out a couple of diet colas and handed one to Lainie. "Is this an interview?"

Lainie let out a little laugh. "No, not an interview. Just a question."

Tori shook her head and flipped the top of her soda can. "The guards there were one step above a rent-a-cop."

They sat on the sofa, a dark blue velvet sectional that was in serious need of repair.

"I honestly don't remember much of that place. I consider the memory loss to be a chief benefit of the passage of time."

Lainie looked around her sister's apartment. *Would she be living in a place like this if that car accident hadn't occurred? What would she be doing now?*

"Something happened to me that time I was there," Lainie finally said.

Tori put her hand on Lainie's knee. "You were raped?"

Lainie hesitated. She wasn't ready to tell her sister *that*. "No," she said, testing Tori a little. "But I could have been."

Tori sighed. "God, you're not going to be one of those stupid journalists who lives the story, are you, Lainie?"

"I wasn't raped," Lainie said, "but that one guard got rough with me."

Tori looked incredulous, then concerned. "Really?"

Lainie nodded. "Yes, really."

In a flash, the concern faded. Tori shrugged. "Maybe you should put that in your story. Might sell some papers."

"Nothing happened. I just thought, you know."

"No, I don't."

"I thought maybe something might have happened to *you*."

"Don't be a twit, Lainie. Sometimes I think we couldn't possibly be related—except for the fact we're twins, of course."

Lainie laughed, nervously. "Thanks. I guess I feel better now. Knowing that nothing happened to you."

"It wouldn't be because you are worried about me, Lainie. I know that much. You'd just feel guilty. You swim in guilt. You blame yourself for everything, don't you?"

"Sometimes I do."

Tori finished her cola. "Maybe we can switch again sometime. You can sing for me at the casino and I can make the world a better place." She started to laugh. "Wouldn't that be funny?"

Lainie pretended to think so, but deep down she knew what her sister thought. Her words almost never matched the truth of her heart.

If she had one, that is.

After they made their false promises to get together soon, Tori said good-bye to her sister. Her apartment was a dump. The clothes in the closet were tacky. The '70s cover tunes she was forced to sing with the subpar band were inane. She loathed almost everything about her life right then except one thing. She threw herself on the bed and started to laugh. It felt so good to know that Lainie still hurt.

Lainie's pain always made her smile.

CHAPTER FORTY-FOUR

Lakewood, Washington

Parker paid fifty-five dollars to the front desk clerk at the American Inn in Lakewood, just south of Tacoma, and went to his room. It was an old-style motel, the kind that Norman Bates would run if he'd never been arrested for being a psycho. It was a dump, used mostly by military guys cheating on their wives or the wives cheating on their husbands. A faded lithograph of a bald eagle in flight hung over the double bed, a nod to the military patrons who kept the place busy. In a way, Parker liked the crappy accommodations. It would be the last time he ever stayed in a place as dank and dirty. The world that he and Tori would inhabit would be as stunning as the sunset over the Olympic Mountains that they shared that first time they'd made love. *Real love.* Not the kid's stuff of a hand on her breasts or her mouth on his penis. But when they'd united their bodies in intercourse. It was in her car parked on a side road near Titlow Beach.

He remembered how she cried. How the tears streamed down her face as he'd given her the kind of pleasure that his father had denied her.

"I love you. I hate myself for it," she had said. "I do."

"Don't," he answered, as he touched her cheek to wipe away the tears.

"Nothing good will come of this," she said.

"You're wrong, Tori."

"This is so dangerous," she said.

Parker nodded. "But I also know how much we mean to each other."

She stared at him with her big blue eyes, shiny with tears.

"We are soul mates, star-crossed soul mates," she said. "We can never be together."

He snuggled next to her, but she pushed him away. She was thinking.

"Don't say that," he said. "There has to be a way."

Tori adjusted her blouse. She'd removed her bra and put it in her purse. Next, she slid her panties up her thighs and straightened out her skirt. She let Parker take in the silkiness of her legs and lifted her hips.

"I'll think about it," she said. "I'll find a way."

They stepped out of her car and walked to a bench with a view of the Tacoma Narrows Bridge. A man was jogging and winked at them as he ran by.

"Everyone will want this for us," he said.

"Everyone but your father," she said.

The air was cool and they felt the chill on their sweaty skin. They watched as the sun crawled behind the Olympics, burnishing the waters of the sound orange and pink.

"Reminds me of Hawaii," she said.

"I've never been there."

Tori paused a moment, thinking of the last time she'd been there.

Her first husband's death? How things had transpired on that remote beach? At the beach house?

"Oh, where we're going to live is even more beautiful,"

she said. "We'll have servants. You'll have a new car in whatever make and model you like."

"Really? Any car that I want?"

"Yes, but remember, there won't be a lot of places to drive on an island. We'll just have to find other ways to keep ourselves occupied."

She touched his inner thigh.

Parker closed his eyes and grinned at the memory of that evening rendezvous, but his smile faded as he thought of his mother. She wasn't part of this, and he shouldn't have dragged her into it by being so stupid about the money pouch from the church. His dad had been competition for his love for Tori, but his mom had never really done anything but love him.

He wished he could tell her that he loved her and that he was sorry that he'd never see her again.

CHAPTER FORTY-FIVE

Haleiwa, Hawaii
Ten years ago

It had been a warm night with trade winds that barely fluttered the knife-blade fronds of the coconut palms that leaned over the beach. Kiwana Morimoto went about her business of straightening up the lanai and the patio. She stacked chairs and pulled the cover over the bubbling cauldron that was the hot tub. Next, she turned her attention to the trio of tiki torches to make sure they were refueled so Tori Campbell didn't complain about that detail a second time.

"Look," Tori said, "I don't think we should have to haul that smelly fuel and pour it into the torch basins. That's a smelly, smelly job suitable for support staff, not guests."

The snotty tone still rankled Kiwana. She shook her head as she poured the citronella-scented oil until the liquid pooled slightly in the cone of a funnel.

Support staff, indeed, she thought.

She looked up as the sound of an argument reverberated through the jalousies of the master bedroom.

"I don't like her and I don't like the way you look at her."

It was Tori's voice. It was harsh and full of anger.

The next voice belonged to Zach. "Look at her? How is it that I look at her?"

"Like a hungry dog. Like what you are half the time."

"Why are you pulling this shit, Tori?"

Kiwana noticed that Zach's voice was resigned rather than irritated, as if they were engulfed in the continuation of a conversation they'd started earlier. The postponed Hawaiian honeymoon must have been over before they got off the plane from Seattle.

Kiwana lingered only a moment.

"Don't get me started," Tori said. "You make me sick sometimes. You act like you're tough, but you are weak. A little boy. A goddamn middle-aged man-boy who doesn't know how to take care of his wife. Yeah, you make me sick, Zach."

"Tori," he said, his voice holding a measure of anger, but as quiet as he could be.

"I don't care if she hears me," Tori said. "She means as much to me as that bitch you're banging back home."

"I'm not banging anyone. I love you."

"You don't know what love is and you don't care about me."

A door shut and Zach appeared on the lanai. He caught a glimpse of Kiwana down below on the patio, but he didn't acknowledge her presence as she hurried the lamp fuel to its storage location under the stairs.

"I'm sorry about all of that," he said.

Kiwana turned to see Zach right behind her.

"Not a problem," she said. "Sometimes sunshine makes people cranky. Too much of a good thing, you know."

He smiled at her. It was a sad smile, meant to convey appreciation of what she was saying without betraying his wife with too much of an apology for her behavior.

"Trade winds are supposed to pick up," she said, looking past him, the awkwardness of the encounter passing in the breeze.

"That'll be nice," he said.

"The morning will bring a better day than today. That's just how it is here on the North Shore. Every single day is better than the one that preceded it."

"Sounds like you should be working for the Chamber of Commerce or something," he said.

She smiled at Zach. "Actually, I'm on the board. Have been for twenty years." Her demeanor was disarming. So much so, he didn't expect the next words from her mouth.

"Your wife is maintenance high, isn't she?"

He looked at her quizzically. "You mean high mainte-nance," he said. "And, yes, she is."

"Of course you've known this all along."

He felt a little redness and it wasn't sunburn. "Yes, I have."

"She's pretty," she said.

"Yes, very."

Kiwana turned the key on the storage locker. "Pretty isn't always easy to live with."

He nodded. Kiwana told him good night. Though they were in the middle of their stay, she would never see him again.

If Kendall Stark had been surprised by the candor of the Pacific Islander in pearl-decorated slippers and a fuchsia-and-bird-of-paradise-patterned shift, she didn't say so.

She sipped her tea, the sweetness no longer nearly as cloying as it had been before the ice cubes began to melt. "You call it like it is, don't you?"

"As much as I can. At that moment, I felt sorry for the guy, but I wanted him to know that whatever he'd gotten himself into was his own doing. You know?"

Kendall nodded.

"Tori is beautiful, no doubt, but so are these." Kiwana touched a necklace of shark's teeth that she wore low, almost into the slightly crinkly cleavage that spilled over the front of her dress.

"So you think she had something to do with Zach's death."

"It isn't for me to say."

"But you want to say something about it, don't you?"

"More tea?"

"No, thanks." Kendall left her eyes on Kiwana, demanding an answer with a smile on her face at the same time.

"You know what I think. I told the police. I cannot add any more. I wasn't on the beach. I didn't see the accident."

Kendall asked Kiwana about the photograph of the paddle.

"Do you want what I know or what I think?"

Kendall nodded at her and sipped her tea. "Thinking is good, but what do you know?"

She looked upward, pondering what she knew. "I know of only one thing for sure. When they went off that morning, I sent them with boogie boards and paddles."

"So I saw," Kendall said, still conjuring up the image of the photograph.

"No, what you saw was one paddle."

"One paddle," Kendall repeated.

"The police only recovered one paddle. *Hers*. The other one was gone."

"Lost in the ocean."

"Maybe," she said.

"Paddles are small and the Pacific is enormous. I know what you're getting at."

"I know—*not think*—that the paddle would have come ashore right there. The current is dependable as Sunday dinner with Grandma."

Kendall sized her up. Kiwana was a no-nonsense type and her certainty was convincing.

"So you're suggesting that the missing paddle was something else. A weapon."

"I'm not *Hawaii 5-0*, Detective Stark. I'm a landlady. All I know is that I made a note of the missing paddle and I billed Tori for it when she returned to the mainland. She put up a real fuss, that one. She never paid me."

"You are tough," Kendall said, with enough of a rise in her voice to convey a touch of humor, a little irony.

Kiwana didn't care much for it.

"You can think whatever you want. But I'd still like to be paid. Maybe you'll pay. She's your friend's twin sister. I'll go get the bill."

Kiwana got up and went inside. Kendall watched a trio of sea turtles toss like green Frisbees in the surf. When Kiwana returned, she handed Kendall a handwritten bill and she found herself digging into her overstuffed purse for her checkbook. It was an old debt that Kendall was sure should have been forgiven long ago.

"I'm a businesswoman," Kiwana said. "Your friend's sister got the best of me those years ago. Now the score is settled. You pay. We're even."

Kendall was tempted to say that the score between Tori and Lainie could never be made even, but she refrained from doing so.

It could never be settled fairly between her and Tori, either.

* * *

Kendall drove through Haleiwa with its macaw-colored shaved ice and overpriced beachwear before heading up the coast toward the place where Tori and Zach had spent their last moments together. She had a map and GPS in her rental car, but didn't need either. Oahu was an island with mountains so rugged that there was no way, and probably no need, to traverse them with a highway. The melty-hot roadways hug the coast, and though the speed limits are ridiculously slow, there usually is no rush to get anywhere.

She parked in a small lot across from the mosquito-buzzing small planes of the Dillingham Airport. Save for the noise of shorebirds, the surf, and the small sightseeing planes, the beach felt desolate.

Kiwana had told her only the locals really got that far out of the way. Tori had asked the night before things went so wrong where they could go to celebrate their marriage "as if we were on a desert island all to ourselves."

"So I told her where to go," she had said. "Not really *where* to go, if you know what I mean. Now I wished I'd done just that. When I had the chance, you know."

"We can't like everyone," Kendall had said.

"No, we can't. God wants us to. But in my years doing what I do, I have to accept what I cannot change. That woman was one of those."

Kendall walked over the leaf-littered sand to where the foam of the waves lapped things clean every day. She went past a couple of young men with fishing spears and a cache of beer in a Styrofoam chest. A few steps closer on the hot sands and she could see they were younger than she thought, no more than fifteen. Kendall was certain the beer and the spears were a bad idea, but she said nothing. She looked down at the photo of the beach taken by the Honolulu Police Department the afternoon of the accident. Her eyes ran the flat line of the horizon. A lone surfer plied the waves breaking a mile offshore where coral and basalt had formed a broad reef. The sun was lower in the sky than in the photo. She looked up the coast where she could see the outcroppings of Kaena Point, partly veiled in a thin layer of volcanic ash and fog the locals called vog. Kendall didn't know what she was really looking for because so many years had passed, it was possible the sands had shifted and moved the most desirable part of the beach out past the landmark that Kiwana had given her.

"The place where it happened is directly in front of the palm swallowed by the banyan," she had said.

That was easy enough to find. In the way that only God could devise, a coconut palm had somehow managed to punch a hole in the canopy of a sprawling banyan tree just off the highway. It looked like the tufted head of a peacock emerging from a mountain of dark green foliage. It could not be missed by anyone with a sense of imagination or a need for shade.

The heat was getting to Kendall once more. She'd coated her exposed skin in a waterproof sunblock that made her sweat. Every time she touched her arms, she felt the oily slick of a product she'd never use again. It was called Banana Boat, but she figured Banana Peel would have been a more appropriate moniker.

Kendall looked at the second photo, the one retrieved from the victim's camera. It was Tori. She was wearing a hot pink bikini and no one would argue that she could get away with donning one. In fact, if she'd wandered past one of those Hawaiian Tropic bikini contests on Waikiki Beach, she might have been confused with the winner. Without oil and the help of the implants yet to come. Probably without an entry form, too. She was simply stunning. Her blond hair seemed more golden than in any other photo Kendall had seen. Her eyes were blue, but not the vapid kind of blue that suggests a swimming pool or charmless sky. There was intensity, a depth of lapis.

Kendall looked at the necklace around her friend's sister's neck. It seemed so fitting.

Shark's teeth, she thought.

CHAPTER FORTY-SIX

Haleiwa
Ten years ago

Maryanne Milton was mad at her husband, an airman stationed in Hawaii. *Mad* was hardly the word. She was bitter, angry, and hell-bent on revenge. He'd cheated on her with another woman, a secretary who worked at the base. To add insult to injury, it was a woman Maryanne had known and admired. Maryanne filled a cooler with beer and drove out to the beach near Dillingham. She figured that she'd drink the beer, then walk out into the creamy surf and let the waves carry her to something that approximated peace. *Tranquility.* A place away from the embarrassment and torment of marrying the wrong man and having a father who'd been right on the money about the louse. Other unhinged women might have sought revenge by killing their husbands, but not Maryanne. She figured that the burden of her suicide would haunt him for the rest of his life. She parked her yellow VW and dragged her cooler to a deserted spot where the waves struck the shoreline with a fury that suited her mood.

She turned the dial on her radio to find the last song she'd hear before she died. A suicide soundtrack is harder to come by than the happy can imagine. Alanis Morissette was too angsty. A tears-in-her-beer country song she couldn't place was too maudlin. Maryanne wanted something melancholy, but settled on an angry woman's anthem, Linda Ronstadt's "You're No Good."

Old school, but oh-so-right.

As she settled into her misery, she noticed a man and a woman down the beach. The woman in a pink bathing suit was on top of the man while another man kneeled behind her. Maryanne averted her eyes when she figured out what they were doing.

They were making love.

Great, she thought. *Rub my face in it. I can't get one man. And she has two. I wonder if they are cheating on their spouses as they act out their little* From Here to Eternity *scene.*

The next time Maryanne looked, the woman had moved her blanket closer to shore and was sitting alone.

Maryanne was planning her next move, her last act of desperation and revenge. She was wondering how her family would react, how the woman who'd stolen her husband would feel.

She looked up to the sound of sirens as police and aid cars converged on the road up the beach. The woman in the pink bathing suit was waving her arms and screaming. In less than an hour, paradise had turned into a nightmare.

Half drunk but sobering up quickly, Maryanne ditched her remaining beer in a trash can, and returned to her car. The hot sands of the beach crunched like tin cans under her feet. A dose of reality had saved her life.

But not the man who'd been making love with the woman on the beach.

She saw on the news that night that one of the men had

died during a boogie board accident. As far as she knew, the trio hadn't been boogying on anything, much less a board. She didn't say anything to anyone about what she'd seen.

She didn't want to explain why she'd driven up to the North Shore.

A fifty-five-year-old woman named Selena Jonas sat at her kitchen table in Haleiwa. Her toes tapped a Morse code of agitation on a well-worn linoleum floor. She shook her head at the late-night circumstances as she eyed the wall-mounted kitchen phone. It stayed mute as it had all day. *What did you do now, Ronnie?* It was a rhetorical question, one she had asked over and over from the time he was small. Shoplifting at seven. Drugs at eleven. Juvenile detention at fourteen. Ronnie had been nothing but trouble. Over and over. He'd promised to get his act together. He said that he'd sober up, go back to school. He agreed to a curfew. All of that had been a big, sad lie.

She only moved from her chair to unhook the receiver to make sure that the line was not dead. Cigarettes piled up like Pickup sticks in a Scotch plaid beanbag-based ashtray. Her husband, a Haleiwa boat mechanic, entered the kitchen and patted her gently on the shoulder. He told her that whatever had happened, Ronnie would be all right.

It was a hope. Nothing more. Deep down, Selena knew it.

The police arrived three days after Ronnie went missing. The teenager's body had washed up on the northern shore of Kauai, the island neighbor to the west of Oahu. A female tourist walking the beach near Kilauea found him. The sight was horrific beyond imagination.

Parts of his face and the soft tissue of his abdomen were missing.

"Juvenile sea turtles," the officer told her, "made a mess of your boy. You don't want to see him."

Serena had braced herself for the news, and yet her resolve to hold it together was crumbling. "How did he die?"

"Looks like he hit his head on a rock or something."

"You aren't going to cut him up, are you?" Her eyes were raining tears.

"Yes, ma'am. If you mean are we going to do an autopsy? The answer is yes."

Selena cried until she could cry no more. After that she could never look at the image of a green sea turtle without thinking of what had happened to her boy.

In Haleiwa that was very hard to do. Turtles were everywhere.

The next day the Honolulu *Advertiser* carried a story in the back of the news section. It was only five lines, the kind of article that means nothing to anyone but those who loved Ronnie Jonas.

Haleiwa Boy Dies
In Surfing Accident

Without mentioning Zach Campbell by name, the piece noted that the Jonas boy's death been the second of two deaths in the area in three days.

It was the only time the deaths were linked in any manner.

The boy was loading his beat-up Chevy Cavalier with a stereo when Tori Campbell first saw him. She'd been walking in the neighborhood at first light; an obnoxious cacophony of tropical birds fed the irritation and anger she'd felt toward Zach. With each step, the anger bubbled over.

"Shut up," she said to the birds. "Shut it up!"

She thought of all the things she could do to make her life better. She could leave him, of course. He'd only married her as arm candy and there was no genuine love between them. And yet, the idea of just walking away seemed like a futile waste of resources.

His resources.

He had the house before they married. He had the bank account. He had everything she ever wanted. The only problem was *him*.

Then she saw the boy. A beat later, he saw her.

"My stereo," he said.

"Your stereo, my ass," she said moving closer to his car. The backseat was filled with valuables that she knew never could have belonged to him. She reached for her cell phone.

"Please," he said. "Do not call the police. It will mean big trouble for me."

She moved closer, unafraid. "You should have thought about that before you stole from that house, you stupid little thug," Tori said, indicating the beachfront two-story that had been the source of his booty.

"I can put it back," he said, his eyes widening.

She had been young like that boy and she knew how hard it was to climb back toward respectability after the world decides who and *what* you are. His fear was useful to her.

"No, keep it."

"I can go?"

She held a camera to her eye and clicked twice, first an image of Ronnie. The second time, she took a photo of the car, its Hawaiian license plate clearly visible.

Like the proverbial frog in the cool water on boil, Ronnie Jonas had no idea that the kettle was over a flame.

"I want you to come back here tonight. I will have something for you to do."

"I don't want any trouble," he said.

"Baby, you don't have anything to worry about." She turned and walked away. If the boy came as she thought he might, everything would be perfect. Taking another party into her plan had really no risk. The other party would never live long enough to say a word.

Tori knew that she'd made a mistake on Banner Road. She would think twice about letting a witness live again.

CHAPTER FORTY-SEVEN

Haleiwa
The present

In her room at the Haleiwa Beach Inn Kendall fiddled with the AC, which someone had set on chill-blaster mode. She'd gone from 90 degrees to 55 and was shaking from the unpleasantly cold air. She'd packed light, too light. She found a beach towel and wrapped it around her shoulders like a shawl. All she'd learned that day was that no one liked Lainie's sister, and her husband had died in a tragic accident. *Things she already knew.*

She changed into an ice blue sundress and sandals and touched up her makeup. A few hours on the beach and she'd already lost the pallid skin that characterizes those from Seattle or the undead. Not a burn, but almost. Even so, she looked pretty good. Rikki Tyler, the retired Honolulu detective who had investigated the Zach Campbell beach accident, had agreed to meet her for dinner in the bar at Haleiwa Joe's. She took the towel-shawl off her shoulders, stepped into the warmth of a beautiful Hawaiian evening, and made her way to the restaurant.

Tyler, half English and half Hawaiian, had all the good attributes of both. His hair was jet black and thick, and his brown eyes sparkled with intelligence.

Kendall introduced herself at the hostess station. She explained the situation with Jason Reed and her role in the investigation in Kitsap County. By way of full disclosure, she also confirmed that she had gone to high school with the O'Neal sisters.

"I used to be a friend of Tori's," she said.

"Well, I used to be a cop," Rikki said, his white teeth gleaming in the dim light of the restaurant. "Until my wife told me she'd had enough. She wanted to return to Idaho. We moved. But Idaho is no place for a Hawaiian boy."

Kendall understood completely. "There's no ocean beach, for sure."

"That's why I'm back here, working at the Walmart in Aiea as a security guard. You caught me on my day off and, frankly, you reminded me of a case that I always wondered about."

"What did you wonder about, Rikki?" she asked as they took their seats next to a boisterous group from the mainland.

He shook his head. "Want a drink?"

Kendall ordered a Blue Hawaiian.

"When in Haleiwa," she said.

Rikki might have been retired, but he was still very interested in Tori Campbell. "What happened after your friend returned to the mainland?"

Kendall studied her unnaturally blue drink, fiddled with the pink paper umbrella that came with it, and took her time answering. "Good question. She put the house she and Zach shared up on the market within the first day or two. She sold it in a week. She bought an expensive house on Oyster Bay about three months later. It was way more money than I thought she had, but of course I hadn't considered the life insurance."

"Do you know how much she got?"

"Not really. Lainie was working at the *P-I* then. She told me she asked a friend on the business desk to look into the real estate deal. This was prior to the whole world being at your fingertips on the Internet. When a cell phone was only good for calling someone. She paid cash."

"Must have made some major dough selling the first place," Rikki said.

"Not really. They owed a lot on it. She maybe came away with a few thousand."

"How much was the new house?"

"Four hundred grand. That's chump change for a place here, but in Bremerton, we're talking a Bill Gates–type property." She paused a second, rethinking her statement. "Maybe not quite Gates."

"She paid for it with insurance proceeds," he said.

She nodded. "I guess so."

Rikki gulped the last of his drink, and motioned to the bartender for another. "What's the victim in Tacoma worth to her?"

"Two million."

"She's trading up, isn't she?"

"Tori was always was that kind of a girl."

They talked a bit more after a waitress left a plate of coconut shrimp and mango chutney—just delicious enough to halt the conversation a moment.

"You brought something for me," Kendall said, indicating his briefcase.

"Like all retired detectives working at Walmart," Rikki said with a self-deprecating smile, "I have photocopies of some of my old cases stashed at home. The criteria, not surprising to you, I'm sure, were the cases that I felt would be the subject of interest someday.

"How many of those? Just four. Your friend's sister's case made the cut."

He opened his beat-up alligator briefcase and produced a small stack of papers. Lainie could see a few more than what she'd found in the North Junett house.

"What did you make of the crime scene?"

"Other than what I wrote?"

"Right. I mean you mention the terrain, the wide grooves in the sand, but you don't really say what they were. Or if it was related."

Rikki nodded. "Yeah, the grooves in the sand, as you call them, were strange indeed. They led from the parking lot to where they were sitting on the beach. We thought there might have been a cooler or a board dragged, but we couldn't track 'em."

"How come there were no photos showing them?"

Rikki fanned out the remaining pages. "I guess I blame myself for that. We didn't do a good job securing the scene. We focused on the body and recovering it, not the entire stretch of beach. It is, after all, a pretty big beach."

Kendall, adept at reading upside down as any reporter, noticed the toxicology report.

"What did tox say?" she asked.

Rikki flipped through the three pages that were the sum of the finding from the lab in Honolulu.

"Alcohol in his system, some trace of a sleeping pill, and—this was the only interesting part—there was some chlorine in the seawater in his lungs."

"Chlorine?"

"Trace, really. But interesting."

"Yeah, I mean, you keep Hawaii's beaches spotless, but not *that* clean."

Rikki laughed nervously, then became completely serious. "I think it was an error at the lab, Kendall. We were going through a bad time back then. Had a flake in the lab who thought that processing evidence was ignoring it."

Kendall understood. While Kitsap County had never had such a scandal, other jurisdictions had a rash of them.

"Tell me about her. Tell me about your interview with her."

"Memorable," he said, grateful for the change in topic.

"Do you mean to make me cry? Do you get off on seeing a girl tormented for no reason?"

Rikki Tyler rolled his eyes and sipped his iced tea. The air-conditioning in the police station was working overtime, sending a cool stream throughout the space. After her husband's body was recovered, the young woman with the stunning tan, blond hair, and slender body had exhibited enough evasive and combative behavior that an interview off scene was in order.

"You are something else, aren't you?"

Tori Campbell looked at the mirrored surface of the window behind him. She knew there were prying eyes looking at her, studying her like she was an exhibit in a greenhouse or maybe even a zoo.

Yes, that's how they'd been treating her. Like a caged animal.

"Do you mean to offend me, officer? I'm a visitor here in your so-called island paradise and my husband has died."

"Detective," Tyler said, now drilling his stare into her blue swimming-pool eyes. "The officers around here are the

man and woman waiting outside to escort you to the bathroom. Should you need to go."

Tori shifted in her chair. It was metal, wobbly, and not at all comfortable. It made a grating noise when she moved. She sat still.

"I don't need to go anywhere but back to the mainland. Home."

"You're not going home."

"Oh, but I am. I watch Law and Order. *I know my rights and I know you can't hold me."*

She stopped herself for a second, thinking about the possibility of using the Flirt she knew so well. The Flirt was definitely a skill not to be wasted. "My lawyer will be here in five minutes."

"All right," he said. "Maybe you'll want to pass the time telling me about your husband and his little swimming accident. I talked with the rental house owner. Says you two weren't getting along."

"She's a bitch," she said, pressing her palms into the table. "I won't say anything more about it."

"What happened out there at the beach, Ms. Campbell?"

She stared at him. Her eyes were now glacial. She wasn't saying another word.

"Don't want to talk about it, do you?"

"I don't—I won't—talk about any of it. None of it whatsoever. But nice try, officer."

"Detective."

"So you keep reminding me. Or maybe you're just reminding yourself."

Tori had meant to get a rise out of him and she could see by the redness of his cheeks she'd been somewhat successful.

Rikki Tyler's lips tightened. His tenseness and anger made Tori relax. It was as if she was sucking the power from

*him and she wound him tighter and tighter around her fin-
ger. He wanted her, she was sure. All men did. He wanted to
rip her clothes off right then and there, and make love to her
on that crummy metal table. Banging around. Dragging its
legs over the cement floor where all the people on the other
side of the two-way mirror could just watch.*

Sure, he wanted her. They all did.

*Tori didn't say another word. She let the detective stew in
his own juices. He'd be better at that than what he was trying
to do with her. That's how she saw it.*

*The pair sat there silently, fluorescents buzzing overhead,
the rat-tat-tat of a woman's heels against the tiled floor outside. People were moving on the other side of the glass, and
then the door swung open.*

*Lyndon Knox, a fiftyish man with a slight belly but the
posture of a man who knew how to wear a really good suit,
entered the room. He was sweaty and in a hurry. He was
well known among Honolulu law enforcement as a gun for
hire who delivered the goods.*

"She's done," he said. "I'm here. We're all done."

The detective gave the lawyer an almost sheepish grin.
"Hi, Lyn. Didn't figure she'd have the dough and the con-
nections to hire the likes of you."

Tori smiled at her newly hired lawyer. "I'm tired. Can I
go home? Maybe we could stop somewhere and get something to eat. As rough as this ordeal has been, I still find the
need to have something to eat."

*The detective held his tongue. He wanted more than any-
thing to say to her,* Eat? Said the spider to the fly?

*Instead, he stood, poked his head out of the interview
room. He spoke in low tones with a couple of other police
department suits and returned.*

"Okay," he said. "You're right. She can go."

He spoke directly to the lawyer, without even looking at the beautiful woman sitting there.

"Don't go far," he said. "We're not done with you."

Tori looked at her lawyer. "Tell him that I have plans. My sister's in from out of town and I'm going to take her on a little trip."

Lyn Knox didn't see any need to relay the message. It was clear what she said.

"I'll make sure Ms. Campbell is available if you need her again."

Tori Campbell uncrossed her long, shapely legs and stood. She smoothed out the wrinkles in her sheer skirt and swung her big white leather purse with the oversize silver buckle over her shoulder and started walking toward the door. She rounded her shoulder with a stretch of her arm, exhaled.

"Lyndon," she said, sweetly, "I really want to have dinner with you tonight. I've been so lonely. I've been through so much."

The detective shook his head.

This lady has game. And I doubt I've heard the last of her.

"One more thing," Kendall said, getting out the photos that Lainie had sent to her. From her side of the table, she slid the image of the Hawaiian boy, his dark eyes flashing fear into the lens of the camera. "Do you know why this photo was among Tori's things?"

Rikki held the photo in his fingertips to the flame of the candle in the center of the table. He shook his head, thinking.

"Wait a second," he said. "That's Ronnie Jonas."

"Who's that?"

"He's a local kid. Died the same week that Zach Campbell did."

"Is there a connection?" Kendall asked.

"There is now."

Her bag packed, Kendall Stark made a beeline through the hotel lobby past the brochure rack that touted all of the luaus, booze cruises, and authentic lei-making classes that promised tourists "a real Hawaiian" experience. She'd had none of that on this trip. She got in her rental Jeep and drove past the farmers' market and along the beach road to the highway to Honolulu. She had one last stop before heading home.

She wanted to say good-bye to Kiwana at Bali House.

She found her just inside the turtle-decorated gate, cutting a bouquet of bird-of-paradise, long green stems topped with spikes of orange and purple.

"Did you find what you were looking for?" Kiwana asked.

"I don't know. Maybe. I talked with the detective last night. He told me something that got me thinking a little."

"What was that?" She put down the flowers and opened the gate.

She pulled her rental car inside and Kiwana shut the gate.

"Come on. I have more of the tea you loved so much."

Kendall didn't have the heart to tell her host that the tea was beyond sickeningly sweet.

"No, thank you."

Kiwana laughed. "No worries. I know it wasn't your favorite. I have pop, too. Come and sit. Let's watch the ocean. Turtles are coming today."

They sat on the white wooden lounge chairs facing the pummeling surf. Kiwana looked over at the spa and shook her head. "Darn thing's turning green." She got up, fished around the closet that held the boogie boards and tiki torch oil, and produced a bottle of Clorox.

"Seawater is lovely when the sea can churn it and keep it clean."

"The spa is seawater?"

"Yes. Don't tell anyone, but I do spike it with chlorine bleach. Just enough to keep it fresh."

Kendall set down her cola, but she missed the rattan side table and the plastic glass scuttled to the patio.

"Oh, no," she said. "I'm sorry. I have to leave."

"It's all right, dear. That's why we use plastic."

"It isn't all right. Not at all," she said, getting up. "I have to go. I have a flight to catch."

And, she knew, the truth to confront.

Across the Pacific, another dream came. Lainie reached for a sleeping pill. She curled up in the empty bed, pulling the sheets up high to her neck as if she would choke the life out of herself just to get some sleep.

Sleep without dreams. Slumber without nightmares. Was that too much to ask?

The images came to her slowly. The water boiled and roiled . . . a seemingly toxic brew. She was naked and she wasn't alone. She felt a man's hands on her waist.

"I'm going down," he said.

His voice was husky, deep.

She watched as he lowered himself in the water, as she arched her back and spread her thighs apart.

She turned and spoke in the direction of some bushes.

"Now," she said.

"All right," another voice answered, also male, but much younger.

She clamped her thighs around the man's head and

grabbed his hair with both hands. She pressed with all her might. The man, who'd gone down to please her, was fighting under the roiling waters.

"Hit him now!" she said.

An oar dropped into the hot tub. A small amount of red bloomed in the water.

"Let's get him in the car," she said.

CHAPTER FORTY-EIGHT

Kitsap County

"Tori! What am I going to do now?"

Lainie and Tori stood outside their car. The smell of gasoline and the crunch of broken glass, torn leather, and acrid striations of burned rubber fell over Banner Road like the remnants of an S&M parade gone terribly wrong. Or, at the very least, more wrong than usual.

"We've got to get Jason out of the car," Lainie said. Her blue eyes were nearly black as her pupils soaked in every drop of light in the darkness of the stretch by the Banner Jump. The fun of the rise and fall of the car had ended in a nightmare. Airborne had become terror. The sisters, working in tandem, battered and bleeding from the crash, hoisted the limp teenage boy from the overturned car and laid him out by the roadside.

"Is he alive?" Lainie asked. She was shaking and bleeding from a small gash in her forehead. "I didn't mean for this to happen. I was going too fast. We were having fun. I thought it was fun."

"He's alive," Tori said, bending closer.

"What am I going to do? I'm going to go to jail!"

Tori put her hand on her sister's shoulder. She was bleeding, too. "He's going to be fine."

Lainie was crying then, bending over Jason and looking up at Tori.

"I already have one ticket! I'm going to be in so much trouble. I'm going to go to jail!"

She was referring to a minor-in-possession ticket that she got after a party in Manchester earlier in the year. Their father had gone ballistic and Tori had reveled in the fact that "Lainie the Perfect" had gotten a little taste of being on the outs.

Lainie, inconsolable and in full panic mode, was crying as she bent over her sister's boyfriend. Tori went to turn off the ignition. She looked up to see the headlights of an approaching car.

The sheriff already? Couldn't be. It would take ten minutes to get anyone out in that southernmost part of the county.

She squinted in the headlights as the vehicle parked on the opposite side of the road. The door opened and the driver stepped onto the pavement, which was glittering with glass.

"It's that druggie Mikey Walsh," Tori said.

"That's okay," Lainie said. "Jason's alive. He's going to be all right."

Jason Reed's voice was weak. Not really a whisper, but the kind of soft voice one uses when speaking from the heart, which he was. Tori cradled his head in her arms, while Lainie went over to talk to Mikey Walsh.

"I'm not gonna make it," he said.

"You are, too," Tori said. "Help will be here in a few minutes. God, I hate this county!"

"I made a big mistake," he said.

"It wasn't your fault. Lainie went too fast."

He shook his head. "No, not that."

Tori heard Mikey talking with Lainie, telling her to calm down.

"This is my fault! All my fault!"

She leaned closer to her boyfriend.

"I don't love you, Tori. I love Kendall. But I screwed things up."

She didn't think she heard him correctly and she leaned closer. She wanted to scream at Lainie and Mikey for talking so loudly.

"What are you saying?" she asked.

His pale blue eyes were open, staring at her, unblinking. He spoke and his words trailed off to a whisper, caught up in the wind of the night, but indelible in Tori's memory.

Tori O'Neal was crouched over Jason Reed as Mikey Walsh rounded the Taurus. The young man who was tweaking and partying just moments before was now in a sweat. He held his arms close to his chest in an attempt to control his pounding heart. He didn't know what to do. He thought of the drugs in his vehicle, and he'd hoped that if the sheriff came, they'd consider him a Good Samaritan and not someone who they needed to bust.

Why didn't I take the Valley Road? I could have avoided this mess.

It appeared as if Tori was consoling Jason, though she was not saying anything. Her eyes were rimmed in red. Even in the stabbing beam of the headlights across the road, it was obvious that the unthinkable had just occurred.

"He's dead," she said. "Jason is dead!"

By then Lainie joined them, slumping onto the gravel roadside and crying so loudly that the nearest neighbors surely would have heard her, even if they'd missed the sound of the breaking glass, twisting metal, and the skidding tires of the crash itself.

"Oh, God," Lainie said. "What have I done?"

Tori reached for her sister and hugged her. "You didn't do anything," she said. "I was driving. This is my fault."

Lainie studied Tori's face. She was offering a solution, an unselfish gift if ever there was one.

Had she heard her right?

"What are you saying, Tori?"

"I'm saying that *I* was driving. This accident is on me."

As Tori spoke, she caught a glimpse of something in Mikey Walsh's expression. She was adept at reading people. Better than her sister. But she wasn't sure what it was that his drugged-out and fearful expression meant.

Just how much had he heard? How much had he seen?

Mikey turned to Lainie.

"I thought you said you were driving."

Lainie was practically on top of Jason's body, sobbing. She looked at Mikey and started to speak, but Tori cut her off.

"Are you on something right now? Do you need to have a drug test when the sheriff gets here? Or are you just stupid? I was driving. I said so."

Lainie never told anyone about what happened that night. There was no point in it. She was sure that Tori would get off without having to go to jail. It was an accident and she'd never done anything wrong. What she didn't know was that the Kitsap County authorities had reached their limit when it came to teenagers and their dangerous joyriding around the county.

Tori O'Neal was going to be the example that everyone remembered.

* * *

Mikey Walsh had been a loose end and a pathetic one at that. The former speed-freak-turned preacher had been lurking in the darkness of Tori's memory for fifteen years. She reviled loose ends. She knew from experience that she alone was the only one worthy of being a witness to whatever it was she'd done. As she packed her suitcase, she knew that her plan had its share of risks. But the rewards were so very great. Two million reasons would easily tip the scales in favor of taking the risk.

She wasn't sure if she was being watched by the police, reporters, anyone. With Darius Fulton's arrest and the refusal of bail, eyes were not on her right then.

"He called me from the jail," she told Kaminski. "Threatened to kill me. He said that if he couldn't have me, no one could."

Despite all of that, Tori was not a woman who wanted to take any unnecessary chances. Not when she was so close to the prize.

When Lainie arrived to "help" after the shooting, Tori sized up the one attribute that she needed to alter.

Her hair.

Lainie's hair was at least two shades darker, and shorter. It was the kind of haircut and color that screamed "average" and she knew it wouldn't be hard to mimic. Tori went into the bathroom with a pair of scissors and a box of honey wheat hair coloring. A few snips, a slathering of the drugstore-brand dye, and it was over.

It took all of a half hour to alter her appearance from stunning to merely attractive. It was a trade-off she was willing to make for a very short time. The matter of her breasts, however, was a slight problem. They were larger than Lainie's. She purchased a bra that, while uncomfortable, would minimize what her surgeon had given her. Tori didn't mind binding them. They were never for her anyway.

Finally, she put on a little black dress that was a duplicate of the one that Lainie had bought at Nordstrom for the class reunion. It was not something that Tori would ever have picked for herself. Lainie's taste in attire was lackluster—from dress to heels to accessories. She was a road map to mediocrity.

Always had been.

She studied herself in the mirror.

Something wasn't right. What was it?

Tori smiled at her reflection. "Oh, yes, that," she said aloud. It was a small detail, but one that might be noticed. She picked up a rattail comb and changed the direction of her part.

"Hi, Lainie," she said into the mirror.

Inside, she knew relief would come once she took care of the final loose end in her life.

Her sister.

CHAPTER FORTY-NINE

Tacoma

Parker opened his laptop and clicked on the icon for the web-cam. Tori had her back to the camera. She was wearing the red teddy. She'd told him that she only wore that on special occasions—the times when they'd be together. In the hotel in Seattle that first summer. The time they'd made love on the soapstone island in the kitchen. The night his father was set aside for good. Parker was about to speak when he noticed a man's voice, then some laughter. He turned up the volume because he couldn't quite make out what was being said. Despite what the Radio Shack clerk had promised when he made the purchase, the sound quality was only good when the person talking directed his or her attention right at the built-in microphone.

"He thinks I'm pregnant," she said.

"I know. Stupid sap," the male voice said.

Parker couldn't believe what he was hearing. *It had to be some kind of a joke. Who was Tori talking to?*

Tori crawled onto the bed, unaware that she was being watched.

"The other day when I had a glass of wine, he told me that it might hurt our baby. I told him that the doctor said that a glass of wine or two is good for it."

"You've got him wrapped around your finger," the man said.

Parker started to shake. None of this could or should be happening—she was his soul mate. They'd done the unthinkable, all for love. All that they'd ever wanted had been built on a big lie.

"Young, dumb, and full of cum," she said.

Who was she talking to? He couldn't see. The voice seemed a little familiar, but not so much that he could identify it.

Parker slammed the laptop shut, imagining that the noise reverberated all the way to North Junett Street and startled her.

Her. She. The woman he loves. The woman who told him he was a man. The woman who had asked him to prove his love with a gun and a knife.

Parker started to cry, guttural, deep—heart-wrenchingly so. He buried his face in a pillow as he sobbed and screamed. It was his eighteenth birthday. Everything that he thought was true was a lie. He was not a man. He was a fool. He got up and rifled through his bag as if there was something he could take to end his life. The medicine to control his acne probably couldn't do that much. He looked for a razor, but he'd forgotten to pack one.

He only shaved once a week.

He thought of his dad. How his dad had showed him how to shave with the back of a comb when he was five.

"Dad, I'm sorry. Dad, can you hear me? Forgive me."

Parker was frantic. There was nothing there to end his life, and once that thought was accepted as reality, perfect, clear, there was only one thing to do. If he could not die, he'd have to face up to what he'd done.

* * *

When Parker Connelly closed his eyes, all he saw was a river of red. When he held his hand over his ears, he could still hear the guttural sounds made by the minister he'd murdered. His hand could still feel the grip of the blade and the ease with which he sunk it into Mikey Walsh's neck and abdomen, draining him of blood and life. And while he doubted he could ever shake the images, the smells, the experience of murder, he didn't want to give voice to what he did afterward. Not to her. Not to Tori. He didn't tell her how he'd sat down and cried before going inside to do what she needed done.

He knew he was in love with her. That he wanted to be with her for the rest of his life. But he also knew how wrong all of that was. How twisted the fantasy had become. It was as if he'd been sleeping, dreaming, and now he was awake.

He closed his eyes.

Red.

He started to cry out, but the sounds he made into the pillow were the same sounds that Pastor Mikey had made.

That his father had made.

He felt that his life was over. That there was nothing to do but kill himself. Stop the pain. Stop all of the red.

But he couldn't. He couldn't do that to his mother. She deserved more than that.

He opened his phone and called her.

"Mom," he said.

"Parker. I've been worried sick. Where are you?"

"Mom, I want to come home."

"Come home, baby. I'll come and get you."

"Mom, I killed that man."

Laura refused to cry. "I know. I know you did. Why? Honey?"

"I can't talk about it."

"You're calling me because you can. I'll come and get you."

"Mom, it's Tori," he said.

"Why?" she asked.

"She's in love with me. I'm in love with her. She said we could be together. She wants us to get married."

"Parker, I don't know. . . ." Laura wanted her son to come home. She didn't want to push him away. "We can talk about all of that."

"She shot Dad. She made me shoot him, too. He was dead when I shot him. I just couldn't do what she wanted."

Laura was crying now but fighting hard to sound calm.

"Where are you? I'll come and get you."

"Mom, she's going to kill her sister. She's going to switch places with Lainie."

"Where are you, Parker?"

"I'm at the American Inn off I-5, south of Tacoma."

"Don't move. I'm coming to get you."

Laura Connelly had not held her son that closely in a long time. He'd not said a word the entire way home from the motel. He stared out the window, and she let him be quiet. Whatever was really hurting him was deep, deeper than she could understand. She knew enough not to provoke him. When they got inside, she led him to the sofa, where they sat together. Almost immediately, he'd slumped against her, letting her absorb his pain. In every way, except for the awareness she had that he was nearly a grown man, it felt like a mother holding her baby. He was taller than her, stronger than her. Yet there he was warm, sweating, sobbing quietly in her arms.

Between gulps of air and a torrent of tears he let some words pass his lips.

"I thought she loved me," he said. "She said she did."

Laura patted him gently, almost so softly that she wasn't sure he'd even feel it.

"I know," she said, though she did not know at all. "I'm sure she did."

He shuddered a little, unwinding, unspooling. "She and I were going to get married on Monday. We were going to fly away to Bermuda."

Laura knew how fragile Parker was just then. She knew what kind of a manipulator Tori could be, but even this was far beyond anything she could have guessed.

There was no girlfriend. At least not a girlfriend that she could have imagined for her son.

"You were wanting that to happen," she said, almost a question.

Parker took a breath. "No, Mom. She and I were soul mates. We're going to have a baby."

A baby? This was too much. It seemed an impossibility. He was only a teenager. She was a grown woman. There was no way that there was going to be any baby. If it was true, there was a deep sickness inside Tori. If it was not true, her son was deluded, and dangerously so. Every explanation, every excuse she could conjure, came at her like Niagara. With so many explanations, so many possibilities, there had to be one that made absolute sense.

There had to be one that would save her little boy.

Laura didn't want to offend her son, scare him off, do anything to break the bond they'd somehow managed to forge in that moment of crisis. Parker needed his mother more than ever. She felt that she'd failed him in the past. She owed him the help that he needed.

"Was Tori your girlfriend?" The words were delivered as flatly as possible. Laura Connelly used all that she possessed to try to keep the tone of judgment out of her words. To judge him was to push him away.

To push him away at that moment would be to lose him forever.

"Mom! I told you, she's pregnant. I'm going to be a father. I'm going to be a better dad than Dad ever was."

She patted him gently. The touch of his heaving body scared her. He was going to disintegrate. "I have no doubt," she said, softly, but with all the conviction of someone desperate to keep her son safe.

No matter what he did.

Parker fixed his stare on his mother.

"She lied to me, Mom. She lied to me. She wasn't going to be with me. She was going to take our baby and run off with someone else."

Laura was crying now, but silently. "How do you know?"

"I heard her. She was talking to him on the computer. I've been tricked. She made me do things that I shouldn't have."

"Parker, what things?"

He tucked his head down on his mother's chest, and she held him like a baby.

"Bad things, Mom."

Laura tried to remain calm. Her son was in serious trouble and on some level it felt like calmness was needed. Like the time he'd split his knee open after falling from the backyard swing when he was seven. The wound looked bad, but she acted as though it was nothing. She knew, like all moms do, that her fear would be reflected back at her boy.

"What kind of bad things?" she asked.

Parker didn't answer.

"You can tell me, Parker. Tell me."

He looked up at her. "She wanted me to kill Dad, but I couldn't. I was too weak. I didn't do what a man would do that time, but later, Mom, I did. I really did."

Laura could feel her muscles tighten. She willed herself to stay calm, as though she really could.

"What did you do, Parker?"

"That minister. She made me kill him. She told me that he was going to hurt her. That he would send her to prison and we'd never be together. She said that our baby would be aborted by the state. I couldn't let that happen. A baby needs a father. I needed a father."

Laura was crying, but she didn't make a sound. Her tears rolled from the corners of her eyes and landed in the tangle of her son's hair while she cradled him in her arms. She could only think of one thing. She needed to get her son out of harm's way.

"We have to get you away from here. Get you out of here. Somewhere where the police can't find you."

"That's just it, Mom. I don't want to do this. I don't want anyone else to die. I don't want to hide."

CHAPTER FIFTY

Bremerton, Washington

Mary Reed could no longer hold her secret. It took everything she had—and her reserves were substantial—to break her silence. She had made a promise. Her word meant something. It always had.

But with all that was being said about Jason, Tori, Kendall, Lainie, and the whole Class of '95 reunion, she knew that the time was right. It was as if God had called her and told her that it was time to shine a light on the past.

It was her day off from her job at the courthouse. For some reason, maybe pride, she decided to dress up a little. She put on a pretty new pink top and dark trousers that made her look slim and stylish. It was as if she was going out for a lunch date with a girlfriend. She wanted to look her best when she said what she had to say.

"You look like a million bucks today," Doug said as he sipped his coffee over a stack of brochures from Poulsbo RV. Retirement from the shipyard was beckoning, and Doug was sure that a recreational vehicle would be ideal for their new "footloose and fancy-free" lifestyle.

"We're going to need a million bucks to afford one of those," she said, heading out the door.

So wrapped up in the brochure, Doug hadn't noticed that his wife had been crying.

I can do this, she told herself as she drove to the sheriff's department. *What I'm about to do is for good, not to hurt.*

Mary parked her car and went through the back door. She told the receptionist who she needed to see and waited in one of those uncomfortable visitor's chairs.

"Mary?" Kendall said, emerging from the door by the front desk. She was exhausted and exhilarated from her trip, though she told no one that she'd just returned. She'd come to work directly from SeaTac Airport. She hadn't slept in twenty-four hours, but didn't really feel the need to. She was sure that Tori had murdered her husband Zach and Ronnie in Hawaii. She was running on adrenaline, but the look on Mary's face brought that all to a halt.

"Kendall, I have something to tell you," she said, looking as if she was going to burst into tears.

Kendall hurried toward Mary, her face full of concern. She wondered if the exhumation had been too much, brought back too many memories.

"What is it? Are you all right?"

"Not here," Mary said. "Is there some place we can go?"

"Some place" meant somewhere private—not an interview room or her office.

"Let's take a walk," Kendall said.

It had warmed up considerably and it finally felt like spring. Kendall didn't see a need for a jacket, so they started out along Division Street until they came upon a row of old maple trees banking one of the uglier courthouse complex's parking lots. She hadn't told Mary about the bloody message on the dollhouse and she wondered if she'd somehow heard about it.

Penny? Adam?

But it wasn't that.

"Kendall, I really need to get something off my chest."

"Mary, the investigation is moving along, slowly. But we're making progress. I'm sorry that it has been taking so long."

Mary shook her head.

That wasn't it, either.

"I've done something to you. Something I shouldn't have."

Mary stopped talking for a moment. It was as if her words were suddenly lodged in her throat. Kendall had no idea what she was talking about, but the pain was so evident that her own eyes began to pool with tears.

Losing a child is something that can never really be over.

"It can't be that bad," Kendall finally said.

Mary looked down. "I sent those messages through the website."

Kendall was confused. The conversation wasn't going in the direction that she'd imagined at all. It wasn't about Jason's investigation.

"I'm sorry. I don't follow you," she said.

"When the class reunion card came in the mail for Jason—I guess the class of '95 forgot that Jason was dead—I just couldn't stop myself. I dropped the note in your office, too."

Kendall's heart raced. "The 'I know everything' message?"

Mary nodded.

"I also e-mailed the committee. I wrote a message about how the truth will set you free."

"I still don't understand," Kendall said, though she had an idea.

"Kendall, I talked to your mother. I took a part-time job at the Landing last fall to make some extra money. When I cleaned your mother's room, she told me the truth."

The truth.

Kendall knew what was coming and she felt her knees weaken. She sat down on the curb and Mary joined her.

"What did she tell you?"

There was still hope that her secret was safe, though a part of her wanted it to be out, over. Finished. Keeping silent all those years had made it the forefront of her thoughts, not forgotten.

"That you had a baby. Jason's baby. My grandson."

Kendall tried to come up with the right words for a conversation she'd never intended on having.

"You must hate me, Mary," she said.

Mary put her arms around Kendall.

"You were so young," Mary said. "I'm sure it was the hardest time of your life."

Kendall hugged her back. Her words came in pieces. "After we broke up . . . I found out I was pregnant, but it was too late. He'd started seeing Tori O'Neal. I'm so sorry."

Jason's mother lifted Kendall's head and looked into her eyes.

"Don't be. I'm happy. Knowing that a part of Jason is alive is the greatest gift I could have."

Maddie Crane looked out over Commencement Bay as she absentmindedly scrolled though e-mails while talking on speakerphone with Darius Fulton from the Pierce County Jail. She looked at the time and wondered what had delayed the bank transfer. She also wondered what had delayed her afternoon tea. *Where was Chad?* If anything, Maddie was the consummate multitasker. She felt a surge of power that she hadn't experienced in some time. It had been a long, hard road since the DUI that nearly cost her everything. But it was behind her. It had faded from the news. She thanked God that she'd been given another chance, and she promised herself that the second time she was stopped for driving drunk would be the last time. While the deal she made compromised her ethics, it was all she could do.

She was not going to be the sad woman who'd lost everything.

"I'm sorry, Darius, but you're just going to have to be patient. Your threats to Ms. Connelly have done you in."

"I did not threaten her."

"She says you did. Phone records bear out her claims."

"I never called her."

Maddie logged on to a secure server and doubled-checked the bank transfer she'd initiated for a client's offshore account.

She smiled at the confirmation that $2 million in life insurance benefits had been deposited.

"Hang tight," she said. "I'll do my best to get you out of there after the weekend."

"Don't be so vague. Say you'll get me out of here on Monday."

She swiveled in her chair at the sound of her assistant coming into her office.

Finally, the tea.

"I have to go now, Darius."

She clicked off speakerphone and took the tea from the tray. She dropped two cubes of sugar into the steaming amber liquid—the color of whiskey, the way she liked it.

"Chad, will you let Tori Connelly know that her business is completed?"

Chad nodded. "Will do."

Tori Connelly set down her phone and made her way to her Lexus. The house was locked, but not because she cared about anything inside. The contents were not important. Where she was going, she'd be starting over with the man of her dreams. The only one who understood both her beauty and her power.

She carried an overnight bag with the bare essentials she needed for the trip later that night.

And then she'd be rich and free.

She texted Lainie, her last loose end.

RUNNING LATE. CALL U WHEN I GET TO YR PLACE. MEET ME IN GARAGE.

She sent one final text message:

LOVE U. SEE U SOON.

She selected two names and pressed send.

It was so easy to stay connected.

CHAPTER FIFTY-ONE

Port Orchard

Kendall Stark stood in front of the mirror, looking at herself. She was not a woman given to overt displays of vanity, but she could not help but wonder how well she'd really held up over the past fifteen years. It was hard to know. Age was a funny thing. It seemed to work so slowly, sneakily, against the beholder. It was as if one day you look in the mirror and you see a line that surely must have been there the day before, but it had gone unnoticed. Unrecorded. Ignored. She thought she looked pretty good. Adam Canfield had reminded her that since she hadn't been a cheerleader or a prom queen, no one would be giving her the critical and cruel eye.

"I'm not saying you don't look great, because, honestly, Kendall, you do. But the truth is that no one cares about what the B-listers look like now. They only want to see how fat the cheerleaders are and how bald the jocks have gotten since graduation."

B-lister?

She wore a black dress that was short enough to show

some leg, but not so much that it looked like she was a Bremerton girl who tried too hard to snare a sailor by the navy base. She almost never wore them, but that evening she put on the single strand of pearls that her mother had insisted she keep when she moved into the Landing.

"Wow, look at Mommy," Steven said as he and Cody appeared in the doorway.

"Look, indeed," she said, dangling the pearls. "Will you hook the clasp?"

Cody sat on the edge of the bed, smiling at his mom.

"You look pretty," he said.

"Well, aren't you the charmer," she said, looking down at Cody. She held her hair above the nape of her neck while Steven fiddled with the tiny lobster-claw clasp. "Your daddy looks pretty good, too."

Steven wore a dark gray jacket, black slacks, and an electric blue tie that was youthful and cool.

Like he always was.

"Tonight should be fun," he said.

"Memorable for the right reasons, too."

"*Fifteen Minutes of Fame*, here we come."

On the drive over to Gold Mountain, Kendall asked Steven to take a detour and drive down Banner Road.

"That's out of the way," he said.

"I know, but I need you to do this for me. I need to talk to you."

He could see the anguish in her eyes.

"All right, we can do that."

It wasn't dark yet. In fact, the sky was blue and the sun turned the tops of the enormous firs along Banner Forest into gold-tipped spears.

"Steven," she said, "Park down by the Jump."

He didn't like the idea, but he could plainly see that whatever it was that Kendall wanted—needed—to say was dark, deep, and difficult. He'd notice how stressed she'd been in the past few weeks and he knew her well enough to know it was more than the murder cases she was working, more than the reunion, or the last-minute forensics conference.

He found a spot, pulled over, and turned off the ignition. A deer and her impossibly tiny twin fawns ambled across the roadway.

"Her babies are beautiful," she said, as she watched the trio disappear into the blackberries and ferns off the edge of the roadway.

Kendall kept her gaze toward the deer, though they were gone.

"You look like you're going to crumble," he said.

"I am," she said. "I've lied to you. I've pretty much lied to everyone."

Steven reached over and put his hand on her knee. "What is it? It can't be that bad," he said, though he could easily see that it was.

"After we broke up, I saw someone."

"You mean in high school, right?"

"Yes," she said.

"That's fine. I dated, too. While you were away."

"That's why I went away."

"To study. Yes, I know."

"I was in trouble. I got pregnant. I left because I had to do something about it."

Steven could feel his own eyes misting. He had no idea that was coming.

"Kendall," he said. "Lots of women have abortions."

She shook her head. "I know. I understand that. I couldn't, I just couldn't."

"You couldn't? You had the baby?"

Steven clenched his fists. Not in rage, but in an attempt to hold his emotions inside.

She nodded.

"Whose baby was it?"

"Jason's," she said.

The name didn't surprise Steven. Nothing could surprise him after hearing that Kendall had given birth before Cody. He wondered what he missed. How he didn't notice anything about her that might have tipped him off. After Cody's birth, her body changed in subtle ways. Why hadn't he noticed it?

"What happened to the baby?"

"He was adopted. I don't know by whom."

"Who else knows? Do the Reeds know?"

"My mom. Mary Reed. I told her today. Are you disgusted with me?"

Steven folded his arms; his face was red, but he wasn't angry. Not really. He could see that his wife was in torment then. It was a huge burden.

"Not disgusted, just disappointed that you've lived with this and didn't think enough of our relationship to tell me."

"It wasn't that. I was so ashamed. I waited so long and then it seemed like it was too late. That it didn't need to be brought up anymore."

Steven embraced her and kissed her. It was a soft, gentle kiss. Almost the kind of kiss that a parent gives a child to make them feel better.

"I love you, Kendall. You know that. My heart aches for all you've gone through. You're going to be all right. We all are. You want to bag this reunion and go home?"

She shook her head. "I can't. Adam and Penny would kill me. And we've had too much of that around here lately."

CHAPTER FIFTY-TWO

Bremerton

The Olympic Room at the Gold Mountain Golf Club had been decorated with balloons and posters that highlighted the class theme "Fifteen Minutes of Fame." Images of popular '90s bands, TV and film actors, and political figures were interspersed with blowups from the yearbook. Side-by-side comparisons of celebrities and classmates made it all too clear—that Port Orchard was slightly behind the times when it came to being stylish. The South Kitsap version of "the Rachel" was a little bigger in volume, decidedly less sleek. Some of the men who rocked a '90s goatee still wore them. Long sideburns, thankfully, had been replaced by a slightly more contemporary look.

The Bremerton band Penny Salazar had fought for was playing its maudlin version of Céline Dion's "The Power of Love" as Kendall and Steven surveyed the room. Most of the faces were familiar in the sense that, fifteen years after graduation, most still held on to the characteristics that marked them in high school. Blondes were still blond. Most athletes still looked reasonably trim. Maybe slightly beefier around the middle, but good.

"Not the train wreck we thought," Adam said, carrying a glass of white wine from the bar and offering it to Kendall. "Are you on duty or here for what passes for a good time in Port Orchard?"

She took the glass.

"Good time, I guess."

"Penny's already overdoing it," Steven said, indicating the primary organizer of the event. Penny wore a flowing low-cut gown that looked as if it used up the entire yardage at JoAnn's fabric store in Port Orchard.

Penny, they all knew, sewed her own clothes and never saw a "designer look" that didn't invite her improvements.

"Michael Kors?" Kendall said.

"More like Bob Mackie," Adam said.

Kendall sipped her wine. She was exhausted from her trip and reeling from the disclosure she'd made to Steven. She didn't feel like being anywhere close to the reunion festivities. But she had no choice. She'd agreed to it long ago. She'd already planned on coming up with an excuse for the next reunion.

Let's share the fun with other people, Penny. It would be wrong for me to be so selfish to do it again.

"Maybe we should mingle," she said to Steven.

"All right, honey," he said, squeezing her hand as if to tell her everything would be okay.

Kendall's phone buzzed and looked down at the screen. It was Laura Connelly.

"Hang on," she said, turning toward the door to the patio that overlooked the golf course. "I'll take this outside."

"Laura?" she asked as she found an empty place by the rail.

"Kendall, I'm sorry to bother you. But Parker and I need to see you. It's about Tori and Lainie."

"What is it? Did you say you found Parker?"

"Yes, and I'm scared, Kendall. I didn't know who else to call."

"That's all right. You can call anytime."

The band started in on their version of Ace of Base's "All That She Wants." It was louder than the Céline cover, and Kendall tried to move to a quieter section of the patio, away from a couple who'd had too much to drink and were arguing about who had dumped whom first.

"I'm at a function right now," Kendall said. "I can't get away."

"You're at Gold Mountain, right? We're coming to you."

"Why, yes. How did you know? Who is 'we'?"

The phone went dead.

Kendall dialed Josh Anderson.

"Josh, I need you to get over here. Laura Connelly found her son, and she's bringing him here. She sounds terrified."

"I can be there in a half hour. Backup needed?"

"No," said. "This is a mom and a boy. We can handle it."

"Got it. On my way."

CHAPTER FIFTY-THREE

Bremerton

Lainie was sure she was dead. The world had gone completely dark. The last thing that happened—before she was dispatched into the darkness—was a sudden, sharp pain to her head. *Had there been an earthquake? Had something fallen?* As she was ruminating over what might have happened, Lainie O'Neal realized that she was alive.

But where was she?

She was curled up in the darkness. She was not bound, but free to move. Although any movement was difficult, the space was so confining.

Am I underground?

She continued to wriggle and shift her body as much as she could, all the while feeling around in the darkness. She touched something round. Hard. Her fingertips felt the grooves of what she knew to be tire treads.

A spare tire.

Lainie was in the trunk of a car.

She shifted her body again and tried to roll in the opposite direction. She was sure that if she was in a trunk, she was facing the wrong way. Because the right way, she hoped, would have a pinprick of light.

Wouldn't it?

Lainie stopped her efforts. She was getting nowhere. She knew there was only one more thing she could do to get help.

She could scream.

"Help! Help!" The words came out of her mouth, but she was unsure just how loud they were. Inside the car trunk everything seemed wrapped in silence. She tasted blood on her lip and remembered that she'd banged her face against something as she fell into the trunk.

"Get me out of here!"

Deirdre Jericho Landers planted herself by the bartender stationed outside the Olympic Room. If she'd thought for a moment that the class reunion was a good way to get reacquainted with her high school pals, she was wrong. The reality of her senior year had just come sharply into focus. She'd only gone to South Kitsap for her senior year. She was a perpetual outsider. Despite all that she'd done to fit in, she was scooted aside by girls and guys with friendships that went from elementary school to adulthood.

Dee Dee drank a gin and tonic at a bar in Gorst before her arrival at the reunion. She was between husbands and boyfriends and felt a little self-conscious. She wanted to take the edge off. Unfortunately, she followed that with a couple more once she arrived. She wasn't an alcoholic, just a woman who was tired of being on the outside looking in.

"I know you," she called over to Eddie Kaminski, standing by the door. Kendall looked over, surprised that Kaminski was there. Josh had likely given him the heads-up on Parker and he was there to keep his hand in the case. The boys' club, she figured, would never really die.

"Sorry," he said, barely looking at her. "I'm not a member of the class."

Dee Dee looked him over. Closely. Her first thought was that he was handsome, fit, and the kind of guy she'd fallen for more than once. She wondered for a second if he seemed familiar because he was the type of guy she usually went home with.

Masculine. Military. Sure of himself. She liked the vibe.

"No, I know you," she said, rethinking her approach. "Are you on TV or something?"

He shook his head. "Not really. Sometimes for my work."

"What kind of work?"

By then, Dee Dee had examined his left hand for a wedding band.

Good. This one's available.

"Police. Tacoma."

"Tacoma?" The wheels were turning, but Dee Dee had had one too many drinks and they weren't all going in the same direction.

"Have a good night," he said, walking away.

Laura and Parker Connelly stood in the turnaround in front of the golf course clubhouse. Kaminski stayed put, waiting for Tori to show up. Kendall and Josh led mother and son to a quiet place near a lineup of golf carts. Laura's face was pinched in anguish. She'd implored her son to do the right thing and he was there.

"She lied to me," Parker said.

"Tori?" Kendall asked.

Parker nodded.

"She totally used and manipulated Parker. She's an evil bitch," Laura said, obviously unable to hold back.

Kendall acknowledged the mother's anger but turned her attention to the teenager.

"Tell us, Parker."

Parker swallowed hard and took a seat on the back of a golf cart. "She shot my dad. I shot him, too. But he was dead. I swear he was dead."

Josh moved in closer and Kendall motioned for him to back off. This wasn't the time to intimidate. The kid was talking.

"I'm really sorry for what I did to that minister," he said.

"What did you do to Pastor Mike?"

"I killed the dude. I shouldn't have. But she told me that it was the only way we could stay together. She thought that you—" He stopped and looked directly at Kendall. "You were going to ruin things with that stupid investigation into that Jason kid's death. All of this is your fault."

"Parker," Laura said. "You know that's not true."

He buried his face in his hands. "I guess so. I mean, I know so."

In that moment Kendall could see clearly that the boy who killed the minister was really very much a boy, listening to his mother, deferring to her.

Like he might have deferred to Tori.

"Tori lied to me," he said.

"We get that, Parker," Josh said. "Specifically, about what?"

"She said I was the only one for her. That I was her soul mate. But she lied. I put a webcam in her bedroom . . . I heard her talking tonight on the webcam."

He stopped and looked at his mother, who had taken a seat next to him and wrapped an arm around his shoulders.

"Go on," Kendall said.

"There's someone else. They were laughing at me."

He turned to his mother and started to cry. "She was laughing at me, Mom."

Laura cradled her son. "I'm sorry, honey. I'm so sorry."

Kendall couldn't help but think of the connection between Jason and Parker. Both of their lives had been ruined at seventeen by Tori O'Neal.

"Please don't hurt her," Parker said. "She's going to have our baby."

Josh turned to Kendall and said in a low voice, "Jesus, this couldn't get any better, could it?"

Of course, like almost always, Josh Anderson was wrong.

Laura pulled Kendall aside.

"What's going to happen to Parker? Is he going to go to prison?"

Kendall hated to answer. She could barely imagine what Laura was feeling. She sometimes wondered—though she would never say it aloud—if the burden on the parents of a killer was equal to the anguish of the parents of a victim. For the rest of their lives, those parents walk each footstep in shame. They wonder if they'd done something to create the monster. There is never, ever any closure.

"I can't say how they'll charge this, but he was a juvenile."

The hope was false, and Kendall knew it. More and more, prosecutors charged young people as adults. Parker was looking at serious jail time.

"He is a good boy. She was using him."

That was true, but it probably wasn't enough.

"Laura, the prosecutor will surely consider those as mitigating factors."

"He's not lost forever," Laura said.

Kendall gripped Laura's hand. "No, no one is."

"Wait a second!" A voice called over to Kendall, Josh, and Kaminski as they compared notes over what Parker had just told investigators.

It was Dee Dee Landers.

"I remember now. You're the guy I saw with Lainie or Tori at the El Gaucho last summer. You're her boyfriend."

Kaminski took a step toward Dee Dee. "Sorry, you must have me mixed up with someone else."

The slightly drunk brunette staggered on her heels, four-inchers that didn't exactly do her any favors in the agility department.

"No. No. I haven't," she said.

"She's had too much to drink," Josh said. "Let's get her out of here so she can dry out."

Kaminski locked his arm on hers and started to take her out the door.

"Detective, wait a sec," Kendall said, ushering them to the breezeway between the Olympic Room and the main clubhouse. "I want to hear what she has to say."

Dee Dee nodded, a little wobbly, but in the affirmative.

"Yes. Thank you. Do I know you?" She looked at Kendall. "Oh, yes. You're Kendall. As I was saying—do you mind letting go of me?—as I was saying, I ran into you and one of those O'Neal twins last year. I talked with Lainie about it this fall when I saw her in Seattle. She didn't remember, so it must have been Tori. The other twin. The one no one around here seems to like."

Kendall looked over at Josh and then locked eyes on Kaminski.

Dee Dee would not be denied. She was not *that* drunk. "I saw him on TV the other day. I know he's the man that was in El Gaucho."

In the dark of what she now knew was her sister's car trunk, Lainie O'Neal began to reconstruct what happened to her. She'd met Tori in her condo's garage.

"Let's move this bag to the trunk," Tori had said. "I forgot to stop at Goodwill with these odds and ends."

Tori never thought her sister was the Goodwill type, but she helped her move the bag from the passenger seat to the trunk.

"Shove it in the back," she said. Lainie bent over, and all of a sudden everything went black. Just like that. It was instantaneous.

Tori had struck her. Hard.

When she worked for the *P-I* she'd written a story about what to do if one is trapped in a trunk. She looked for the taillight to kick it out and wriggle her hand or foot to attract attention. She was so turned around she didn't know which direction the back was. She felt along the top of the trunk for the other tip—the reason for her news story—look for the escape latch and pull.

Found it.

A flash of light.

She was free. A sign in the parking lot told her where she was.

WELCOME TO GOLD MOUNTAIN
Drive Friendly.

Jesus, she thought, feeling the blood dripping from her head. *This is the worst appearance by a schoolmate since Carrie went to her prom.*

Kendall and Steven huddled with Lainie. It was obvious that something major was going on. Kitsap County deputies and detectives were swarming the parking lot. Penny Salazar told the band to play louder, but Ace of Base didn't get better with volume. Penny was beginning to feel her theme had been a bit prophetic.

But not in a good way.

"Parker confessed that your sister killed her husband," Kendall said.

Lainie steadied herself. "It doesn't surprise me, but it still hurts. Knowing that she could do something like that."

"You'll need to tell your father. It'll be in all the papers."

Lainie said she would.

"This will kill him, you know," she said.

"There's more, Lainie. I think your sister killed some other people, too."

Lainie looked incredulous. "What other people?"

"Jason, a boy in Hawaii, Zach . . . maybe even your mother."

"That couldn't be. You're wrong about that."

Kendall felt so sorry for her, but she had to know.

Eddie Kaminski, who caught the last few words of the conversation, offered to take Lainie somewhere if she wanted to clear her head.

"That would be nice. I really don't feel like partying."

Even an unbudgeted round of extra hors d'oeuvres barely captured the attention of the Class of '95. There was too much drama in the parking lot. That was about to change when a second blonde in a little black dress showed up.

"Tori's here," someone said.

All eyes went to the entryway.

"I'm Lainie and that bitch of a sister of mine whacked me."

Kendall looked over at Lainie and Kaminski as they started toward the door.

"You're Tori," she said to the twin who'd just arrived. "That's Lainie." She pointed to the woman with Kaminski.

The first blond twin shook her head.

"Oh, Tori, why are you saying that? Don't you ever stop?"

"I *am* Lainie," said the second, as she hurried across the room to face the other.

"I can't tell the difference," Kendall said.

"I am Lainie and I'm getting out of here," she said, grabbing Kaminski's arm and tugging.

"You're not going anywhere!"

"Can someone calm her down? Please. This is embarrassing."

The bleeding blonde grabbed the other, but she pulled away. The contents of her Coach purse spilled onto the polished aggregate floor. Tubes of makeup, plane tickets, and a wallet tumbled out.

"I can prove she's not me," the second said snatching up the wallet. "Her driver's license. I'll show you."

She tore open the wallet and her face fell.

"I don't understand. I don't . . ."

Kendall bent down and picked up the plane tickets. Two hundred classmates stopped in their tracks to watch the spectacle. Kendall pushed people away in that way cops often do to "give people some air."

Penny told the band to play something else—and fast.

"She's bleeding," a former cheerleader called out. "Someone get a bandage."

The woman felt her head and stepped backward. She bumped into the guest registration table.

"Make her sign her name!" she said.

Kaminski rolled his eyes, clearly exasperated. "This is stupid."

"We don't know who is who," Kendall said. "And considering what we found out tonight, we need to."

A former geek-turned-hottie who was hosting the table handed over the guest book and a pen. The woman signed her name and handed the pen to her sister. She knew her sister was a practiced forger, but there was one thing she couldn't do.

The sister complied and the tip of the pen ran over the paper.

"They look the same," Kaminski said, looking down at the signatures.

"Better do that again," the bleeding one said. "This time use your left hand. Like I did. Lefty Lainie."

Kendall eyed Josh. No words were needed between them.

"Tori Connelly," Kendall said. "You're under arrest for the murder of Mikey Walsh."

"She's my collar," Kaminski said.

"Not so fast," she said.

Kendall held out the airline tickets. One ticket had been made out for Lainie O'Neal; the other, Edmund Kaminski. She looked at the Tacoma Police detective with the kind of disgust that cops use for the scourge of their brotherhood—the dirty cop.

"And you're mine," she said.

Tori was cuffed and sitting in the back of a Kitsap County sheriff's cruiser. Her makeup was smeared, her dress disheveled, and her hair looked like it had been styled by an immersion blender. Tori probably never looked worse in her life and Lainie figured that probably bothered her as much as anything.

Even the reason why she was cuffed in that car.

Lainie went over to Tori. A deputy put his arm out to stop her.

"Let her," Kendall said.

Lainie nodded at the detective and walked past the deputy barricade. She stood by the open car door and faced her twin sister.

"I won't even begin to ask you why. I doubt you know," Lainie said.

Tori barely looked at her. "My life would have been different if I hadn't been forced to share it with you from the minute we came onto this earth."

"I thought your life was wonderful, Tori."

"I hate you," she said, this time looking right into Lainie's eyes. "I always have."

Lainie stood her ground. Her sister could say nothing to make her hurt, to make her cry. She'd done that over and over and there was no emotion left.

"I know. Maybe you have reason to hate me."

Lainie and Tori watched as Parker was escorted to another cruiser. The teenager held his head down, looking only at the pavement. He looked like a boy who'd been caught smoking by the school principal.

Except he'd killed a minister. Except he plotted to kill his father.

"You mean about going to jail for you? That was a mistake. A spur-of-the-moment decision that I regretted."

"I'm sorry," Tori said halfheartedly. "I've told you that."

"I guess sorry doesn't do much after all, Tori."

"It wasn't easy for me. You think I'm tough, but I got raped in that hellhole by that asshole prison guard," Tori said.

Lainie's heart raced, something that seemed a physiological impossibility given all the stress she'd been through. She thought she might have a heart attack.

"You, too? You were raped, too?"

Tori allowed a faint smile to cross her lips.

"Yeah, Lainie, join the club."

Lainie's face was red. "My own sister handed me over to be raped. Who could do that but you, Tori?"

"I figured you deserved it for what happened to me. Besides, I knew how you operate. All I had to do was ask. You live on guilt the way some people live on Diet Coke."

Lainie was reeling then, and Kendall came over and pulled her by the shoulder.

"I'm not finished here," she said.

"Let her go," Kendall said gently.

Lainie turned to face her sister one more time.

"Were you going to switch identities, pretend you were me and live your life?"

Tori rotated her shoulders as if she were bored. She waited a beat before she turned her laserlike eyes toward her sister.

"Something like that," she said. "But really, just long enough to get past airport security and get out of this country."

"You killed Mom, too, didn't you?"

"Not sure what you're getting at."

Lainie started to ball up her fists, though she never would have hit her sister. She was tense, angry, and still reeling from her ordeal in the trunk.

"I know you did," she said, refusing to cry. "I saw you do it in my dreams. I told you . . . I saw things like that."

"Your dreams were stupid, Lainie," she said.

Lainie turned away and started walking, but she had one more parting shot.

"You're sick, Tori."

Tori held her hard gaze at her sister. "Look who you're talking to. Remember, I'm a mirror of all that you are. Everything I am, you are. Our genes and DNA are the same."

"We're not the same," she said. "We *never* were."

EPILOGUE

Port Orchard

Sunday morning all over Puget Sound people did what they always did. Some woke up to brewing coffee, sizzling bacon, or the frenzy that comes with getting ready for church. Some hurried out the door to walk their dogs or take a run along a path. May in the Northwest is stunningly unpredictable.

The night before it had rained buckets, soaking the streets, filling swollen gutters from Bremerton to Seattle, but that morning the whole region was blessed with the blue skies and soft marine winds that make the region among the most beautiful places on Earth to live.

All across the Puget Sound region, people connected to Tori's crimes stirred.

In their cozy Harper bungalow, Kendall snuggled next to Steven, relieved that there were no more secrets between them. He'd been so understanding and forgiving that she wondered how she could have doubted him at all. The fact that she'd given birth so many years ago hadn't changed who she was to him or to Cody. That she'd made the decision to give her son up for adoption hadn't changed who she was. It was not a mark against her.

Her oldest son. He'd be eighteen in a couple of years. She wondered if he'd look for her. She hoped so. She wanted more than anything for Mary and Doug Reed to see their grandson.

As she drifted off toward much-needed sleep, Kendall made a list in her head. Vonnie, Jason, Zach, Ronnie, Alex, Mikey . . . Lainie would have been Tori's seventh victim. Tori was only thirty-three. She'd had decades of killing to do. There was no telling how many people she might have killed during the ten years that she'd vanished. The FBI was working the case along with the Kitsap County Sheriff's Office. Seattle, Tacoma, and Bremerton police were also scouring their records for any connection she might have had.

It was possible that the only murder she'd do time for was Alex's.

Kendall didn't think it was fair, but murder and justice usually weren't.

When Parker Connelly was being booked into the Kitsap County Jail, all of his personal effects were cataloged, bagged, and placed into bins for storage.

The booking officer looked quizzically at the ID retrieved from his duct-tape wallet.

"This is you, but the name's not right," the officer said.

Parker shrugged. "I know. My girlfriend had it made for me."

"You don't look like an Eddie Kaminski. Maybe a Teddy Kaczynski."

"I guess she thought it was funny," Parker said. "You know, naming me after the guy she was using until we got out of here."

The officer closed the lid to the plastic tote.

"Look, kid, I'll tell you something about that woman. Forget about her. Forget you ever laid eyes on her. I married a gal like that. Maybe not that bad. But the type. You meant nothing to her."

Parker kept his mouth shut.

I don't care what you say, asshole, he thought. *She's my soul mate. I can forgive her.*

It took two minutes for Darius Fulton to hear the news that a new guy had joined the ranks of those killing time at the Pierce County Jail. Edmund Kaminski was locked up in a segregation cell.

"That piece-of-shit cop is going away big-time," a guard said. "So is that woman. You'll be out of here by tomorrow. This thing's big."

Darius assumed he was talking about Tori, but he wasn't.

By the time police came knocking on her North Tacoma door, Maddie Crane had downed her fourth whiskey sour and retired for the night. She looked at her watch, satisfied that everything was over. The plane had taken off from SeaTac to Miami. She was free. She was grateful for the second chance that Edmund Kaminski had given her the night he found her car in a ditch by the railroad tracks along Ruston Way. Instead of arresting her and destroying her once-damaged reputation, he'd offered her a deal. At the time, it didn't seem too much of a compromise. Being a lawyer had always been about give-and-take.

The knocking on her door woke her, and she put on a robe and went to answer. It was Tacoma Police Detective Daniel Davis and two uniformed officers. Blue lights showered her garden with an eerily pretty light.

"Madeline Andrea Crane?"

"You know who I am, Dan," she said.

"You're under arrest for conspiracy and fraud."

In her cell at the Kitsap County Jail, Tori Connelly lay awake, staring at the ceiling. The woman next to her smelled of vomit and body odor, and Tori pulled the scratchy blanket up over her mouth and nose to filter out the stink. She thought of a million reasons why she'd ended up there. She'd miscalculated. She blamed Jason, her sister, Kendall, Kaminski, Parker, even Maddie Crane.

She blamed everyone but herself.

"You're that bitch who killed her husband, aren't you?"

The smelly woman on the other bed had awakened, and she was coming toward her.

"Excuse me?" Tori asked, suddenly ramrod upright.

"I saw you on TV. You're something. We're going to be friends. Come over here and sit next to me."

Tori flinched a little at the invitation. "I'd rather die."

"You're too pretty to die."

A smile came to Tori's face. She knew the woman was right.

Lainie O'Neal didn't lie awake all night like she had night after night. After she'd been treated at Harrison Hospital and released, Adam Canfield took her to her Seattle condo. They'd arrived very, very late, and Adam curled up on the couch. Without Ambien, without counting games to numb her mind, she simply and sweetly fell asleep. When she finally opened her eyes she remembered nothing of her dreams. She could remember what happened the night before and the drama that came with it, but that was all a true memory. It wasn't one of those transplanted dreams that her sister seemed to send her.

Her eyes lingered over the photograph of her sister and her sitting on the top of her dresser. It showed the two of them in their ballet recital costumes.

Lainie shifted in her bed and grabbed the extra pillow. She flung it across the room, knocking the photo and its silver frame to the floor.

Adam Canfield scurried into the room and turned on the light.

"You all right?" he said. "I thought I heard something."

She glanced in the direction of the broken photograph and Adam nodded at the splinters of glass and the black-and-white photo. No comment was needed.

"My head hurts," Lainie said, pressing her palm against the spot that had been shaved and bandaged.

"That's because your twin bitch-ter smacked you with a crowbar or something."

"Right," she said, though she hadn't forgotten anything. "What time is it?"

"Eleven forty-five."

"A.M. or P.M.?"

Adam laughed. "Morning. You've been out, but not that long."

"I'm going back to sleep," she said.

Adam reached for the light switch. "No problem. You need the rest. I'll be here."

"Thanks, Adam," Lainie said, slipping back deeper under the covers. "Thanks for bringing me home."

She closed her eyes, thinking that the bad dreams would come back to taunt her.

But they didn't. They couldn't. She was safe and free.

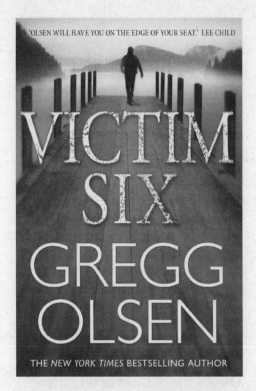

'OLSEN WILL HAVE YOU ON THE EDGE OF YOUR SEAT.' LEE CHILD

VICTIM SIX

GREGG OLSEN

THE *NEW YORK TIMES* BESTSELLING AUTHOR

The next kill is always the best

The bodies are found in towns and cities around Puget Sound, Washington. The young female victims had nothing in common, except the agony of their final moments. But somebody carefully chose them to stalk, capture and torture – a depraved killer whose cunning is only matched by the depth of his bloodlust.

And his next victim – number six – will be the most shocking of all.

Available now
£7.99

Visit www.constablerobinson.com for more information

SERIAL

'LUTZ KNOWS HOW TO MAKE YOU SHIVER.'
HARLAN COBEN

JOHN LUTZ

NEW YORK TIMES BESTSELLING AUTHOR OF *SINGLE WHITE FEMALE*

Once wronged, never forgotten …

A New York restaurateur, Millie Graff, is followed home from work by a man who forces her into her apartment and tortures her before killing her. She is found with her hand wrapped around a silver cross on a necklace. She's been gagged, sexually violated and then skinned alive.

As former NYPD detective Frank Quinn and his associates follow the path of the killer known as The Skinner, another woman's desperate search for the truth will bring her into the crosshairs of a killer with a burning desire to settle old scores.

'A heart-pounding roller coaster of a tale.' Jeffrey Deaver

'Lutz is in rare form.' *New York Times Book Review*

Available now
£7.99

Visit www.constablerobinson.com for more information

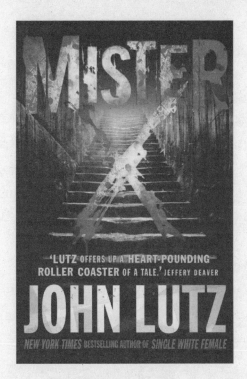

'LUTZ OFFERS UP A HEART-POUNDING ROLLER COASTER OF A TALE.' JEFFERY DEAVER

JOHN LUTZ

NEW YORK TIMES BESTSELLING AUTHOR OF *SINGLE WHITE FEMALE*

Fear leaves a mark …

He mutilates his victims. Cuts their throats. And then carves an X into their flesh. Five years ago he claimed the lives of six women and then the killings stopped. And no one knows why.

Ex-homicide detective Frank Quinn remembers – which is why he's shocked to see one of the dead women in his office. In fact, she is the identical twin of the last victim, and she wants Quinn to find her sister's murderer. But when the cold case heats up, it attracts the media spotlight – and suddenly the killings start again.

'Lutz knows how to make you shiver.' Harlan Coben

Available now
£7.99

Visit www.constablerobinson.com for more information

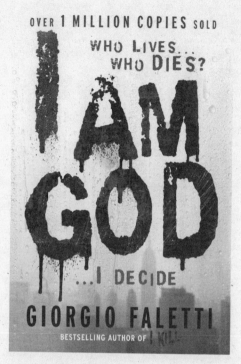

OVER **1 MILLION COPIES** SOLD

WHO LIVES...
WHO DIES?

I AM
GOD
...I DECIDE

GIORGIO FALETTI

BESTSELLING AUTHOR OF I KILL

A serial killer holds New York in his grip

The bombing of a twenty-two-storey building, followed by the discovery of a letter, lead the police to face up to a dreadful reality: some of New York's buildings were mined at the time of their construction. But which ones? And how many?

A young female detective, who hides her demons behind a tough facade, and a former press photographer with a past he'd rather forget, are the only hope of stopping this psychopath.

A man who does not claim responsibility for his actions.
A man who believes himself to be God …

'Italy's publishing sensation finally arrives in Britain.'
Financial Times

Available now
£7.99

Visit www.constablerobinson.com for more information

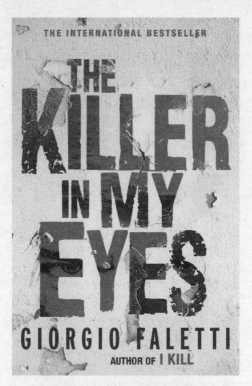

THE INTERNATIONAL BESTSELLER

THE KILLER IN MY EYES

GIORGIO FALETTI

AUTHOR OF I KILL

A killer drawn to obsession

Mayor Marsalis's son is found dead in his New York studio, his body stained red and arranged like the cartoon character Linus – with a blanket next to his ear and his thumb in his mouth. Desperate, Marsalis asks his ex-cop brother, Jordan, to investigate.

As the killer strikes again and again, Jordan is thrown together with beautiful young detective Maureen Martini, newly moved from Rome to forget her boyfriend's brutal murder. They begin a race against time to unmask the killer – a murderer seemingly obsessed with comic strips. But in New York nothing is ever quite what it seems …

Available now
£7.99